MATRONS

and
Madams

MATRONS
and *Madams*

Sharon Johnston

DUNDURN
TORONTO

Editors: Sylvia McConnell and Shannon Whibbs
Interior Design: Janette Thompson (Jansom)
Cover design: Laura Boyle
Cover image: © Image Zoo Illustration/marketplace.veer.com
Printer: Marquis

Library and Archives Canada Cataloguing in Publication
    Johnston, Sharon, author
       Matrons and madams / Sharon Johnston.

    Issued in print and electronic formats.
    ISBN 978-1-4597-2896-7 (pbk.).—ISBN 978-1-4597-2897-4 (pdf).—
    ISBN 978-1-4597-2898-1 (epub)

       I. Title.

PS8619.O4875M38 2015   C813'.6   C2014-907104-3
                                               C2014-907105-1

    2   3   4   5   19   18   17   16   15

Conseil des Arts   Canada Council   Canada   ONTARIO ARTS COUNCIL
du Canada   for the Arts   CONSEIL DES ARTS DE L'ONTARIO

We acknowledge the support of the **Canada Council for the Arts** and the **Ontario Arts Council** for our publishing program. We also acknowledge the financial support of the **Government of Canada** through the **Canada Book Fund** and **Livres Canada Books**, and the **Government of Ontario** through the **Ontario Book Publishing Tax Credit** and the **Ontario Media Development Corporation**.

VISIT US AT
Dundurn.com | *@dundurnpress* | *Facebook.com/dundurnpress* | *Pinterest.com/dundurnpress*

Dundurn
3 Church Street, Suite 500
Toronto, Ontario, Canada
M5E 1M2

War can end families
and war can begin families.

In memory of my grandmother and mother,
whose fortitude led to my five daughters and
eleven grandchildren.

CHAPTER 1

London, England, 1918

Sister Clara Durling looked up from her notes as though she had just experienced an electric shock. Maidenhead Red Cross Hospital was so close to London that it received news of the truce almost as it happened. Clara's heart pounded when she heard the clipped British voice break with emotion as he announced: "The war is over!" She stood in the middle of the ward, observing the carnage around her. The soldiers were so heavily sedated she could not share the glorious news. Three women from the voluntary aid detachment, tears wetting their cheeks, continued checking on the state of bandages. The strong odour of antiseptic was a stark reminder that lethal bacteria lurked in every wound.

"I need to take a few minutes to digest what this means," Clara said to the volunteers. All three women looked exhausted. Rationing of food and the absence of all toiletries showed on their thin, pale faces.

"I wish the end of the war meant the end of the wounded," Clara said, her voice hoarse with fatigue. "Casualties are coming in so fast, the foyer is filled with beds. I'll take a moment in the chapel if you don't mind. And the men on the east wing need new bandages. I'll be back shortly to help you."

As Sister Durling entered the chapel, she thought of the millions of lives lost for freedom. Sliding into the single pew, she looked up at the wooden cross on the altar. Tears of pride, fear, relief, and longing flowed down her cheeks. "I still have my children," she whispered to no one and wiped her eyes.

She could still picture it as if it were yesterday: five-year-old Billy and four-year-old Ivy burrowing under the sheets on George's convalescent bed to make a tent. George had been exposed to gas early in the war and suffered repeated lung infections. After the Battle of the Somme, he was sent home to heal and rest. The children would giggle when their father tickled them with his foot, but the moment they heard his raspy breathing, they'd slip out from under the sheets. Clara would put warm steam under his nose and rub camphor on his throat and chest. Her sense of duty outweighed the thought that she was getting her husband well enough to go back to his certain death. Soldiers with damaged lungs rarely left the hospital, but engineers were so desperately needed that even a sick one would, in the parlance of the War Office, give Britain one more fighting chance.

Billy and Ivy would rush off to play and wait for their father to breathe normally again. Some days this did not happen. But on every good day, picnics, safaris, trips to the moon, and treks through the desert had taken place in the convalescent room. George had had a sense of fun that he would not let the war take away. When he was deemed well enough to return to the front, he had the children promise to continue flying to the moon so they could watch over him. Every evening they looked out the window, plotting their lunar adventure.

George returned to France, but his lungs did not hold up

in the mud-swamped trenches. He was transported to a coastal clearing station and back to England. Barely able to breathe, he must have prayed, as the horse-drawn ambulance trundled along the railway to the coast, that he would make it home to say goodbye to his family.

When the cortege of Red Cross ambulances from the casualty ships had arrived at the Maidenhead Hospital, Clara had rushed out to meet her husband.

The driver descended from the ambulance and walked toward her. "Major Durling did not survive the journey, ma'am," he said, bowing his head respectfully. "I have the last letter he wrote. He told me his greatest wish was to make it back for your thirtieth birthday. Major Durling struggled with every breath, but we kept him comfortable with morphine. I'm so sorry, Sister Durling, to have to deliver such sad news on what was to be a special day."

There were three soldiers who had died in transport. Clara had no illusions; the battlefield was strewn with body parts. The bravest risked open fire to retrieve their blown-apart comrades so there could be a burial. She was grateful to have an entire George. He was buried in Knockholt Cemetery on the outskirts of Woodside. St. Katherine's Anglican Church had been his family's parish for generations. Two weeks after his shortened funeral service, Clara took the two-hour train ride back to Maidenhead Hospital. Britain was still at war.

Clara's quiet reflections in the hospital chapel were interrupted by an alarming thud on the floor above the chapel. She raced up the stairs to find a young soldier who had flipped his iron cot on its side. He was swearing incoherently and swinging frantically at the two orderlies trying to subdue him.

"I want to go home!" he screamed. He was built like a milk wagon, but blind, and his mouth was so disfigured he could not feed himself. His parents said they could not handle him until he could eat properly. Only time and surgery would determine if the young man would ever be reunited with his parents.

Clara gripped the soldier's hands to avoid being struck. "We'll get you home, but you must get well first. Let's start by putting your bed upright." She placed the soldier's hands on the iron frame. "One, two, three, flip." She put her arm around his waist and, holding one hand, walked him to the end of the corridor while the orderlies remade his bed.

She returned to find Dr. Newbury in blood-spattered operating scrubs ready to give the soldier a dose of morphine. He had just finished a bilateral above-knee amputation.

"Great news! Finally!" he said, putting his arm around Clara's shoulder. "I wanted to say goodbye, Sister Durling, before you go on your well-deserved break."

Clara smiled. "Thank you. I'm aching to see Billy and Ivy. It's been four weeks since I've laid eyes on my children."

Dr. Newbury was a Canadian surgeon who had joined the war effort at the age of sixty, despite the War Office considering him too old to enlist. When war broke out, he had just been appointed head of the department of surgery at the University of Alberta. He was small in stature with a booming voice that lifted everyone's spirits, including Clara's. *I'll miss him*, she thought, *when he returns to Canada.* He distracted wounded soldiers with ribald tales as they waited for their next shot of morphine. He loved to recount life in Lethbridge, Alberta, where he had begun his surgical practice at the Galt Hospital. During one of these often risqué conversations, Clara heard that the mayor of Lethbridge, a friend of the doctor's, treated prostitution like any other municipal service, providing the ladies of the night a safe, regulated area close to the hospital. The listening soldiers, in

MATRONS AND MADAMS · 11

their fog of morphine, vowed to move to the infamous city if they survived the war.

"I'm off to 11 Pickwick Place this evening," Dr. Newbury said, chuckling. "I spoke with your brother-in-law and he's offered to open his oldest brandy to celebrate."

Miff was a successful London solicitor who had married Clara's younger sister, Addy. He had been rejected for service because of a mild heart condition. As his war effort, he offered free legal services to families of soldiers who had died. He and the Canadian doctor had become good friends. Miff had told Dr. Newbury one of the family's secrets: his wife's eldest sister had been sent to Canada at the age of nineteen. The doctor had nodded knowingly, his delicate way of saying: *An unexpected pregnancy can happen to anyone.*

Clara was six years old and the seventh of eight Ives children when her sister had suddenly departed. To her question "What's Canada?" she received an unsatisfactory response: "Canada is a large, cold country where explorers go to find the North Pole."

"Then why did you send Amelia there?" asked Clara. She never received a satisfactory answer.

The local vicar had arranged for the girl to leave. It was only when Clara eavesdropped on her parents' conversations that she learned why her sister had been sent away. Amelia had given birth a few months after arriving in Canada. For many years, the sister lost contact with the family until she wrote one day to say that she had married a pharmacist and was living in Nova Scotia with her daughter. Clara herself had no idea where or how Amelia had lived before her marriage. Now, thinking about her Canadian connection, she wanted to write to tell her sister she had lost George. *But then my sister wouldn't even know I was married,* she thought. She gave her last set of directions to the ladies and headed for the stairs.

Clara was an experienced nurse who could distinguish a fever due to influenza from a rise in temperature caused by a bacterial infection in a wound. Seeing younger staff overwhelmed by the rapid onset of the highly contagious flu, she had offered to sleep at the hospital for the past month. Now she was finally getting a week's leave of absence.

At the entrance to the hospital, she stopped to observe the commotion. Eighteen beds were squeezed into the foyer. Outside the main door, a Red Cross ambulance driver and a nurse were unloading four new casualties. Clara removed her cape and began pushing together the iron cots in the foyer to make room for the new arrivals. The volunteer nurse was flustered because they had run out of cots.

"Get mattresses," Clara snapped. The volunteer sped off and came back with an armful of blankets. "That will do for now," Clara said in a softer tone. "The men won't feel the floor through the morphine. Go tell Matron we received four more."

"Sister Durling, we must get you to the station or you'll miss your train," the hovering ambulance driver interjected. With order established, she joined four ambulant soldiers waiting for the outgoing truck. They were helped into the back and Clara stepped up beside the driver. During the one-hour drive into central London, she would have time to plan what she would do with Billy and Ivy during the week. Until the fast-spreading flu, Clara had been home most weekends, but now she had the dark circles under her eyes of someone who had often worked through the night.

On the train, Clara sat beside a young soldier, who, after a few minutes of chit-chat, suddenly began to cry. "I was to be shipped back to the front in two weeks," he said. "My ma's already lost two sons and she was terrified. I sent her a telegram right away when I heard the good news. I hope she checks at the post office."

Clara's moss-green eyes filled with tears. "Your mother will be overjoyed to know you were in England when the truce was announced."

"I expect so, ma'am." The soldier wiped his nose on his sleeve and apologized.

The train buzzed with stories and occasionally audible tears. Clara rested her head on the window and slept until the train whistled her arrival. She dreamt that Dr. Newbury had suggested war widows would have better opportunities to raise their children in Canada. Her response before she woke up was: "I'd never leave England."

There was a symphony of church bells ringing through the cool air as she stepped onto the platform. Shouts of joy rose from the village square. Woodside was in a frenzy of celebration. Someone began banging a drum. Then an entire band began playing "God Save the King." *What a contrast from the hospital,* Clara thought. Tears of joy and sorrow were streaming down beaming faces. Everyone in the village had lost someone. People hugged, sang patriotic songs, and tipped metal flasks to their smiling lips. The occasional face covered with a protective mask was a stark reminder that England's troubles were not over. She overcame her exhaustion and broke into a run.

Mrs. Drake, wife of the neighbouring farmer, was waiting at the gate with Billy and Ivy. She was a short, hefty woman, suited for farm work. Clara had confessed to Mrs. Drake that her parents could not help her financially. Seeing Clara facing hardship and having to work, she'd offered to babysit during the week. During the month that Clara had remained at the hospital, Mrs. Drake had just moved the children to the farm permanently so she only had one household to look after. At the end of each school day, she stood with the mothers waiting for the children to be dismissed. It was worrying to hear that closing the schools might be necessary to prevent the rapid spread of flu. The health council had sent a notice to all families stating that children were more vulnerable than older adults.

Mrs. Drake's chubby cheeks broke into a broad smile as she pushed the children forward to meet Clara.

"We made you a cake," they pronounced simultaneously.

"My husband got us an extra ration of butter and sugar," Mrs. Drake said with a satisfied smile.

"And did that cost a chicken?" Clara asked, her eyes wide.

"It did."

"We're a lucky family to have the Drakes as neighbours. Now, what do we say?"

"Thank you, Mrs. Drake."

"Oh, I *am* glad to be home, even for a week."

"Why do you have to go back to the hospital?" Billy asked.

"Because there are some sick soldiers, and we need money to live." Clara buried her face in Billy's thick blond curls. "You've inherited my hair gene," she said, smiling. "Now, let's go see this special cake."

Clara relieved Mrs. Drake after the cake ceremony and spent the day joyfully entering into the children's play. In the evening, to counter Billy's bedtime negotiations, Clara reminded him that Mrs. Drake had said seven o'clock. "You're tired and Mummy won't be far behind you."

The next morning, as the children gobbled up their eggs, Clara said, "We're fortunate to live next to a farm. Manners, please."

"Do I have to leave something for the butler?" Ivy asked.

"Manners would like a small bit of your egg," Clara said, laughing. Ivy burst into giggles. "Let's go for a walk in Farmer Drake's woods. Best to avoid the shops with this flu virus."

Watching her children scurry about to find their boots, hats, gloves, and raincoats, Clara was struck by how normal her children were in spite of the tragedy around them. She wondered how long it would be before *England* was normal once more. *Children are more resilient than adults*, she thought, setting out for their walk in the woods with a new sense of confidence. She felt fortunate to be a nurse and saddened for those women who had filled men's jobs during the war. Most of them would now be replaced.

Ivy perched on a log at the edge of the woods. "I want to see the birds, Mummy. I promise to stay put." She bent the rim of her hat back off her eyes and looked up at an enormous flock of rooks. The birds made a deafening noise. Billy dashed into the woods after a rabbit. Clara felt her exhaustion return as she ran behind while he darted around trees and jumped over logs.

After the first day's outing, Ivy decided to keep a diary. She noted birds, animals, trees, and flowers in her tidy, compact printing. She offered a page to Billy, but he said he kept everything he saw in his head.

Near the end of Clara's week of leave, she suggested they visit Mr. Drake's barn at milking time. When they arrived, a young farmhand was sitting on a stool rhythmically pulling at the udders of an enormous black-and-white cow. Ivy wandered to the end of the barn and asked why there was a cow in a cage.

"That one there is a bull. He doesn't give us any milk," the farmhand said.

"Then why would you keep him?" Ivy asked.

"Hmm, I think you ought to ask Mr. Drake," he said. Ivy shrugged and headed off to explore.

"My daughter questions everything," Clara said, laughing. She turned to find Billy trying to climb from the fence onto a cow's back. The farmhand managed to remove him without getting kicked.

When they arrived home, Mrs. Drake had prepared a modest goodbye tea. "This was the best I could manage," she said. "But we still have some of the cake."

After tea, Billy dragged Clara outside to show her his rose garden. She was always touched that he shared her love of flowers. She had bought him an expensive set of children's gardening tools, which he used eagerly to tend his roses. "One day I shall own a greenhouse," he said as he marched her around the outside of the house. The garden was on the west side, next to the farmer's field. The sun was slipping rapidly below the horizon.

"I see you've clipped the stems," Clara said, running her fingers through Billy's curls. He gave her such a smile, and she felt a sharp pain in her left breast. "You are a fine gardener," Clara said. "I wish I didn't have to go back to the hospital."

Ivy came rushing out onto the back stoop. "Can we listen to the birds go to sleep?" she asked.

"If you promise not to argue about bedtime," Clara said, laughing. She hugged Billy and Ivy as they sat on the last step quietly watching the moon replace the sun. The chatter of birds gave way to rustlings in the woods.

"We were supposed to watch over Daddy," Ivy said, looking up. "But now he's looking down on us."

Clara's hands brushed over Ivy's wet cheeks. "He sees us, my darlings. I'm sure of that."

The aroma of suet pudding, simmering on the stove for three hours, had permeated the house. "Oh, this will taste good," said Clara. Slow cooking of tough meat encased in a suet crust was part of her childhood. Wartime had restored the pudding to favour.

"Can we visit you at the hospital, Mummy?" Ivy asked. "Mrs. Drake can bring us on the train."

"I wish that were possible. But there is something very contagious going around the hospital. Not even adult visitors are allowed. I will just have to come home more often." Clara was grateful her children didn't detect the doubt in her voice. The sickness had left the hospital short-staffed.

"Give your face the once-over," Clara said, passing each child a warm wet cloth.

"Mrs. Drake makes us have a bum bath twice a week," Ivy said, giggling.

"She doesn't like to put on the water tank," Billy added.

Clara feigned disapproval at the rude word, but inwardly she laughed and recalled how she had been spanked for using such a word. She had had to write fifty times "not bum but bottom."

"Ah, but Mummy gave you a full bath. And I let you splash around until the water got cold." Clara made an exaggerated shiver. "Brrrr."

Billy and Ivy pulled their pajamas from under their pillows and began arguing as to whose bed Clara would sit on to listen to them read.

"I won't listen to anyone until your clothes are folded. Why don't I compromise and sit on Ivy's bed first and let Billy start the story."

"Girls should go first," Ivy retorted.

"You are a bossy toad," Clara said.

Billy read a few pages, and then laid the book on his lap. "My eyes hurt, Mummy. I don't want to read."

"All right, give the book to Ivy." She switched over to sit on Billy's bed and put her hand on his forehead. "Your head feels warm."

"But I'm cold," Billy said. Clara tucked blankets around

him. There was no thermometer in the house; she had taken hers to Maidenhead when there had been an urgent plea for medical supplies.

Ivy had stopped reading.

"Go on with the story," Clara urged. "I want to know who's going to win, the tortoise or the hare."

"I don't want to read, either."

"All right. Both of you snuggle down, and I'll tell a story after I get something to cool Billy down."

Clara came back with a mixture of water and alcohol and began sponging Billy's head.

"Does Billy have flu, Mummy?" Ivy asked.

"Of course not. It must have been something he ate," said Clara. "It doesn't surprise me with this shortage of fresh food."

Billy closed his eyes, complaining of a headache, and promptly vomited.

Clara turned off the lamp and shouted down to Mrs. Drake, who was clattering away in the kitchen. "Edna, call Dr. Westoll. His home number is beside the telephone. His wife will know where to find him. Tell him it's an emergency." She wiped Billy's face and propped him up. "Ivy, wait downstairs until the doctor comes." Ivy began to cry.

"You'll be fine, little man." She knew the symptoms and prayed to a merciful God. Half an hour later, Dr. Westoll came rushing into the bedroom wearing a face mask. He examined Billy's pupils and put a thermometer under his tongue. He put on eyeglasses after shaking it. "His temperature is one hundred and two. If it continues to go up, he risks having a febrile convulsion." Clara stiffened at his words. "All you can do is sponge him to lower his temperature. Billy's a sturdy six-year-old. He'll pull through. I'm sure this will be a short-lived virus."

Mrs. Drake was standing at the bedroom door holding

Dr. Westoll's hat and coat. She followed him down the stairs. Clara sat on the side of the bed wringing out the cloth and sponging Billy's forehead and chest. Her mind reeled at the rapid onset. Mere hours earlier she had been admiring how he had put his prized rose garden to bed.

After an hour, Mrs. Drake came upstairs to ask if she should take Ivy to her house and let her teenage daughter stand by in case the doctor was needed.

"Yes, I think it best that Ivy leave," Clara said. Her eyes looked frantic, but her movements were deliberate and slow.

"Put on your clothes, Ivy, and I'll get your hat and coat," Mrs. Drake said. Ivy's face was a frightened mask as she descended the stairs.

Around midnight Billy's body arched in a severe convulsion. An hour later he had another and Clara called down for the Drake girl to get Dr. Westoll.

"He's *here*," the girl called in reply, and a moment later the doctor came into the room.

"The young lady fetched me after the first seizure," he said. "Rather than go home I just napped on your sofa. My wife knew where to find me if there was another emergency." The doctor put his stethoscope on Billy's chest. He sat down beside Clara and put his arm around her shoulders.

"Prepare for the worst," he said to Clara. "I don't think Billy will make it to morning." His eyes filled with tears. "I brought Billy into the world. I never thought I'd see him out. What have we done to deserve this flu, after losing so many to win the war?"

Billy's temperature stayed relentlessly high. Clara's arms had become expert at knowing when a life had succumbed, and in the early morning, one week after the glorious truce, Billy died.

Dr. Westoll told Clara what she already knew: "Had Billy

survived such severe convulsions he would have lived the rest of his life handicapped or brain damaged in some way."

Clara grieved to the point of sickness, but returned nevertheless to Maidenhead Hospital after two weeks, believing she could bury her sorrow. But trying to save the lives around her only highlighted how helpless she had been to save her own son. As she cared for the wounded soldiers she tried to comfort herself that some mother would be happy. But her drawn face and thin body were visible reminders that she had suffered a double loss. Seeing Clara sobbing in a supply cupboard, the matron ordered her to take more time to grieve.

"Young Ivy will be a comfort to you if you return home for a few weeks," the matron said. "We can manage." She unexpectedly put her arms around Clara and smiled. "I know you don't believe *that*, Sister Durling."

Clara's eyes smiled through her tears.

By late spring, Billy's death had become a diffuse ache through Clara's entire body. She scratched about in his small rose garden imagining her son's delight at the appearance of early buds. Billy would have checked on the new growth repeatedly, not wanting to miss the first flowering. Clara had met her son's expectant behaviour with "Watched kettles never boil." The memory of her adage produced a flood of tears, but she brushed them away and forced her thoughts beyond the garden.

Dr. Newbury, preparing to return to Edmonton and seeing Clara's despair, pressed her even harder to move to Canada. Once back in Alberta, he wrote a letter urging her to respond to the advertisement for a lady superintendent at his alma mater, the Galt Hospital in Lethbridge. He explained that this position was the same as a British matron. "The lady superintendent is responsible for all hospital staff except the doctors," he wrote.

Clara had spent two weeks discussing the possible move and reflecting on what decision would be better: to try a new life or stay and struggle on in England. Staring at the prickly rose stems, she felt they held the answer. *The garden was brown and flowerless when Billy died,* she thought, *and now it's ready to bloom again.* Clara clipped a rose and placed it in an envelope of parchment paper. Her decision to move to Canada was made, and the rose would be her reminder that Billy's short life had been a happy one. She wrote to Dr. Newbury asking him to write a letter of recommendation to the Galt Hospital board. Very shortly afterwards, he sent her a copy of the letter he had written to Mayor Harwood. Clara smiled as she read, thinking that all she knew about the mayor was his lenience toward prostitutes. *Lethbridge,* she mused, *will be a challenge.*

> *Dear Alistair,*
>
> *I hope this letter finds you well and Mrs. Harwood on the mend. Morris has kept me informed about your wife's illness. Your worries about the Galt Hospital are well founded. Before I left for England, I was quite concerned by the deterioration of the place. Nursing standards had slipped badly, as you know from your own wife's unfortunate stay in the hospital.*
>
> *While Acting Surgeon at the Red Cross Hospital in London, I worked closely with a nursing sister, Mrs. Clara Durling. She comes from a lovely family, whom I also had the privilege to meet. I believe she is the person we need to bring back the Galt. I have worked cheek-by-jowl with her, and she is quite simply the best nurse I have ever encountered. She received her training at St. George's Hospital in London and was Assistant Matron at St. Bartholomew's until she married her husband, George. Unfortunately, he*

died before war's end from gas exposure. In spite of her grief, she continued to work tirelessly. But tragedy did not end there. As the war ended, her six-year-old son died of the flu.

Mrs. Durling remained a consummate professional and faithfully kind to her patients. The soldiers could not have received better care. The one drawback is that she will need someone to be responsible for her five-year-old daughter, Ivy, while she is running the hospital. I might add Ivy is a lovely little girl.

Alistair, I am asking Mrs. Durling to send her résumé directly to you. As hospital chairman, would you be so kind as to send it on to the hospital committee to consider her as the new lady superintendent? I am confident that as matron she will re-establish standards in my alma mater hospital.

I send my fond regards to Mrs. Harwood.

Yours faithfully,
Francis Newbury, M.D.

CHAPTER 2

Sydney, Nova Scotia, 1912

Two years before the Great War erupted, Lily White entered her graduation year at Sydney Academy. She had applied for a scholarship to teachers' college in Truro, Nova Scotia, for the following year, but the scholarship was conditional on Lily maintaining at least a 75 percent average in all subjects. Being prudent and heeding her father's advice that a bird in the hand is worth two in the bush, she planned to earn money for her tuition during her final school year.

Lily's father, Robert White, was a pharmacist, and he had taught Lily the value of money when she was only twelve by hiring her to deliver medicines to clients. People in Sydney would smile as she pedalled down the street with a carrier filled with packages. She would return the smile and wave.

The outward happiness did not reveal the real turmoil within. Lily's mother, Amelia, had always favoured her younger daughter, and Lily felt her preference for Beth very keenly. Beth was a year younger than Lily, but stylish and brash. She had her father's lapis lazuli eyes and Amelia's brown wavy hair. Once, during an argument, Beth had taunted Lily with the fact that she didn't look like either of her parents. This comment made Lily feel even further estranged from her mother and slowly she began to consider the idea that she might be adopted. At sixteen she decided to ask.

She stopped at the door that connected the house and the pharmacy and watched her father shake, stir, pound, and bottle various potions for breathlessness, stiffness, infections, rashes, sleeplessness, coughs, and headaches, wondering how she would ask the question: "Are you my real father?" Her nerve gathered up, Lily stepped forward just as an elderly client tottered into the pharmacy from the street. Robert pulled up a chair for Mrs. Birch then knelt on one knee to see what was bothering her. Lily had to smile while she watched: he looked as though he were going to propose. Mrs. Birch complained of terrible back pain and Robert suggested she might need stronger pain medication. "Or perhaps a new mattress," he said with a sympathetic grin. "I'll send Mrs. White over next week with the Sears catalogue and she can help you choose."

"How did you know I slept on a lumpy old thing?" Mrs. Birch chirped. She looked up at Robert with an adoring smile.

"Because every old-timer in Sydney does the same thing. Or perhaps I'm clairvoyant."

Lily had tears in her eyes. She adored her dad. "He has to be my real father," she whispered, wiping her tears away with her fist. Robert helped Mrs. Birch to the door, promising to have the new pills delivered as soon as they arrived at the pharmacy.

Lily stumbled across the large room. "Are you my real father?" she blurted.

Robert gripped her shaking shoulders, then pulled her forward into his arms. "I knew this day would come and I'm prepared." He led Lily to Mrs. Birch's chair and knelt as he had before. He was a tall man, who often lowered himself so his elderly clients could hear. "Lily, I helped deliver you into this world. Your mother was staying at the Anglican rectory when you decided to announce yourself. I'm not a doctor, but I am a pharmacist and your mother was in great pain. I gave her a little morphine. I was there from the beginning, Lily. So to answer your question, yes, I am *your* dad. As real as you need me to be."

Over the following weeks, the story was gradually revealed. Lily's mother, Amelia, pregnant and unmarried, had been sent from England to board with an Anglican minister and his family in Halifax, Nova Scotia. After her arrival she had provided light housekeeping services in the rectory. Before her condition was noticeable, the minister had asked her to be a live-in companion to a dying parishioner, assuring her she could move back to the rectory during her confinement. This is how she met Robert White, the grandson of the elderly man she was caring for. Robert's habit was to visit his grandfather once a week. Daily pop-ins began after he discovered Amelia. Pregnancy had not prevented Amelia from looking stylish and attractive, and her bright personality captivated Robert. He proposed. In a quiet ceremony, attended by his wife, the Anglican minister joined Amelia and Robert in marriage and Lily was born five months later.

Robert had grown up in Halifax, where his father was an officer in the Royal Navy. His mother had often cared for sailors with prolonged illness in her home, and Robert became very interested in healing and medicines. He greatly disappointed his father when he chose to study pharmacy instead of following his father's career path.

After his marriage, he bought an old building in the centre of town in Sydney and put up a sign reading WHITE'S PHARMACY. Customers warmed to the young pharmacist who treated their illnesses. When Lily was born they put suspicions aside and cooed over Lily as she lay swaddled in a cot behind the counter. Robert would explain with a sheepish grin that he was just giving his wife a rest.

Lily began her final year at Sydney Academy full of optimism that she would win a scholarship. Remembering the "bird in the hand," however, she marched into the principal's office and introduced herself in the third week of the school year. She had scanned the notice board and found, among requests for child minders, dog walkers, and help in an old folks' home, that there was a student who needed help to pass a mandatory English comprehension test. She offered her assistance.

"That would be nice," the secretary said, giving Lily an appraising look. "What are your qualifications?"

"I'm smart." Lily instantly regretted her flip remark and added, "I'm smart about people. I like them."

"Well, you'll have to be smart with Ed Parsons. He doesn't like school. His father told me Ed would be the first of his boys to have more than a grade eight education, and he's upset that we're making Ed repeat his school year. But the rule is you must pass an English comprehension test to enter the matriculation year and Ed failed it."

"I plan to go to teachers' college next year. Tutoring Mr. Parsons will give me some practice."

Lily agreed to the twenty-five-cent hourly rate and arranged to meet Ed after school. He arrived at the end of the school day just as the other students were piling out to smoke or hurry to part-time jobs. They cast knowing glances at him as though he were there to fetch his sweetheart, not to be tutored in English. Lily play-acted the part by handing her bag of books to Ed. The ruse seemed to work. He had deep-set blue-black eyes that reminded her of anthracite. His dark stubble, short-cropped black hair, and six-foot stature made him look more adult than his classmates, but he was actually a year older than Lily.

"I'm the dolt on the notice board," he said with a sarcastic edge.

"What did you find difficult on the test?" Lily asked.

"I had one hour to answer questions after reading a passage from a book. I panicked and wrote whatever nonsense came into my head. I'm no scholar."

"That's not true! You're almost through high school and that's more than your brothers achieved. Don't you want to graduate with a diploma?"

Ed's eyes became iridescent with moisture. "Everyone in the school will know that I need special help."

"Look, as soon as the bell rings and the students have cleared out, come to my classroom. If someone asks why you're there, say you've come to carry my books."

Ed shrugged and gave Lily an appraising look that embarrassed her. She ignored the flirtatious look in his eyes.

"English is just words, and words make up stories. People from Cape Breton make up their own stories. But you need to be able to read and hear a story and know what you've read and heard. Panic cuts concentration. I know that. Let's start with stories and leave grammar out." She pulled out a book that had taken several days to find amongst the old-fashioned British Annuals, which Lily considered boring.

Lily opened the book and handed it to Ed. "What am I supposed to do with this?" Ed asked.

"You're to write the first paragraph on the board and then read it. The only way to improve your illegible handwriting is to have you read what you've written. Let's start here."

Ed groaned as Lily handed him a piece of chalk. She stood beside him as he scribbled the words on the board. Lily had chosen an adventure story about a young stowaway being tied to the mast of a ship. At the end of the first hour, they were well into the story and Ed had seemed to enjoy it.

"Were you ever tied up as a boy and not able to free yourself?" Lily asked while Ed was doing his best to write the words legibly. She recalled Beth tying her to a tree when she was six years old, and then running into the house when a storm hit. Although Beth had been practising slipknots, the knot would not budge, and Lily, terrified, was left with a deep fear of storms. "I wonder if your older brothers did mean things. I'm sure you got your share of torture, being the youngest of six boys. Or maybe boys are not as cruel as girls." She shivered, recalling the enormous claps of thunder and the zigzag flashes she was sure would strike her tree.

"I don't think being tied to a mast or a tree is torture," Ed said.

"I guess boys from Glace Bay are pretty tough. You're lucky if your brothers weren't mean."

"My brothers were rough, but they never beat me up. We used to have wrestling matches in the parlour that drove my mom crazy. Always worried we'd damage her furniture."

"Mothers are like that," Lily said. "But your parents have your best interests at heart. That's why they want you to get your diploma."

A janitor was spreading septic-smelling sawdust down the aisles and sweeping it up with a wide broom just as Ed dropped a piece of chalk in Lily's cleavage. His action was so quick she almost didn't notice, but felt the hard lump at her bodice. The janitor witnessed her furious slap on Ed's cheek. Ed slouched away embarrassed, and Lily muttered, "I hope I never see you again, Ed Parsons!"

*   *   *

Both Lily and Beth had dreams of being on the stage. While they were at Sydney Academy, they buried their rivalry and joined the same theatre group. The school play for the year was *Macbeth*. Beth gave a star performance as Lady Macbeth while Lily played a minor character. However, once in Truro at teachers' college, Lily tried out for the lead female role in the school play that had been written by the drama teacher.

It was during the auditions when Lily noticed a fair-skinned handsome young man constructing the props. She went off stage and introduced herself. James Barnaby blushed as he described himself as the school handyman. Unlike Ed Parsons, who was all bravado, Barnaby — as he liked to be called — exuded a quiet confidence. He laughed, saying he was constructing the stage for a formidable actress. They talked awhile before he returned to sawing and hammering the pieces of wood. At each rehearsal Lily chatted with Barnaby, hoping he might wait around and ask her out. But before each practice session ended, he would rush off without explanation.

The night of the sellout performance, Barnaby stood in the wings with an ear-to-ear grin as Lily bowed to a standing ovation. The Sunday after her acting debut, Lily took advantage of the crisp fall day to relax. It was her custom on weekends to take an early morning walk to explore different neighbourhoods. She was pleased and surprised when Barnaby caught up with her.

"Are you following me?" she asked, not disguising her pleasure at seeing him.

"I'm not following you. I'm trying to catch up," Barnaby said blushing. They walked along silently, stopping on a road where the houses looked like unfinished repair projects. One single-storey house was still waiting to be clad. Loose insulation flapped haplessly in the breeze.

Lily suddenly turned to Barnaby, looking perplexed. "The drama teacher told me you studied medicine. So why are you at teachers' college?"

"You were asking the teacher about me?" Barnaby asked with a smile, raising an eyebrow.

Lily blushed this time.

"I'll need to teach for a year or two to earn enough to start a specialty in surgery," Barnaby explained. "I had a scholarship for my first degree."

Lily had a pang of anguish, feeling her life was so much easier than Barnaby's. *My scholarship is a source of pride, but not essential to my going to teachers' college,* she thought, as she returned Barnaby's smile.

He gestured toward the flapping tarpaper. "That's what I call a do-it-yourself project. I grew up in a house like that. My father died before he could finish the exterior. A teacher's salary won't be enough to finish a surgery internship. Fortunately, my father taught me basic carpentry skills and that's what I do in my spare time. Surgery is a good choice for a handyman."

"You *do* have your life well planned," Lily said, aware now of why Barnaby rushed off after rehearsals.

"My father at least lived to see me become the junior light-weight boxing champion," Barnaby said. "He taught me to box and how never to lose a match."

Lily's eyebrows popped up in surprise at this statement. Barnaby shot her a boyish grin.

"He also instructed me how to be a gentleman in the ring."

Lily smiled. "You seem more cherubic than pugnacious, Barnaby, with those pink cheeks."

Barnaby gripped her arms gently and swivelled her around to head in another direction. Lily felt her heart beat faster, just as it had while watching him build the stage.

"Let's go see where we'll practise-teach," Lily said, embarrassed by her thoughts. "It's in an equally poor area."

They stopped suddenly as they saw a large man cuffing a small boy's ears. Lily dashed across the street to intervene in the bullying, and Barnaby followed her. "Please stop that," Lily said firmly to the man.

"The boy sings in the church choir like an angel, but speaks like a clown," the father said, finally taking his hands off the boy.

"I, I, I don't m-m-m-mean to," blurted the boy, who looked to be about seven years old.

"Come see for yourself," the father said angrily, gesturing to the nearby church.

Curious, Lily and Barnaby followed the pair into church and listened to Bobby's unhampered voice as he sang.

Several weeks after this incident, Lily began her teaching practicum at Bobby's school, and the incident of the stuttering boy who could sing so beautifully stayed in her mind.

After a rehearsal one evening, Lily told the drama teacher about the boy's stuttering. The teacher had studied in Paris for a year and recounted the story of the famous French actor Louis Jouvet, who could act his parts perfectly, yet not speak in a normal conversation without stuttering. The teacher had concluded that a singsong voice allows a stutterer to control his speech. Lily approached the principal to see if she could set up an after-class program for three boys, including Bobby. The principal agreed to let her try, and Lily began her speech classes. The sessions were kept to half an hour as the boys couldn't tolerate more than thirty minutes of trying to speak properly.

On those afternoons, Lily walked into the classroom with her tools. Using mirrors, feathers, balloons, handkerchiefs, and songbooks, she worked with the little boys on breath control. She had noticed within the first lesson that each boy took a huge breath before trying to speak. She also noticed that they were speaking when almost out of air. Another startling moment occurred when a frustrated boy shouted at Lily without stammering. Lily ended each session with songs, and they would trudge home to their disappointed parents.

Disappointment turned to pride when the stuttering boys sang in the Christmas concert. The seasonal choir was featured on the front page of the local newspaper. At the end of Lily's practicum, she met with the parents to show them the exercises she had taught the boys. And with this lesson, she extracted with her broad smile and thoughtful brown eyes, a promise: the parents would no longer shout at the boys. "Pressure," Lily told them, "is the root of a stutterer's problem."

Lily won the best teaching practicum on graduation. She and Barnaby exchanged their parents' addresses, not knowing exactly where they would end up living. Barnaby had accepted a teaching post at a high school in Halifax. They were both filled with uncertainty now that war had erupted. Lily had been disappointed that Barnaby had not declared himself for she was sure that he fancied her. Why else would he have asked her to come to watch him box on Saturday afternoons? The wistful memory of sitting on a front bench and cheering Barnaby on was disheartening. Her heart had taken a flip when he'd looked at her from the ring and winked. He had singled her out, but when the match was over he would leave immediately, saying that he had to finish a carpentry job.

Amelia was frustrated when Lily arrived home without a serious beau. When she admitted she had exchanged addresses with a fellow student, Amelia shrugged. "What good is that?"

"He's going to become a surgeon," Lily bleated. "He's years of studying ahead of him."

"But he didn't propose!" Amelia retorted, throwing her arms up in exasperation.

Despite this initial tension, Lily decided she would like to spend a summer month with her parents before leaving to teach. Lily had been offered teaching jobs in Sydney, but she chose a post in Glace Bay to be close to her parents, but not underfoot. Glace Bay was only ten miles from Sydney. The onset of war had made many families closer, with the constant worry and fear of not knowing who might be lost. Robert White was a liberal, bordering on pacifist. He would have enlisted against his beliefs to please his military father, but circumstances saved him. The Sydney Hospital needed a pharmacist, and Robert volunteered his services, thus avoiding the war.

Lily's sister Beth had joined an amateur acting troupe for the summer that had ended up in New York City. She sent cheery letters home, describing her exciting life in New York and the young crowd of actors she hung out with. The year away from Beth had given Lily a broader perspective on her sister, who was not just their mother's favourite, but the embodiment of all that Amelia had not been able to do in her life. Lily was now aware of her mother's unintended pregnancy. As much as she disliked the English family she had never met, the family that had sent Amelia away, she realized that Robert would not have been her father if they had not shipped Amelia off in disgrace to Halifax. Many nights Lily comforted herself with this thought.

While she was at home with her parents for the summer, Lily received a letter from Beth asking her to come to New York. The acting group had disbanded at the end of the summer but Beth had stayed on, telling her parents she had been offered another job in the theatre. In the letter to Lily, Beth had scrawled in large letters: PLEASE COME AS SOON AS POSSIBLE!

Lily decided to tell her parents during the midday meal that she wanted to visit Beth before she left for Glace Bay. She wouldn't mention the letter because it sounded so ominous. Robert had just come in from the pharmacy and they were all sitting down at the table when Lily announced her plan. "A capon — my favourite dish!" he said, beaming at his wife. He carefully sliced the breast after removing the wings and legs. "I think it's a good idea that older sister is going to check on Beth," Robert said, as he placed chicken pieces on their plates. Lily smiled at her dad's impeccable manners, mentally comparing him with the young men at college who had spoken with their mouths full and didn't have Robert's refined etiquette.

"You'll get to see Beth on stage," Amelia said, with her usual admiring tone. "We received a brochure for a play at the Playhouse Theatre, although there was no indication Beth had a part."

"Young actresses aren't prima donnas," Robert said, wagging a cautionary finger. "They learn to act by working *behind* the scenes. These jobs don't get mentioned in the brochure. Beth would be quite lucky to have a small part alongside a seasoned actor."

As Lily climbed the stairs, Amelia called out, "Pack something fashionable."

Opening the closet door, Lily grimaced, pushing aside the plain wool dresses of her teenage years. She frowned, recalling Beth's superior tone while advising her on clothes that boys would find attractive.

"Look, it's not enough to have brains," Beth had said. "A girl has to have style to get the right man. Look at Mom, a poor girl who ends up marrying the son of a naval captain. Why, Dad grew up sailing at the Halifax Yacht Club! He wouldn't have married her if she had been a bad dresser."

"Blood must be thicker than water," Lily muttered as she dragged her suitcase out from the bottom of the closet. Sleepy, she stretched out on her bed, thinking she might never marry. She wondered if Ed Parsons was still in Glace Bay. She recalled that two weeks after the chalk incident she had bumped into him on Rogue's Row, a forested path where students went to smoke and romance. Lily had gone there to stroll with a friend. She urged him to begin his English lessons again, saying she'd forgiven his rudeness.

He had tossed his cigarette, planted a lingering kiss on her mouth, and then wheeled around and disappeared. The next day, Lily watched in horror as Ed poked his head into the girls' washroom, knowing the incident would be reported and he would be expelled.

Lily wondered if Ed had gone overseas or stayed at home because of the need for miners. Lily sighed, thinking that Barnaby might soon be at the front as well. She could recall the intimacy of exploring the Truro neighbourhood with Barnaby just as she could still remember Ed's kiss.

CHAPTER 3

Knockholt Cemetery, England, 1919

"I don't want to visit any dead people," Ivy protested as Clara coaxed her through the creaky gate of the Knockholt Cemetery. Ivy had become saucy, spending most of her time with the Drakes, who spoiled her. Schools had been closed because of the flu pandemic and Clara considered herself fortunate to have Ivy so well cared for. She had been terrified that Ivy, like Billy, might catch the flu. The Drakes provided a safe way of keeping Ivy isolated. Today, Ivy had not wanted to leave the farm.

"Ivy, we must put flowers on your brother's and your father's graves," Clara said softly. "It could be a very long time before we return. Canada is far from England." She stopped on the gravel path to put her arms around her daughter. Clara had struggled to make ends meet since her husband had died, selling her engagement ring to meet a mortgage payment. She was relieved that she had been offered the well-paying position of lady superintendent of the Galt Hospital. *I'm doing what Dr. Newbury suggested: setting my sail anew. But I'm only accepting the job in Lethbridge for Ivy's sake.*

A sudden clang of church bells was an abrupt reminder that the war had ended a year ago that day. Visitors to the cemetery looked up at St. Katherine's Church tower as the bells pealed out the eleventh hour. Knockholt Cemetery was crowded with families looking for their loved ones' graves.

"Over here!" someone shouted. "I've found Chester!" A group hurried past, scuffling the pebbles as they rushed to join the discoverer of Chester's tombstone.

Like war, peacetime is to be shared, Clara thought as she listened to three women talking to one another about the slow emergence of fresh food on the market.

"We're expected at the pub in less than an hour," Clara said, taking Ivy's hand as they wound along the pathway. Clara looked up at the cloudless blue November sky. "Ivy, let's be positive! Pretend we're explorers to the New World. We're going to see cowboys, Indians, galloping horses, enormous lakes, towering mountains, pristine snow, and year-round sunshine. Aren't you breathless with excitement?" She kissed Ivy's wispy blond head and continued to hold her. She could feel the wetness of her daughter's tears through her dress. Both of them remained motionless, wrapped in each other's arms.

Clara's mind drifted to the grim day she had spent in the Knockholt Cemetery only a year before. Mourners had lined up where she now stood with Ivy. The influenza pandemic had spread so rapidly throughout England that it had put immense pressure on the burial system.

At the time, a horse-drawn hearse was the only vehicle available to transport Billy. The back doors of the hearse, hand-carved in the form of draperies, were held closed by huge brass springs. Clara swallowed hard, remembering the sharp clack of the doors as they were shut — dealing a note of finality — and the shocking words of the driver. Knocking one of the springs with his fist, he'd said, "These will ensure no indignity will occur while I'm driving."

Clara had driven to the cemetery in the hearse, while Miff and Addy had followed in their car with Di Shaw, Clara's friend since her nursing school days. Clara's parents had contributed well beyond their means for the purchase of a magnificent gravestone that would honour George, and now Billy. Only a modest stone had been laid on George's grave in the midst of war. Clara received loving notes from her siblings from as far away as Gallipoli. Even from a distance, she felt their grief.

Light drizzle had begun to fall on that sad day of the funeral as Clara arrived at the cemetery with Billy in his small coffin. The horses' backs glistened in the rain. The driver, forced to wait on the High Road outside the graveyard and fearful that the horses might bolt if a car passed, had stood beside the carriage with a tight hold on the reins. It was an hour's wait before they were handed a piece of paper with the plot number and permission to proceed. Two men stepped up to unload the coffin and carry it to the designated spot behind St. Katherine's Church. The young vicar was waiting for them at the grave. He looked haggard and dishevelled in his damp suit and soiled clerical collar. For a young man, his face was heavily lined. He had already performed six burials that day, but Billy was the first child.

Billy's casket was lowered onto his father's. Clara shivered, recalling the dug-out rat-infested trenches George had crawled through to repair communication lines. Everything became blurry around her.

The minister offered his condolences and began his shortened service. The last thing Clara could remember was "earth to earth," followed by thumping sounds as clumps of mud hit father and son's boxes. Overwhelmed, she collapsed forward and toppled into the grave. Miff immediately stepped down onto the coffin, trying not to lose his footing in the slippery mud. The vicar reached down, and together they hauled Clara up into Addy's arms. Di began to sob until Miff pulled her away. Overwhelmed with anguish, Clara leaned on the men for support. Streaks of clay mixed with blood smeared her face. Di climbed into the hearse beside her, and Clara was taken to hospital, where they cleaned the deep cut on her forehead.

A young man, balancing himself on crutches, stopped in front of Clara, "Are you all right, ma'am?" he asked. "You don't look so good."

"Oh, thank you for your concern. I suppose being in the graveyard has brought back some terrible memories. My husband and son are buried here." Clara motioned to the plots not far from a giant yew tree.

"Was it the flu?" the man asked.

"For my son, yes."

"My brother would be almost seven," Ivy said, tears glistening on her eyelashes. "We're moving to Canada now that my daddy is dead."

Seeing the look of pain on Clara's face, the man said quietly, "Death doesn't mean the same to a child." After a quiet moment, he asked, "And your husband?"

"Died in the service of his country."

The man, not more than twenty years old, smiled as Ivy stared bug-eyed at his useless-looking legs.

"We all lose something to win a war," the young man said, tapping his leg. "Want to see how fast I can go on these things?" He set out, swinging his legs through the crutches. "C'mon. I'll race ya to that big tree."

Ivy trotted beside him toward the enormous yew and Clara followed. The eight-hundred-year-old tree attracted visitors from miles around, and, according to the vicar, had even increased attendance at church.

"I must leave ya here," the man said, turning along another path.

"Thank you for cheering us up," Clara said.

"Good luck, ma'am. You have a pretty little daughter."

Whistling, the man swung away in another direction. Clara began to walk on, then stopped abruptly and broke into a grin. Di Shaw was leaning back against the wide trunk of the old yew, reading a book. Ten years earlier, Clara had walked out of St. George's Hospital with Di, both proudly holding their nursing diplomas. They had, however, followed different paths; Di married immediately upon graduating and soon had a family. *How life's circumstances change*, she thought.

"You look elegant just sitting by a tree," Clara said. Di jumped up and rushed over with her arms extended. She was wearing a grey wool coat, a beige silk head scarf, matching gloves, and fashionable stockings. Despite the war, she had retained her taste for fashion.

"I wasn't expecting you," Clara said, looking happy and surprised.

Ivy wrapped her arms around Di's middle. "Can't I live with Auntie Di?" she asked.

Clara covered her hurt with a smile. "Miff said you would meet us at the pub. Now that you're here I can show you the headstone."

They stomped through overgrown grass to the grave. Beyond the church hedge there was a meadow filled with late autumn flowers. "Such a peaceful place," Di said, resting her hand on the granite. "This must have cost a fortune."

"My parents helped me. It was the least we could do for Billy and George."

"What is this black stuff?" Di asked as she traced the inscription with a finger.

"It's molten lead. The village blacksmith did the lettering as a favour to my father. It will last several lifetimes." Clara handed Di a handkerchief. "No more tears, Di. I've been asked so many times how I could still go to church after God dealt me such a sorrowful hand. He has his reasons. And if I'm lucky, the day will come when He will reveal them to me."

"Sorry," Di said as she sniffed and wiped her eyes. "I want to be a comfort."

"You are."

Ivy buried her head in Di's chest. "Why do people have to die?"

"People are like trees," Di said. "Some trees live for a long time and others die early. Billy and your daddy are like trees that died early, especially poor Billy, a mere sapling." Di led Ivy away from the grave and back to the yew tree.

"Will I die like Billy?" Ivy asked.

"Don't be silly. You're going to live to be as old as this tree," Di said.

Ivy grimaced, looking back at the grave.

"Canada won't be at all like my gentle old England," Clara said wistfully, glancing at the blooming meadow beyond the hedge.

"Don't be a dreamer," Di said with the confidence of an old friend. "This class-bound country would be rough on a widow with limited funds. It takes money or extreme luck for a young girl to succeed socially in England." She put her hands on Clara's shoulders. "Clara, it was sheer good fortune that you got to nursing school. Do you want *Ivy* to be a tweenie?"

"I wasn't a real tweenie," Clara said. Her goal as a young woman had always been to avoid the fate of being a tweenie, a job that was higher than a scullery maid, but lower than a cook. "Whatever I was in the Pinks' house," she said defensively, "I received an excellent education as Harold Pink's niece." She regretted having told Di that her mother, Lydia Pink, had run off with the family blacksmith, Clara's father, and had a daughter four months later, whom she named Amelia.

Lydia's brother, Harold Pink, had visited when Clara was eight years old, and, admiring her brightness, invited her to live with his family. He had long since forgiven his sister for her indiscretion and wanted to help. He was impressed with Clara's intelligence and industry as she scurried around organizing the messy cottage. He offered to provide her with a proper education. He gracefully made no comment on what he thought of the ne'er-do-well blacksmith, who called himself a gentleman farmer. Addy had been too young at the time to be of interest to Harold Pink and had stayed with her parents.

Di hugged Clara. "You've made the right decision to emigrate. Take a few minutes to reflect on your good fortune, and I'll go ahead with Ivy."

Clara leaned against the yew tree and waited for the calm to come. She let her mind drift into the little patch of garden Billy had so energetically cultivated. She could feel the sting of the nettles he had weeded from the beds. She imagined him holding up his muddy hands as he entered the house for her to wash them in the bucket by the back door. Many nights, it was the memory of Billy in the garden that helped her fall asleep.

Remembering her family's circumstances when she was a child, Clara began to think again that she might try to find her older sister. *A pharmacist can't be hard to find*, she thought. Feeling more relaxed and quite excited, she abandoned the tree and headed for the pub.

*   *   *

Clara caught up with Di and Ivy as she turned up Knockholt's High Street. Stopping to catch her breath, she stood watching Mrs. Peck, the pub-owner's wife, waddle underneath some rusty old scaffolding erected to give the Double Crown a much-needed facelift. She was picking up the debris left from the workmen's lunches and throwing it in a dented bin. The newly painted white stucco stood out against the dark oak beams. Several patrons, who stood outside chatting, nodded approvingly at the changes.

"Nice job ya done, Missus Peck," a man in uniform shouted through the scaffolds.

She stood up quickly, knocked her head on a board, cursed, and waved. "Glad you've lived to enjoy a pint, love," she said, grinning. She crouched down and continued removing debris.

"This scaffolding is too much like a ladder," Clara said as she stepped into the street to avoid walking under it.

Di laughed, shaking her head. "You *are* superstitious!"

"I need to be. I've had my share of bad luck."

"I know you have." Di reached out and squeezed her friend's hand. "Let's be happy," Clara said. "For Ivy's sake. It's all so confusing. I've made the best decision, *but* I will always miss my homeland." Di pressed her finger to Clara's lips. They had already had this conversation.

A man dressed in a shapeless brown tweed suit stepped out of the pub and motioned for the incoming customers to stop. "You'll need to wait in the entryway 'cause we got a full house. 'Bout ten minutes should do it. Judge a pub by its lineups," he said, grinning, then scooted back inside.

"Phew! I can smell the musty beer from here," Clara said, screwing up her nose in distaste.

"With prohibition you won't have any damp pubs in Canada," Di said, laughing.

"Ah, well, that's why some Scotch whisky and brandy will

be crossing the Atlantic in my steamer trunk." Clara chuckled. "I remember returning to the hospital after purchasing my libation to find Dr. Newbury imitating Canadian temperance ladies marching in large feathered hats to seize all the medicinal beer in the Galt Hospital. The soldiers had been asking about his hometown, Lethbridge. They stopped laughing when they saw me, of course, but I pretended to be absorbed in reading a chart. But Dr. Newbury had his back to me and didn't notice. 'Lethbridge ladies of the night work in cozy brothels,' he was saying. 'In Montreal, they work on the street in the midst of danger and crime.'" Clara's face became thoughtful. "Dr. Newbury is as wise as he is witty. I would never have made the decision to go where my sister was banished without his encouragement."

Di put her arms around Clara and they held this embrace until Miff marched into the entryway and said: "Ladies, we've been waiting. I didn't notice you'd arrived. The waiter has asked us to move to a smaller booth to make way for a larger party."

"Hurry on in, mates," the man in the rumpled suit urged. "We're filled to the rafters."

The atmosphere in the Double Crown was jovial, and lively conversations echoed through the smoke-filled room. Everyone seemed to be talking at once. Across the room, the offer "Want a Players?" resonated, suggesting rationing of cigarettes was slowly easing. Waiters wearing white shirts and black trousers wove through rows of heavy oak tables, holding up trays topped with jugs or glasses filled to the brim. They had towels draped over their shoulders, ready to mop up spilled beer. Several tables, pushed together to seat larger groups, made it difficult for the waiters to pass. A waiter's swinging hip knocked one of the tables, causing a huge splash of beer and a clatter of broken glass as a jug tipped onto the floor. "If that happened at the club," exclaimed Miff, "the waiter would lose his job."

"Women aren't allowed at your club, Miff, so don't fuss about spilled beer," Addy retorted.

Di interjected, pulling a box from under the table, "Your auntie and I have a present for you, Ivy, to keep you warm at the North Pole."

"You know I'm not going to the North Pole," Ivy said, putting her hands on her hips and smiling. "Can I try it on?" she asked, bouncing on her seat as she tore open the box and saw what it contained.

"Oh my, rabbit fur!" Clara said as she let Ivy slip out to try on the coat. There was a matching hat that she set on the table.

"Don't that little miss look smart," a man sitting opposite said to his companion.

Ivy blushed and refused to put on the hat, but she went around the table to give Di and her aunt each a big hug.

With Ivy momentarily out of earshot while she went to the washroom, Miff began questioning Clara. "What do you expect to be doing exactly at the hospital? Do you know anything about the Galt? With whom have you corresponded?" Miff looked concerned. He had attended to Clara's finances and, finding them tight due to George's poor planning, he had advanced her a hundred pound sterling "to be paid back at any time."

Clara lowered her voice. "I've communicated with Dr. Orr, who is the medical officer of public health for Alberta. He wrote me that there's a serious problem in that province with the rapid spread of venereal disease brought back by the soldiers. The highest incidence is in Lethbridge. He explained that it's not surprising since the city had the highest enlistment for its population in all of the Dominion."

"Well, that suggests great loyalty to our country," Miff said, nodding approval.

"What about your living arrangement?" Di asked, joining

the conversation. "We worry about you being so far away."

"I'll have a small flat in the nurses' home. I was sent a photo, and it seems that the home is attached to the hospital. The nursing students, or what we call probationers, live there as well."

"What's this segregated area you've talked about, Clara?" Addy asked, frowning.

"It sounds very American," Di interjected.

"No, it's quite Canadian." Clara laughed.

"But you're a surgical nurse, not a social worker," Addy added.

"Well, it looks as though I'll be both. Lethbridge began as a mining town filled with amorous bachelors, so it tolerated prostitutes. The segregated area is a red-light district for brothels and some Chinese merchants that citizens refuse to have in the downtown area. Prohibition complicates things, according to Dr. Orr. He indicated that brothels are also a place to have a drink and as such most prosecutions are for liquor infractions. The ladies of the night themselves are rarely charged. I won't know much more than that until I arrive."

Ivy was now sitting down again beside her mother, and Addy gave Miff a censoring look.

"Dr. Orr covers the entire province. I'll be working more closely with Dr. Morris Lafayette, the medical officer of health for Lethbridge."

"What a strange combination of English and French," Miff said.

"Dr. Newbury explained that Dr. Lafayette's mother changed Maurice to Morris when her husband died to appease her Scottish family, who never approved of her marriage to a Frenchman." Clara looked at her brother-in-law. "I'll have my challenges, Miff. I know that."

Miff put his arm around Clara. "We're going to miss you both terribly."

CHAPTER 4

New York City, 1914

All the way to New York, Lily had made up scenarios: Beth needed money; was engaged; had a serious illness; was moving back home. She stepped out of the taxi and took a deep breath of the big city air. She gaped at the strange surroundings — tall apartment buildings bookended by little shops and eateries. She plastered herself against the taxi as a bicycle whizzed past.

"Nice place ya got here," the taxi driver said as he smiled at the twenty-five-cent tip. Lily gawked at the eight-storey brick building where Beth lived. Shimmering late August heat rose up from the sidewalk. The driver plopped her suitcase down and puttered off, looking for the next customer. Lily entered the apartment lobby and scanned the mailboxes until she found the name Mac Whittaker, and under it, Beth White. She pushed the buzzer for apartment 302.

"It's Lily! Are you going to let me in?"

There was a giggle, followed by a click. Lily pulled open the wrought-iron door and started up the carpeted stairs. Her nose crinkled at the musty smell. As she knocked at the door of 302, she heard a door slam inside the apartment and then light footsteps. Beth opened the door slightly and poked her head out.

"I'm not dressed," she whispered. Stepping back momentarily, she opened the door wide. Her satin slip clung to her body with the humidity. Her chestnut hair was tied back, making her face with its aquiline features and striking blue eyes seem gaunt.

Embracing Beth, Lily could feel the round hardness of her sister's belly. "How are you faring in New York?" Lily asked. "Mom and Dad made me promise to bring back details."

"Let's not stand at the door. The building is filled with nosy tenants." Beth closed the door behind Lily and dragged her to a sofa upholstered in a nubby green fabric, pushing several theatre reviews to the floor. She plopped down, pulling Lily beside her.

"Lily, I'm pregnant. I don't think that's the kind of news Mom and Dad want to hear."

"I can't believe it! You're going to have a baby?"

Beth slipped a cigarette from a Pall Mall package and knocked the end gently on the coffee table. She took a match from a glass box and struck it under the table, lighting her cigarette and inhaling deeply.

"Want one?" she asked.

"Not a habit I've started." Lily shifted to face her. "When are you due?"

"The baby would be born close to Christmas. I'm five months along. But I don't want a baby. I'm going to have an abortion — and I wanted you with me. Please don't judge me, Lily. Life in New York has been complicated and not what I planned."

Several minutes passed before they spoke again.

"Beth, tell me what's been going on. Who's the father? Why can't you have the baby and put it up for adoption? Why can't you keep it? Come home, and Mom will look after it."

Beth tossed her head and scoffed. "Me, the favoured

daughter, bringing home an illegitimate son or daughter? It doesn't matter. I'm not going to have this baby." Her tears softened the hardness of her voice.

Lily got up and sat on the end of the sofa. She couldn't remember ever having seen her sister cry.

"Beth, you can't go through with this. At five months you might injure yourself, or harm the baby and still deliver it alive. You could end up with a defective child." She shook her head in dismay that Beth was being so foolish. "Come home and I'll look after you. I'm not afraid of Mom's opinion. I'm begging you!"

Lily scanned the room for evidence of another person. "I saw the name Mac Whittaker beside yours. Is Mac the father of the baby?" An end table was scarred with cigarette burns. Lily put her finger on a burn mark and picked up a butt smeared with lipstick. "Someone's a careless smoker. Who else lives in this apartment?" Lily stared at the two closed doors off the living room.

"Are you conducting an investigation?" asked Beth. She got up and went to the kitchenette, which was separated from the living room by a serving hatch that looked like a home-made adaptation. Lily watched her sister pour two glasses of water.

"I'm guessing Mac is the careless-smoking father."

"He is a smoker, but he's not the father."

Lily gulped down the water, plunking the glass beside the ashtray. "Phew, I hate the smell of cigarettes!"

Beth let out a snort and smiled. "Getting back to Mac. He's an aspiring actor. Ben Shenker is the owner of the theatre and he adores Mac, *but* he's also married with two daughters." Lily cocked her head, looking pensive. "Neither Mac nor I can afford the forty-dollars-a-month rent for this place on our own, but the next step down is pretty awful. I don't really know if Mac's queer or not, but he does need help with the rent."

"So you're saying Mac is a kept man?" Lily said, wrinkling up her nose in distaste.

"Mac's a nice man and we get along. But he's certainly not the father."

Lily narrowed her eyes. "How do you pay your half, Beth?" Lily reached out and took Beth's hand, shaking her head with slow comprehension. "So you and Mac are both being looked after."

"Don't distort the situation."

"Who *is* the father?"

"The father's unimportant. I'm getting rid of the baby. But it's worth noting that he didn't offer to care for the child. Men like a sign of their virility, but not the responsibility."

"I don't know what is worse: Mac in a secret relationship with a man who has a family, or you having an abortion."

"Don't judge me, Lily! In the theatre you sleep with someone who will advance your career. It was my bad luck to get pregnant."

Lily groaned and put her head in her hands. She was surprised at her sister's coarseness. Beth was spoiled, but she'd never been coarse. *Beth's right,* she thought. *She would be a huge disappointment to our parents.* Lily wondered what story she could fabricate about her visit to New York.

"Beth, how on earth did you ever get into such a seedy situation?" Lily threw up her hands and walked to the window. Cars whizzed by in the street below, honking as they dodged pedestrians. She was surprised at how much love she felt for her younger sister. How could she have suffered such a reversal of fortune? She let out a long sigh and turned back to Beth.

"There are hundreds of couples who would adopt your child."

"Sorry, Lily. I've made up my mind. There's a woman doctor who's going to do the abortion tomorrow night."

"Beth, I pinched some laudanum from Dad, thinking you might be sick. I wouldn't have if I'd known you were having an abortion."

"I used to pilfer laudanum and sell it for cigarettes." Beth broke into a guilty grin. "I always knew when a delivery of narcotics was arriving. Dad had a calendar of shipments in his desk, and I'd look through, noting the dates. The delivery boy could kiss me for one bottle and touch my breast for two."

Lily shook her head. "Beth, you could fall in a cesspool and come up smelling like a rose."

"Let's hope I come up like a rose tomorrow."

"All right, enough for now. Where should I put my suitcase?"

Beth led Lily into a small bedroom with a double bed, its iron frame painted white. Lily recognized the quilt her parents had given her sister when she'd left for New York. She heaved her suitcase onto the bed and retrieved the laudanum.

Later, Lily and Beth lay on the bed listening to the night noises: laughter, shouts, curses, tires screeching, horns honking. "This is nighttime in New York," Beth said.

Lily tucked the threadbare blanket under her head and said, "I can't believe you brought this horrid old relic of your childhood to New York!"

Beth laughed in response. Then Lily asked, "What happens when Mac's friend comes over?"

"I stay for a while and then leave discreetly."

"Neither of us likes each other's noises."

They both laughed.

Once Beth had fallen asleep, Lily curled herself around her. She lay awake listening to Beth's rhythmic breathing, then pulled the blanket from under her head and tucked it around her sister.

In the early morning, Lily unwound herself from Beth and slipped out of bed. She put on Beth's red satin dressing gown, another going-away gift from her parents. The dressing gown reminded Lily of her parents, and she wondered again what she would tell them when she returned. She knew she couldn't say anything about Beth's abortion. Lily's mood darkened at the thought of it.

Beth came into the kitchen, rubbing her eyes. "I thought you might have gone back home," she said, with a panicked expression.

"You know I wouldn't walk out on you. But I haven't changed my mind about the abortion. It's a dumb idea."

"Lily, let's not bicker. I'm starved!" Beth opened the icebox door and an odour of uncomplimentary smells wafted out. Dill pickles, chocolate and caramel sauce, sliced onions, Polish sausage, russet apples, and hard cheese were stored in jars, plastic plates, or bits of paper on the upper shelf. A glass container marked MAC sat on the bottom rack. Beth piled onion slices on a plate and covered them with the chocolate. Lily's brown eyes became owl-like as her sister gobbled the onions and chocolate sauce.

"Are you having cravings?" she asked, screwing her nose up in disgust, and they laughed. Then Beth clasped her hand over her mouth and rushed to the toilet. Lily put her hand on her own mouth hearing Beth heaving in the bathroom. She had a weak stomach at the best of times.

A couple of minutes later, she heard Beth flushing the toilet and brushing her teeth. She reappeared looking perfectly composed.

"Is there someplace nearby where I can eat *normal* food?" Lily groaned.

"There's a cheap diner down the street called Dingley Place.

People know me at the diner, so please don't mention the abortion." Beth narrowed her eyes, and for a brief moment Lily recalled Beth's face when she was being unkind.

The morning was cooler than when she had stepped out of the taxi the evening before. Older residents were sitting on steps or parked on chairs they had dragged to the sidewalk.

"Hi, Beth. Who's the friend?" A plump, olive-skinned lady sat with her feet well apart to keep her fleshy thighs cool as she shelled peas into a bowl on her lap. She smiled broadly when Beth indicated that Lily was her sister. The lady had perfect false teeth.

"This is Signora Bumbacco," Beth said with an exaggerated Italian accent. "She's the building super, and she makes the best calzone in America."

"I make some for the dinner tonight?"

The elderly woman took Lily's hand and gave it a little shake. Lily returned her smile with a knot in her stomach, as she remembered that after dinner there would be an abortion. In a flash of panic, she hoped she wouldn't faint during the procedure.

"We both have dates tonight," Beth said.

Signora Bumbacco gave Lily an appraising look and grinned. "I bring the calzone early?"

"That would be nice. I love calzone," Beth said.

At the diner, Lily ordered coffee and cinnamon toast, and Beth asked for an egg, sunny-side up, and hot chocolate. "I promise I'll hold this down."

"I hope so!"

"Women are so free in New York," Lily said, glancing around. "Mom would go shopping alone, but she'd never sit alone in a diner. And women smoke in public! Beth, return to New York if you want *after* the birth, but please come home first." She leaned close. "If you still want to date men who will pay for your apartment, then Dad has things at the pharmacy that you can get with a doctor's order. You just have to say you're married. Or I can filch a few."

"You mean condoms," Beth whispered.

"Exactly. You never want to go through this again!"

Beth's expression darkened. She looked around the diner and shrugged. "It's a man's world, Lily. You and I grew up with Dad. He's the anomaly. Let's get off the abortion. Tell me about you."

Lily regaled her sister with tales about her year in Truro, opting to concentrate on the lighter stories. She admitted to being spurned by James Barnaby, who preferred medicine to girls. They reminisced about high-school experiences. Recalling the story of Ed Parsons looking under the washroom door, they both laughed. It was the first time Lily had seen a true smile on her sister's face since she'd arrived. She was glad she had put their rancour behind her and come to New York when asked.

After they'd paid their bill, the two sisters headed to a nearby park, where they threw peanuts to grey, black, and brown squirrels until one got too aggressive and hopped on Lily's purse. She shook off the pesky animal with a little shriek. Then the squirrel landed up on Beth's bag and she dropped it, jumping aside. They grabbed their handbags and hurried out of the park, laughing.

They walked twenty blocks to the theatre where Beth was to have had a small part before the mayor of New York objected to the play. "When the manager tried to argue that the *Girl with the Whooping Cough* was *not* an obscene play, the mayor closed the theatre," Beth said. "I hope to have a part in the next production here."

They returned in the late afternoon to find that while they had been exploring, Signora Bumbacco had deposited the calzone in Beth's icebox. She had also wiped down the icebox and thrown out the food that had gone bad.

"Not everyone on the street gets calzone from the matriarch of the street," Beth said, pulling it out of the icebox. She poked at the crust to inspect the filling.

"I don't think you should eat if you're going to be anesthetized," Lily said.

"Who says she's going to put me out? All it takes is nerve, a coat hanger, water, and heat." Beth looked her sister in the eye with bravado and then added, "Lily, I'm scared. That's why I underlined 'please come.' You have the nerve. You've always been stronger than me. Now, let me eat a bit and stop treating this as though it's the Last Supper."

Lily found she had no appetite and put the remainder of the calzone back in the icebox. Then she went into the bedroom to make sure everything was clean and tidy. Feeling helpless, she pulled the sheets taut, plumped the pillows, folded Beth's quilt, and put it aside. Every mean thing she had ever said to Beth came back like a chorus. She'd always thought she was the only one under pressure at home because their mother was so critical of her. But poor Beth had to be her mother's alter ego. It was their mother who had encouraged Beth to go to New York.

Lily wanted to cry, but she couldn't. At six-thirty, a knock at the door signalled the doctor's arrival. She wore a white cotton dress and a kerchief tied at the nape of her neck. She had a crisp, cold look that frightened Lily. She stood in the living room, holding a black bag, staring at her. Lily met her stare with a hard look of her own. Then she softened, realizing that in a few moments this woman would have her sister's life in her hands.

"So, where do you want me to do the job?" the woman asked, looking at the sofa.

"It's my sister, not me. She's in the bedroom." Lily nodded

her head in that direction. "Are you a qualified doctor?"

"I have enough medical training to do the procedure I'm about to perform. It's simple. If you're pregnant and don't want to have a baby, there's no alternative."

The woman, who had not offered her name, went into the bedroom, where Beth was lying covered by a top sheet. Her face was pale and taut, without an ounce of her old bravado.

"I'll have to heat this on the stove," the woman said as she pulled a wire from her bag. "Put an apron on so you can help me. I'll need some hot water."

Lily turned on the gas and watched, half paralyzed, as the woman rotated the wire over the flame holding a pair of tongs.

She returned to the bedroom and poured iodine on a sponge. "Roll on your side," she said and began wiping Beth's buttocks and thighs.

"Are you ready?" the woman asked.

Lily checked her urge to flee. She gripped Beth's hand and whispered, "It will soon be over."

The woman folded a piece of gauze several times, and then soaked it in a clear liquid. The smell of ether nauseated Lily. The woman positioned Beth's legs wide apart and slipped a towel under her. She put on cotton gloves.

"I'm going to put this cloth over your face. Breathe normally."

Beth reached for Lily's hand. She breathed for three breaths and was out.

"Keep her legs apart," the woman said.

Beth's breathing was even. The woman took the coat hanger wire and slowly inserted it into Beth's vagina. She put a few more drops of ether on the cloth over Beth's mouth and nose and continued the wire on its journey. Lily's entire body winced when the woman nodded, indicating the wire was doing its job. She moved it around in a circular motion. Blood trickled onto the towel.

"Stop," Lily said and put her ear next to Beth's mouth. "My sister's gagging. She can't breathe under that cloth." There was a pinkish spot on the gauze. Lily tore the cloth off Beth's face. Beth's mouth was covered in partially digested food. She took a shallow breath and began coughing. Her heart was pounding under her slip.

"She's aspirating," the woman said, and she tipped Beth over onto her side. With each raspy attempt to take in air, Beth's body shook with spasms. The woman, who had pulled out the wire, scrambled up on the bed. She straddled Beth, encircled her chest with her arms, and squeezed hard repeatedly until a bolus of food spewed out on the floor.

"I've got to get out of here," the woman said. "I've disturbed things enough that the abortion will occur spontaneously. I *told* your sister not to eat beforehand."

"If you had, she would have followed your instructions," Lily spat.

"I'm sorry, but she'll have to abort without an anesthetic. She will have a lot of pain." The woman threw her things into her bag and scurried out of the apartment and down the stairs.

"What am I supposed to do?" Lily screamed after her.

She propped pillows behind Beth's back so she would remain on her side. She waited until Beth could breathe without going into a spasm, then she raced down the stairs to Signora Bumbacco, who was eating dinner with her husband.

"You like my calzone?" the woman asked, shovelling in a big mouthful.

"Signora, please come. Beth is losing her baby." Signora Bumbacco made the sign of the cross. "I'll explain when we get there. We need to hurry."

CHAPTER 5

Boarding the Scotian, 1919

Clara took the ten-mile train ride back to Woodside after saying goodbye to her family. Ivy slept the entire way. The fast rhythmical click of the train made her feel anxious. She'd hardly had time to think in the past few months as she'd prepared to leave her homeland. She placed her finger on her wrist, breathing slowly until her pulse slowed down. As the train rolled forward she thought of ways she might connect with Amelia once in Canada. Her sister had inherited their father's dark-eyed gypsy look; that she remembered, but as events turned out, also their mother's careless ways. Clara marvelled that her unmarried sister with a child had captured the heart of a pharmacist. As an adult reflecting on her parents' decision to send Amelia away to avoid scandal, Clara felt Amelia's good fortune was poetic justice. She believed her parents could have handled the situation less harshly.

"Three more nights in the house," Clara said when they arrived back in Woodside. Boxes were piled and marked, waiting to be picked up by the local auctioneers. Their contents defined her domestic life. She pictured the auctioneer holding up her twin crystal decanters with their matching sherry and port glasses. She hoped they would go to someone who liked entertaining.

The pungent aroma of camphor wafted up from the dining-room table. Clara had surrounded her silver tea-and-coffee service with camphor-soaked cloths to prevent tarnishing. The set was packed and ready for shipping along with eleven Limoges demitasse cups. George had bought them directly from the Laternier factory during a visit to France. Clara thought the decorative Limoges stamp on the bottom of the cups was as lovely as the pink, gold, green, and blue border. She loved to serve after-dinner coffee in them when she was entertaining. George, unable to smoke himself, would offer guests a round of cigarettes with the coffee.

It was during a pleasant dinner for a visiting officer that one of her precious Limoges cups had been broken. As she passed a cup of steaming coffee to a guest sitting beside her, the officer made a quick gesture with his outstretched arm. The hot liquid was knocked onto the lap of the guest. When he stood up, yelping in discomfort, the cup on his lap tumbled to the ground, shattering into countless pieces. Clara rushed the afflicted gentleman to the kitchen, alternately reassuring the officer and apologizing to the guest. She handed him a jar of salve she had taken from the hospital for her children's rashes and left him to administer its soothing effects in private. When the guest returned, he quipped, in a falsetto voice, that he still wanted coffee. The clumsy officer broke into relieved laughter. This, Clara recalled nostalgically, was her final dinner party, the one that had sent George, still breathing with difficulty, back to the front.

Clara went outside to look at the Drakes' cows basking in the late-day sun. She heard the mooing, suggesting it was milking time. The sun disappeared in the woods at the western edge of the fields. A little laugh escaped her lips at the recollection of a walk in the forest one spring day with George. He had put his hand down the front of her dress, not noticing a pair of elderly neighbours behind them. She had screamed, "Get this wasp away from me!" Swatting at her dress, she pretended George was trying to capture the offending insect. The couple turned modestly away and later asked if she was allergic. George teased her that she would make a great actress. "You are naughty, George," she said.

The memory comforted her, and gave her thought as she went back in the house to fetch Ivy.

"Let's go for a walk. Maybe we'll see a rabbit or a fox before sundown. That's when they are most active. Settling down for the night, I suppose."

After she'd gathered up Ivy and they'd started their walk, Clara stopped to chat with the same neighbouring couple that had caught her with George's hand down her dress. Mr. Hewson, clad in breeches and green wellingtons, leaned with both hands on his silver-handled walking stick as he chatted. *He looks so British in his gentleman's walking uniform,* she thought. Mrs. Hewson wore a kerchief that allowed strands of salt-and-pepper hair to escape. Her tweed coat, the same colour as her hair, was loose and baggy, leaving her figure formless.

"Do you remember when Margaret tripped over the laundry basket hanging out the washing, Mrs. Durling?" Mr. Hewson asked, referring to his wife. "Her face was covered in blood and dirt, and she couldn't move her arm. There weren't many doctors on call during the war, but you came right away and popped her arm back into its socket. Then you made a splint before I took her to the hospital. The doctor was pleased with your quick reaction." Mrs. Hewson lifted her arm and made circling motions to show how well she could move it. Clara nodded approvingly.

Bringing the conversation to the present day, Clara said, "James and Dorothy Aston are the new owners of my house." After a thoughtful pause, she added, "Let them know that despite the sadness at the end, we were a happy home. I'm leaving behind some good memories. When we get settled, I'll send you news."

An officious-looking man in a blue uniform shouted, "Cabin-class passengers with children, board first."

"That's us," Clara said, pushing Ivy gently in the direction of the gangplank, grateful that Miff had provided the needed cash to upgrade their travel.

They walked along the deck to a spot where they could watch what was happening below on the quay. Clara tried to focus on the commotion and ignore the inner voice insisting it wasn't too late to change her mind. She watched Ivy affectionately as she chattered away with fellow passengers on deck.

"Once them that's on the upper deck is boarded, we'll load on the handicapped," announced the official down on the quay. "Third-class passengers go last," he continued, in case anyone stepped out of turn. Clara imagined this puffed-up man with his dissolute red face bicycling back to his modest two-room cottage after the ship departed. She did not resent him relishing his short-lived importance. She pictured him enjoying his pint of beer at the end of the day.

"Oh, my goodness," Clara said, looking down at the quay. "Auntie Di's down there, arguing with the official."

Dressed in a black sheared-lamb coat and hat, Di was shooing away well-dressed passengers who were starting up the gangplank. "Please, make way for the wounded," she said. "The able-bodied can wait." She started up the ramp with a man in a wheelchair. His head and eyes were wrapped in white gauze.

"You've got no ticket, lady," the official yelled as though Di were a stowaway.

"Auntie Di is bossier than you, Mummy," Ivy said. Clara nodded her head in agreement as she watched Di block the boarding passengers. She drew Ivy close and let her snuggle into her old wool coat. Di had urged her to buy a warmer coat before leaving for Canada. "I know, I know. I wasn't born yesterday," had been Clara's irritable reply. She smiled down at Ivy in her white rabbit fur. "I might look a bit tatty, but you look splendid, darling." Ivy's arms tightened around Clara's waist.

Within minutes, the scene below them on the quay was transformed as strapping Canadian officers helped their rank-and-file soldiers get on board. Nurses in blue capes stepped up their pace, fearing another scolding from Di, who they thought must be the matron of the nearby military hospital. Di had no financial worries with her husband a successful financier, but with the onset of war she'd hired a nanny and gone back to nurse at St. George's Hospital.

Watching Di commandeer captains to push injured enlisted men reminded Clara of her last visit with her friend at St. George's. There had been a peace parade that day, and it had passed in front of the hospital on its way into Hyde Park. Clara and Di had watched from a second-floor window overlooking the park. Decorated generals and ordinary soldiers in their distinctive uniforms were a vivid reminder that the war had been won through the collaboration of many countries. After the spectators dispersed, Di and Clara had crossed over to the park to sit one last time at their chosen meeting spot as nursing students. Di had liked to smoke there, and it used to be Clara's job to keep watch so she wouldn't get caught.

The day after the peace parade, *The Times* had published an editorial describing how rich and poor had mingled as one for the celebration, "high-born ladies making way for modestly dressed onlookers." After reading it, Di had put the newspaper down, unimpressed. "Clara, this is the reason you're moving to Canada. Even the war couldn't unite the classes here for more than one day."

Di continued as the self-appointed chargé d'affaires until twenty-five soldiers — some of them amputees, some with head injuries, and some blinded or coughing — were on board.

"Thank you for your kindness," Di said to the first-class passengers, now embarking behind them. They shook her hand as she stood at the bottom of the gangway.

Clara grabbed Ivy's hand and rushed down the boarding ramp to meet Di. "You're the consummate nurse," she said, linking her arm through Di's and laughing to hold back her tears.

"Ivy looks wonderful in the fur coat," Di said, equally emotional. "Promise me you will return soon, Clara. I'll be waiting at this same dock." Di took out a lace handkerchief and dabbed at her eyes. "You'll do well. I know you will."

"We're going to miss you, Di." And then the officious man shouted for Clara to get back on the ship as though it were a car that could drive away fast.

"When you're lonely, think of Hyde Park," Di said, puffing an imaginary cigarette. She turned to leave, still dabbing her eyes.

Clara watched her until she was out of sight; she had curled her fingers into her palms so hard she looked to see if they were bleeding. She took Ivy's hand and rushed up the plank.

Passengers were settling into their cabins. The steward, who introduced himself as Joseph, answered questions as to various services, mealtimes, and activities. "What sort of entertainment is offered on the ship?" a woman dressed in a smart brown wool dress asked him. She held on to her wide-brimmed hat with her left hand and slapped at the hem of her dress with the other. Each gust of wind exposed her fancy stockings. "Oh, dear," she said, "I think I shall return to my cabin until the wind dies down." As she retreated, she removed her hat and used it to hold down her dress.

"How old is the ship?" a decorated officer asked. Clara recognized the Canadian uniform.

"I'm not sure of the age, but she's recently been refitted in Glasgow," the steward said. "We're down to six hundred passengers in Cabin Class, or Third. The vessel was redesigned to take more cargo. Rest assured, Canadian Pacific will provide you with excellent service."

"Are you a shareholder?" The soldier laughed.

The steward smiled and made a barely perceptible bow of his head.

Ivy's wispy hair was blowing all over. "Let's get out of this wind," Clara said, brushing a strand off her daughter's face. They scurried into the lounge, where three green upholstered benches provided seating against the walls. At the near end were shelves with well-worn books, a pair of binoculars, bowls of mints, and some dog-eared playing cards. Above the shelves, a partially rolled-down map bore a description of the ship's history: *The Scotian transported Canadian Expeditionary Forces to Britain in 1914, but at the end of the war served as accommodation for German prisoners on the Isle of Wight.*

Other passengers hurried into the lounge to get out of the wind. A tall, thin man with steel-grey hair, identifying himself as Mr. Mason, said, "I have the latest weather report. Captain Haines said our departure will be stormy, but fair weather will arrive when we clear England and be with us for the rest of the journey. I'm off to Canada to check on my daughter who's married a Canadian soldier." He spoke the last sentence proudly and had the look of a man who laughed often. The lounge was filled with British, English, and French-Canadian accents. Everyone seemed eager to tell his story.

A soldier in his mid-twenties stood in a corner of the lounge, observing the happy commotion. Noticing his medical insignia cap badge, Clara asked if he was a doctor.

"I am the doctor on the *Scotian*, a post that offers the benefit of free passage." He held up his right stump and a thumbless left hand. "Let's hope we don't have a surgical emergency." His grey-green eyes crinkled with amusement while his mop of straight auburn hair gave him a boyish look "You're Sister Durling! Do you remember me from Maidenhead Hospital?"

"My goodness, I do! You're Dr. James Barnaby, a protégé of Francis Newbury's. You were part of the Second Canadian Division from Nova Scotia if my memory serves me."

Dr. Barnaby laughed. "I recall waiting outside Dr. Newbury's operating room, watching you march around the ward as though you were in charge of a battalion." Dr. Barnaby's eyes brightened at the memory, and they both chuckled.

"After losing my right hand and left thumb, being a surgeon was no longer an option. Learning of my dashed hopes, Dr. Newbury arranged for me to finish my medical studies in Scotland with an emphasis on neuropsychiatry. I did my practicum at Craiglockhart Psychiatric Hospital treating shell shock. That was worse than accepting my change in plans. I was on the committee that decided when a soldier was ready to go back to the front. I felt I was letting a soldier commit suicide with my blessing each time I signed a *Return to Front* order."

"Dr. Newbury is head of the department of surgery in Edmonton now. Are you going to join him?'

"Yes." Dr. Barnaby's eyes were serious but happy.

"Such a coincidence," Clara said. "I'm also off to Alberta to assume a position, thanks to Dr. Newbury.

"What will you be doing?" he asked.

"I will be the lady superintendent of the Galt Hospital in Lethbridge."

"That makes two of us owing our second chance to Dr. Newbury."

Clara excused herself as Ivy tugged on her arm to go and explore the ship. "I hope we won't be needing your services," she said with a broad smile.

CHAPTER 6

Glace Bay, 1914

Beth didn't abort, but spent the following few days tended by Signora Bumbacco. Unable to face the procedure again, she decided to travel back to Sydney with Lily. Upon their return, Lily left it to her parents to sort out what to do with Beth and the future baby and moved to Glace Bay, resigned to Barnaby's ambition and hoping Ed Parsons had grown up.

She scouted out the possible boarding houses, and, after checking out several landladies, she settled on Mrs. O'Dea, whose house was on the side of town closest to the school where she would teach. Mrs. O'Dea was a childless widow who had always rented out a room in her house. She was pleased to show Lily a large room overlooking the street — the only problem being light from the streetlamp.

Lily moved in with her belongings, and, as was her custom, set out to discover her surroundings on foot. She settled into a local restaurant for a cup of coffee and to get her bearings. The waitress, a chatty girl, mentioned that on Saturday evenings young people go to the Dew Drop Inn. "I wonder if an old classmate of mine is still in Glace Bay," Lily said. "We were both at Sydney Academy."

The waitress screwed up her face as if to say "aren't you grand?" She volunteered that Ed, who was no schooler, now worked in the Caledonia mine.

Lily thought back on the conversation when he had said, "Us Parsons are miners through and through." Still blushing from the "look," Lily thanked the waitress for sharing local news.

Lily tentatively set out for the Dew Drop Inn the following Saturday evening and was pleased when Ed turned up at the dance. Cleaned up and smelling of cologne, he stood out from the other miners. Tall and heavily muscled from the mine work, he looked incredibly handsome. He seemed livelier and more confident than at high school. He wore the top two buttons of his shirt open to expose thick tufts of chest hair. "Is my tutor going to dance with me?" He smiled down at her.

Lily, remembering the chalk down her dress, retorted, "I see you're still irritating, Ed Parsons." He ignored the remark, pulled her onto the dance floor, and drew her close. His firm hand on her back made it easy for her to follow him. Lily smirked, recalling how Barnaby had apologized to her during a college dance. He had drawn her into the waltz position, then turned scarlet as he uttered, "Oops, I'm sorry." There was no apology from Ed.

"Nice rhythm," Ed whispered. Goosebumps erupted on her arms as his breath brushed her face. After the dance, he threw his jacket over her shoulders and led her outside. Avoiding the bootlegger pocketing cash, they made a quick about face and walked off. Ed spread his jacket on the ground so Lily could sit down. She pulled up her knees and leaned against a tree.

"I like coming to Dewdrop," Ed said. Lily compared his

happy face to the worried look he always had at school.

"I see you like dancing," Lily said. "I took lessons when I was at teachers' college."

Ed frowned. "Who'd you dance with?"

"The teacher designated our partners." Lily giggled. "Sometimes it was a girl. I always wanted to dance like my parents. They would push back the living-room furniture and roll up the rug, creating a makeshift dance floor, thinking my sister and I were asleep. They didn't have a gramophone, so my dad would whistle a tune as though he were whirling my mother in front of a live orchestra. I would sit unnoticed on the stairs peeking through the bannister. It was in that darkened room with nothing but moonlight where I realized how much my parents were in love. It was beautiful watching them dance."

Ed raised Lily's chin and kissed her. Tears were trickling down her cheeks.

"What's wrong?" Ed asked, pulling away.

"I get emotional when I talk about my dad."

Ed stood up brusquely, walking away impatiently. "I hate emotions," he said. He brushed aside the bootleggers pressing him to buy alcohol. Lily followed him back into the inn and squeezed into the booth where his friends were sitting. They were debating whether a square dance should be the next request. A man with pockmarked skin slid out and crossed the floor to ask the caller if he would oblige. He reported the caller would start once he'd downed his drink. "Don't imagine he's drinking water," he said, snickering.

Once on the dance floor, the group arranged themselves into four couples with Ed claiming Lily as his partner. The fiddle started playing, and they joined other foursomes as they began stomping their feet and clapping to the music. People on the side whooped at their friends. The girls wove in and out under the arms of the boys, skipped forward and back to "do-si-do," and then linked arms for the promenade. Lily slipped her arm through Ed's and they began skipping forward in a circle. As they passed the sidelined hooters, a young man made a suggestive comment about Lily's ample breasts. Ed swirled around so quickly that Lily didn't see what happened. But the man had blood on his lips.

"She's sweet on a boxer named Barnaby!" the bloody-mouthed man goaded. Lily recalled now he was the "creep" at teachers' college who hadn't made it. She had been relieved to think he would never be in a classroom. Dancing stopped as the partiers egged the men on from the sidelines.

"You're asking for it," Ed said as he delivered another punch.

Lily and the other girls scurried out of the inn and along the path as quickly as possible in order to stand at a safe distance. They could hear taunts, insults, and blows as they rushed away.

"Now they've all joined in," a girl said, giggling nervously. "Last year there was a ruckus that ended with a fiddle being slammed over the caller's head, I don't think my parents are going to let me come here anymore."

"I wonder if we could forbid alcohol for the first part of the evening so the gals can dance before a fight gets started?" Lily said.

The girls, traipsing behind her let out a skeptical laugh. "Why do you think the boys go to Dew Drop?" the girl who had recounted the fiddle bashing piped up. "Moonshine!"

When Ed caught up with Lily later, he grabbed her arm to stop her.

"You should have told me you had a boyfriend," he said. "I don't like being made a fool in front of my friends."

"Are you jealous, Ed?" Lily regretted her teasing as soon as she saw the hurt in Ed's eyes. "Look, if you promise not to fight, I'll come with you next Saturday. But one punch and I'll find other amusements in Glace Bay." Lily felt she was back at school lecturing Ed. Her heart was filled with tender and frustrated emotions.

Ed gave her a prolonged kiss while the other girls stood gawking. Lily looked at the audience and blushed. She had been slow to resist Ed's advances.

Sunday family dinner seemed the right occasion to introduce Lily to the Parsons family. She and Ed had been dating now for almost four months. His invitation to meet his parents came with a rider: "Don't be surprised if my mother treats me like a five-year-old." Ed's older brothers, Tim and Andrew, had left home to train at Val Cartier before being shipped overseas, but three married brothers with their families came for the noontime meal to meet Lily.

"How would you keep boys who want to be miners in school?" Mr. Parsons asked, lamenting his grade-eight education. They were all gathered in the living room, the children playing with a train set that was brought out whenever they visited.

"We can't force them to stay in school, but we can lay the foundation," Lily said. "I just concentrate on the three R's; reading, writing, and arithmetic. Girls already love to read. It's the boys who hate books. Except to throw them." The family joined Lily in laughter. "I do try to give the boys books that will interest them, but it's not easy."

Mr. Parsons brought up Ed's misdemeanor in the washroom, but Ed protested. Lily adroitly turned the conversation to the Christmas play.

Before the meal, Lily stood up and offered to help Mrs. Parsons serve the food, following her into the kitchen.

"No need to help," Mrs. Parsons said as Lily stepped out of her way.

Despite her plump figure, Mrs. Parsons spun around the kitchen like a top. Lily wondered what Mrs. Parsons would have done with a daughter. The bustling about her kitchen, however, resulted in a delicious pot roast in a rich tomato-and-onion sauce. Mr. Parsons said grace, and the family members crossed themselves, a reminder to Lily that Ed had been raised Catholic. Mrs. Parsons ladled the meat onto the plates along with a large scoop of buttered mashed potatoes.

"My mother isn't a good cook," Lily confessed, relishing the tender beef and gravy. "Dinner in our house consists of high-level conversation and low-level food."

"Well, if that's the case, Lily," Mr. Parsons said, "why don't ya stay with us for Christmas and enjoy a right big meal with all the trimmings made by Mrs. Parsons? Then ya'd meet Tim and Andrew." Mrs. Parsons's eyes welled up with tears, and she crossed herself again.

"I would like to meet Tim and Andrew, but I would miss spending Christmas with my aunt Marjorie. She's my father's sister and always comes to our house for Christmas."

"Help me clear the plates, dear, and you can tell me more about your aunt," Mrs. Parsons said kindly as she bustled about clearing dishes.

"I don't know how much longer she'll be with us," Lily said, her voice quivering as she brought the first load of dirty dishes to the kitchen sink. "She would be appalled that I'm so emotional with strangers."

"We're not strangers, Lily. Ed talks about you constantly. Especially how you helped him at school."

"Well, until he peeked into that washroom." Lily laughed. "It was a unique way of getting expelled."

"Are the two of you going to the Christmas dance at the Dew Drop?"

"I'm not," Lily said. "The man who runs the place is serving free punch. It will be mayhem."

Mrs. Parsons turned from the sink and looked at Lily. "I've spent my life sticking up for Ed. According to him, every antic was someone else's fault."

"I think moms always have a favourite," Lily said thoughtfully. She recalled Beth's hard fall from grace as the special daughter. Lily wanted to tell Mrs. Parsons about her sister's baby, but realized she couldn't discuss this with such a devout Catholic. Beth was adamant that she would not keep it, so Amelia had gone hat-in-hand to the Anglican Parish to see who might adopt the child once it arrived. Beatrice, a cousin of the vicar whose husband had a fishing boat, offered. Lily joined her mother and Beth when they'd gone to Peggy's Cove to make the arrangements. They were greeted with homemade bread and deep-fried cod. Beatrice's four children, ranging from eight to fifteen years of age, were excited about having a baby in the house. "We all have to share a room," the fifteen-year-old said. She looked at Beatrice. "Could I share the room with the baby?" she asked. Beatrice nodded, eliciting a broad grin.

When everything was settled regarding Beth's confinement, Amelia turned to Beatrice and asked if she would like to visit Sydney. "We own a pharmacy," Amelia said.

"Do you sell candy?" the youngest child asked.

"For a penny, but perhaps you can have some for free," Amelia said, ruffling the boy's hair. "There're lots of things to do in Sydney."

Beatrice laughed, and her children let out a whoop of enthusiasm.

"It's settled, then. You'll come with the whole gang." Lily and Beth had grinned. They had never heard their mother use slang words.

Mrs. Parsons brought Lily back to their conversation in the kitchen. "I'll have to help Ed decide what to buy you for Christmas."

Lily chuckled. Mrs. Parsons did indeed treat her son like a five-year-old.

A few days after the Sunday dinner with the Parsonses, Lily went out to purchase gifts for her family before heading home for the Christmas holiday. The first winter storm had just hit, but she struggled through the blowing snow from shop to shop to buy Beth a box of face powders in varying shades of beige and a silk wrap for Aunt Marjorie. Heavy flakes of wet snow dampened her wool hat. She blinked away the ice crystals that were forming on her eyelashes. Commercial Street was almost empty as shoppers headed away home. She looked at her watch. "My goodness," she muttered, "an hour of shopping and I only have two gifts."

As Lily hurried back to Mrs. O'Dea's, she realized it would be appropriate to buy her a Christmas gift as well. Lily appreciated that her landlady allowed her some privacy. When she had been looking for a place to live, she was surprised at the nosiness of ladies renting parts of their house.

Lily stepped into the small vestibule to find Ed's boots standing in a puddle of melted snow. She smelled coffee and felt a wave of panic. If Ed had used her landlady's kitchen, Mrs. O'Dea would know he was in her room. There were no other boarders. Lily had never brought up the subject of entertaining visitors. Her body felt tingly as she mounted the stairs. She was excited yet angry that Ed had let himself into her room.

When she opened her door at the top of the stairs, she was momentarily speechless. Ed was stretched out in his underclothes, sipping a mug of coffee. His clothes lay in a pile beside him. She bolted across the room and closed the curtains, then grabbed her blue wool dressing gown from the back of the door and threw it at him.

"Put this on!" she said as she hastily adjusted a crack in the curtains. "What if someone saw you?" She had visions of a pupil or parent leaning against the lamppost looking up at her room. Everyone knew where she lived.

Ed tried to pull her onto the bed. "Come on, Lily. You know you want it."

"It!" Lily said hoarsely. "What's it to you, Ed? Something to boast about?" Lily realized her words sounded harsh and she softened her voice. "What I want is love, like my parents had."

Lily's body was awash in mixed emotions as she watched Ed go from excitement to shame. She turned her back as Ed dressed. "What went through your head?" she asked, angrily. Ed turned and picked up a chair, setting it down so hard again that the front leg broke off. Tears spilled from his dark eyes as he stomped down the stairs.

Lily knelt on her bed, parted the curtains, and watched him disappear into the falling snow. She smoothed the mark Ed's body had made on the bedcovers. A shudder coursed through her. What would have happened if he had stayed? She turned off the light and leaned on the windowsill looking out at the falling snow reflected by the street lamp. "It's time you stopped acting like your mother's five-year-old," she whispered. "I'll never have a serious relationship with someone so unpredictable." She lay down on her bed and rolled onto her side, tucking her childhood blanket under her head. It smelled of hair pomade.

In spite of these thoughts, Lily continued to see Ed, although her feelings for him often went from tenderness to anger. Ed presented Lily with a heart-shaped locket at Easter and asked her to be his girl. As summer approached he suggested taking a picnic to the swimming hole where he had learned to swim as a boy. It was a salty inlet, warmer than the ocean. When Lily said she couldn't swim, he offered to teach her. But she refused, saying she was terrified of water.

"I'm happy just enjoying the sun," she said, as she spread out a blanket and unpacked the pastries, fresh bread, and sliced ham his mother had prepared. She felt a wave of irritation that Mrs. Parsons had added a flask of liquor. Ed didn't need any encouragement.

The dessert had melted all over the picnic basket. "What a mess!" Lily said, laughing. They scooped at the puddle of chocolate and licked each other's fingers. Then Lily waded into the inlet to rinse out the picnic hamper. Dark water marked a sudden drop-off. She hurried back to the sandy beach and was raising the liquor flask to pour what was left on the ground just as Ed emerged from the bushes in his bathing costume.

"Don't waste it," Ed said, grabbing the flask and screwing on the lid.

He rushed toward the water. "I'm going to swim out to Baldy Rock." Lily watched in amazement at the powerful stroke of his arms and rhythmical kicking. Every few strokes he brought his arms forward simultaneously, arching his body like a dolphin.

"I've got a cramp," Ed shouted as he swam back. Forcing herself to overcome her fear, Lily high-stepped into deeper water to help him. At the edge of the drop-off, he put his hands on her waist and hoisted her toward him. She shrieked with terror as her skirt billowed up over her face.

"Hold your breath," he shouted. He dunked her under, and she came up coughing sputtering and gagging.

"Ed, you know I can't swim!"

Ed held her waist, treading water with his powerful legs. Lily pummelled his head when he dunked her under a second time. This time she screamed as she came up for air.

"We live by water. You need to be able to swim," Ed said forcefully.

"What the hell are you doing with that girl?" a man shouted from the shore. He was rushing toward them, his daughter and wife watching on the beach. Ed lifted Lily up and set her down in the shallow water. She was sobbing between deep breaths. The man put his arm around her and led her back to shore.

"I wouldn't have anything to do with that young man, Miss. Scaring a poor girl like that. If I were you, I'd get swimming lessons real quick and never go near that bully again."

"He *was* my boyfriend," Lily said.

"No kidding?" The man looked at his wife and child. "You wouldn't find me doing that."

Ed rushed past the glaring family to sit down on their picnic blanket. Lily joined him, dripping and still breathless.

"I didn't believe anyone could be *so* afraid of water," he said.

"Well, I didn't believe anyone could be *so* mean. We're both surprised, Ed Parsons."

"Lily, I'm sorry. That's how I learned to swim. My brothers tossed me off a wharf."

"Ed, I have a mean sister and I don't intend to have a mean beau. I need a break from you. Aunt Marjorie has asked me to spend the summer with her in Sydney, to help out. I've decided to say yes." Lily's eyes filled with tears. "Ed, I can't take this push and pull. One minute you act as though I'm your girlfriend, and the next you act as if you don't care. I don't know what you're afraid of, but it shouldn't be me."

When she saw Ed's defensive expression, Lily fought to keep her resolve.

"You're right," he said. "You deserve better than a coal miner."

"You're missing the point. This has nothing to do with you being a miner." Lily ran her fingers through her wet hair in exasperation. "I can't stand these moods."

Ed's eyes glistened, but Lily couldn't interpret his silence. He dressed, and they walked silently back to town, Lily in her sopping dress.

As soon as Lily got back, she used Mrs. O'Dea's phone to call her aunt in Sydney. She broke into a broad grin when she heard Marjorie's voice at the other end. "Aunt Marjorie, I'd like to accept your invitation. I can't cook, but I'd be helpful in everything else." Marjorie chuckled. Lily was surprised at how strong her aunt sounded, despite the fact that the breast cancer had spread to her lungs.

"Lily, it would be wonderful to have your help. When can you come?"

"In two weeks, when school ends. I need some practical advice."

"Well, you know your aunt has an opinion on everything."

Marjorie understood the delicate interaction between Lily and her mother. She had met Amelia in her compromised circumstances when Amelia was the housekeeper to the elderly Mr. White. Marjorie was working at the time as a full-time nurse and was unable to care for her grandfather. She understood that Lily reminded her mother of something she wanted to forget. Marjorie had intentionally filled the emotional gap when Beth was born by making Lily her *special* niece.

When Lily hung up the phone, she began to cry. Marjorie had called her beautiful even when she was at her most ungainly. Beth, so sure of herself, didn't need compliments. The proof of her self-confidence and resilience was found in the fact that even a botched abortion and the birth of an illegitimate child had not daunted her. Beth had returned to New York after the birth of the baby.

After her first full year of teaching, and her tumultuous relationship with Ed Parsons, what Lily wanted most now was to rekindle her family relationships and forget her former beau.

"What was I like when I was young?" Lily asked one evening, curled up on the sofa. The weather had turned cool and her aunt had stoked up the coal stove.

"My goodness, you make yourself sound so old," Aunt Marjorie said, laughing. She held the glass door open for a moment, staring at the orange embers. "You would stretch out by this stove reading your page-worn books and eating my cookies."

"I remember the cookies," Lily said. "Two cookies bound together by homemade jam. Sometimes you used a date mixture, but I preferred the jam."

"Your uncle Ned paid a full month's wages for this New Silver Moon stove on our first anniversary," Aunt Marjorie said, looking fondly at the stove. "You were always intrigued by the name. That's why I want you, the daughter we never had, to inherit it. I've set aside money to transport this stove wherever you are, so long as it's not Timbuktu."

Lily laughed. "I don't want to inherit the stove anytime soon, Aunt Marjorie."

"Just remember, there were never more than six hundred New Silver Moons manufactured."

"And God only made *one* Aunt Marjorie." Lily took her aunt's bony hand and held it against her cheek. "Mom's pleased that I've broken up with Ed Parsons. What do you think, Aunt Marjorie? Mom never liked me dating a miner. And all her hopes are pinned on *me* now ... after Beth's humiliation."

"Well, your uncle never went beyond grade school. Never judge a man by his diplomas! Tell me what you liked about Ed."

Lily knitted her brow and released Marjorie's hand. "I don't know exactly." She blushed, imagining Ed stretched out on her bed drinking a cup of coffee. "I suppose I was *attracted*," Lily said, not looking at Marjorie.

"Attraction is not reason enough to marry a man. When I was in nursing school, an engineer swept me off my feet. He was a master at ballroom dancing."

Observing Marjorie's translucent skin stretched over her high cheekbones, Lily realized how beautiful her aunt was, despite her illness.

"I've kept in touch with him over the years. He's now the mayor of Lethbridge. Imagine that!" Marjorie eyes sparkled. "I suspect I would have had a more exciting life with him than with your uncle Ned. He was larger than life even as a young man. But your uncle and I were always like two old friends. And married to him, I could pursue my career in nursing. My engineer has a most unhappy marriage, he tells me." Marjorie laughed. "Uncle Ned was quiet and modest. We had a peaceful marriage."

"Well, Ed and I wouldn't have that," Lily said, frowning.

Lily received a long letter from Ed that disturbed her peaceful sojourn with her aunt. Labour tensions had escalated at the mine, and before Lily had left Glace Bay for the summer, Ed had gotten mixed up with some Americans led by a man named Bob Glimp. Ed's father called the man a Bolshevik troublemaker, but Ed distrusted the managers of the mine and ignored his father's suggestion to try to get along with them. Lily had laughed when Mr. Parsons said the troublemakers courted Ed because he was a hothead. But now his letter suggested he was now in the middle of the violence.

The company had hired police from the local detachment, paying them more than the regular constables. Families were divided. Some miners thought they were lucky to have a job. Others believed they should join the Americans. Shoving and shouting in front of the company store had ended with no one certain whose side he was on. Someone had threatened to burn down the manager's house, and he had retaliated by turning off the electricity in the miners' company-owned homes.

Ed is right, Lily thought as she read his letter. Low pay, double shifts, and rigged seniority along with dismal safety checks and absence of health care were reason to complain. But, like Mr. Parsons, she believed the Americans were recruiting Canadian miners to join their union out of self-interest. *They want money*, Lily mused, *not change*. She thought of returning to Glace Bay before the school year began, but then changed her mind because she still needed time to decide if she would permanently end her relationship with Ed.

In early August, Lily received a letter from Ed begging her to return to Glace Bay. She wrote back, correcting his spelling, but, realizing the unkindness of that and imagining the tears in his eyes, she tossed that letter out and wrote simply that she wouldn't return before school started.

Two weeks after the worrisome letter, she was surprised by a visit from Father Michael, the new priest at St. Patrick's Church in Glace Bay, who had walked the ten miles to Sydney. He was a young priest, recently graduated from St. Francis Xavier, where he had earned a reputation as an excellent boxer. Months earlier, while Lily was sorting clothes with Mrs. Parsons in the church basement, the two women had watched the priest hop from foot to foot in boxing slippers and cassock. He'd been so absorbed in practising his moves that he'd seemed unaware of their presence. They had quietly retreated, giggling with their hands over their mouths, all the way up the old wooden stairs of the church.

Lily had met Ed when he moved to Sydney to finish high school. Sydney Academy had combined academic and technical programs and Mr. Parsons had visions of his son managing a mine rather than working underground. He was willing to pay for boarding so Ed could get a better education. Most of Ed's friends in Glace Bay had quit school before graduating to work in the mines. While Lily did not have a personal connection to Father Michael, she did know that he was the Parsons family's priest. She was taken aback that he had walked such a distance just to talk with her. The priest had blue-black eyes, similar to Ed's, but they were not wary like Ed's.

"Has something happened to Ed?" Lily asked, surprised by her sense of urgency. "Will you stay for tea and something to eat, Father?"

"It's a long walk home on an empty stomach." He chuckled.

Aunt Marjorie retreated and clanged about the kitchen, hoping the noise would allow her niece some privacy.

"No, nothing has happened, Lily. But Ed has confided something to me. Of course, as his confessor, I can't divulge what that is, but I've asked him to tell you himself. Certainly, it's not for a bachelor priest to interfere in relationships, but if you had certain information you might better understand this young man's erratic behaviour. I'd like the two of you to talk."

"I wrote him that I would be back in Glace Bay at the end of August. I won't change my plans." Lily stretched her long legs in front of her, arched her back, and clasped her hands behind her. Then she let out a loud sigh and shook her head. "Tell Ed Parsons I'm looking forward to seeing him." *Love*, she thought, *shouldn't be so complicated.*

Father Michael left with a box of Marjorie's jam cookies. He thrust his hand in the box before he closed Marjorie's gate.

Lily watched him walk briskly down the road. "Funny," she said to Marjorie, "that he feels so responsible for Ed."

Three days before classes resumed, Robert drove Lily back to Glace Bay.

"Are you excited to start a new school year?" he asked.

"I am, Dad. I'm thinking of starting a music group, perhaps a choir."

"That's interesting. I never thought you had any special liking for music. Books, yes, but Beth was our singer and dancer. I suppose that's what drove her toward the theatre. Tell me more about your plans."

"Do you remember my telling you about a little boy, Bobby, in Truro, who stuttered badly yet sang beautifully in the church choir? Well, this summer Aunt Marjorie urged me to work with a group of children with speech impediments who came for day treatments at the hospital. The parents of stutterers were at their wits end thinking speech was mind over matter." Lily laughed. "I taught the children to speak in a singsong manner as though they were reciting poetry." She imitated the lilting speech, "May ... I go to ... the bathroom."

Robert leaned back and laughed heartily.

"Watch the road, Dad." Lily grinned. "I was paid for the work, by the way. I haven't forgotten that bird."

"That's my girl! A bird in the hand! What will you do with the extra money?"

"Buy sheet music and perhaps rent a piano. Last year we had six pupils with speech problems in the school; two started stuttering when their fathers left for war." The car ride became less jocular as both Lily and her dad contemplated the war. As

Robert pulled up to Mrs. O'Dea's, she was waiting, smiling, arms akimbo in front of the garage. He was careful not to block it.

"Do you have a car?" he asked Mrs. O'Dea.

"Nope. I sold it after my husband died. The garage is filled with junk." She shook Robert's hand and disappeared into the house, leaving him to carry the suitcases up to Lily's room on the second floor. Lily was relieved that her landlady had not divulged the ruckus overhead when Ed had broken the chair and stomped out. Lily had concluded she must be slightly deaf, but decided now it would be best to tell her father the whole story.

As though Robert could read her thoughts, he asked, "Has Mrs. O'Dea met Ed?"

Lily shrugged and laughed. "She's either heard him or she's deaf. He got upset one evening and stomped out."

"Hmmm. So Mrs. O'Dea allows visitors in her boarders' room. Be sensible. You don't want to follow in Beth's footsteps." Lily looked at the ground to hide her smile. *My parents still think of me as their child,* she thought.

"Don't worry, Dad. The Parsonses' priest asked if I'd talk with Ed so he could get something off his chest. I don't want an entanglement, but I can listen." Lily cocked her head. "Since Beth's predicament, Mom has loosened up. Isn't that a good thing?"

Robert raised his arms in resignation. "Women! I'll never understand them." Lily gave her father an impish grin. "Just use your judgment, Lily. I'm sure Ed Parsons can weave a good story."

"There's a lot of good in him, Dad." She laughed. "It's just hard to find it sometimes."

Robert knocked on Mrs. O'Dea's door before leaving and handed her a large jar of pickled beets from his wife. She beamed.

My father is a woman charmer.

"Keep an eye on my daughter," he said, handing over the jar. "She's no trouble at all," Mrs. O'Dea replied, heading for the kitchen.

Lily sprinted up to her room once her dad had driven off, and changed into a pretty dress, fluffing her hair, pinching her cheeks, and applying a light pink lipstick. Her sister's words about how to catch a man flickered then disappeared from mind. *I only want a conversation with Ed,* she thought. She expected him to arrive in an hour. Why Father Michael had walked ten miles to deliver his request still mystified her. She hurried out to buy a few items before he arrived. On the main street, children dragged their mothers into stores to buy new outfits and supplies to start the school year. *Not every child in my class has the privilege of new clothes,* she thought. Parents, recognizing her, greeted her and said they were glad she had come back. She suspected they had heard she'd ended her romance and assumed she'd moved elsewhere. There was no such thing as privacy in a small town.

Ed was waiting in the downstairs hall at Mrs. O'Dea's when Lily arrived back home with an armful of parcels. He reached out to relieve her. "You look great, Lily. A summer at your aunt's has done you good." He shuffled his feet awkwardly. "Is it all right if I carry these bags up to your room?"

"Just keep your clothes on," Lily said with a hard stare that quickly relented. "Come on. Let's go up and have a talk. Father Michael suggested you had things you needed to say to me. So here I am."

Once upstairs, Ed picked up the chair that had had the broken leg and examined it.

"Mrs. O'Dea fixed it," Lily said. Ed twirled it round and sat on it backwards. He cracked his knuckles and stared at the floor.

Lily slid back on her bed and waited for the talk to begin.

She interrupted the prolonged silence. "Ed, speak to me honestly about what's on your mind. I understand from Father Michael that he's asked you to be frank. He spoke so mysteriously that I thought you had killed someone. I've seen you lose your temper, but I know you're not violent."

"Lily, I did kill someone. Murder is murder even if it's an accident."

"You're joking!" Lily's normally pale skin became deathly white. "How did such a horrid thing happen?" Her eyes narrowed. "Surely, you didn't murder someone at the Dew Drop Inn. I hated the way everyone got liquored up with cheap alcohol. I couldn't believe it when you nearly knocked a man cold just because he taunted you."

"That twerp joked about your breasts, knowing you were *my* date." Ed shrugged and let out an audible sigh. "I didn't kill anyone at the inn."

"Then where, Ed? What happened?"

"I have a story I don't want to tell. But telling it is the only way you can understand me. Before Father Michael came to St. Patrick's, we had an old priest called Father MacDonnell, and he retired in Glace Bay. One day, the old man slipped off a cliff while out walking and a fishing crew discovered his body. The police stated in the newspaper that his death was not due to foul play. But Father Mac wouldn't have slipped if I hadn't run at him with my brother's dog. I had been exercising the dog on the flats when I noticed him walking on the path along the cliff. I ran toward him and the dog bounded ahead. He was terrified of dogs."

"If you knew that, why did you try to scare him?"

Ed's normally full mouth was thin and taut. "Because I hated him."

"Did you push him? I mean, actually put your hands on him?"

"No, but I wanted to. He spun backwards off the cliff before I could do that."

"But, Ed, it was an accident. Wanting to murder someone and actually killing them is not the same thing. Was that all there was to it? Why did you hate him? What else did you tell Father Michael?"

"That Father Mac stole my childhood."

"Sometimes I think my sister stole mine. I had to learn to defend myself against her meanness," Lily said, trying to thaw him out.

"I was eight years old, Lily, when I learned during a camping trip what it meant to be Father Mac's favoured boy. *I* got to share his sleeping bag while the others boys just had blankets on the ground. I crawled out in the night and told my friend what had happened. He didn't believe me, and I was afraid my mother wouldn't either. That same year Father Mac selected me as an altar boy. There were ten boys hoping to be chosen, but he picked me. When he showered special attention on me, Mom crowed to the other church ladies. She adored him. He promised to get me into a seminary or private college. Back then I loved school. And my mother had ideas of me being a priest." Ed let out a bitter laugh.

"Until I went camping, I thought Father Mac looked serene in his black cassock and purple stole."

Ed plopped his chair next to the bed and put his head on the mattress. Lily ran her fingers through his thick pomaded hair. She felt the same tightness in her chest that she'd experienced during Beth's failed abortion. She had believed the body was sacred until that woman had rotated a coat hanger in Beth's womb. A violating priest was no better than an unlicensed abortionist. Lily leaned over and kissed the top of Ed's head. She had difficulty reconciling her kindly Presbyterian minister with the idea of this predatory priest. "Ed, I'm so sorry," she whispered.

"My job was to return the holy vessels to the church office after mass. The other altar boy delivered the missals to the back of the church where his parents would wait for him. I knew I couldn't escape the instant I heard the click of the lock on the huge carved door of his office. Father Mac once said, 'Altar boys prevent priests from going crazy. Otherwise they'd leave Mother Church. God doesn't want that to happen.' Lily, I can't tell you the rest. I feel dirty even talking about it. But I need you to know why I get so angry. It happened many times."

"Why didn't you tell your mother, Ed, the first time you were hurt?"

"She wouldn't have believed me. At eight years of age, you're afraid of making your mother angry, let alone God and the priest. She treated Father Mac as though he were the living Jesus."

Lily felt dizzy with rage.

"But there's something more frightening than God. Father Mac said my schoolmates would blame me for what happened, so I shouldn't even think of telling them. I thought of ways to kill him. But each time, all I could do was fix my eyes on a religious tapestry opposite the desk and try to pretend it wasn't happening."

"Where were your brothers when all this was going on? Did they know about Father Mac?"

"There's a three-year gap between Tim and me. When he was an altar boy, my brothers fetched him after mass. Father Mac would have known not to tangle with them. By the time I became an altar boy, they no longer attended church."

Ed stood up abruptly and grabbed the chair.

"Breaking another chair won't change things, Ed." Lily got up and took it from him, placing it behind her. She did not want Mrs. O'Dea checking on her now.

"I have days when I can feel Father Mac all over me. It was one of those days that made me lie on your bed the way I did. I don't know what I was expecting. And I'm sorry I was so crude."

"When there's love, sex isn't dirty, Ed."

Ed's face was contorted and Lily buried her head in his chest. She dropped her hand to his buttocks and pulled him forward.

"I have wanted, until now, to be a virgin when I married. But I'm willing to lose my innocence to recapture yours. Put Father Mac out of your mind forever. Let him be dead." She hugged him tightly to her and he responded.

Lily slipped her dress over her head while Ed unbuttoned his trousers. She jammed the wooden chair under the doorknob. She prayed silently, *Please, God, don't let Mrs. O'Dea hear, and don't let me end up like Beth.*

CHAPTER 7

~~

Atlantic Crossing

The first night aboard ship the storm erupted and Clara ordered a dinner of eggs and toast to be served in the cabin. Ivy had fallen asleep during the light meal and Clara soon snuggled in beside her. "Spoon or jam?" she whispered. Ivy awakened, and they both started to giggle as they listed toward the edge of the bed. Ivy let out a toot. "That *is* smelly," Clara said, flapping the sheet. "Eggs never agree with you, Ivy."

The sheet-flapping recalled a funny incident from Clara's nurse's training. She and Di had been busily changing patients' dressings on the male surgical ward when across the room a young naval officer, whose surgery to his thigh had become infected, let out a loud and smelly fart. He apologized immediately to the young probationer in charge of dressing his wound, who indicated this was not a problem. "We'll let the gas escape," she said quickly, folding back the top sheet and shaking it.

Suddenly, Di and Clara heard a gasp, and the probationer called out, "Please, call Matron!" When they looked in the direction of the distressed probationer, they had to suppress their giggles. The officer, who was not wearing pajama bottoms, was sporting an erection. When Matron appeared, the naive student reported, "I think the infection has spread. Officer Jackson's member is red and swollen hard."

Di and Clara only just managed to leave the ward before they exploded with laughter. Years later, they still recounted this resurrection story.

During the night, Clara woke up and, wrapping a shawl around her, stepped out of the cabin, wanting to feel the rage of the storm. When she reached the open deck, she gripped the gunwale of a lifeboat and stared at the churning sea, letting the heave and dip of the ship calm her. Her thoughts wandered to what Lethbridge might have in store for her. As a nursing student Clara had been renowned for telling fortunes. At the end of a meal in the student dining room, teacups were lined up for her to read. But no one had ever read *her* fortune. She pondered the coincidence of Dr. Barnaby, who was a Nova Scotian, and also a protégé of Dr. Newbury, being on the same ship.

By morning the storm had abated and Clara could venture on deck with Ivy. They ate breakfast in the dining room and then made their way to the lounge. Mr. Mason soon breezed in, looking dapper in deck shoes, grey flannels, and a crimson sweater over a white shirt. "How did everyone fare during the storm last night?"

Several passengers who knew that Clara was a nurse had crowded around her to ask advice on nausea, dizziness, headache, chills, and diarrhea. Dr. Barnaby arrived in the lounge and joked, "Sister Durling, you should never have said you are a nurse."

Mr. Mason circulated a notepad and Dr. Barnaby signed up to play bridge.

"How do you hold your cards, Dr. Barnaby?" a lady asked kindly.

"I have a special cardholder. This handicap does not undermine my bridge." He flashed a challenging grin.

"Happily, we have a self-appointed social director on the ship," the lady with the hat said with a sigh. "Before the war, everything was planned from morning to night on these crossings, and nobody was ever bored."

While passengers were writing their names and cabin numbers in the notepad, a modestly dressed girl of about twenty peered into the lounge, looking lost. Clara, who had never been to Italy, thought the girl looked Italian with her olive complexion and dark brown hair. She wore a brown wool skirt and a white cotton blouse covered by a rough tweed coat. She was holding a baby with fat rosy cheeks and strawberry curls. She was surprised that a family would hire an Italian girl so soon after the war. *Perhaps she's Welsh*, Clara thought.

"I wonder if she's looking for the child's parents," Clara said. Several people shrugged and went on signing up to play bridge. Clara went to the door of the lounge, but the girl had hurried off along the deck. She signed up for an afternoon game and then went off with Ivy to find the lounge for younger passengers.

"I met some new friends today," Ivy said as she put on her pajamas that night.

"Having friends on board will make the trip seem shorter," Clara said. "You need a good night's sleep so you can have fun with them tomorrow."

Once Ivy was asleep, Clara, bothered by the musty smell in the cabin, bundled up again and stepped out to get some fresh air. She grimaced, thinking a German had slept in her bed, and then reminded herself that Germany had widows, too. Despite her stolid patriotism, Clara had often accused Britain's leaders of hubris, thinking they could win a war without fighting on the continent. For a moment she felt the full weight of her double loss, then, shrugging off the gloom, she walked fifty yards along the deck to join Mr. Mason, who was engaged in lively conversation with an elderly couple using blankets as shawls. They shifted to let Clara into the circle. She glanced in the direction of her cabin. "My daughter is not an adventurer," she explained apologetically, "but I still worry that she might come looking for me if she wakes up. I won't stay out long."

When the group broke up, Mr. Mason accompanied Clara back to her cabin. Stopping abruptly, he whispered, "That's the same girl who passed the lounge earlier today. What on earth is she doing out in the cold with that baby? At least she's put a wool cap on the child's head."

"We saw you looking for the parents today," Clara called to her with an encouraging smile. "Did you find them?" Seeing the girl's distress, she added, "It's easy to get lost on a ship."

"This is *my* daughter," the girl said. "Her father was killed in the war. I'm taking Florence to see his parents."

"You're awfully young to be a widow," Clara said, shaking her head. "What is your name?"

"Annabel Nurser. If the father had lived, my name would be Dupuis." Annabel's face became wistful. "We never had a chance to get married."

"How very sad," Mr. Mason said, shaking his head and putting his arms out to hold Florence. She started wailing and clung to Annabel's neck. Her mother rocked her until she quieted.

"Isn't she tired at this late hour?" Clara asked.

"My cabinmates lie around and smoke all day," Annabel said. "I came up to give Florence some fresh air. I must go back down now." She pulled away as the steward, Joseph, walked briskly toward them.

"Wait, Miss Nurser," Clara said, grabbing her arm.

"It's highly irregular for a third-class passenger to be on this deck," Joseph said indignantly. "I might lose my job if I allow this."

"This young lady has brought her baby up for some fresh air," Mr. Mason said. "Her little daughter is suffocating from the smoke down below."

"Perhaps irregular, but not impossible," Clara chimed in. "I think this baby should be in the play lounge each day if Miss Nurser looks after her."

"I'm sorry I've caused trouble," Annabel said and pulled her arm away.

The metal of the steps reverberated as she hurried down the stairs.

The young widow's fear of authority bothered Clara. She detested British snobbery that wouldn't make an exception for a child suffocating down below from smoke. As much as she hated elitism, she disliked cigarettes even more. When Joseph refused to let Annabel use the children's lounge, Clara went to the bursar the next day and paid what was deemed a fair increase for a third-class passenger sharing her cabin. Negotiating a financial arrangement was easier than convincing Annabel she should move. Mr. Mason thought Clara was being too hasty. Dr. Barnaby hailed her lack of British reserve. "But of course I'm Canadian," he said, laughing. Mr. Mason came round and offered to help Annabel move to Clara's quarters. Annabel gave way, and the move was quickly made.

"May I call you Annabel?" Clara asked.

"That's my name," Annabel said shyly, as she arranged Florence's baby items in a drawer below the bed. "Don't you want your daughter to sleep in the second bed? I feel I'm imposing."

"Nonsense. I pin Ivy against the wall so she won't fall out. She's a sleepwalker on occasion." Clara picked up Florence, who was no longer making strange. "Will the Dupuis family meet you in Montreal?"

"I expect so," Annabel said. "I need to have the letter they sent me translated." She pulled an envelope from a bag and handed it to Clara. "The Deceased Veterans' Office wrote to tell the Dupuis that Florence and I would be on this ship, arriving in Montreal. Their reply arrived two days before my departure. I didn't have time to have it translated."

"They must be looking forward to seeing their granddaughter."

"Réjean never spoke about his family. But Florence is all they have left of their son. I think they'll be very happy to see us."

"My French is pretty limited," Clara said. "Perhaps Dr. Barnaby could translate? Let's change Florence before I fetch the doctor."

"Can I help?" Ivy asked. Clara handed her the pins, and she hopped on the bed beside Florence.

Annabel frowned. "When I complained about the ladies smoking in our berth, they said that *their* smoke smelled better than Florence's arse. I tried not to let them hurt my feelings — but they did." Annabel let out a little sigh. "Until I met Réjean, I had not felt much kindness."

Clara walked along the starboard deck until she saw the medical station insignia, a snake entwined on a staff, and knocked at the door. "I need a translator," she said when she saw Barnaby at his desk. "Don't all Canadians read French even if they can't carry on a conversation?" She grinned impishly.

"That just about describes my French," Dr. Barnaby retorted. "Now Gaelic is a different story." He laughed and pulled on his jacket. A double amputee soldier was resting on a cot in the corner. His artificial legs lay beside the cot. He dipped his hand in a large metal tin of salve and rubbed a glob on his stumps.

"I'll be back to put on your bandages," Barnaby said and followed Clara to her cabin. "You have a letter you need me to translate?" He sat at the end of Annabel's bed. "How old are you, Annabel?"

"Nineteen."

Clara felt a lump in her throat making it hard to swallow as she watched Annabel leaning against her pillow holding her small baby. Clara handed the letter with the large, ominous script to Dr. Barnaby. "Tell me about Réjean. I should know something about him before I read the letter from his parents." Annabel's face lit up with a happiness Clara had not yet seen.

"His barracks were near the munitions factory where I worked. In the evening, I would go over to help the cook. Réjean was lining up to get his food when he first saw me. He called it a thunderbolt, except he said it in French."

There was a knock at the door and Annabel looked startled.

"It's only Joseph bringing some tea," Clara said. "Don't worry, everyone is happy about the arrangement."

Joseph left the tea tray and plate of yellow sponge cake covered in grated coconut on the bedside table and left. He looked back and nodded as he closed the door.

Annabel breathed a sigh of relief and accepted some tea and cake. "Réjean asked for a leave to come back for the birth of the baby, but it didn't happen and I didn't hear from him. A fellow soldier returned my letters. He wrote that his brave comrade had spoken of me often." Her eyes filled with tears.

Ivy stood up. "Don't cry, Annabel."

"We know a lot about tears, don't we, Ivy?" Clara said, planting a kiss on Ivy's cheek.

"How old was Réjean?" Dr. Barnaby brushed Annabel's shoulder with his stump.

She stared at his infirmity and shook her head.

"War is horrible!" Dr. Barnaby nodded agreement. "The veteran's office said he was eighteen when he was killed at Amiens. He would be almost twenty now." Tears welled up again in her eyes.

Barnaby took the opened letter and translated its contents.

Mademoiselle,

My son was married to a local girl. He joined the war on the advice of his English boss. I told him this is not our war and he best stay home and look after his family. I never like the English. They only let us speak our language in our own foyer. I warn you not to come because you are not welcome. Réjean would not cheat on his wife. She lives with us now, so do not come to our house with your baby. We do not want to see you or your daughter.

Odette Dupuis

"This is quite a shock," Dr. Barnaby said sadly. "I'm so sorry."

Clara tried to disguise her dismay at the letter's meaning. "Did you ever wonder if your lover proposed marriage to take advantage?" she asked.

Annabel grabbed her handbag and opened it. She pulled a packet out of her purse, saying, "These letters are not the letters of a liar."

War, thought Clara, *can make monsters or cowards out of ordinary people.* But she had hoped that Réjean Dupuis had not been one of them.

Clara recalled Ricky Roberts, a short, skinny, pimple-faced soldier with a mop of unruly brown hair and eyes that had never seemed to focus on the same spot. Shifty, some of the nurses had called him. Ricky had been admitted to Clara's ward with a severely dislocated shoulder. He was terrified of dying on the front, but after four weeks in hospital, he was deemed ready to go back to France.

"Tomorrow, I'm going off to die," Ricky said to Clara. "But tonight, I'll have fun. I'll be back before morning, Sister Durling." But he wasn't.

Six months later, he was returned to the hospital, gaunt, pale, and running a high fever. He had advanced gonorrhea. He received a quick court martial and was shot before they could treat him.

Annabel continued. "Réjean's boss encouraged him to enlist in order to take advantage of the program for returning soldiers to get a college education. He spoke highly of his boss. I don't believe Réjean was married." She collapsed back on the bed and, as the shock wore off, began sobbing.

"Put that letter away," Ivy shouted.

"What am I going to do with a dead man's baby? I had hoped Réjean's parents would help me. My parents won't, and I can't support her on my own."

"Florence is not a dead man's baby," Clara said. "She's your baby, and you must look after her. Perhaps I can find work and accommodation for you both at my hospital. You're lucky to have Florence, and I'm lucky to have Ivy."

"I feel more jinxed than lucky, Mrs. Durling," said Annabel tearfully. "After Florence was born, I suffered from melancholia. My parents didn't know what to do with me, so they admitted me to Fulbourn Hospital. That's where they send wacky people and women like me. The doctor wanted me to stay with my parents and be treated as an outpatient, but they said they were too old to cope with a baby in the house."

"How long were you in the psychiatric hospital?" Dr. Barnaby asked.

"A month. I had terrible thoughts of drowning Florence when I bathed her. I would scream for the nurse when the thoughts came over me, and she would shout for the doctor. He would sit next to me in the bathroom and hold my hand and reassure me that that my thoughts were normal. 'It's the fear of being entirely responsible,' he told me. He called it the post-baby blues. He recommended I stay at a nearby cottage hospital until I felt confident about caring for Florence. That's when I decided to make contact with the Dupuis family."

"I worked in a psychiatric hospital in Scotland," Dr. Barnaby said. "It's good that you had help available."

Clara looked at Florence, who was swinging her bottle up and down, hitting the side of the bed and giggling. White drops splashed everywhere. Clara removed the bottle before it smashed. She picked up Florence and held her on her lap. "Even if I have to delay getting to Lethbridge, I'll find a way to reach Madame Dupuis. I know she will change her mind once she sees Florence."

Clara couldn't help but think of her sister, and she wondered if Dr. Barnaby had ever encountered a pharmacist named White in Nova Scotia. Amelia's child must be twenty-five by now, she thought. Her heart skipped at the thought she might meet her sister one day.

"Let's walk the deck, Annabel. You've had enough for one day." Clara reached out and pulled her off the bed. "Tomorrow we can figure out how to charm Madame Dupuis.

The translation of Madame Dupuis' letter sent Annabel into a downward spiral of fear and anger. Clara tried to console her with truths she had learned after Billy and George's deaths.

"No two sorrows are alike," Clara said the following afternoon, "but the way to happiness is often the same. Let's start right now, here on the ship. The musicians down below are striking up some lively tunes. It sounds like they're playing homemade instruments. This can be part of our Canadian education, or French-Canadian if you're going to live in Quebec."

Annabel's shoulders drooped. "I don't want the third-class passengers to think I'm rubbing it in that I'm staying with you," she said, on the verge of tears.

"What the passengers would resent is you looking sad when you've had a bit of good luck. Just follow me and put on a smile."

"Can I go down too?" Ivy asked.

"Of course, you can. Mummy wants to find out what instruments are making music so strange to my British ears." Clara picked up Florence from the bed and handed her to Annabel.

They stopped at the top of the stairs leading down to third class. Mr. Mason sauntered along the deck. "I was wondering if you would be my bridge partner this evening, Mrs. Durling, now that you have Annabel to mind Ivy."

"Thank you, I'll let you know. Right now we're going to see what's going on down below. It certainly sounds happy. Come with us."

"More lively than the classical music we're offered up here," Mr. Mason said as he led the way down the staircase.

They entered a wide-open area with a low white ceiling and slick black floor filled with people. A long corridor ran off the far end of the common area. Through a glass partition they could see rows of wooden tables all set for the next morning's meal. Napkins, folded like dunce caps, stood at each place setting.

A drum, fiddle, tambourine, washboard, and accordion made up the orchestra. Passengers clapped in time to the music and a few older ladies danced with each other. They grinned as they twirled one another around.

"They must be playing by ear," Clara said as she watched the men tap the beat with their feet.

"Tum, duddy, tum, duddy, tum, duddy, tum," a washboard player sang as his hands bounced up and down the instrument. Perspiration glistened on his bulbous forehead and slick, black ponytail. His pointy nose curved down to meet his protruding jaw. A man with the same concave face as the washboard player began to move his feet rapidly in time to the music, letting his arms hang loosely at his sides. His body rose up and down like a piston while he stayed in the same spot. The metal heels on his soft leather shoes clicked rhythmically, alternating between the left and right foot. The movement was so rapid that Clara couldn't tell if it was eight or ten beats. When the dancers, dripping with sweat, stopped, the square-bodied accordion player struck up a quieter tune and a couple began to waltz. Others stood around and swayed to the music.

Clara looked up and met Dr. Barnaby's broad grin as he bounced down the stairs.

"So this is where I'll find some action!" he said, standing on the last step. "Everyone on the ship is healthy. I've nothing to do."

A bright-eyed girl moved toward the stairs. "Want to dance?" she asked. Barnaby hopped off the step and circled her waist with his stump. She glanced at his hand.

"Welcome to down below!" the burly accordion player shouted in broken English. He began a faster tempo and Clara grabbed Florence, lifting her as though she were a dance partner. The baby wiggled and waved, making it hard for Clara to hold her. Then Clara switched to swing dance with Ivy. Annabel, looking glum, held Florence on the sidelines. Mr. Mason pulled Clara into a foxtrot, exaggerating his movements. Soon the open area at the bottom of the stairs was completely crowded with dancers. Mr. Mason requested a tango and took hold of Clara again. His firm hand on her back made it easy to follow the advance and retreat of his feet as he led her in the classic form of the dance. The passengers moved aside and watched, and Clara smiled, remembering how George would exaggerate the backward bends until her long hair touched the floor. Surrounded by dancing third-class passengers, she became aware of how important her memories would be to her. In their shortened marriage, they'd had so much fun.

Soon they were all tired from the vigorous activity and sat for a while to watch the other dancers. Later, as they were leaving, a pasty-faced woman came up to Annabel. She inhaled deeply, rounded her lips, and puffed out multiple smoke rings.

"Florence is a real cute baby," the smoker said, kindly. "Come down and visit us, Annabel. We got no problems with Florence during the day." She had the husky voice of a chain smoker, and when she smiled, she displayed yellowish-brown teeth.

"I was sorry to be a bother," Annabel said.

"Ah, maybe we was a bit hard on you," the woman said.

"Everyone's happy now," Clara said. "Annabel is entertaining my daughter, Ivy."

"Does that mean you can be my partner at bridge this evening?" Mr. Mason asked, his eyes twinkling.

"I'd be happy to mind Ivy," Annabel said softly. "You've been so kind to me."

Once Ivy was in her pajamas, Clara went off to the lounge to play bridge. Annabel seemed settled and happy to be useful when Clara left.

They had set up three tables. Clara was paired with Mr. Mason and Barnaby with the lady who had grumbled about the lack of planned activities. Within minutes, Barnaby had her laughing.

It was a cold, starlit night when the bridge game finally ended. Clara and Mr. Mason had been the evening's winners.

The players, not ready to return to their cabins, strolled along the starboard deck to stargaze. The waves slapped the side of the hull and flipped backward in a white spray. The streams of moonlight were broken by a flock of migrating birds, swooping down in unison to catch prey on the well-lit surface of the water. "Such tenacity," Mr. Mason said, as the birds flew off into the darkness. "They still have thousands of miles to go. Thank God, the stars can guide them." Everyone looked skyward to gaze upon the blanket of stars and planets.

As Dr. Barnaby was seeing Clara to her cabin, they suddenly heard screams.

"Oh, dear!" Clara rushed toward her cabin, followed by Dr. Barnaby.

Annabel, crouched at the head of the bed, was pounding on the wall. Ivy looked on, wide-eyed and terrified, with Florence wailing behind her. Clara sat, and, slowly putting her arms around the young woman, coaxed her to sit back down beside her on the bed. The letters were strewn on the floor. Clara leaned forward and gathered what she could. She placed them on Annabel's lap. "You'll want these one day," she said, tucking them under Annabel's hand. "I believe this young man loved you, Annabel, and that's what matters. So many war widows have comforted themselves by thinking it is better to have loved and lost then to have never loved at all." Clara got up and changed places with Dr. Barnaby. Annabel let out a moan and started to sob again.

"I put Florence against the wall so she wouldn't fall out," Ivy said, her high child's voice showing her alarm. "I wanted to get Joseph, but I couldn't leave Florence."

"You did just the right thing, Ivy."

It took several minutes before Annabel began breathing almost normally. Dr. Barnaby assured Annabel that he had something in the infirmary that would make her feel better and went off to fetch some laudanum.

Annabel slumped back on the bed while Clara sat opposite, speaking softly to Ivy. Ivy crawled under the sheets and Clara tucked Florence in beside her. She hummed, rubbing first Ivy's and then Florence's back. "She'll be all right," she reassured Ivy. "You sleep now. Annabel will need you to be cheery in the morning."

Dr. Barnaby returned with a glass vial and syringe, telling Clara that he had whisked by Mr. Mason and the other passengers still on deck identifying stars. The doctor had just waved his hand at them, indicating he couldn't stop and talk.

He gave Annabel an injection and said, "Keep a close eye on her, Sister Durling."

Clara motioned to a chair. "Please stay until Annabel is asleep."

Dr. Barnaby nodded pensively. Ivy and Florence were already dozing. He pulled the only chair in the cabin over beside Annabel's bed.

"I wouldn't mind a bit of conversation after all this excitement," Clara said, releasing a large breath. "Tell me, where was your home in Nova Scotia?"

"It depended on what I was doing. I grew up in Halifax and studied medicine there, but moved to Truro for teachers' college and then back to Halifax to teach for a year before beginning training to be a specialist." He smiled wistfully. "I was the provincial lightweight boxing champion. I'll miss my boxing more than being a surgeon.

"When did you decide between teaching and being a doctor?" she asked.

"I always wanted to be a surgeon, but I needed to earn enough to specialize after graduating from med school on a scholarship. I had just begun teaching when the war broke out. I enlisted soon after."

In the dim light of the cabin, Clara asked him the question that had been on her mind. "Did you ever have dealings with a pharmacist named White?"

"I was in love with a girl named White — Lily White — but I don't know if her father was a pharmacist. White is a common name in Nova Scotia, even for a pharmacy." Dr. Barnaby let out a weary sigh. In the darkness, Clara could still see his sombre face. "I never showed my feelings for my classmate, and she ended up marrying a miner from Glace Bay. She led our class at teachers' college." Dr. Barnaby shook his head slowly. "At her wedding I realized I'd made a mistake. But money was scarce and I wanted to be a surgeon. I couldn't let love get in the way. I needed to concentrate on earning money. In my spare time I earned extra cash doing odd jobs."

Dr. Barnaby leaned over Annabel. "She's in a deep sleep now. I think I should go."

Barnaby returned to his cabin, stretching out on his bed in the gloom. *How different my life would be if I'd let my heart rule my head.* He massaged his stump as a reminder that his life had followed a different course. *War changed everything*, he thought. *But Lily could have been my constant.*

Looking back, it seemed strange that Lily's only mention of Ed Parsons was that she had tutored him, and that he was expelled and never graduated. A deep sadness came over Barnaby, recalling that she had married Ed. *That should have been our story.* He drifted back to Truro, seeing Lily in his mind's eye, with her brown owl-like eyes and unruly hair as she was doing her practise-teaching in front of a classroom of youngsters. He remembered the director of the teachers' college had said: "Miss White, you are a natural."

CHAPTER 8

Lily Marries Ed and Moves to Lethbridge, 1916

Lily was relieved at her parents' straightforward response when she told them that she was going to marry Ed Parsons.

"Other than a bit of a wild streak, Ed's a good man," her father said when she called him.

"Your decisions are certainly more practical then Beth's," Amelia said when she took the phone. Amelia had relaxed so much, Lily hardly recognized her. Both her parents were sad that she would be moving out west after the marriage, but there were good prospects in the mines there and Lily felt a total break with the past would be a good thing for them both and help Ed recover from the trauma he had experienced.

And the intended move to Lethbridge gave Aunt Marjorie a reason to reconnect with the mayor, Alistair Harwood, her engineer beau of yore.

"I hope he still remembers me," she said with a girlish candour. "It has been a while since we were in touch."

Aunt Marjorie wrote Alistair about Lily and Ed's impending move, and he was quick to reply.

My dear Marjorie,
How wonderful to hear from you. I look forward to meeting your niece. Is she like you? I still hold on to those happy memories of your nursing student days.

Marjorie touched her thin arms as she read the letter, glad the mayor would not see her in failing health.

There are not many teaching jobs available out west. Our schools have adopted a modern curriculum and hire American teachers or those from Ontario. I know the Maritime Provinces still use British texts and we Westerners consider that old-fashioned. I am, however, confident that a personal interview will lead to a job. In the meantime, I propose volunteer work at a local veterans' hospice for wounded amputees requiring rehabilitation. Many soldiers can barely read enough to follow a written order. Teaching male adults should be an interesting challenge for your niece.
Have her get in touch with me as soon as she arrives.
I hope you are keeping well.

Your old friend,
Alistair

The news of the upcoming marriage of the Parsonses' youngest boy to a schoolteacher spread quickly through the Glace Bay community. Lily blushed and cheerily accepted the many compliments. When a passerby suggested Lily might tame Ed, she smiled and retorted that perhaps he would make *her* livelier.

Seeing no reasonable alternative, and grateful to Father Michael for his kindness, Ed agreed to be married in St. Patrick's Church. When they entered the church office the first time, the place where he had ceased to be an innocent child, Lily noticed how he eyed the desk that Father Mac had used as cover and she felt his unease. Seeing Ed's discomfort, Father Michael made a few boxing moves that made him lift his fists and laugh. Lily smiled with relief at the priest's cleverness. *Father Michael is no Father Mac.* She thought about how he was going to make her a temporary Catholic so she could be married in the Catholic Church.

While Father Michael danced about play-boxing with Ed, the church housekeeper bustled in to offer them tea. She was a chatty soul and admitted she loved housekeeping for the young priest. With her hands on her hips, she described the many jars of pickled beets, the applesauce, relishes, casseroles, breads, and desserts that had been delivered for the wedding. She raved about the butcher's offer to roast an entire pig. Wagging her finger at Father Michael, she said, "This is all because of your popularity." Then she added, "The Parsonses are a much admired family as well."

Ed left the church with an enormous grin on his face and holding Lily's hand.

Lily's wedding dress of cream satin was trimmed with Venetian lace that her father had bought in Montreal at Ogilvy's department store. On the day of the wedding, Amelia helped Lily get dressed. She passed a loving eye over her daughter. "Sometimes mothers and daughters don't always see eye to eye," she said, as she fastened the pearl buttons at the back of the gown. "You've been a wonderful daughter, Lily, and I'm proud of you. I didn't have an easy start and perhaps I blamed you for that."

"You've been the love of Dad's life," Lily said. "I hope I'm that to Ed." They both wiped their eyes.

"A bit of face colour?" Amelia asked.

"Just a tad. Remember, I started the Old Maid's International at school. Dab on just enough so I won't be a plain Jane."

They both laughed and hugged, and in that instant all the past hurts vanished.

The wedding behind them, the Parsons household, where the newlyweds were staying, became a whirl of packing and unpacking. Lily groaned good-naturedly as Mrs. Parsons replaced her treasured literary works with cookbooks, eggbeaters, bowls, knives, cutlery, and a heavy iron frying pan.

"These are the basics," Mrs. Parsons said. "You can't live on love." They both laughed as Mrs. Parsons nestled spice packets amongst the clothing and domestic articles.

"Ed's been fully warned that I'm a dreadful cook, but we'll manage somehow," Lily said cheerily, but inside she was feeling Ed's coldness when they were alone. Every morning when Mrs. Parsons shot them a knowing look, Lily returned it with a false grin. Ed's old bedroom where he had fled after leaving Father Mac was no place to consummate their marriage.

Lily had mixed emotions when she recalled her wedding day. Her father had walked her down the aisle to "O Perfect Love." Ed looked remarkably handsome in his dark suit and royal-purple tie against a crisp white shirt. She had restrained a grin, knowing how much he hated to dress up. But in that instance he looked relaxed and content to receive Lily's hand from her father. But during the reception he took offence to a casual remark from an inebriated guest. A former classmate in Truro, in loud slurred language, reported that Barnaby had been smitten with Lily during her teachers' college days. Ed insisted he fight for his honour. Barnaby accepted the challenge. Father Michael tried unsuccessfully to dissuade the men. The priest jumped up on a chair, careful not to trip on his cassock, and directed guests to clear a space. Like the young woman whose remarks started the fight, they had consumed enough libation to think a wedding boxing match was quite normal. The fight ended after Mr. Parsons intervened. He was a short, strong man and had no difficulty separating the boxers. It ended with a reluctant handshake and Barnaby left. But not before he had a few private words with Lily while Ed was in the washroom. She easily recalled them. *If things get tough, come home. I'll be your doctor.*

The newly minted Parsons finally escaped to a small inn whose proprietor was a lonely old lady named Mrs. Brownlee. She had closed the inn at the end of summer when her son had returned to Halifax. However, she agreed to rent the newlyweds the room overlooking the ocean. When they were finally alone, Lily led her husband in a tender lovemaking dance. She pulled him onto the window ledge, opening the window so they could feel the wind and hear the ocean. She leaned back on Ed's chest and he wrapped his arms around her.

"A penny?" she said, locking her hands behind Ed's neck. He unbuttoned her bodice.

"I *feel* married," he said putting his hand on his bride's soft skin.

At seven the next morning, Mrs. Brownlee knocked on the door. Ed groaned. "I forgot to tell her we didn't want breakfast in our room."

Their landlady was holding a breakfast tray and pushed the door open with her foot. "I'll come by later to see what you need," she said.

"Nothing but privacy," Lily retorted, but Mrs. Brownlee was either deaf or ignored her. Their only time alone was in the short interval when the old dear walked into town to buy food for their evening meal. As soon as they heard the front door bang shut behind her, they would "make hay while the sun shines." When the dark cloud of Father Mac appeared, Lily brushed it away with her hands.

The happiness of their brief holiday was dampened when they returned to Glace Bay. The Parsons family waited constantly for bad news from the front, and Lily finished packing with an anxious heart. It had been a month since news had arrived from Tim and Andrew. A tunnel had collapsed on ten soldiers somewhere near Arras. A week earlier, Germans discovered another tunnel, killing all the occupants. Each time Lily saw the young man from the telegraph office, she prayed he wasn't heading for the Parsonses' home. "Positive thoughts are what will ensure your sons' safety," she said, putting her arm around her mother-in-law, who always feared the worst.

At Ed's insistence, no one came to the train station. "I'm married now, Ma, so stop treating me like a five-year-old," he said when his mother objected to them leaving without a send-off.

The train was crowded with young soldiers singing ribald songs. One chap with a peach-fuzzed face passed around a package of Chesterfield cigarettes and offered an engraved silver flask. His uniform didn't disguise his private-school manner, but alcohol had left red patches on his plump cheeks. A rough-looking older soldier refused the packaged cigarettes, saying kindly, "I prefer to roll my own." *These men, regardless of their background, will have to be friends*, thought Lily. *Their lives will depend on it.* The rolled-cigarette man began singing, repeating the last two lines until someone shouted at him to shut up. The train jerked into motion, and another soldier lurched forward onto the laps of his friends and vomited. Lily got up quickly as the men tossed their friend onto a bench and sought the conductor.

"I'm going to another car," she said. Ed opened his eyes wide, staring as though this would improve his hearing. She shook her head disapprovingly. Ed was already showing the signs of having had a few swigs. Rolling her eyes at his companions, Lily marched off down the aisle.

When she returned, she saw Ed had continued to take advantage of the free-flowing liquor and asked the conductor to make up their upper berth as soon as possible. Still singing, and obviously drunk, the soldiers settled in around them. Lily plugged her ears against the dissonant chorus and let the rocking motion of the train lull her to sleep.

Lily had only a pictorial knowledge of the Canadian Shield from teachers' college. She was in awe of the rugged geography as the train sped through the Ottawa Valley past Georgian Bay and then beyond to the wild terrain of Lake Superior. "How sturdy the roots of those evergreens and birch trees must be to grow out of the barren rock," she commented as they stared out at the fast-changing scenery. She recorded her tree observations in her diary and then added that the lakes were still open, but swamps and bogs were covered in ice. Ed grabbed her pencil and scribbled, I LOVE LILY PARSONS.

"I hope our love lasts as long as this granite," Lily replied. Her breath had created frost on the window and she wiped it with her sleeve just as a bull moose stepped out of the woods, knocking clumps of snow from the branches with his antlers. The moose pawed nonchalantly at the deep snow to find protruding grass. Much farther along the track, several deer leapt back into the woods and turned to fix their startled eyes on the passing train. Lily recorded both scenes in her diary. Arriving in Port Arthur, the giant grain elevators provided her first link with the west.

They ate in the dining car, ordering the cheapest items on the menu, letting repeat cups of tea prolong their meal as the waiter stood impatiently by. Once the soldiers had disembarked in Quebec, Lily and Ed had begun acting like honeymooners. By the time they arrived in Lethbridge, they were happy and exhausted.

CHAPTER 9

Grosse Île, 1919

Happy to be alone, Clara walked to the prow of the ship to watch the sun rise over Grosse Île. How exciting it was to be finally approaching their destination. Annabel had been kept calm for the last seven days on laudanum. *During the war years, surrounded by suffering so much larger than my own, I didn't fall apart,* she mused. *I found courage in looking forward, not back.* She sighed. *That's what poor Annabel was doing when she wrote to the Dupuis family.*

In the evening, when the children were asleep, Clara coaxed Annabel out of the cabin to enjoy the freshness of the night air. Neither had proper winter clothing, but they wrapped themselves in the grey wool blankets that Joseph provided. As they leaned on the railing, Clara mostly listened as Annabel told her story.

"My mother rejected me because I was the late and unexpected arrival after she thought that she had passed the change in life. She didn't want any more children after having already raised a large family. I didn't get much mothering."

Annabel paused, then sighed. "My father is a professor of modern languages at Cambridge, but when the war broke out, he left the university to decipher German codes for the War Office. My parents were disappointed, even ashamed, when I went to work in the kitchen of a munitions factory. *I* thought I was doing my patriotic duty," she added thoughtfully. "In any case, that's where I met Réjean. He spoke pretty good English, and we had no trouble communicating."

Clara held Annabel's hand while she reminisced about the love notes she received over the food counter at the barracks; the few hours in her rented room; their plans for a marriage; a heart-wrenching goodbye; the wording of the death notice. Clara let the lapping of the waves be the background music to the doleful conversation.

In the morning, Clara watched the small steamers carrying immigration and health officials chug toward the ship. She hoped the inspection would not delay their arrival. Grosse Île, a sombre reminder of high hopes dashed, had served as an isolation and health inspection station for almost a century. After years of potato-crop failure in the 1840s that had been met with cruel English indifference, thousands of Irish immigrants had arrived here, half-starved and weakened by typhus and dysentery. Many had failed to make it beyond the island, which became an enormous burial ground. Clara had learned about this shameful part of British history at St. George's, where she was taught that cleanliness was the godliness that would stop the spread of disease. She anticipated the health inspectors arriving on board would be very cautious now, so soon after the flu pandemic that had killed millions in Europe.

Clara waved at Captain Haines as he stood on the bridge, his collar turned up and the earflaps of his cap pulled down against the cold. An icy film covered the frigid waters. The Canadian winter was not far off. She formed a brighter picture in her mind of a white Christmas, a novelty for Ivy, who had seen pictures, but never touched snow. In England, even ice cubes were rare, so her daughter did not even have that as a comparison. *Good thing whales have blubber*, she thought, shuddering. Her fatigue had made her feel the chill more deeply.

Other early-rising passengers joined her at the bow. Joseph set up a sixty-cup silver urn filled with hot chocolate; waiters brought plates of sliced fruit and cheese to pass as people milled restlessly about. "Grosse Île is the hardest part of the journey," Joseph said to those crowded around the urn. "Everyone is impatient to be finished with the inspection so they can proceed to port and their final destinations."

Clara took a large cup of hot chocolate to her cabin, where Annabel sat flushed and agitated after realizing she had used up the doctor's supply of laudanum. "I'm not sure I can cope until Montreal," she lamented.

"You'll have to, Annabel," Clara said softly. "I won't abandon you. I plan to stay in Montreal until we have contacted the Dupuis. The news of a child must have come as a bitter surprise knowing they had lost their son, but I'm sure the family will warm to Florence when they see how much she looks like their son." She shrugged. "Unmarried sex during a war is expected. The Dupuis will not be the first family to take in a bastard child. Call this noblesse oblige or just plain kindness. I'm sure now that you've arrived they won't reject their own grandchild."

Immigration officials and health inspectors came on board and asked Dr. Barnaby about the passengers' health. Satisfied there was no illness to report and that everyone's papers were in order, they descended to the lower quarters.

Finished with the inspection, cabin passengers headed to the dining room.

Clara's heart jumped when she noticed Annabel walking back and forth along the railing holding Florence. "Florence could slip out of your arms!" Clara said sharply, urging her back from the edge.

"I feel like a caged animal," Annabel retorted, her face rigid with anxiety.

"Time for a good breakfast," Clara said. "We'll soon be over this inspection and on our way."

Clara took Florence from Annabel's arms and started toward the dining room, her heart beating fast with worry about Annabel's frantic pacing, but Annabel followed her quietly toward the dining room. Florence flailed her wool-clad legs when Clara hoisted her into the sunlight. She pointed at the floor, wanting to get down. While on the ship, she had begun to walk with a little help. *The grandparents will adore her,* Clara thought, smiling at the little girl's strawberry curls poking out from her bonnet. She gave Annabel a smile, which was not returned.

Clara waved when she saw Mr. Mason seated at the far end of the dining room. He stood and waved back.

"We'll miss this fine gentleman, won't we?" Clara handed Florence to Annabel and put her arm around her shoulders, giving her a reassuring squeeze.

"Buck up, my girl," Mr. Mason said as they arrived at the table. "You'll need a good breakfast to charm Madame Dupuis." Clara had confided Annabel's difficulties to him and he had treated her with kindness. Dr. Barnaby, too, had checked in on her every day.

"I do love a buffet where I can take an extra pat of butter," Clara said as she cast an appreciative eye at the long table.

Mr. Mason teased her that she spread butter on her toast as though it were an exotic cheese. "War rationing is my excuse," she retorted.

Mr. Mason held Florence while Annabel chose from the buffet. The toddler chewed on a small piece of toast and then tossed the gummy lump on the buffet table, earning some disapproving looks. Annabel put down her plate and took hold of Florence. She strapped her into the wooden high chair at their table just as Ivy arrived with a full plate of eggs and sausage. Ivy grimaced when Clara accused her of having eyes bigger than her belly. When Florence began dropping bits of food on the floor, the waiter laughed good-naturedly, causing Clara to remark that he must be a Canadian. Everyone within earshot laughed.

"I forgot the bottle," Annabel said, rising from her place. "I'll go back to the cabin."

"Joseph can fetch it," Clara said and beckoned the waiter. "The waiter will know where to find him. Just enjoy your breakfast."

The waiter apologized. He was not free to leave the dining room, and Joseph, he said, would be occupied organizing the passengers' luggage.

"I won't be long," Annabel said as she stood up. She kissed Florence. "Be good while Mummy's gone." Clara smiled, feeling Annabel was taking charge. She'd need all her self-confidence with the Dupuis.

From the window in the dining room they could see Captain Haines talking with the inspectors. They handed the captain some papers. "The government had been planning to close the island until the flu pandemic erupted," Mr. Mason said. "It was like a small city on the island, with schools, hospitals, churches, graveyards, hotels, and houses for the people who worked there. It was a busy place during the shipping season."

"I hate graveyards," Ivy chimed in.

"Waste not, want not," Clara said as she finished the food that Ivy had left. "Annabel *is* taking a long time just to fetch a bottle. I hope she's not getting herself all riled up again. I'll go check on her quickly if you'll keep an eye on the children, Mr. Mason?"

As Clara stood up, she noticed that many in the dining room had risen and were rushing to the windows on the starboard side of the ship. Even from the dining room they could hear cries of alarm. She noticed through the window the captain and Dr. Barnaby standing together looking along the deck. Clara ran from the dining room and saw Annabel: she was halfway along the deck and holding a ten-foot boat hook. She jabbed it in the direction of the captain and the doctor to warn them back. "Don't try to stop me," she screamed above the wind that was rocking the ship. "I don't want to live." Then she leaned out over the railing, staring at the dark, icy water below.

Clara had joined the men. "Put it down, Annabel," she called calmly. "Then we can talk."

The captain motioned passengers to remain silent as they stood on the deck, paralyzed, and unable to do more than exchange terrified looks.

Clara could hear Ivy crying and looked back, putting her finger to her lips to indicate quiet. Mr. Mason had pulled Florence out of her high chair, soothing her with a rocking motion, and brought her to the door of the dining room.

Annabel's eyes were large and frightened as she eyed the stoker in the steamer below. He looked up motionless with his hands together in prayer. He held this posture, afraid any movement might encourage her to jump.

"Annabel, I want you to come to Lethbridge," Clara called out. "Florence will be like a sister to Ivy. Then neither of you will be lonely. Wouldn't you like that?"

Annabel shifted slightly, as though she might be changing

her mind. Except for the idling engines and a flapping flag, there was silence. It was broken when the second mate stormed indignantly onto the upper deck behind her. "What's this delay?" he shouted. He had been waiting below for the inspection to begin.

In the split second when everyone's attention turned to the second mate, Annabel catapulted herself over the rail, still holding the boat hook. She torpedoed into the freezing water and emerged seconds later at the surface. Her dress billowed up around her shoulders. The stoker down below in the steamer ripped off his coat and threw himself into the water. Annabel jabbed at him as he tried to grab her. His heavy work boots made it hard to tread water, but he dipped under Annabel and grabbed her wrist, twisting it until she let go of the boat hook. She began choking, and he tried to lift her head out of the water. Another member of the crew threw out a life ring. When the stoker grabbed for it, he lost hold of Annabel. He tried to take hold of her wrist again, but she kicked her feet to push him away and went under. The stoker was able to grab the hem of her dress and pull her toward the boat. She had stopped thrashing, and, with the help of his mate, they were able to haul her up over the side of the steamer.

Dr. Barnaby backed awkwardly down the ladder to join the stoker in the smaller boat, and Clara followed. The stoker had thrown his heavy coat over the sodden figure as she lay on her side, her chestnut hair strewn across her face. Dr. Barnaby put a finger on Annabel's neck. He shook his head. There was no sign of a pulse. "It's over, I'm afraid. If she hadn't struggled, we might have saved her." He turned to the stoker. "You did a valiant job, sir. I should think that the impact with the frigid water caused her to take a deep breath. Or the shock alone from the cold might have stopped her heart." He turned toward Clara, distressed and angry with himself. "I knew she was distraught. I should have kept a closer eye on her."

"As should I," Clara said. She could hear crying. She looked up and saw Mr. Mason with his arm around Ivy and with Florence on his hip. Tears streamed down their faces.

Captain Haines and the chief medical officer from Grosse Île joined them in the steamer. "We still have a coroner on the island," the medical officer said. "He can provide an official death certificate and arrange for the young woman's burial. I'll arrange for a second boat to fetch our people once they've done the inspection." He looked apologetic. "I'm afraid the inspection must continue before the ship can go on, but we'll take the young woman's body to shore."

"We have six hundred traumatized passengers who will be anxious to leave this ship," Captain Haines said. "The whole thing is tragic. I don't relish informing the parents of their daughter's suicide."

Clara's head swirled with the knowledge that Annabel's parents had rejected her. She sat down quietly on a bench, watching while the medical officer covered Annabel's body with a brown canvas tarpaulin, which flapped wildly in the wind. Clara wondered who was going to inherit little Florence.

"What will happen to the baby?" the inspector asked as though he could read Clara's thoughts.

"As captain of the ship, I have legal authority to appoint a temporary guardian," Captain Haines interjected. "I hope I can name you, Mrs. Durling, since you've had the most contact with the deceased since she boarded the ship. You're in a position to arrange an adoption at your hospital. If I allow Florence to be a ward of Quebec, she will be put in a Catholic institution, and then there will be arguments. I'm assuming Annabel was Protestant."

"She was, but intended to convert when she married the baby's father, who was Catholic." Clara sighed. "I will certainly take care of Florence until we have a proper solution for her. But I can't imagine at the moment what that will be. Annabel's parents abandoned her in her difficulties, so I doubt they will offer to keep her child. The letter from Madame Dupuis that sent Annabel spiralling down into melancholia made a family union seem unlikely."

"Meanwhile," said the captain, "will you accompany us as we take her body to the shore?"

As the boat reached land, Clara turned to wave at Ivy, who was standing with Mr. Mason, watching their progress. The sight of a white wooden church perched on the rocky embankment comforted Clara. "I'd like to say a final prayer for Annabel before leaving the island," she said. "I'll contact the Dupuis after I get to Montreal. I'm not sure if they'll want to meet their granddaughter, but if they do I'll wait for them at the immigration office."

"Thank goodness you're in charge of little Florence," Captain Haines said. "If you hadn't befriended young Annabel, who knows who would be caring for her."

"I wonder what Annabel would have done if the noxious letter from the Dupuis had been translated while she was still in England?" Clara's shoulders sank. "We'll never know now."

CHAPTER 10

Young Marrieds Arrive in Lethbridge, 1916

The Lethbridge train station was bustling with well-dressed families, single girls, uniformed soldiers, and nurses with blue capes waiting to receive the wounded. A Red Cross ambulance was parked nearby. People stood back as two veterans, both with above-the-knee amputations, were carried to the waiting vehicle. One of the nurses smiled and chatted with the soldiers as she tucked blankets around their stumps. Then an ambulatory burn patient wearing an eye patch, his head wrapped in gauze, was helped up. The door was closed and the driver headed for the hospital. Another Red Cross truck pulled up, and the nurses repeated the procedure. The war, now well into its second year, required such efficiency as the casualties were mounting fast.

Lily and Ed stepped down onto the platform, being careful not to get in the way. They went inside the station building to consult a map of the town while they waited for the baggage cart to be unloaded. Lily noted points of interest and directions to them in her diary.

"Are you afraid we might get lost?" Ed teased.

"Let's check into the station hotel and then go for a walk and explore," Lily suggested. Ed looked reluctant. "Come on, Ed Parsons. You've never been beyond Nova Scotia."

The Royal Hotel was situated across from the railway station, next to a row of rundown buildings. Lily and Ed retrieved their suitcases from the baggage cart and headed across the dusty road to the hotel. The hotel clerk handed them the key to a ground-floor room and barked at the bellboy to take care of their luggage. From the reservation desk they could see through to the bar where several men stood around, dragging idly on cigarettes and swigging occasionally from mugs. Lily looked down at the red-and-black carpet scarred with cigarette burns and splotches of beer and coffee. Her attention shifted from the soiled rug to the bar when she heard an American drawl. "That Virginian accent is unmistakable," she said, frowning at Ed as she saw the look of astonishment and recognition on his face. "Is this the American your father calls a Bolshevik?"

Ed's surprise was genuine as he turned quickly and approached the speaker. "Bob Glimp! What on earth are you doing here?"

Lily followed to see the two men shaking hands. "Did you know he was in Lethbridge?" she asked her husband.

Bob answered for Ed. "Just coincidence," he said. "I'm not following your husband, but that don't mean I'm not glad to see him. I knew he was coming out west, and I'm happy to see he's arrived." He lifted his mug in salutation. He and Ed exchanged some news before Lily grabbed Ed's arm and steered him toward the hotel restaurant.

They sat near a window overlooking the street and picked up the menu. "No service less than 10 cents," Ed reported. "Guess we can't eat, Mrs. Parsons." Reluctantly, the youthful waiter agreed to let them order from a cheaper breakfast menu. The total bill came to less than one dollar.

Ed opted to stay at the hotel to catch up on sleep while Lily went for her daily walk. She thought if he slept while she was gone, he would avoid getting hooked up with the Americans. She strode onto First Avenue under the bright September sun, eager to explore her new environment. A weather-faded CLOSED sign hung on the door of what must have been a saloon. She asked a passerby about the city's dry laws. "We voted against prohibition, but opposition, especially by religious leaders, has sent the sale of liquor underground," the man said. He raised his eyebrows. "In Lethbridge, brothels are sometimes the only place a man can get a drink. Our religious zealots rarely venture into the segregated area — that's where the ladies of the night ply their trade. That area is one of the town's main tourist attractions." The man laughed at Lily's wide-eyed expression. "National prohibition isn't likely to be repealed anytime soon. Not until the war is over."

Lily shrugged and thanked the man. *I hope I can find a place to live that isn't over a secret drinking establishment*, she thought.

She walked west about a mile until she reached the Oldman River with its ice age coulees. The sight of the bizarre geology stopped her in her tracks. The coulees, with their flat faces and long spines, seemed like magnificent dinosaurs lumbering down the embankment to scold the humans for making a mess along the meandering river. Beyond the dilapidated shacks and debris, an enormous trestle bridge spanned the river to the northwest. The shaft of an old mine protruded as a reminder that the city had previously been known as Coal Banks.

Lily consulted her mental map and headed south. Streets ran north and south, avenues east and west. *Glace Bay isn't so orderly*, she thought with a smile.

A passerby directed her to the rehabilitation hospice. "It's behind the hospital," he said. "Stay on First Street."

Galt Hospital had more interesting architecture than the red-brick hospital in Sydney. Lily walked up the front stairs of the main building and inquired at reception as to where she could find the soldiers' hospice.

"It's the corrugated iron hangar out back. It used to be a storage area for old equipment," the woman at reception said. "It's been fixed up to house the soldiers. There's nowhere else they can go," she said matter-of-factly. She pointed in the direction Lily should take.

Lily began to have misgivings about accepting the mayor's advice. The memory of antiseptics and eucalyptus in her father's pharmacy rose up in her nostrils. She walked around the south side of the hospital to the backfield, crossing an uncultivated field toward the revamped warehouse. Deep in thought, she stopped for a minute and took a deep breath of the crisp fall air, watching the sun set over the coulees. A maniacal scream, loud banging and swearing escaped from somewhere inside as she entered the hospice. She froze. A nurse rushed past her, followed by a man in a white coat.

Lily ran the entire eight blocks back to the hotel.

CHAPTER 11

Montreal Port, 1919

How desolate Grosse Île seemed on this damp November morning. While Annabel was being prepared for burial, Clara walked through the avenues of gravestones inscribed with Irish names and prayed that the next burial she attended would be her own. *Six thousand Irish gravestones on the island*, she thought. Shaking off the feeling that death surrounded her, she started toward the mortuary. Seagulls flew overhead, looking for dead fish or any refuse washed ashore.

Dr. Barnaby was standing with the coroner at the head of Annabel's modest wood casket.

"The casket was made from local trees," the coroner offered. "We still have dozens left from the old days. She was a beautiful young woman," he added softly.

Clara looked away. "I have no idea how I'm going to cope with a baby if the Dupuis don't take her," she said, her voice cracking.

"Don't be ashamed, Sister Durling. There's no harm in tears." Dr. Barnaby put his arm through Clara's. "Will you walk up to the church with me?"

"I'd like that. I want to say a final prayer."

She and the doctor climbed the steep path to the church and sat on the steps looking across the bay at the ship. Clara's body shook with sobs.

"You've had so much to deal with," Dr. Barnaby said. "Some people are called upon to bear bigger burdens than others."

"Death during war isn't the same as when a child dies in a plague of influenza. I loved my country and was willing to sacrifice for the war effort, but there was no sacrificial cause to ease the loss of my son. Now Annabel's suicide is another kind of senseless tragedy. I should have suspected that the letter from the Dupuis would be malign."

"Don't blame yourself. War puts many soldiers in confusing situations. At the heart of it all was fear of death and great loneliness. I'm sure her young lover meant no harm. He just needed comfort before returning to what would seem like certain death."

"Time to pray," Clara said, wiping her eyes. Stepping inside the white clapboard church, she genuflected and made the sign of the cross. "I'm high Anglican," she explained, seeing Dr. Barnaby's curious look. They sat in the front pew for several minutes. Captain Haines walked into the church, and, nodding at them, headed for the organ. His hands danced over the keyboard as he sang. "I feel the winds of God today. Today my sail I lift." Clara turned to Dr. Barnaby when the captain finished. They were all crying.

It had taken monetary persuasion to have the priest inter Annabel on Grosse Île. "I have never buried a Protestant," the priest said as he reached for Clara's fifteen dollars. She ignored the transactional nature of the priest and resolved that if more unexpected expenses occurred, she would swallow her pride and send a wire to Miff. He would not understand how she was temporarily responsible for a nine-month-old baby, but he would send the money. Miff had called her a magnet for lost souls, and Florence would be the proof.

The *Scotian* docked at the Port of Montreal eight hours behind schedule. In contrast to the subdued atmosphere on the ship, the port buzzed with activity. Clara gave fat little Florence an affectionate squeeze as she looked down at the crowd. The baby, wriggling with excitement, was hard to hold.

"Look at the men in red coats riding horses, Mummy," Ivy shouted over the din. *Not many six-year-olds have been so closely acquainted with death*, Clara thought. She was relieved that Ivy seemed happy.

"They're officers of the Royal Canadian Mounted Police. There must be something special going on since they're wearing their dress uniform. It does look fancy, doesn't it, Ivy?"

She walked across the deck so she could see outgoing ships moored at the eastern wharves. Some would be heading back to England. Annabel's suicide had shaken Clara's confidence; she could almost feel her own body falling through the air toward the freezing water. She shuddered as the image of the young woman vaulting over the railing returned to her yet again.

Clara tried to focus her attention on the activity below. Well-muscled stevedores, sleeves rolled up, pushed wooden barrels out of the *Scotian* onto the docks. Light brown horses, harnessed to flatbed carts, pranced on the spot, waiting to haul the cargo. The mounted police officers weaved their horses through the crowd of onlookers who waited patiently for the disembarkation to start. Vendors cried out in English and French from makeshift stalls set up against the temporary Port Authority building; a drab metal-and-wood structure covered in dust and grime. Trying to put her worries aside, Clara focused her eyes on the stalls below. Bolts of bright coloured cloth flapped in the breeze. A short, stout man held up a bolt of light-blue material and hollered, "Dress cloth for the ladies!" Blue-and-white crockery, tarnished silver flatware, iron and copper pots, paintings on unframed canvases, tattered second-hand books, embroidered table clothes, metal wares, and wooden crosses were enticingly displayed to attract customers. The man walked back and forth in front of his wares, picking up one item at a time and describing the object's virtue in a singsong voice.

"Everything to set your table, ma'am!" he shouted to Clara, who was staring wide-eyed.

A group of lady volunteers stood at the bottom of the debarkation plank. They held up a sign reading: WELCOME TO OUR SOLDIERS' DEPENDENTS. The shipping season would soon be at an end and their job would be done. Clara had heard that for the last year these women had helped war brides — arriving by the thousands — to reach their final destinations. In many cases, they provided newcomers with money, food, and babysitting services. But now the arrivals of dependents were dwindling, so the host ladies would be gathering elsewhere to welcome the new families into the community.

"That must be the nurse with the orphaned kid," a man shouted pointing at Clara. He wore a fedora pushed up off his brow and a pencil behind his ear.

Captain Haines came up behind Clara. "The ship's arrival is always published in the paper," he said. "Normally, passengers' names, bad weather on the voyage, or a dignitary on board are what's reported. But the suicide will make headlines."

Mr. Mason organized several passengers to precede Clara down the plank. "Mrs. Durling needs to blow off the reporter with a few curt words," he said. He offered to escort her and the children to the notary's office before he boarded the train to Toronto, where his daughter would meet him. But the newshound deftly bypassed Mr. Mason as soon as Clara's foot hit the pavement. He had bloodshot eyes from sleeplessness or drink, Clara couldn't tell which. "Will the baby of the woman who committed suicide be adopted in Quebec?" he asked. His pencil was poised to write.

"It's undecided," Clara said coolly. "I may take her to Lethbridge until I hear from the deceased girl's parents." She held on to Florence a little more tightly.

"You're squishing me," Ivy said to the reporter, giving him a sharp poke with her elbow.

"Ouch! That's not nice, little girl," he exclaimed and shot her a dirty look.

He handed Clara an English-language newspaper: SCOTIAN PASSENGERS WITNESS YOUNG MOTHER'S SUICIDE. BABY LEFT TO BRITISH NURSE.

"That's an inaccurate statement," Clara said. "I am the child's temporary guardian."

"Shouldn't the Dupuis family have custody?" the reporter asked. "They *are* the grandparents."

"No one should have custody until we have informed the dead girl's parents. And how did *you* know about the Dupuis?" Clara said, glaring.

"The priest who buried the girl contacted our newspaper. A little bit of digging and I came up with the Dupuis. I'm just here to report the story."

"We must clear immigration before *any* decision is made," Clara retorted. *I should never have told that mercenary priest Annabel's story*, she thought to herself. To shake off the reporter, she turned to look at the stevedores unloading the cargo. "Are those barrels of wine being imported from Europe?"

"Why, yes, of course," the reporter answered, caught off-guard.

Clara kept her quizzical face although she was laughing inside. The inquisitor's focus was no longer on the orphaned baby.

"But isn't that against Canadian prohibition? I thought you could only sell alcohol for medicinal purposes. You can't all be sick in Quebec."

"No ban on hooch in Quebec," he said. "We're not like the rest of Canada."

Clara let out a laugh. Tension lifted from her shoulders. "Good heavens!" she said. "I know I'm in Canada when I hear the word *hooch*." She smiled politely at the reporter, signalling the end of their conversation, and turned back to Mr. Mason.

"Whew, what a bother!" Clara said to Mr. Mason as they slipped quickly into the Port Authority building.

A few minutes later, she was sitting in front of the notary, relieved the pressman was no longer bothering her. The notary was a short, heavy-set man with raven hair and wire-rimmed glasses attached to a gold chain that draped over his ears like earrings. He reeked of stale tobacco, which did not surprise Clara, given his stained fingers. He spoke English clearly enough, but with a rough French accent. She imagined he had little to do between ships but smoke and eat. Captain Haines and Mr. Mason sat on either side of her. She handed Florence to Mr. Mason, fearing the child might rip the custody documents. She had learned the hard way on the ship when Florence had torn up her map.

"Good morning. My name is Yves Monet. Welcome to Quebec," the notary said without rising. As he was surveying this newly arrived group, a tall, bullish-looking man of about fifty, wearing a greatcoat and fedora, barged into the office.

"Are you part of this party?" the notary asked irritably. "If you're here to sign a bill of purchase, you'll have to wait until I'm finished with this matter."

"I'm Alistair Harwood, the mayor of Lethbridge," he replied, to Clara's astonishment.

He looks like an American gangster, she thought in alarm. *Why is he here? Will he ask me to refuse custody of the orphaned baby or lose my job?* Her pulse quickened, but she stood and held out her hand. "I'm Clara Durling. This is my daughter, Ivy. I'm very pleased to meet you."

Before Clara could introduce the others, Mayor Harwood continued. "I'm here in Montreal at the invitation of the mayor's office. It's a nice coincidence that my meeting overlapped with the disembarkation of your ship. I read about the tragedy in this morning's newspaper and hurried down, thinking that you might need some support."

"I do, Mayor Harwood! An aggressive reporter is waiting for me to make a statement. Nothing can be decided until we have informed both sets of grandparents. It is unfortunate that the suicide made front-page news."

"Oh, don't worry, Mrs. Durling. I also had some unfortunate press." The mayor opened the newspaper he'd been carrying under his arm. Clara read: MAYOR OF LETHBRIDGE MANAGES PROSTITUTION LIKE ANY OTHER MUNICIPAL SERVICE. "I didn't appreciate that reporter eavesdropping on my private conversation," he remarked. "I expected him to report our public discussion about roads, sewage, and taxes."

The mayor shrugged and let out a quick laugh. "I've unwittingly become a Montreal hit," he added. Seeing Clara's grave expression, Harwood's face became less jocular.

The notary, who thought awarding temporary custody of an orphan was the issue, became confused by the conversation. "What or where is Lethbridge," he interrupted, "and what does that have to do with our proceedings?"

Before Harwood could answer, a priest followed by a stocky man in a red-and-black-checked jacket and a thin woman in a belted wool coat entered the office. The woman's dark brown hair was braided and wrapped around her head like a Roman crown. The man had leather-like skin and the woman's tanned face looked like a corrugated washboard, clearly suggesting that they worked outdoors.

"I'm Father Anselme, and this is Monsieur and Madame Dupuis," the priest said in accented English. "The Dupuis are the grandparents to this little girl." The priest arched his hand, and let it rest on Florence as though he had just baptized her.

Noticing the spiteful look on Madame Dupuis' face, Clara's heart sank. The priest had a supercilious air and the husband one of resignation. *Why haven't they brought Réjean's wife,* she wondered? *How could an army romance in a cafeteria end so sadly?* She could make no connection between the downturned face of Madame Dupuis and the upturned smile of Florence.

The woman took Florence's hand and gave it an awkward shake, saying: *"Coucou, ma petite chouette."* Florence dove her head into Mr. Mason's neck.

Clara stood and offered a disheartened handshake to the priest and the Dupuis. Monsieur Monet rose and dragged over some chairs. "Sit down, all of you, so we can get on with the decision at hand."

"Madame Dupuis has come to claim her grandchild," said the priest.

"How do the Dupuis know this baby is their grandchild?" Clara asked.

"Monsieur and Madame Dupuis received this letter." The priest waved the crumpled paper, poked his thumb in his chest and said with a smile: "*I* translated it!"

"But Madame Dupuis wrote back that the mother of this

baby mustn't come, that they didn't want to see the baby," Clara said. "She would not be expecting Miss Annabel on the *Scotian*."

"Ah, ha!" The priest wagged his finger with a pithy air. "The priest who bury the girl on Grosse Île send message to my *paroisse* that a Catholic *orphelin* arrive in Montreal."

The room fell silent as a thunderous look filled Clara's moss-green eyes.

Madame Dupuis looked defiant and her husband alarmed. She shrugged and took the letter from the priest. "I write my son already have wife and she don't want no baby of another girl. Me, too. I don't want no English baby. But the girl's dead, and so I change my mind."

"Annabel was a trusting but naive English girl who could not read French," Clara said. "How cruel that your son deceived her in proposing marriage. She was sure you would welcome your grandchild until she learned her lover was married. She was devastated that Réjean had lied. She expected to be his war bride."

The priest glanced at Monsieur Dupuis.

"My son was *not* married," Monsieur Dupuis said. He turned to his wife. "What have you done, Odette? We had one son. And you want we lose our granddaughter?"

Clara stood abruptly and approached Madame Dupuis. "You caused the suicide of a young woman."

The captain leaned forward and held Clara's arm, afraid she might shake the woman.

"Your lies had fatal consequences," Clara continued angrily.

She went over to the door and beckoned the reporter, who had been hovering outside. She handed him the letter. "Now you can write the story of how a young woman, duped by Madame Dupuis, committed suicide." Clara stared at the woman, who glared back.

"I need some fresh air," Harwood said. He left the notary's

office, followed by Mr. Mason and Ivy. Clara took Florence back into her arms.

The priest took Clara by the arm. "Mrs. Durling, Madame Dupuis' lie is a sin. But taking your own life is a mortal sin. God does not want Madame Dupuis to be punished for Annabel's suicide."

"I'm not interested in your theological arguments," she countered. "Annabel was not just 'somebody.' She was a young mother who believed that Florence's father loved her — until she got that letter. And now that she is dead, you wish to claim her baby. Not as long as I'm in charge."

"Monsieur Monet," Captain Haines interjected, "I am asking you to give Mrs. Durling legal custody of the baby until the parents of the deceased are informed. She is the best person to arrange an adoption if this becomes necessary. She feels a personal obligation to Annabel. We all do. Such a vulnerable young girl so tragically misled. Florence would be a constant reminder to Madame Dupuis of her wrongdoing."

Monsieur Dupuis looked heartbroken. "If I knowed my wife do such a letter, I make stop her. I only ask you, let us know where you take the little girl. She look like Réjean as a baby. She is our granddaughter. Oh, Odette, what you have done?" He touched Florence's cheek with his hand. Her chubby cheeks dimpled.

Monsieur Monet sighed and shook his head. He signed the custody document and handed it to Clara.

Madame Dupuis looked angrily at Clara. "What you know about losing son?"

Clara was instantly returned to Knockholt Cemetery. "Nothing, Madame Dupuis. Nothing you could understand." She hoisted Florence onto her hip and stepped outside into the bright morning sunshine, leaving Odette Dupuis in the care of her priest. She looked up at the sky as though Annabel might hear her. "I'll take care of her," she promised.

She could hear Mr. Mason giving the mayor an account of the dancing, the bands, the dinners, and charades during their Atlantic crossing. "We had an enjoyable time, until the end. Mrs. Durling will be an excellent matron of your hospital. I very much liked her company."

"Well, I hope I'm as good a travelling companion on the train as you were on the ship," Harwood said to Mr. Mason. "I'll travel with Mrs. Durling as far as Regina, where I have some business to attend to."

Ivy stood beside Mr. Mason, still holding his hand.

"Let me know how you're doing once you're at your daughter's, Mr. Mason. You know where I am — the Galt Hospital," Clara said. She was disappointed she had not said a proper goodbye to Dr. Barnaby. He was tidying up the surgery for the outgoing doctor.

Barnaby had business in Montreal so he would not be on the same train. He promised to forward his address once in Edmonton so she could inform him of Florence's fate. Clara appreciated the doctor's concern.

CHAPTER 12

Housing in Lethbridge, 1916

Lily had slept fitfully, tossing and turning, thinking about whether she would volunteer at the hospice. Determined to make her second day in Lethbridge happy, she shook Ed awake and announced, "I'm starved!"

When they entered the restaurant with the ten-cent minimum charge, the same waiter as the night before said sarcastically, "*Now* you can order from the breakfast menu."

"Perhaps we prefer lunch," Lily countered. The waiter did not smile. He hurried off with an order for bacon and sunny-side-up eggs. She turned to Ed. "After breakfast, while you report for work, I'll look for a place for us to live." The waiter brought them coffee while they waited.

"What kind of place do you think we can afford?" Ed asked.

"Probably something in the segregated area will suit us. A man called Sam McKlintock owns most of the properties — everything from brothels to Chinese laundries."

"How do you know that?" Ed asked.

"The mayor of Lethbridge wrote to my aunt Marjorie, suggesting that the segregated area was cheap, safe, and had some nice apartments. I think 'safety' means it's well-patrolled. I'm going to Mr. McKlintock's office this morning to get started on my search."

The hotel receptionist gave Lily Mr. McKlintock's business card and directions to the centre of town. It was a short walk and Lily arrived quickly at the two-storey red-brick building. She wondered why his office wasn't in the same place as his real estate. *Maybe he doesn't like his tenants bothering him,* she thought. She climbed the dusty wooden stairs and walked to the end of the corridor to a door advertising his office. She glanced at the other building occupants. Her eye caught Alberta Job Placement on the right side of the hallway. She planned to come back and visit that employment office once she had her lodgings. Lily knocked on the door, opening it when a voice shouted to come in. Sam McKlintock sat behind a desk covered in papers and took a moment before looking up. His penetrating blue eyes scanned her from head to toe and he smiled. Except for his small moustache, he was clean-shaven. His copious jet-black hair and well-muscled shoulders suggested a fortyish athlete who still kept in good physical shape. Sam exuded confidence.

She introduced herself and said, "I've just moved here with my husband and we need a place to live." Although fit, Sam seemed a small man, and Lily imagined that when he stood she would tower over him. "We've come from Glace Bay, Nova Scotia, and my husband will be working in the mine."

"How will you pay the rent, Mrs. Parsons?"

"What do you prefer?" Lily asked, squaring her shoulders. "Cash or cheques? My husband has a job at number four mine and I'm looking for a teaching job. While I'm searching, I might volunteer at the rehabilitation hospice behind the hospital. The segregated area will be convenient for both of us."

"Doesn't your husband want to see the apartment?" Sam asked incredulously "He's going to be paying for it."

"My husband trusts my judgment."

Sam leaned back in his chair, putting his hands behind his head, then bounced up and came round the desk. He was small and wiry, and not much over five feet. "I store furniture for my rental apartments in a warehouse at the corner of Third Avenue and Fourth Street. The apartment on the second floor is available at thirty dollars a month. It has three small rooms and a bathroom. Would you like to see it?"

The apartment was situated between two Chinese laundries. Lily commented on the strong smell of chlorine as she climbed the stairs. "I'll just have to close the windows if the odour gets too strong," she said. "But it will be convenient just to go down the stairs with my laundry. Miners clothes can get quite dirty."

Sam gave Lily a quizzical look. "How does a teacher like you end up marrying a miner?"

"In Cape Breton, people marry for love."

Sam laughed. "What will your husband feel about living next to some Chinese?"

"He'll have to develop a taste for Chinese food."

"I bet there weren't many Chinese in Glace Bay."

"Our mines attracted every nationality *but* Chinese. Yet I believe they would have been well received since they're hard workers."

After looking around the small but clean apartment, Lily shook Sam's hand to seal the deal.

"I see you're quite adaptable, Mrs. Parsons." Sam handed Lily two sets of keys. "Welcome to the neighbourhood. I'll look forward to meeting Mr. Parsons. Other than the smell of chlorine, I don't expect you'll have any problems."

After signing the contract, Lily walked over to the hospice, hoping things would be calmer than at her aborted visit the day before. Summoning up her nerve, she pushed open the metal door and introduced herself to the charge nurse. Miss Duffy wore a crisp white uniform that contrasted with her genial manner. She looked to be about Aunt Marjorie's age, and Lily wondered if the nurse had come out of retirement because of the war.

Miss Duffy inquired about Lily's background and thanked her warmly for her offer to volunteer. She suggested she read a few patients' charts before talking with them. "Some of the injuries are pretty awful," she admitted, "but these men have more than physical scars, Mrs. Parsons." She sat Lily down in her office and wheeled over the charts. "Go ahead. You'll find more than enough to do at the hospice."

Lily picked up three metal clipboards and deciphered the nearly illegible daily scrawls. The first chart noted details of Daniel (Dan) MacIntyre: "Unmarried double-above-knee amputee. Enlisted before he finished high school. Transferred from main hospital in August." She recalled the reception nurse's sober words: "There's nowhere else they can go." The chart indicated that Dan's family "could not handle the violent outbursts that accompanied his bouts of phantom limb." Treatment was morphine.

Lily picked up a second chart for Ken Smyth. This patient had enlisted before he finished his degree at military college. He was twenty-two years old and depressed that his fiancée refused to marry him. She had returned to live with her parents unable to accept his amputations. Treatment was morphine.

One more chart, she thought, *and then I'll go to see the soldiers.* She was beginning to feel her usual hospital queasiness.

Just as she opened a chart for Harold Beasley, Duffy walked into the makeshift office. The nurse glanced at the name on the chart and then took it from her. "Mrs. Parsons, Harry is our worst case. There's nothing we can do but give him large doses of morphine and compassion. Surgical amputations due to infections have left him with no forearms or lower legs. That was about all they could do in the field hospital. Basically, he was sent back from England to die in his homeland, something thousands of our soldiers were never able to do. Come, let's go on the ward and I'll introduce you."

"Did most of these injuries occur in the first battle at Ypres?" Lily asked.

"Yes. Few survived the second battle because the Bosch had begun to use gas." Nurse Duffy lowered her voice. "Most of these men wish they had died with their comrades."

Duffy swung open the rattling double doors to reveal a long, open space with ten beds crowded on either side against the walls. The windows were high up, so there was no view. As she entered the room, Lily found the disconnection from the outside world depressing.

"We're a stripped-down unit," Duffy explained. "The hospice functions more as a residence than a hospital."

The men who were not sleeping off their dose of morphine stared at the visitor.

"Mrs. Parsons has just moved here from Nova Scotia," Duffy explained to the curious men. "She'll volunteer here until she finds a teaching job."

When they reached the end of the room, a young man rolled over onto his stomach, and slid to the floor, grabbing Nurse Duffy's hand for balance. His stumps were covered with thick wool stockings. He waddled toward Lily, still holding the nurse's hand.

"I'm Dan," he said, looking up at Lily.

"Dan screams when his phantom limb bothers him," Nurse Duffy said. "Otherwise, he's a model patient." A few guffaws erupted.

As Lily walked about the ward patting a leg or touching a shoulder, learning names, she tried not to recoil at the deformities. There seemed nothing worthwhile she could do. As she was leaving, she glanced at Harry, out cold with sedation, and then stopped and turned to face the other men, who were all watching her. "Learning is a life-long process. I can see your physical losses. You still have brains, though. I know that many of you quit school to join the war."

"I had trouble reading orders — which got me demoted," a voice piped up. "I'd like to get more education now that I'm back home."

"Until I find a teaching job, I'll look forward to seeing you each day," Lily said, surprised by her own determination. After meeting the rest of the soldiers and getting more familiar with the layout of the building, she bid the men and Nurse Duffy goodbye for the day. Once outside the hospice, she took a deep breath to restore fresh air to her lungs. She headed for Millie Schuster's brothel on Third Street, also known as "the pink house." According to Bob Glimp, Millie's was the best place to get a drink in town. He had ushered Ed there the previous evening. Lily had a plan to curb Ed's drinking; something he did with friends.

Chinese laundries and small restaurants dotted the streets around their new apartment. Despite the area being patrolled, Lily wondered if she would feel safe at night there. She entered a restaurant, hoping to get a feel for her surroundings before going to the brothel. She introduced herself to what appeared to be the owners. They stood, arms akimbo, talking with the cook in his grease-spattered apron. They looked happy to have their first customer of the day. The couple smiled broadly, exposing some missing teeth.

"I be Lee Wong and this my wife Peking Duck." They both chuckled loudly and scurried away to set tables.

"Hold on," Lily said cheerily. "I just came by to introduce myself. We live next to the laundry on Second Avenue. Maybe I'll come back with my husband. He's never tasted Chinese food. I know he will like it." Lily smiled inwardly, thinking she had never eaten Chinese food, either. Lee Wong bobbed his head encouragingly. She marvelled how brothels could be situated in such respectable-seeming surroundings.

As Lily started up Third Street, she recalled Sam McKlintock's words about the brothels: "I'm the landlord, but as long as the rent comes in and the houses are kept tidy, I don't care what they do inside or out." The street was empty this early except for a woman pushing a baby carriage. She wore a typical Ukrainian babushka. The woman gave Lily a disapproving look as she passed. Lily felt like saying "I'm a schoolteacher" to those censuring eyes.

"Oh my goodness!" she muttered. "There must have been a paint sale." Five brightly coloured houses dotted both sides of the street. They stood out saucily as though they were making a statement. Other than the paint, they looked like every other two-storey house on the street with their neatly winterized postage-stamp-size gardens. Dead grass had been raked and bushes were wrapped in burlap. The brothels, at least in physical appearance, had not shamed the street. The absence of litter shocked Lily. She had expected liquor bottles and cigarette packages to be littering the ground. She tucked her head into her coat collar and started up the walk to the pink house where Ed had gone to drink the previous evening.

Lily's body was taut with misgivings as she knocked at the door. She had no idea how she would start a conversation with a woman who ran a brothel. In that moment of indecision, a no-nonsense-looking woman answered the door. She had a well-worn face adorned with heavy makeup and bluish-black hair like a starling. She assessed the visitor with a well-practised glance.

"My name is Lily Parsons."

"And I'm Millie Schuster, Are you looking for employment?"

"No," Lily said, bristling with dismay. "I'm volunteering at the military hospice behind the hospital. I'm a teacher, but haven't found a job yet."

"I *was* a teacher," Millie retorted. Lily didn't hide her surprise. Millie rubbed her fingers together as though she were fingering change. "Money," she said. "No comparison. If you're not looking for work, I don't know what I can do for you, Mrs. Parsons." Millie stood stolidly, blocking the door.

"I was hoping I could talk with you," Lily said.

Millie stood aside and gestured toward a parlour furnished with large comfortable furniture.

Lily plopped into one of the armchairs that faced the kitchen, where three girls laughed and fussed with each other's hair. "I suppose no one comes here during the day," Lily said.

"Have you ever been in a bordello?" Millie asked as she eased into a chair opposite.

"Well, no," Lily said, reddening. "I *have* seen Cape Breton girls hanging about on the main street hoping to be picked up."

"And did you disapprove of that?" Millie asked.

"Well, I'm not really one to judge. But I don't think a girl is safe when she gets picked up by a stranger," Lily said. She crossed her hands on her lap. She could feel the hot rush of blood in her cheeks. She didn't know how to steer the conversation to Ed.

Millie snorted and spelled: "*S-A-F-E-T-Y* is the *reason* for our brothels. Girls who sell sex on the street get knifed or killed. Meet *my* girls. *I* look after them."

Lily followed her into the kitchen, wishing she had never knocked on Millie's door. A magazine picture of Lillian Gish wearing a broad hat and well-applied makeup was pinned on the kitchen wall above an oak sideboard covered with liquor bottles. Beside the photo of Lillian Gish a headline from the *Lethbridge Herald* read: IF MAN HAS NEEDS, HAS NOT NATURE PROVIDED FOR THEM?

"Are those the words of Lillian Gish?" Lily asked wide-eyed.

"Of course not," Millie said as the kitchen girls burst out laughing. "These are the words of our mayor. A statement made when he was interviewed after the council meeting had voted for a segregated area." Millie gestured at the girls. "They are the 'nature' Mayor Harwood is speaking about. There is nowhere else in the Dominion where prostitutes work with the protection of the mayor and constabulary!" Millie wagged her finger. "The brothels are the first place the police come when there's trouble in town. If there's someone the police are looking for, he usually ends up in a brothel. Men involved in strikes, thefts, assaults, murders, kidnappings, extortions, arsons, anything out of order, sooner or later come through here it seems. We are the hidden part of any police investigation, and we're happy to co-operate. And so, unless there is fighting and disorderliness, the police ignore us. If there's a fight, we call the police, who then arrest the culprits, but otherwise leave us alone. There are about thirty people besides the prostitutes who work in the brothels in this part of town. That's a lot of informers.

"I think it was your husband who was here drinking with a man called Glimp last night," Millie continued. "He was so proud to tell us his wife was a schoolteacher." Lily was on the verge of angry tears, thinking that Ed had so quickly turned into an embarrassment. "Your husband was a gentleman even though he was a bit drunk. But Glimp is a pig, dead drunk or sober!"

Lily felt like a supplicant asking for a favour. "Would you let me know if my husband's drinking gets out of hand?"

"You aren't the first missus to ask for help," Millie said, putting her hand on Lily's shoulder. "A distraught wife came by last week accusing us of supplying her husband with morphine. We do have drugs, but we were not this man's supplier."

"Let me be frank, Mrs. Parsons. The police don't trust Glimp. If your husband hangs around with him, they won't trust him, either."

Within a month of her first unsettling experience at the hospice, Lily had a plan to get the wounded soldiers out of the dreary building and into an available classroom in the basement of the Galt Hospital. She needed supplies and a means of transporting the men across the rough fields. She burst with energy and enthusiasm at the prospect of engaging her unhappy charges. Advertising in the *Lethbridge Herald* resulted in a wealth of art-and-crafts supplies from stores and ordinary citizens; leather hides, blocks of basswood, pieces of cloth, a sewing machine, typewriter, scissors, knives, bobbins, and carving tools trickled in. The hospital board readily agreed that she should have use of the classroom providing there was no rowdiness. Lily gave the board her promise.

"What the hell am I going to do with a sewing machine?" Dan growled the moment he stepped into the well-equipped room with his fellow veterans.

"You'll have plenty to do, so stop your complaining," Lily retorted. She surveyed the skeptical men with her large brown owlish eyes, ignoring their derisive snorts.

"You sound like old men," she said with her hands on her hips. "But you are *not* old men. Old men don't go to war. There will still be many more young men coming home just like you before this war has ended. I refuse to accept your depressing attitudes. Write your stories, and they will be published. Paint your stories, and I'll hang them up. And if they're good enough, you'll sell them. It's a way to get things off your chest. You can have a brighter future. So let's deal with the past and all that you've experienced, then plan ahead. There is still something good you can do."

And so Lily's work with the veterans began.

Ken Smyth was the most educated of her charges. Ken began by writing to the advice column in the regional paper: "Lonely Hearts." He was advised to send his fiancée a picture of himself in his uniform, standing proudly on his new legs so that she could see he was still the same man she had been going to marry. But it would take months to fit artificial legs and Ken became even more depressed. Lily pushed him to write and submit his stories to various magazines. She had already challenged the most popular ladies' magazine to publish stories with photographs of amputees doing normal things, like dancing or driving a car.

Dan never did use the sewing machine. He used paint, brush, and canvas to conquer his demons, portraying trench warfare as smears of blood, mud, and ditchwater. At first, on each canvas, he painted a perfectly formed body part; you were left to guess where the rest of the body might lie in the obscene muck. They were macabre and haunting, but also beautiful. No one bought them, so he donated them to the new armoury. Looking forward now, not back, Dan began painting portraits. These works had an ethereal tone; soldiers, pictured in various aspects of repose, looking up at a waning moon. The details of each expressive face were portrayed with such visceral tenderness, it was as though a mother had painted them. These made Dan popular locally with families who had sons and fathers at war. People wanted to possess them and give them meaning of their own. And they were willing to pay. They could see in those faces a father, a husband, a brother, or a son, and felt that if they owned one of them, it was as if they were bringing a loved one home.

Meanwhile, Ed was working at the mine. Lily was so absorbed in organizing her workshop that she hadn't noticed a strike was imminent. She arrived home one evening to find Ed sitting at the kitchen table with Bob Glimp. Until this moment, she had never noticed Glimp's cold grey eyes. He stood and offered her his chair.

Slick, she thought. "I'll stand," she said coldly.

Glimp held up a packet of papers. "We're drawing up memberships to join the United Mine Workers of America," he said. "Strength in numbers if we decide to strike."

"Best time to threaten a strike is during a war," she said sarcastically. "Ed's brothers are in Europe fighting. Shouldn't you be fighting Germans, not mine managers?"

"The war ain't nothing to do with Americans," he said.

"You haven't heard of the *Lusitania*, then?"

Bob shrugged as though a hundred rich Americans losing their lives didn't matter.

"Well, it does have something to do with Ed," said Lily. "There's talk of conscription." She left them and went into the bedroom, flinging herself on the bed. She opened her father's letter telling her that Barnaby had been deployed to Europe. After Bob left, she pulled on her housecoat and joined Ed in the kitchen.

"Ed, please listen to *me*, not that piggish American. Britain is desperate for Canadian miners and Canadian coal. Stopping production would be dishonourable. You're right that managers are taking advantage of the war. But you can't justify a strike when your brothers are overseas digging in conditions more dangerous than here."

"I know Canadian miners are dying in Europe," Ed said. "But when my brothers come back, I want them to return to safe standards and fair wages."

"You can pick up the fight when we've won the war. But there's no pride in halting mine production when they're so desperate for coal." Ed's eyes had that hangdog look Lily so hated. "You would feel more pride by joining your brothers overseas than closing the mines. Your brothers are risking their lives against tyranny. I think these American agitators are tyrants, coming into Canada when we're at war with Germany and convincing us to shut down our mines."

Ed pushed back his chair, went to the stove, and poured some coffee. Lily felt tense waiting for him to respond to her arguments. He sat down again and pushed aside the papers that were strewn across the table. "All right," he said quietly. "I'll give the membership cards back to Bob tomorrow. But I feel like I'm letting down a friend."

"He's not a friend," Lily said softly. She got up and stood behind her husband, resting her hands on his shoulders.

"Lily, I'm going to enlist and pick up the union fight when I come back. I can ask to be in the same unit as Tim and Andrew."

Lily pulled his head back onto her chest and hugged his shoulders. "I'm scared, but I think it's the right thing to do. I'm proud of you."

*   *   *

The next day they walked nervously to the recruitment office in the centre of town where Dr. Lafayette and other doctors did physical examinations for prospective recruits. The doctor looked exhausted. "Our boys are lining up to enlist by the hundreds. Conscription won't be needed for our hardy lot." Lily was shocked at the youthful faces that sat in the waiting area, some with wives or girlfriends sitting close and looking scared.

Ed had been with Dr. Lafayette twenty minutes when the doctor came out into the waiting area and said, "Come in, Mrs. Parsons. I'd like to speak with you." Lily entered the examining room and her heart ached to see Ed perched like a child on the plinth, bare-chested and worried. "Your husband is passing bloody urine. More tests are warranted before I can sign his attestation forms."

Lily reeled at this news. She recalled hearing the story of Ed, as a young man, chatting with Mr. Finnegan beside his milk wagon when suddenly the old man gave his horse a sharp crack with his whip. The startled animal kicked out, catching Ed on his right side with her ironclad hoof. Ed dropped the crate of milk he was holding and doubled over, lurched toward the house. By evening, he was vomiting, running a fever, and urinating blood. The company doctor thought the kick had bruised his right kidney.

"The doctor in Cape Breton said his left kidney would take over if the injured one failed," Lily said.

Dr. Lafayette put his hand on Ed's shoulder. "Mrs. Parsons, I won't sign these forms, even if conscription *is* imposed. It would be medical malpractice to send a young man to war with kidney problems."

Ed, humiliated that he was not fit to fight, waged his own war against the owners and managers of the coalmines. Soon, he was back with Bob Glimp and his friends.

*   *   *

Later in the year, Lily was offered a job teaching grades three and four in Fort Macleod, thirty miles from Lethbridge. Now well settled and happy volunteering at the military hospice, she had greeted the offer with mixed feelings.

"So you're going to leave us," Dan said.

Lily put her arm around him. "I need the money, Dan, and I'm trained to teach."

"You're teaching *us*," he retorted. "Isn't that enough?"

Lily had difficulty swallowing. *I've scolded, bullied, praised, and felt the pride of a parent seeing a child launched*, she thought as she looked at him, trying to surmise if he was disappointed or angry. A knot in her stomach tightened recalling the struggle of the men to get mobile and nimble with their artificial limbs.

Lily was confident the veterans could look after themselves, but less certain about Ed. As well as planning a strike at the mine, he was now stopping off at Millie's after his shifts. However, he was arriving home sober, and Lily wondered if he was seeing one of Millie's girls.

She marched off unannounced to Millie's to see what was going on. Standing in the entrance, her jaw dropped; Ed was hunched over the kitchen table engrossed in a card game with the girls. Lily stifled a laugh as Millie waved her away with a hand and an exaggerated wink.

"Don't interrupt us," she said, snapping her cards on the table. "We're playing cribbage." Lily shook her head in disbelief. Millie had added gambling to her services! She smiled as she watched the two rough diamonds. She knew Ed wouldn't let alcohol get in the way of his winning at cards. She'd asked Millie to keep her husband in check, but Millie had never promised she could do that. But she had. *That's friendship*, Lily thought as she left them to their game.

CHAPTER 13

Mining Accident, 1917

The school in Fort Macleod provided weekly room and board. On Friday afternoons, Lily returned home in the dusty old car of a Mounted Police officer. Still overseeing the veterans' projects, Lily was disturbed when Bob Glimp arrived at the hospice with two tough-looking friends. She intercepted them at the door.

"Mrs. Parsons," Glimp said, pushing himself into the ward, "we need veterans to make a show of supporting labour, especially if they ain't got no legs. They're mad as hell 'cause the government don't help 'em. I plan to take advantage of that anger."

"You're not welcome here," Lily said. She grabbed a wooden leg from a bed and raised it. "I mean what I say. Get out and take your cronies with you."

Glimp looked at her as though he might take the leg and use it on her. "No one speaks to me like that," he said as he stormed out.

Lily shivered, seeing the rage on his face. "You've already done enough damage!" she shouted after him.

A strike at the mine began soon after the altercation at the hospice. Glimp got his retribution: Ed joined the picket line. "We need better pay and safety," Ed said when Lily begged him to stay home. "Do you want to be a widow with no pension?"

"Of course not, but I'm working and can look after myself." He looked hurt, and she put her arms around him. "We're not underdogs. I've got a job and you can start back to work when the strike's over. Glimp should go back to the States and agitate. He has no business up here. We're not militant like the Americans."

"That's why he's here," he said, pulling away from Lily.

"Because we can't look after ourselves?" she said, raising her eyebrows in mock surprise. "Stay out of the shenanigans, Ed. Apparently the Americans roughed up a scab worker and cut the queue off the poor Chinese man delivering food to the manager's house."

"The scab workers are foreigners," he said.

"So are the Americans."

"But they speak our language."

"Look, we could go on arguing all night. Please, just stay away from the picketers and nothing will happen. I don't want you around those rabble-rousers."

"You shouldn't have told him off at the hospice in front of his men. I heard about that."

"Those Americans," she said, "they're nothing but cowards."

For two weeks, the police patrolled the picket lines to prevent any violence. Monday mornings, Lily left with the officer for Fort Macleod, hoping Ed would not get into a violent clash while she was away for the week. The Americans had warned that the strike would continue until the mine met their demands. Although Bob Glimp knew how to fill the miners with righteous indignation, he wasn't the one to provide their paycheques. Lily realized her modest salary would not sustain them if the strike were prolonged. Being prudent, she had tucked away her earnings from the Sydney hospital and a small amount of money she had received as a wedding gift.

Driving back to Fort Macleod on a Monday morning, the officer said: "I spoke with a constable patrolling the strikers, knowing you were worried about your husband being on the picket line. He told me that Ed walks the line well away from the Americans, but he also said he does have a bit of an edge to him. I hope I'm not too frank in saying that."

"Not at all," she said wryly. "Ed can be angry, but he has his reasons. I thought marriage would make him more relaxed."

"I guess every woman hopes that, but us men tend to hold on fairly tight to our demons."

"My husband's turning twenty-five next week," Lily interjected, trying to brighten the conversation. "The principal told me to take the day off. He said a quarter-century was worth celebrating. Ed has come to love Chinese food, so I'm going to have Lee Wong prepare his preferred dishes and take a picnic to the mine. Make those nasty Americans jealous. I doubt they have wives who care about them."

"Mrs. Parsons, I'd stay clear of the mine. It would be better to take your husband to Lee Wong's restaurant."

Lily smiled, but inside she felt angry that she should be afraid of the Americans. By the time she arrived to begin her week in Fort Macleod, she had planned the entire picnic menu.

The morning of his birthday, Ed packed two meat sandwiches and an orange in his lunch box. Lily smiled, thinking he had not realized it was a special day.

"Nice that the school is closed for a water repair," he said. She could taste his breakfast on his lips as he kissed her. "I'll get home early and we can go to Galt Park to watch the ball game."

She nodded, and he gave her a pat on the rump. "Hmm, maybe we can do something else." Lily pushed him away with a laugh. Ed turned and waved, and Lily blew him a kiss. She longed to say, "I love you, you silly, sentimental, complicated man."

At noon she strolled over to the Peking House, enjoying her taste of freedom.

Lee Wong was standing at the door, basking in the bright August sun. "I pack everythin' ready, Missus Parsons."

She smiled broadly, imagining how pleased Ed would be. She peeked in the box containing four packages wrapped in greasy brown paper. Lee had marked the packages, SESAME CHIKEN, CHOW MEIN, EGG FOOYUNG, and STICKY RICE. He had put in an old bent fork, aware that Ed had never mastered chopsticks.

"I add fortune cookies," he said, as he slipped in another small parcel. "I want you and Mr. Parsons have plenty good luck."

The day was cloudless, and dozens of crows hovered in the sky, hoping for scraps. Lily perched on a rock, half-hidden by a clump of bushes, observing the railway track. On one side, she saw Ed standing about fifty yards away, talking with another man who was leaning on his placard. Closer to her, but in the other direction, Bob Glimp, surrounded by his goons, stood much farther up the narrow gauge rail. He leaned back on one of the cars with his arms akimbo, observing the strikers from a distance. Lily averted her eyes as the police officer known as Jimbo emerged from behind a tree, buttoning his trousers. She let out a little groan, seeing the food carton had made a grease mark on her skirt. She slid the box under a low tree branch and started up the overgrown track in the direction of her husband's group. Ed was still chatting with his back to her. She called out his name and he turned and saw her.

"I've brought your birthday lunch," she shouted, waving. Ed

smiled awkwardly and began walking briskly toward her. There was a rumble and he looked over her shoulder up the track and saw the coal car Bob had been leaning against. Lily kept walking, oblivious.

"Get off the track! " Ed screamed. He sprinted toward her, shouting, "You bastards!"

"What happened?" Lily stammered, touching the damp bandage on her scalp. She withdrew her hand and winced at the blood. She swung her legs over the bed slowly and stood. A nurse tucked her arm under Lily's to help her balance. "I remember my husband shouting and then everything went blank. *Bastards.* Yes, that's what I heard him shout. *Bastards.*"

"Your husband pushed you out of the way of a runaway rail car and got clipped himself. The doctor is with him now."

As Lily followed the nurse through the men's ward, she tightened with anxiety, seeing the worried faces. She slipped behind the heavy curtain cordoning off Ed's bed.

"This is Dr. Lafayette," the nurse said.

"We've already met. Dr. Lafayette examined my husband when he tried to enlist."

Lily shook hands and reached over to kiss Ed, who, except for his chest, was motionless.

"Your husband's heavily sedated," Morris Lafayette said as he came around the end of the cot. "His right thighbone is broken." He pointed to the pulley suspending Ed's leg. "This system applies traction to the bone ends so his leg will heal straight."

Lily didn't hold back her tears. "Ed didn't deserve this. *I* was the target."

"A police officer witnessed what happened," Dr. Lafayette said, shaking his head in dismay. "An American has been arrested."

"Yes," Lily said softly. "I saw that officer come out of the woods just as I started up the tracks. He would have seen exactly what happened."

"Mrs. Parsons, Ed's leg will heal nicely in six weeks. But his healthy kidney was damaged in the accident. Unfortunately, your husband will have to be treated in the hospital for several weeks."

"I'll have to quit my job. How on earth am I going to pay for all this?"

"Everyone in this hospital has admired what you have accomplished with the veterans. You'll manage, Mrs. Parsons. Perhaps your family could help?"

"My parents live in Nova Scotia. I had hoped not to let them know that Ed was on strike. My father would not have approved of a strike during a war."

"I'll return this evening when some of the sedation has worn off, and we'll talk," Dr. Lafayette said. "Sit down and rest. Your husband will be out for a while."

"Mrs. Parsons, Mrs. Parsons! You were screaming," a nurse said as she gripped Lily's hands. "I rushed in, thinking it was the patient."

"I had an awful nightmare," Lily mumbled, struggling upright in her chair, her hand cupped over her mouth. "I was deep under the ocean floor when I saw a dead canary. I was carrying a lamp and tried to run before there was an explosion. There was a boom and everything went black."

Ed moaned and opened his eyes. Lily leaned over him. "Ed, you put yourself in such danger for me. Do you remember? It's my fault. I should never have come to the mine." He put up his hand to touch her face, drifting back to sleep a moment later. She sat down in the chair, pinching her cheek to stay awake and trying to quell her worried thoughts.

She could only pray that the hospital bill could be paid over time.

*   *   *

"It's been three weeks since the accident," Lily said when Dr. Lafayette passed by on his usual rounds. "How's he doing?"

"The urine has been clear for two days," he answered. "But I've noticed his left leg is swollen. Unfortunately, he can't get up walking until we remove this traction." The doctor pulled aside the sheets, exposing the uninjured leg. He pressed Ed's calf with his thumb, leaving an indentation. "Ed must do exercises to keep the circulation moving in order to avoid a blood clot." He demonstrated circular movements with his foot. "Ed must do this regularly until he's walking. I've spoken to him about this, but maybe you can encourage him?"

Ed nodded, indicating his willingness to try harder.

Lily flopped forward in her chair, cradling her head in her hands. "I should never have goaded Bob Glimp at the hospice. He hated me after that."

"Mrs. Parsons, if it wasn't you, he would have found another target. I've heard all about him. I call this 'fear tactics.' It must have infuriated him that you confronted him at the hospice. He is paid to scare Canadian miners into joining the American union."

"I should have told him to go packing the first time I saw him be rude to Lily," Ed said. "But I really believed us Canadians should join a union. And Bob seemed to have the tools to make it happen."

Dr. Lafayette ran his fingers through his wavy white hair and touched Ed gently on the shoulder. "It will all come right in the end, son." He circled each of his broad shoulders slowly as though he was adjusting a burden. "By the way, Mrs. Parsons, that was quite a show you put on at the hospice," the doctor said as he was about to leave. "I couldn't imagine a better use for that old warehouse. What made you think those veterans had so much talent? My wife bought one of Dan MacIntyre's paintings. His work is very good, quite provocative."

Ed grasped Lily's arm affectionately. "She's a believer, Dr. Lafayette, even in a bad apple like me."

Lily put her finger to his lips. "Shush. You aren't a bad apple. Just a little rotten at times." Ed held her hand until he drifted off to sleep.

CHAPTER 14

Lily Widowed, 1917

The senior nurses were short-handed during Ed's recovery. Having given up her job in Fort McLeod, Lily offered to help them, especially with the management of the awkward traction device. When she had a free moment, she scooted over to the hospice to help with incoming wounded vets struggling to get mobile.

The war was into its third year, and with more casualties arriving, another ten beds were squeezed into the limited hospice space. Lily was a volunteer, and without an income she fretted about her finances. Dr. Lafayette intervened and the hospital bursar set up a schedule of payments she could meet. She doubted a cheaper rent could be negotiated with Sam McKlintock. However, between her small savings and the money they had collected at the wedding, she had two hundred dollars, and that would help cover the hospital bill.

Millie Schuster arrived unexpectedly at the hospital with seventy dollars stuffed in a scented envelope. "Bet you didn't expect this!" she said gleefully as Lily counted the bills. "When trouble hits, we ladies of the night are generous. We drop off cash without tooting our own horn. Some folks don't like to take money from prostitutes, no matter how hard up they are. But money isn't everything," she added, as she pulled out a pack of cards. "I'm here to play cards." The nurse looked away as Millie set out the poker chips on the edge of Ed's bed.

If this is the only thing that will make him smile, so be it, Lily thought.

Dan had dropped by the hospice to see Lily and unfurled a wad of bills. "My art is earning money that I have no desire to spend," he said. He backed away as Lily tried to hand back the money. "You're going to make me have one of my fits if you don't take this," he said, laughing.

Alone in the hospital room while Ed slept, Lily contemplated the unusual direction her life had taken. The gutless Americans had fled after Ed was injured, and the strikers had returned to work, never having achieved their goals of fair wages and safe working conditions. She was sure the manager wouldn't give Ed an office job when he recovered, so it was with bitter satisfaction that she heard Bob Glimp was in jail.

Ed had been in the hospital for six weeks. The splint had been removed and he was now walking with crutches. Dr. Lafayette recommended he be discharged in a few days. Other than being tired after a short walk, Ed seemed to have fully recovered from his accident. A nurse explained the tiredness as a result of inactivity and assured Lily her husband would soon be "as right as rain." Lily's head was full of plans to find a teaching job in Lethbridge. The thought of having Ed at home renewed her confidence.

"My leg hurts," Ed complained, sitting on the bed and flexing his foot. The nurse looked briefly at his leg. "Your calf is a bit

MATRONS AND MADAMS · 163

swollen. Nothing to worry about."

"Should we call Dr. Lafayette, to let him know?" Lily asked.

"I don't like to bother the doctor unduly," the nurse said. "I'll come back later to check on it."

Lily asked the probationer who came in with the evening meal tray to look at Ed's leg "Has the doctor been informed about the swelling?" she asked. The student nurse promised to inquire and left.

"I'm not hungry," Ed said. He had begun to sweat and complained of a pain in his chest. There was no one at the nurses' station. Lily poked her head into the matron's office. The room was empty and everything was packed in boxes. She couldn't tell if the matron was moving in or out. She picked up the phone on the desk and asked to be connected to Dr. Lafayette.

"Who's calling?" the operator asked in a harried tone.

"Mrs. Ketchum," Lily replied, using the name of the matron.

"I'm sorry," she said after a moment, "the doctor isn't answering. Try again in an hour."

I don't want to be an alarmist, she thought. Ed was snoring softly, and she decided not to disturb him. Soon, she was asleep herself, but a raspy cough jolted her awake. Ed's head was tilted back as he struggled to breathe.

"I can't get air," he gasped as he coughed up a bolus of bloody mucus. He gripped the mattress, trying to lift himself up. Lily propped the bloodstained pillows behind him and wiped away some pinkish foam that had accumulated around his mouth.

"Help!" she screamed, throwing back the green curtain. The patient nearest the door shouted for a nurse.

Lily tore through the ward, screaming for help. The nurses' station was still empty. She ran up the stairs to the women's ward as two nurses hurried toward her.

"Get Matron," one of them hissed. The patients looked terrified.

"What's happened?" a shaky female voice asked. Except for a nightlight, the ward was dark.

"The matron's entertaining in her apartment," the other answered. "She's not to be disturbed."

"Such idiocy," the older nurse snapped. "She *wants* to be called in an emergency. Get hold of Dr. Lafayette." The nurse descended the stairs two at a time and was gone.

Lily rushed back to the ward and knelt on the bed, pulling Ed forward. He put his hand on his chest. "It hurts," he wheezed through the foam, looking terrified. He dropped his head onto her shoulder, coughed, and sprayed blood. "Lily, I'm sorry."

"You have nothing to be sorry about, Ed. I have something to tell you. We're going to have a baby. The doctor said I'm three months along." Lily couldn't hold back her tears. "The doctor will be here soon." Ed's face became contorted as he took a small breath in and then resumed coughing blood.

He grabbed Lily's arm. "I love you ... mother ..." Ed's chest stopped heaving.

By the time Matron arrived, it was over. Ed Parsons had died of a pulmonary embolism while Lily and three nurses stood helpless beside him.

Lily repeated the words she had longed to hear: "I love you." She closed Ed's eyes and wiped his chin, then lay down beside him. "Please, don't cover his face," she said as she encircled his head with her arm on the blood-stained pillow.

"What's happened, Matron?" a frightened voice called from the other side of the curtain.

"Shhh, everything's all right," she responded firmly. "I'll be with you in a moment."

*   *   *

Dr. Lafayette arrived at 9:00 p.m. dressed in formal attire. "A blood clot must have travelled to his lungs," he said. "Matron, please leave us alone."

Lily hung over a metal washbasin, retching. The doctor held her by the shoulders and handed her some water. "I felt so confident about Ed," he said. "I joked to a colleague that he must have nine lives. Dear God, Mrs. Parsons, how I wish I had signed those enlistment forms."

He put his hand on Ed's shoulder and adjusted the sheet over him. It was a gesture that Lily found comforting; she felt he was still Dr. Lafayette's patient. "Let the nurses deal with him now," he said.

Ed was buried in his wedding suit in the Catholic cemetery. Lily had written to Mr. and Mrs. Parsons to let them know of their son's death. She didn't think she could feel more sorrow until she received Mr. Parsons's streaked letter saying that a coalmine in the Arras area had collapsed on Tim and Andrew.

"That's three of my sons who are buried away from home," he wrote. Lily had to interpret the bleeding handwriting. But the message was stark: "Mrs. Parsons suffered a stroke on reading the telegram informing us of our boys' death. She now has aphasia, thank God, so she will never understand about Ed. He was her baby."

Lily put down the letter and wondered if she should write back about the baby she was carrying, a child of Ed's. *When it's born, I'll visit Nova Scotia. There is no joy until this war is over.*

A few miners had come to the funeral. Millie, Dan, Ken, and Lee Wong also attended the short mass performed in a side chapel. Lily hadn't expected the mine manager, and yet she'd hoped he might come. Not even a young man's death had moved him, however.

Unexpectedly, Sam McKlintock reduced Lily's rent for a month while she looked for another place to live. She drove out to Fort Macleod with the same officer who had given her regular lifts, but her job was no longer available. A spinster had replaced her while she had been caring for Ed. "She's proving quite satisfactory," the schoolmaster said as he glanced at Lily's increased size. "Having a baby, aren't you? I don't think parents would be happy with a pregnant teacher in the classroom. It would be distracting."

"To you or the parents?" Lily retorted.

"I do need someone to clean the school after hours," the schoolmaster said, avoiding Lily's wide-eyed gaze. She swallowed her pride and thanked the man, but declined his offer.

Mrs. Piper, the mine manager's wife, offered Lily room and board in exchange for domestic service. She had met Mrs. Piper when she'd brought her old linens to the hospice. Lily had wondered at the time how an indifferent manager had married such a caring wife. She accepted the job only when she learned the mine manager was rarely home.

Edward Parsons Jr. arrived in August of 1917. Teddy was over nine pounds at birth, with a head of tight black curls and blue-black eyes like his father. "Oh, you are a chatty soul, so unlike your dad," Lily cooed when Teddy loudly made his wants known. Her joy at having Ed's child was tempered, however, by her continual worry about finances.

"I feel I'm throwing you out on the street," Mrs. Piper said, a month after Lily gave birth. "But I've raised my five children and have no desire to hear a baby crying all night."

"My breasts can't satisfy such a big baby," Lily said. "I'm sorry you were disturbed." Unfortunately, the sincere apology did nothing to change Mrs. Piper's mind.

"You may have the baby cot and clothes as well as bottling

accessories to get you started," Mrs. Piper offered. "But you *must* find another place — although I don't think any household will hire a domestic with a child. You need to get back to teaching so you can afford your own apartment. I'll write you a very good reference."

"There are more teachers than classes," Lily said, softly.

Lily walked through her old familiar neighbourhood with a sense of longing. *Here,* she thought, *was my first home as a newly married bride; where Ed was cared for in the nearby hospital; where he developed a taste for gambling and less drink; where I humiliated Bob Glimp with dire consequences; where I launched the veterans and saw Dan fly.* She was tearful by the time she reached Millie's brothel. Millie had kindly offered to mind Teddy while Lily looked for work.

The proprietress greeted her with a broad smile. "We thought you'd never come back after living high with the Pipers." She picked up Teddy and cradled him in her arms. "He *does* look like Ed," Millie said. "Say, why don't you come and work for *me*? I'd love to have a baby in the house. A little boy would be a fine distraction for the girls on their off-hours."

A bedroom off the kitchen and twenty dollars a month is what Millie offered Lily to keep the house in good order. "You've come at a convenient time because the lady who managed our house has gone to live with a family in Calgary. You'll have to have backbone to keep these girls in check. They can get pretty fond of themselves, forgetting they're here to work. Sometimes they think it's enough to just chat with the clients."

And so, reluctantly within a day or two, Lily moved with her small son into the brothel. She hoped it would only be a temporary arrangement.

She kept Millie's place spotless. In the evening, when Teddy

168 · SHARON JOHNSTON

was sleeping, she helped serve drinks. Dan MacIntyre and his cronies came by the brothel more often now that Lily was there. They'd order a drink and a little love if they could afford it.

Betty Sanchez was the prettiest of Millie's girls. She had Aztec features with thick brown hair and wide-set black eyes, which put her much in demand at the brothel. Dan became her preferred client. One night he had arrived with a gash in his arm and she cleaned and bandaged it. While she did this he slowly uncovered his plan to kill himself. But he decided to have one last fling before doing so. After tending to his wound, Betty gave him his tender finale, hoping he would want more. She was right. Dan came regularly. Sometimes just to talk or cry. Betty had augmented her income from The Last Post by cleaning at the hospital. During a mopping session in Ed's room, Lily had asked her about her schooling. She was surprised to learn that Betty had never attended school. She had looked after her father until he became sick with a lung infection and returned to Mexico. Betty sent half her wages to him even though he had abandoned her at the age of sixteen. Her tale was just one of the sad stories among the women at the brothel.

CHAPTER 15

Lethbridge, Alberta, 1919

It was already dark when Clara, two children in tow, taxied onto the driveway of the Galt Hospital. She was tired from the train journey across the Prairies, but elated to arrive at her new home. Rows of young poplars bowed in the wind to signal her arrival.

"Can you orient me?" she asked the taxi driver.

"The hospital is situated on the south bank of the Oldman River," the driver said. "The back of the hospital has a fine view of the coulees."

"I received a photograph of the hospital. I believe those two windows to the right of the main entrance are the matron's office," said Clara.

The driver looked back, raising his eyebrows. "So *you're* the new lady superintendent everyone's being talking about! Word is you fought in the Great War."

"I did my part," Clara said with a touch of levity.

"My daddy died in the war," Ivy piped up.

"I'm sorry, miss. I should not have spoke lighthearted."

"Lighthearted is good," Clara said. She breathed a tired sigh of relief. "This will be our new home, Ivy."

"Where will *we* live?"

"In the nurses' residence, over there." Clara pointed at the two-storey brick house at the east end of the hospital. It looked austere, but not uncomfortable.

The train passage across Canada had been uneventful, a welcome relief after the tragic events on the ship. Mayor Harwood as board chairman had assured Clara that the hospital would pay for a compartment for her and Ivy, but she had been content with a lower berth. After all, she had slept with both girls on the ship. The mayor laughed good-naturedly at her squished arrangement, but he himself had taken a compartment in the adjoining carriage. A young Cree woman provided Clara some free time during the trip to play cards in the lounge car with the mayor. She was on her way back to the Canoe Lake reserve in Saskatchewan and happy to earn some pocket money babysitting Florence and Ivy. Already a mother of three, she was skilled at keeping the children occupied.

Snuggled in her berth with a child on either side, Clara reflected on their mutual fatherlessness. She wondered if Amelia had lost her pharmacist husband on the battlefield. The thought of Amelia widowed and working at a menial job to support her daughter distressed her. She felt grateful that she had received a nurse's education, an education that was perfected during the war years. *I feel ready for anything,* she thought as she adjusted her body between the two girls. She fell asleep once she'd settled in a comfortable spot.

Mayor Harwood used the train ride to share his worries about the Galt Hospital with Clara. He was frustrated and angry that the American College of Surgeons had not accredited the

Galt after calling its health-care practices non-standardized. "The College's criticisms applied to both the nursing and medical staff," he said. "They cited inconsistent surgical and radiograph practices, and a host of other failings."

"I'm sure I'm up to the challenges — with your support," Clara responded.

The mayor sighed. "I'm often the object of the city's dirty politics, which include attacks on the hospital because I'm chairman."

"Uneasy lies the head that bears the crown," Clara said, grinning. "You're a battler, I can see. I like that. I am too, when it's necessary."

During one of their more lighthearted conversations, Mayor Harwood confessed he had converted the top floor of his house into a dance floor. In turn, Clara described her lessons with George at the Savoy Hotel. "Mrs. Harwood must enjoy dancing to let you take up an entire floor," she said, laughing.

The mayor sighed heavily. "My wife returned recently from Dr. Lulu Hunt Peters's weight-loss clinic in Los Angeles with some strange ideas. They certainly weren't about dancing or having fun. The doctor published a manual called *Diet and Health: with the Key to the Calories* in which she referred to fat people as *fireless cookers*. She used witty illustrations to show how 'fatties' are unable to get the heat out of their packing." The mayor let out a short laugh. "Seriously," he continued, "the idea of measuring the energy content of food as calories is being practised in most Canadian hospitals. Quite revolutionary!" He looked sad. "My wife has taken dieting to extremes and risks getting ill. She weighs everything she eats on a set of scales she can carry in her purse. Then she calculates the calories. Not many friends invite her over anymore. She was an attractive woman when I married her."

"I'll try to convince Mrs. Harwood to follow a sensible diet rather than worrying about her weight," Clara said, regretting having laughed about the mayor's wife.

In Regina, Harwood and the Cree woman both got off the train. The mayor was advising on the formation of a public utility company in Saskatchewan. *It doesn't surprise me that Alistair Harwood is being asked for advice*, Clara thought when she learned the reason he had to get off at Regina.

"See you in a few days," he said to her as he bounced down onto the train platform. "I feel responsible for you since I'm the reason you moved to Canada."

Clara waved and smiled, thinking she was in Canada because of Francis Newbury. Butterflies flew at random in her abdomen as she watched Harwood disappear.

The taxi driver carried the luggage into the hospital, thanking Clara for the tip. With Florence in her arms, she took a moment to admire the elegant ironwork of the original hospital. As she climbed the stairs to the main entrance, she noticed the steps had loose masonry. The exterior lighting was also inadequate. *No one knows better than the British how to keep an old building going*, she thought. She was smiling now as she entered the inner sanctum of the hospital, followed by the driver and Ivy.

In the main foyer, probationers were delivering dinner trays from a metal trolley to patients in a nearby ward. Clara introduced herself to Mrs. Klausen, the receptionist, who logged in her arrival. "Everyone's glad you've arrived safely," she said. "Mayor Harwood wired us about the baby. Unfortunately, the Sunbeam Ward has had an outbreak of chicken pox. We can't expose a baby. She will have to stay with you in the nurses' home for a few days before we can put her in the children's ward."

Clara sighed. "Let's get her settled first and then deal with arrangements for my daughter, Ivy."

At that moment, Florence awoke, stared wide-eyed at Clara, and started to whimper, but she smiled when Ivy tickled her face with her fur hat.

"I'm glad Florence can stay with us, Mummy," Ivy said, beaming.

Miss Sweet, the night nurse on duty, arrived wearing black stockings. A brocade bag with wooden handles and a pair of knitting needles sticking out of it was tucked under her arm. "A sweater for my brother's birthday," she said defensively, noticing Clara's disapproving look. "He just came over from Edmonton to celebrate. I don't see him often, so this will be a nice surprise."

"I'm sure it will," said Clara, taking the knitting bag. "But knitting on duty will not be allowed, Miss Sweet." She smiled to soften her rebuke. "I can't imagine any nurse having free time," she added, clacking the bag's wooden handles together and tucking it under her arm. "Please show us to the matron's apartment now. These children need to eat and get to bed, whatever the sleeping plan." She marched beside Miss Sweet toward the breezeway connecting the nurses' home to the hospital, followed by Mrs. Klausen carrying the bags. Clara stopped momentarily to glance in the kitchen. An open door beside the cookstove revealed a man hunched over a small fire warming his hands. A kerosene lamp lit up a tin-roofed shack that extended twenty feet behind the hospital. Beyond the shack the frost-covered coulees shimmered eerily under a full moon.

"That's Yip, the cook," Miss Sweet said. "He sleeps out back during the week and stays with his brother's family when he has time off. The Chinks run the kitchen and the laundry."

Clara went forward, introduced herself to the cook, and then returned to Miss Sweet. "Miss Sweet, there will be no talk of *Chinks* in my hospital," she said. "Chinese people, Asians, Orientals, but never Chinks."

Miss Sweet's face was by now quite sour.

Clara imagined her inventory list of things that needed attention as a collection of eggs in an egg carton. She put prejudice in the carton, along with black stockings and the shoddy front entrance.

Irritating woman, Clara thought, entering her apartment. She scanned the furnishings; nothing matched, yet everything was in good taste and comfortable. A dark green upholstered Chippendale sofa, two well-stuffed armchairs, tea and card tables, and a sideboard gave the place a homey appearance. The plumbing was efficient and the ceramic tub did not have a ring of scum, which pleased her. Through the bathroom window she could see the poplar trees still bowing.

Miss Blair, a first-year probationer, arrived at the apartment to take Ivy to her own room. She looked surprised when she saw Florence. "I didn't know there were *two* children," she said, looking flustered.

"I'm staying with my mother," Ivy said, glaring at Miss Blair.

"Miss Sweet, you may get back to the ward and I'll work things out with Miss Blair," said Clara. "I'll join you at reception in an hour."

Soon, there was a baby cot in the bedroom, making it hard to manoeuvre, but it was a temporary solution while the Sunbeam Ward wasn't available. Ivy was to have her own room across the hall from her mother's small apartment. This arrangement was to begin the next day, allowing Ivy a night to get comfortable in her new surroundings.

Miss Blair, who had been assigned to look after Ivy while Clara worked, was an organized girl, being the eldest of five sisters. Florence and Ivy were bathed, fed, and in bed within the hour.

Clara unpacked and arrived back at reception. Her nostrils

were assaulted with an unpleasant mixture of smells of stale food and fecal matter. The trolley that normally transported the dinner trays was no longer on the ward, but the tray perched on a filing cabinet did not escape her nose. The metal cover protecting the plate had slipped sideways, exposing the congealed food. "Why is there a tray left here?" she asked.

Miss Sweet stood awkwardly beside her with hands clasped behind her back. "Mr. McIsaac refused his dinner," she retorted.

Her lack of concern as to why a patient didn't eat disturbed Clara. She decided to establish her authority. "Miss Sweet, I wish to speak with Mr. McIsaac." She entered Ward B with the nurse tailing behind. Eight iron beds, on opposite sides of the room, were separated by metal cabinets. Two well-worn, green leather chairs were stationed at the end of the room for mobile patients. Neither the utility cupboard nor the adjacent bathroom doors were closed, thus exposing cleaning supplies and the toilet. Clara closed both doors before turning to the recalcitrant patient in a bed to the left of the entrance. His short grey hair was matted to his forehead and day-old stubble covered his face. Heads popped up from the other beds to see what was happening. Clara's eyes swept across the room like a lighthouse beacon.

"Are you from the Christian union?" a patient wheezed. "My missus is one of them lady prohibitionists."

"Then you're lucky to be in hospital, where 'medicinal spirits' can be served," Clara said. The patient dropped back onto his pillow, exhausted from speaking. She winced at the sound of his poor lungs. His chart would show if it was cancer, emphysema, or gassing that was causing the breathlessness.

"Mr. McIsaac, this is the new matron, Mrs. Durling."

"Why haven't you eaten, Mr. McIsaac?"

"I got no appetite, worrying about my missus doing the farm work since I caught my leg in the threshing machine." He held up the blanket to show his leg and Clara noticed a bedpan jammed against his uninjured leg. "Can you remove this?" he asked, tapping the metal pan. "I managed to get my arse off, but then the nurse never came back."

Clara flicked open a linen towel, slipped it under the covers, and with a quick gesture gripped the pan and removed it to the bathroom, closing the door behind her. She returned to put the emptied and rinsed pan in the metal cabinet beside his bed.

"Do you wear dentures?" she asked, hearing the sucking sound of his gums.

"Yeah, but the nurse took 'em to be repaired. I don't wanna get her in trouble, but I couldn't eat them chops."

Clara lifted the metal chart from the end of the bed and flipped through the pages. "I see the teeth were taken for repairs this morning."

The patient in the next bed piped up to add clarification. "He ain't et all day."

"You must be hungry," she said, patting Mr. McIsaac's arm. "I'll arrange for a tray of soft food to be brought. Is there anything special you would like?"

"Just something I can chew."

Clara whisked out of the ward glaring. "It's no wonder the poor chap didn't eat, with a smelly bedpan left on his bed and no teeth!"

"I didn't know about the bedpan *or* the teeth," Miss Sweet bleated. "The probationers on day shift leave immediately after serving the evening meals. I suppose that's why they forgot the bedpan. And I don't know who took the teeth."

Clara looked furious. "Miss Sweet, you are the charge nurse. It is your job to check on the probationers. My goodness, you have set a poor example. Go and fetch those probationers and tell them they will work a double shift until this ward is spotless. And *you* are going to help them. I want everything stripped. Right down to the rubber sheets. Bed frames to be swabbed and floors thoroughly mopped. When do you turn down the lights on the wards?"

"Ten o'clock," replied Miss Sweet, barely containing the resentment she felt at this intrusion into her evening. "Wouldn't it be better to be doing all this on the day shift?" she asked. "Our cleaning staff is on duty then."

"Miss Sweet, there's a lesson to be learned this evening. Fetch the probationers, and I will arrange for a soft tray. My watch tells me we have two hours to get this ward spotless."

Yip had come in from the cold and was scurrying about the kitchen preparing food for the next day. His pepper-grey pigtail swung back and forth in rhythm with his movements. He stood with his back to the central counter looking worried when he saw the matron.

"I do something wrong?" he asked.

"Not at all," Clara said softly. "Mr. McIsaac was served food he couldn't eat while his dentures were being repaired. Can you make him something he can chew without teeth?" Yip, relieved, returned her smile.

"I make him very nice cheese omelette." The kitchen was filled with mixed odours of onions, custard powder, root vegetables, and oriental spices. The perimeter of the kitchen was lined with milk cans, egg cartons, and sacks of vegetables waiting to be put into patient's meals. Clara yanked open the cold room door, where hip and shoulder joints hung from metal hooks. A dozen large metal pots swung precariously over Yip's head as he whipped up the omelette. She watched him crack eggs on the edge of a bowl with a snap of his wrist. Next he grated cheese, pushing it aside while he beat cream and seasoning into the eggs. A frying pan had been sizzling gently with butter on the six-burner gas stove and he poured the mixture into the pan. He tipped and lightly shook it until the mixture was ready to turn. Finally, he sprinkled clumps of cheese on the flat eggs and then flipped both ends over to complete the omelette.

"You take Mr. McIsaac soft tray now and tell him I sorry." Yip placed a bowl of ice cream on a saucer of ice chips and handed the tray to Clara. She nodded enthusiastic approval.

"I will, Yip. This looks just right."

"Miss Sweet never say he got no teeth."

"She won't do that again," Clara said quietly. Yip grinned, showing gaps in his teeth. *He needs false teeth as badly as Mr. McIsaac,* she thought. She nodded at Mrs. Klausen as she passed the reception area and entered the ward. Removing the lid, she placed Mr. McIsaac's tray on the bedside table. His eyes widened at the cheese dripping out of the steaming omelette. "And chocolate ice cream!" he gasped.

"Once forgotten, twice rewarded," Clara said.

"Can *I* have another dinner?" a patient asked.

She grinned. "Not unless somebody took your teeth."

Laughter. A fart. More laughter.

"Looks like you're going to have to empty another bedpan, Matron," a voice piped up.

"Looks like you're well enough to go home," she replied. She could not quite imitate the Alberta accent.

A general quietness descended as the patients contemplated whether home was better than the hospital. Their thoughts were abruptly interrupted by the incoming scurry of four probationers wearing white aprons over blue uniforms and starched caps. Miss Sweet arrived with an armful of clean sheets.

"Change Mr. McIsaac's linens last. He needs time to eat."

Clara walked back and forth, inspecting the beds.

One by one, patients were rolled on their sides; sheets were pulled off and replaced with clean ones. Used bedding was pushed into a white laundry bag suspended on a wire frame and rolled out into the corridor. Mops, pails, and Izal — the standard hospital cleaning fluid — were retrieved from the utility cupboard. The probationers swished and swiped at the floor, polished and rubbed bed frames. Metal bedpans and tooth trays were washed, dried, and wiped with a disinfectant and returned to the bed tables covered by white cloths.

Clara had made her point. Now, the smell of clean linen and washed floors met her nostrils. She ordered tea and biscuits to be served to the patients before lights out and went back to her quarters, happy that she had established standards without being unkind. She looked forward to complimenting the probationers in the morning.

CHAPTER 16

December, 1919

Clara swung her legs out of bed and expelled a contented breath. The purposeful steps of the nurses as they walked past her door were familiar and comforting. This was her fourth week as lady superintendent of the Galt Hospital and her life was settling into routine. Ivy and Florence were both happy and comfortable, and Ivy was enjoying her own room. With the Sunbeam Ward still quarantined, Clara had asked Miss Blair to share her single room with Florence. Seeing panic on the young probationer's face, she assured her that her duties would not interfere with her courses. "A senior nurse will be responsible for taking Ivy to school each day, so you will still have plenty of time for your own work." Overhearing Ivy say that the coulees could take her away, Miss Blair had set out one day with her charge to explore the scary surroundings. After she'd explained to Ivy how the recession of ice and rocks thousands of years before had caused the unusual landscape, Ivy's fear turned to curiosity.

"Why is there a ladder under my window?" she asked Miss

Blair as they strolled around the hospital grounds. "Someone might climb up and get me."

"It's a fire escape," Miss Blair said. "People go down it." She began to giggle. "Well, not always. If probationers are late getting back, they use the ladder to get into the residence without being noticed. Don't tell your mother or the probationers won't like you."

Ivy, resenting being told what to do, at once revealed the secret to her mother, who immediately directed the gardener to saw off the bottom rung. "In an emergency, it really isn't too far to jump," Clara said as she supervised him cutting through the metal.

Ivy quickly learned that tattletales receive a cold shoulder. When she entered the nurse's residence that evening after school, she was met with cold stares. The first indication of retaliation was the quiet disappearance of her snack. Yip had wrapped individual pieces of fudge that Ivy stored in a tin. Clara had warned him not to indulge her sweet tooth, so the fudge was their secret, and Ivy had carefully stashed it under her bed. At a glance, she knew that someone had stolen the fudge. Intending to discover the thief, she tiptoed into the probationers' dormitory. The open tin sat on a table in plain view. She retreated quietly to her room, understanding the challenge: if she took back her fudge, next time they would steal more than her candy. Ivy sprawled face down on her bed, choking back tears, wondering how to stop the meanness. Hearing the sobbing, Miss Blair came to console her.

"No one wants to be mean to a kid, but we don't want to be scolded for sneaking out either," she told Ivy firmly. "Your mother is too strict. Rules have changed since she was a student."

"I'm sorry I told my mother about the ladder."

"We can't climb up anymore. What would you think of helping us?"

Ivy sat up on her iron cot. "What do you want me to do?" she asked.

"Come here."

Miss Blair opened the window, holding Ivy's hips so she could hang out to see the sawed-off ladder. "What we need is a dangling rope to hoist us to the lowest rung. But the rope can't stay there or your mother will cut it down, just like she cut off the rung. We want you to hide the rope under your bed. You're too small to hold the other end, so we'll have to secure it around the bed leg. When we're down below, you can open the window and throw it out."

"But what if I'm sleeping and I don't hear you?"

"We'll throw pebbles at the window until you hear."

Ivy was doubtful, but she nodded.

"Ivy, if you tell your mother, we'll all be in trouble, even the ones who don't sneak in late." She drew her finger across her throat as if it were being slit.

"I can keep a secret," Ivy said.

"Most six-year-olds can't," Miss Blair said, "but I know you're the exception."

Dr. McNally, the medical superintendent, got on with the new matron very well. He was an old-fashioned doctor with a practical approach that matched Clara's. He had held a meet-and-greet evening soon after she arrived. Clara was comfortable with the doctors and enjoyed the respect they showed her when she was first introduced. *Dr. Newbury has cast me in a good light,* she thought as she shook hands.

There were exceptions, however. Dr. Galbraith, not a staff doctor, was in a legal dispute as to what he owed for patients he had admitted to hospital. He worked for the coal company and treated mostly miners. The hospital had sued him for the back payments and he had refused to pay. He seemed a disagreeable man, and Clara was wary. But she had a more blatant concern when Dr. Loring — interviewed by the *Lethbridge Herald* a week after she arrived — said, "The new lady superintendent lacks the tact to run a hospital." This had not amused Clara. She resolved not to get tangled up with either doctor. Loring, she knew, was spoiling for a fight. She guessed that he either disapproved of her having a child in the hospital or had backed another candidate.

Clara had taken her first month as lady superintendent to familiarize herself with the medical staff. Her next step was to speak with the maintenance engineer, Mr. Lloyd, and the dietician, Miss Muchall. *They are the backbone of the hospital,* she thought as she descended the stairs to the basement, where she found Mr. Lloyd, who looked to be middle-aged, judging from the infiltration of grey in his black hair. He was short and stocky with pale, heavily muscled arms. His indoor pallor was partly disguised by a heavy growth of salt-and-pepper stubble. He slept by the boilers when something was seriously wrong, and today the boilers were making quite a racket. Clara had to shout to get his attention. His wife lived in mortal fear that a furnace explosion would cause her husband's death. The heating system had partially collapsed the previous year, causing havoc to the heating, kitchen steam tables, sterilizers, and laundry, and Mr. Lloyd's concerted effort to keep the system running had earned him a ten percent raise on his hundred-and-fifty-dollar-a-month salary. Except for the doctors and the lady superintendent, he was the highest-paid employee in the hospital.

"They're predicting cattle-killing cold again this winter," Clara warned. "I count on your attentiveness to avoid another major disruption, Mr. Lloyd. It won't be long, I hope, before the hospital can afford to upgrade the heating system. But for now we're relying on you to keep the old system in working order. But your message said you have a health concern. What is it about?"

"The boilers are working good, if you don't mind the noise, and we got a sufficient supply of coal," Mr. Lloyd asserted. "But, well, I'm a bit worried about getting overexposed."

Clara's brow furrowed. "To dust?" she asked.

"Oh no, I'm not talking about coal dust," he said with a laugh. "I'm worried about Dr. Loring's X-ray equipment always breaking down."

"If the machine is not working, there's no radiation, Mr. Lloyd."

"That's true, but once I done my repair, Dr. Loring takes pictures of my hand to verify the machine works. He's got twenty-five pictures of my left hand. I don't let him use my right one, after seeing what's happened to the doctor. His right hand is all shrunk like something burned it."

Clara looked horrified. "You can be sure, Mr. Lloyd, I will investigate this. In the interim, you mustn't allow Dr. Loring to take another X-ray of any part of your body."

Dr. Loring is a most foolhardy physician, she thought, as she headed to find Mrs. Muchall, the hospital's dietician, who had just threatened to resign. Her major complaint was that the ice supply was too irregular for her to do her job properly.

"We can't have spoiled food in the hospital," she explained.

"Well, we can't afford a refrigeration unit, either, so what do you propose we do in the meantime, Mrs. Muchall?"

"I don't know."

"Who's the supplier?"

"Chillers' Ice House."

"Mrs. Muchall, you need to go down and find someone responsible to talk to at Chillers. Don't do it by letter. Go down. And have the name of another supplier with you. There's nothing like a bit of competition to get good service and a cut in price."

But there was another problem the dietician wanted to discuss. Eggs were rising sharply in price.

"Then we'll build our own henhouse," Clara said. "Yip will tend to the birds, I'm sure, and if we sell the surplus eggs at the Chinese market, we'll have something to put toward the purchase of your refrigerator."

Mrs. Muchall seemed surprised. "The other lady superintendent dismissed me as a complainer," she confessed. "Thank you, Mrs. Durling, for listening and making good suggestions. I'll start working on them right away. I'll talk to Yip first."

"Good girl," Clara said, tapping Mrs. Muchall on the shoulder. "Now, get on with it."

Neither the previous matrons nor the hospital doctors had ever thrown a Christmas party. Clara decided to change that. She sent invitations to domestic workers, medical staff, and board members to join her in celebrating the joys of the season. An invitation for a hospital get-together created quite a stir. However, everyone responded promptly to her invitation.

Bridget O'Toole, a nurse on the children's ward, offered to perform an Irish jig. Although Clara had a formidable reputation at home as a reader of tea leaves, she nevertheless delegated this entertainment to one of her staff. The clairvoyant nurse was to analyze teacups in a fortune-telling booth constructed for the occasion by Mr. Lloyd.

A hand-delivered note invited Mrs. Harwood to the party since she was known to throw hospital mail in the wastebasket. Clara wondered if the mayor's wife was suffering from some type of psychosis that would explain her aversion to food. Clara had asked in her note if Mrs. Harwood would pour tea at the party. But she never replied, and Mrs. McNally, the wife of the chief of staff, offered her services. Mrs. McNally made a kind observation about Mrs. Harwood. "It must be difficult being married to such a busy man as the mayor. I imagine the last place she wishes to pour tea is the Galt Hospital."

Prompted by Mrs. McNally's remark, Clara went to the Harwoods and knocked briskly on the door, giving Jessie Harwood no excuse to ignore her. Clara was ushered into the drawing room and the maid scampered upstairs. *The furniture and decor has not been touched in ages*, Clara thought. Family pictures of the Harwood children were displayed on a drop-leaf table behind the sofa. Clara was puzzled that there were no pictures of the children as adults, or of the grandchildren. She looked up from the photos and smiled as Mrs. Harwood walked into the parlour. She wore a lovely silk kimono of a Japanese design over her pajamas. The mayor's wife was shockingly thin. She extended her bony hand to Clara.

"Mrs. Harwood, I apologize for coming unannounced. But your husband said you didn't use calling cards. I just wanted to say how much we would love to have you pour tea at our Christmas party."

Jessie sighed, glancing at the dated photos. "I haven't been up to going out for some time," she said. She didn't offer tea, and so after ten minutes Clara took her leave, repeating Mrs. McNally's comments at the door.

*   *   *

The hospital was spotlessly clean by the time the guests arrived. Clara greeted them inside the main entrance. Probationers took coats and ushered guests into the dining room while on-duty staff filtered in from various parts of the hospital. By four-thirty, the dining room was full, and Clara abandoned her post greeting the last arrivals and joined her guests. She regretted that Mrs. Harwood had not attended the party with her husband.

Cakes, plates, forks, and small linen napkins were spread across the diningroom table so people could serve themselves. Clara had thrown economy to the wind, purchasing nuts and raisins, which students passed around in glass bowls smiling as guests took enthusiastic handfuls.

After a while, Clara noticed the guests had divided themselves into conversational clumps. Doctors spoke with doctors, nurses with nurses, and domestic staff to one another. She picked up a spoon and banged it on a glass bowl. "Put up your hand if you have met somebody new today," she said. Four hands went up. "I'm going to ask the same question in half an hour." Taking her hint, people broke out of their comfortable cliques.

When Clara clinked a glass thirty minutes later, a huge show of hands shot up. Satisfied everyone was mingling, she announced the Irish dancer. Bridget wore an emerald-green dress with a pleated skirt and an orange belt that cinched in her small waist. Her thick curly hair was almost the colour of the belt. She jumped, clicking the heels of her dance shoes forward, back, and sideways. Her dark eyes flashed as she moved deftly over the dining-room floor, while guests clapped in time to the fiddle music. Following the dancing, guests drained their cups and lined up to have their fortunes told. At six o'clock, Clara closed the booth.

Mayor Harwood came over and put his hand on her elbow. "By Jove, you're a formidable host, Mrs. Durling. All of Lethbridge will be talking about your party. Perhaps you should oversee my entertaining."

"If I fail at nursing, perhaps I'll become a caterer. And then I'd be available to assist Mrs. Harwood." Several guests who heard this remark smiled at the mayor.

"It's been many years since anyone has dined at Jessie Harwood's," one of the doctors observed.

Clara saw her guests out and thanked them for coming. After the last person departed, she went back to supervise the cleanup. She was surprised to see Dr. Loring and Dr. Galbraith still in the dining room. Dr. Loring was a short, thin man about the mayor's age. He had thin strands of hair strategically wound around to cover his bald spots. Dr. Galbraith sported a moustache and parted his full head of steel-grey hair in the middle, leaving butterfly wings to fall over his forehead. Sideburns overlapping his ears suggested he should see a barber.

Dr. Loring approached Clara with a scowl on his face. "Mrs. Durling, I didn't appreciate the note I received from Mr. Lloyd. Until last week, he seemed happy to fix the X-ray machine. I feel you are meddling in my medical affairs."

"I asked Mr. Lloyd to stop being a guinea pig. I didn't ask him to stop fixing the machine."

"Why, I often radiograph my own hand," Dr. Loring said. "Doctors frequently request a demonstration."

"Well, that's as unwise as putting Mr. Lloyd's hand in the machine. I'm told you took an X-ray of your wife's purse when you were courting her. Wouldn't it be better to check the workings of the machine on an inanimate object such as a lady's handbag? It would make for an amusing demonstration and yet have no potential harm."

"I think the issue of X-raying Mr. Lloyd should be between him and Dr. Loring," Dr. Galbraith interjected.

"On the contrary. Everything that goes on in this hospital is of concern to me, especially the health of the staff. As a nurse, I'm concerned about the welfare of the patients and the staff, and as matron my job is to insure smooth functioning of the hospital. Effective management makes it easier for the doctors to do their work," Clara said, hoping to end this conversation. She had to admit that it put a damper on her mood after such a successful party.

"This isn't the last of this conversation," Dr. Loring said, looking coldly at Clara.

Clara sat in her office enjoying the warmth of the morning sun, sipping tea and relaxing. Rivulets of melting frost on the floor-to-ceiling window broke the sunrays into shimmering lines on the opposite wall. This was one of those rare moments when she closed her office door and hung a sign signalling that she wanted privacy. She had been looking at the hospital's agenda for Christmas Day, feeling pleased that St. Augustine's church choir would come and sing carols to the patients. It was a British tradition to make the hospitals as homelike as possible on that one day of the year. Clara had discussed the menu with Yip several times. She intended to stay at the hospital at Christmas to allow all senior nurses to spend time with their families.

Ivy had been invited to spend the holiday with the Iverson family. Etta Iverson had befriended Clara the day she'd arrived in Lethbridge. They both had a passion for playing bridge. Etta's daughter, Katherine, in her mother's words, was Ivy's best enemy and worst friend. Despite the childhood arguing, they were inseparable. Clara smiled, thinking that her friendship with Etta had been an attraction of opposites: Etta flourished in her kitchen while Clara delighted in being able to rely on Yip. But Clara was sure Etta found her stimulating. This brief thought of self-congratulation induced a sudden anxiety that Ivy would much prefer Etta's home to the hospital.

Clara's Christmas musings were suddenly interrupted

when Alistair, ignoring her sign, burst into her office with a smart-looking couple whom he introduced as Percy and Mary Sampson. He had mentioned to her that friends were visiting him in Lethbridge over the holiday, but he hadn't said who or why.

"'Percy is a lawyer at the R.B. Bennett law firm in Calgary," Alistair said. "I've known Mary since she was a teenager. She has tried without success to start a family. I told them about Florence, and so here they are, ready to adopt her." Clara wanted to say that Florence had become part of her family, but she kept quiet. She could not let Florence miss a golden opportunity. *Alistair would not have brought them to see me if they would not make excellent parents.*

In the middle of the discussion, Ivy entered the office on her way to school. A nurse always accompanied her, even though the school was only ten blocks away. The nurse stood in the corridor holding Florence, ready to put her in a pram. "Mr. and Mrs. Sampson are here to visit Florence," Clara said. "They are thinking of adopting her."

"But I want her to stay here," Ivy said tearfully.

"Ivy, you'll be late for school," the nurse interjected, poking her head in the door.

Ivy glared at the nurse. "Mummy, why don't *you* adopt Florence?"

"I have my hands full running the hospital," Clara said, trying to disguise her own pain. "Florence needs a real home and parents of her own." She released the stricture in her throat by swallowing. "Go ahead with Ivy and leave Florence here," she said to the impatient nurse. She handed Florence to Mary Sampson, who beamed with pleasure. "I'll be deeply sorry to give this little miss up, but I couldn't afford to pay a lawyer if the Dupuis, backed by the deep pockets of the Catholic Church, decided to try to gain custody of Florence. But you could represent yourself, Mr. Sampson."

"I've been volunteering in the children's wing of the hospital in Calgary to get practice," Mary said, sensing she was being observed.

"I can see that you have a natural way with children."

The nurse reported later that Ivy had wept all the way to school. At the end of the day, she had rushed straight to her room. There was no longer a cot. Then she dashed into Clara's office.

"I hate you!" she shouted.

"We'll go to Calgary to visit Florence in a few weeks," Clara said consolingly. Ivy curled up in the corner of the office and sobbed.

Florence's departure threw Ivy into a downward spiral of anger and resentment. She called Clara "Mrs. Durling" and remained silent when spoken to. This behaviour carried on for days. It was a sad relief when Ivy left with a box filled with seasonal goodies to spend Christmas with the Iversons.

At five o'clock on Christmas Day, Etta phoned saying they were serving dinner in an hour and would Clara join them? She declined again, content that Ivy would enjoy Christmas with a friend while she remained with the patients. She explained to Etta that she was "holding the fort" so the senior nurses could be home with their families. Etta didn't remind Clara that Ivy was *her* family. It wasn't necessary. When Clara hung up, she felt the familiar pain in her gut.

Putting her doubts aside, Clara went to the kitchen to check on every detail of the patients' dinner trays. Sprigs of holly, shortbreads decorated with sparkles, and tall glasses ready to be filled with cold beer, for those whose doctors had ordered it, were ready to put on the trays. Yip had a butcher assist him in deboning and slicing the turkeys that had been cooked the day before. Stuffing was scooped out of the birds' chests before the carving began. Clara smiled with unconcealed pleasure. *Next Christmas*, she thought, *I'll have Ivy help decorate the trays and then we'll both go to the Iversons'.* The pain under her left breast eased.

Yip broke into a missing-tooth smile. "We do good job, Mrs. Durling?"

Clara, as quick with praise as condemnation, replied, "Thank you from the bottom of my heart."

It pleased Clara to see the patients enjoying their food. The beer had unleashed cheerful conversation from the most taciturn patients on the men's ward. After visiting the male patients, she went upstairs to the female ward to see Mrs. Goldenberg, thinking she might feel isolated amongst the merrymakers. "How's my old sweetheart?" she asked as she perched on the bed and squeezed Ruthie Goldenberg's hand to let her know she was there. Her hearing and eyesight had deteriorated.

Ruthie lifted her watery gaze and said, "Merry Christmas, Matron." Taking a hanky from her pocket, Clara dabbed at Ruthie's eyes, where the tears were starting to fall.

"I'll get the doctor to prescribe something for those tear ducts." Ruthie closed her eyes and leaned back. Clara used the hanky to remove some crumbs stuck to Ruthie's lips. Seeing she had drifted off, Clara got up quietly and went back to her apartment. She could hear the high-pitched giggles of two probationers as she entered her apartment. It seemed dreary and anything but a home. She put her head on the table and wept, remembering the Christmas just after Ivy was born, when her little family was settled and content.

"Hey, now. What's going on here?" Clara felt a hand on her convulsing shoulder and recognized the mayor's voice.

"It's just a sudden bout of homesickness, Mayor Harwood," she said, wiping her eyes.

They played two-handed bridge until Clara got up to do a final check on the patients. She then walked the mayor to the front foyer and watched him as he got into his car, holding his fedora.

CHAPTER 17

Matron Meets Madam

Clara had been so busy in her first few months of running the hospital that she had not noticed the strange weather patterns. A Chinook in mid-February caught her off guard. *How can a foot of snow disappear in one day?* she asked herself after Ivy came home crying from school. Her accompanying nurse had forced Ivy to wear her winter clothes back to the hospital. All the other pupils had left school with their coats slung over their arms.

Clara was in her office, trying to figure out the origin of a Chinook when Morris Lafayette arrived. He settled in the chair across from her desk. The doctor was a tall, handsome man with compassionate blue eyes. She had corresponded with Morris before leaving England and regarded him as a friend. He had come to discuss the venereal disease clinic. The board of directors had finally reached a consensus that the clinic should be in the hospital rather than a downtown location. The decision was not unanimous. Three directors argued vehemently that women of ill repute should not be in close proximity to respectable patients. But the remaining men saw venereal disease as a medical problem rather than a moral disgrace and wanted prostitutes to come to the hospital for their weekly inspections. Now that the decision was made, Morris planned to visit the segregated area where the problem of the disease reared its ugly head. Clara was to accompany him. It was four o'clock and she ordered tea before they set out.

Morris smiled appreciatively as a probationer placed a tray of chicken sandwiches, tea, and cakes on the desk beside a stack of neatly arranged files. The student nurse poured two cups of tea and removed the towel covering the sandwiches. "Is there anything else, Mrs. Durling?"

"This is lovely, thank you. Please come back for the tray when we leave. I hate stale food in my office."

"Very nice," Morris said as he picked up a sandwich. He glanced at the files. "You've been busy these past few weeks, Mrs. Durling."

"I have. While I'm not very popular, I *am* pleased with the changes. I have been well supported by the mayor."

"I'm glad you've established a good relationship with Mayor Harwood," Morris said. Clara blushed thinking privately that she called him Alistair.

Morris leaned toward Clara and picked up another sandwich. "Ladies of the night believe hospitals are in cahoots with the police," he said, his eyes serious. "It won't be easy getting them to come to the clinic to be examined. But we need to gain their trust in order to reduce the spread of venereal disease. I know the madam who runs The Last Post, and I believe this brothel is a good place to start."

Morris provided a running commentary as they walked to The Last Post. "Originally, the streets were named after the shareholders of the coal company." Wood Street was engraved in the sidewalk cement. "William Wood was a London entrepreneur

196 · SHARON JOHNSTON

who invested in the coal mine. I imagine he'd be shocked to know the street named in his honour sported brothels." Morris's eyes twinkled with amusement. He looked younger when he was smiling. "Brothels are called *cribs* in Lethbridge."

"What an odd expression," Clara said. "There's no maternal safety in these houses."

"That pink house just ahead is The Last Post." Smoke swirled above the metal chimney and light from the windows formed shadows that danced on the street. Christmas decorations still hung from trees as though there had been a community decorating party.

"The previous madam of The Last Post died in the flu pandemic, poor soul. Millie Schuster was known for her generosity. The flu had no boundaries, Mrs. Durling. It was a cruel blow losing your son. I was so sorry when I learned this from Dr. Newbury."

Clara touched the doctor's arm. "Dr. Lafayette, my son will always remain a blond, curly-haired boy who loved to garden. I still have a mental portrait of Billy that I could paint myself."

"There are so many sad stories," Morris said. "Lily Parsons, who runs the brothel now, lost her husband after a mining accident. She taught school, I believe, until her husband's death. Soon after, she gave birth to a son. Overwhelmed by hospital bills and the need to look after her child, she took over the brothel." Morris faced Clara. "I feel responsible for Ed Parsons's death. It shouldn't have happened."

The conversation ended when a hatless young woman, emerging from a taxi, caught their attention. The driver gave her a smack on the rump. She wiggled it in mock appreciation, then dashed up the stairs of a robin's-egg-blue house and slipped in the door. A gust of wind had caught her skirt, exposing her red net stockings. Then a stocky man with a slight limp walked out of the pink house and crossed the street to the house the girl had just entered. He knocked.

"My God, that's Randy Bulloch," Morris whispered. "What on earth is he doing here?"

"Who's Bulloch?" asked Clara, feeling the tension.

"A charlatan," Morris said, just as they arrived at The Last Post. "I'll tell you about him later."

A metal helmet and a small gong served as a doorknocker. Morris banged loudly. A red-haired woman in her twenties, wearing a black skirt shorter than was the fashion, and a turquoise-and-black top, answered the door.

Morris looked beyond her and said, "Why, that little boy looks *exactly* like Ed Parsons!"

A young woman came forward, "This little boy is Teddy," she said. "I'm the manager here," she continued, looking at Clara. "I'm Lily Parsons, and this is my son."

Morris introduced Clara, and the two women shook hands. It surprised Clara that such a wholesome-looking young woman, with her sad but expressive brown eyes, would be running a brothel. *I only have part of this story*, she thought.

"What on earth was Randy Bulloch doing here?" Morris asked. "I just saw him leave this house and enter the brothel across the street."

"We *need* him," Lily retorted. "He helps us. He keeps the girls clean and provides us with morphine. The pharmacist won't sell it to us. Nor would my father, if he'd known it was for prostitutes. Dr. Bulloch has a practice in this area and makes sixty dollars a month from the five houses."

Morris put his hand on Lily's shoulder; he hadn't forgotten the look of helplessness in those owl-like eyes after Ed's death. "Mrs. Parsons, the man who just left isn't a doctor; he *was* a field ambulance driver during the war. Randy Bulloch is a con artist.

The hospital board fired him when they learned of his deceit. Why do you need morphine?"

"For Betty Sanchez."

"The girl who cleans at the hospital?" Morris said.

"Now I understand why Bulloch wouldn't admit Betty to hospital — even though she's very sick," Lily said. "He can't."

The redhead who had answered the door scooped up Teddy.

"Put me down!" he shouted, laughing and kicking his feet as he tried to wriggle out of her arms.

"How old is your son?" Clara asked.

"Three and a bit."

"Surely a brothel is no place to raise a child," Clara said disapprovingly.

"Nor is a hospital. I understand you have a young daughter."

Feeling the spar, Morris intervened. "He's a fine-looking boy, Mrs. Parsons."

Clara closed her mouth and decided to let the doctor do the talking.

"I'm sorry I haven't checked on you more often since your husband's death," Morris continued. "But it seems I don't even have time for my own family. Where's the sick girl?"

Lily motioned to the stairs. They crossed the landing at the top of the stairs and Lily opened a door next to the bathroom. An acidic smell of vomit filled the hallway. At the head of an iron cot they saw a man with a double amputation balanced on his cotton-covered stumps. Betty lay on her stomach retching into a pan. The man was keeping her raven hair out of the bucket.

"This is Dan MacIntyre." Lily introduced the man by Betty's bed.

Morris stood at the end of the bed. "I know of Dan through his paintings. Tell me what's going on here."

"Betty's been in a lot of pain." Lily picked up a bottle with amber liquid and a grubby syringe that sat on a side table and handed them to Morris.

He let out an audible sigh. "Cheap, dangerous morphine and no doubt a used needle," he said, shaking his head. "Who knows where it's been?" Turning to Betty, he asked softly, "Could you roll onto your back so I can examine your abdomen?" Betty nodded weakly. A few minutes later he spoke to those assembled in the room. "Betty will have to go to the hospital. She has an enlarged liver and spleen. I'm calling an ambulance."

While Morris used the phone, Clara helped Betty get dressed. Dan asked: "Are you going to call the police about the morphine?"

"We're in the business of healing, not arresting, people," Clara said.

As they descended the stairs, Dan on his rump, Lily said softly, "I can't forget the carelessness of the nurses when my husband was in the hospital." Clara regretted her remark about raising a son in a brothel. She watched as the redhead, called Ginger, cuddled the boy. *Mrs. Parsons and I have had to make hard choices*, Clara thought. *Once we're at the hospital, I'll apologize.*

Once there, Betty was put in an isolation room. After taking a blood sample, Morris called Chief Gillespie from Clara's office about Randy Bulloch and left a message for the chief to call him. The receptionist indicated he was out but would be back in an hour. Clara put on her beaver coat and slipped outside to get some fresh air. The coat had belonged to the mayor's mother and he asked Clara to take it. He confessed that his wife was the only woman he knew who didn't like fur. Clara checked her watch to confirm that she had enough time before the chief called back.

A jolt of cold air hit her when she opened the front doors of the hospital. She looked at the steps needing repairs under the poorly lit front entrance and felt the weight of so many shoddy and shocking surprises. She walked the five blocks back to the segregated area. *Why*, she thought, *would these poor girls not come to the hospital when they live so close? Prostitutes working in the Hyde Park area of London didn't hesitate to come into St. George's to be patched up after a violent encounter. I need to understand my new surroundings if I'm ever going to get a venereal disease clinic started. Mayor Harwood's vision hasn't quite turned out.* Clara took a deep breath. *I'll have to be quite creative to get these girls to seek care.*

Shadowed by the darkness, Clara watched a young man leap off his horse and tie it to a nearby lamppost before joining a group of men who stood smoking outside a canary-yellow house. A liquor flask was offered up and the newcomer grabbed it, took a swig, and punched the man who had given it to him on the shoulder. He took one more swig, lit a cigarette, and began blowing smoke rings as he glanced anxiously up at the windows on the second floor of the house. After a few minutes, a hand waved from an upstairs window and a woman with a head of copious blond hair peered down and nodded. The newcomer dropped his cigarette, stamping it out with his foot, and mounted the small front stoop in one leap. He knocked on the door, was admitted, and moments later the upstairs curtains were closed.

Clara saw another man lurching down the sidewalk toward her. Concealed behind a bush, Clara watched the visitor grab the handrail at The Last Post and pull himself up the steps. He banged loudly on the metal helmet doorknocker and a young woman flung open the door and let him in. A few minutes later, Clara noticed the same girl and the male visitor dancing in front of a large window that faced the street, the man's gait unbalanced and awkward. Clara could just make out the sound of music coming from the house. She watched as the dancers stopped and chatted, then began dancing again. *He's having a dance lesson,* Clara thought. Reluctantly, she admitted to herself that these prostitutes had good hearts. She glanced down at her watch, then turned and walked briskly back to the hospital.

When she arrived at her office, she heard Morris's distressed voice: "Randy Bulloch has set up shop in the segregated area as the prostitutes' medicine man. I've just had a young Mexican girl admitted with probable hepatitis. Bulloch diagnosed flu." Clara watched as Morris smacked the desk in frustration.

Clara made some noise as she entered the office and Morris hung up the phone.

But before Clara could ask him what was going on, a nurse knocked and asked to speak with the doctor. "Miss Sanchez is more settled," she reported, "but I wondered if you could look at her friend's stump? He just arrived and seems awfully agitated. I fear it may be infected."

Morris followed the nurse out, but returned a few minutes later to Clara's office. "I gave Mr. MacIntyre a good shot of laudanum. He's a remarkable artist, you know, Mrs. Durling. His work is being shown all over the province."

The conversation was interrupted when Chief Gillespie blustered into the office. He shook both their hands and pulled up a chair beside Morris.

The chief started right in with explanations. "Randy Bulloch was an ambulance driver during the war. He had an elite high school education and wanted to be, but never became, a doctor. We learned from our janitor, who knew him before the war, of Bulloch's lack of qualifications, but not until after we had hired him at the hospital. We immediately reported this bad news to our chief of medical staff, Dr. McNally. He fired Bulloch, warning him to get out of town or we'd prosecute. It never occurred to us that he'd dare to stick around."

"If Bulloch had been our only problem, we would have advised his patients, many of them Chinese," Morris said. "They have their own medicines, but it's not enough for more serious diseases. Like the prostitutes, they prefer not to come to the hospital, so a freelancer was appealing to them." Morris cupped his chin. "At the time of Bulloch's dismissal, the hospital was involved in a nasty lawsuit. Also, a staff doctor, after serving overseas, committed suicide while on holiday. Both the suicide and the negligence lawsuit were covered widely in the newspaper, but Bulloch's dismissal never got reported and we just assumed he'd left town."

"So the hospital's reputation was in decline," Clara said, thoughtfully. "The hospital is only a few blocks from where Bulloch practised, yet it was easy for him to pass unnoticed. The segregated area really *is* segregated. We'll never be able to establish a proper clinic to reduce the spread of venereal disease if we don't have a relationship with the madams and their girls. The hospital needs to serve the whole community, including undesirables."

CHAPTER 18

Revelations

It had been a long day and the discussion with Morris and Chief Gillespie had disturbed Clara. She hurried to her apartment through the passage connecting the nurses' home to the hospital. The wind usually picked up in the evenings, making the windows in the passage rattle. She shivered with the realization that she was now living in a cold climate. Entering her apartment, she smiled widely when she saw the mayor. He had tossed his greatcoat and fedora on the arm of a chair.

"Will you join me?" he said cheerily, lifting his glass from the side table. Within two weeks of Clara assuming her position as matron, the mayor had begun the routine of recapping the day's events in her apartment. She accepted a well-watered Scotch, content to have company.

She recalled with pleasure the first time the mayor had waited unannounced in her apartment. The door had been open when she'd arrived. She'd masked her happy surprise with a frown, seeing Alistair Harwood relaxing on her sofa, legs stretched out and a glass on the side table.

"Who let you in?" she'd asked with mock displeasure.

"Who wouldn't let me in? Aren't you glad to see me?"

"Ah, yes, you're the mayor and chairman of the hospital," she'd retorted playfully.

He'd laughed and gone to the sideboard to pour them each a Scotch. They clinked glasses, settled themselves on the couch, and agreed to use first names outside the hospital.

Betty Sanchez's blood test confirmed hepatitis. The treatment was a healthy diet and rest for several weeks. She was no longer in the isolation room, but had been moved into the general ward. A female patient, discovering Betty was a girl from the segregated area, demanded she be moved back to the isolation room. "If you continue to complain, I'll remove *you*," Clara said. Then she smiled, but it was clear that she would tolerate no more complaints.

Betty was too weak to appreciate the drama going on around her. Nurses complained that it was difficult to work with Dan always at her bedside. They also reported that he used swear words. When Clara went to investigate, her heart ached to see him trying to lower the bed to his shortened height.

"Enough of that blue language, Mr. MacIntyre," she said softly. "Are you having trouble with that crank?"

Dan looked as though he might explode. "Damn right I am!"

"You want the bed lower? There's a safety catch. Let's have Mr. Lloyd come and see what he can do to make it easier to drop down the bed." Clara moved the crank to look at the mechanism. "Another six inches and you'll be able to rest your chin on the mattress."

Dan's eyes watered up. "I just get so goddamned frustrated."

"I know you do, so let's just fix the problem."

Clara checked the bed adjustment in the afternoon. A nurse glowered at Dan, saying the lower height was hard on her back. Clara swung out the crank and raised the bed. "The point of a crank is adjustment. Put it up when you're working with the patient."

"Imagine if I had to do that with every patient," the nurse retorted sourly.

"Well, you don't. There's only one Mr. MacIntyre." Clara sighed. She pictured her imaginary egg carton and dropped in another problem egg in need of attention. She was disappointed by how quickly they still added up.

Mr. Lloyd resurrected the easel and chair formerly used by Dan in the basement workshop. He visibly relaxed when he had a paintbrush in hand.

"Mr. Lloyd, you never do anything to become an unprofessional egg," Clara said, smiling at him.

He looked confused but then broke into a broad grin. "I'm assuming, Mrs. Durling, that you have just given me a compliment."

Rest and a nourishing diet did not restore Betty Sanchez to health. Accusations surfaced that the young prostitute was malingering to avoid returning to the brothel. As well, Clara had to deal with complaints from patients' families, who pressed to get Betty off the women's ward. These people did not think, as she did, that everyone, good or bad, deserved to be treated by a qualified doctor. "This poor girl doesn't have a choice," she said in the face of grumblings.

After his latest visit to see Betty, Morris suggested that she suffered from melancholia and thus didn't respond to the prescribed treatment. His speculation did not, however, get to the heart of the matter as to why Betty — after four weeks — was doing poorly. She was restless, had little appetite, and suffered from back pain. It was a teacup reading that led to the reason for the young woman's continued ill health.

The tradition at bridge club was to have a fortune teller read tea leaves while refreshments were being served. Clara finished the sandwiches and cakes offered and handed up her cup. It was a source of amusement among the bridge players that the pragmatic matron of the hospital had a superstitious side. The tea reader drained the last drop of tea into the saucer, then righted the cup and observed the leaves from different angles. She frowned and smiled in the way tea readers do. "Hmmm." The reader angled the cup so the ladies could see the leaves. For a minute they were quiet as they contemplated the leaves. The reader's manicured finger pointed to a clump resembling a tall figure with a markedly protruding stomach. "Your leaves suggest there is a woman about to deliver a child," she finally proclaimed.

"Well, it's not me!" Clara retorted, to general laughter. There was friendly banter as to who the pregnant lady might be.

Walking back to the hospital, Clara stopped under a streetlamp to look at her watch. *Nine o'clock isn't too late*, she thought. She headed for The Last Post to speak with Lily Parsons. Ginger, the redhead, answered the knocking. The young woman nervously glanced out at the street.

"I'm alone," Clara said. "I'd like to speak with Mrs. Parsons." *Constables protect these brothel ladies, not arrest them*, she thought. She wondered what Ginger was afraid of.

"Lily's in the back room with her son," Ginger said. "I'll go fetch her." Clara could hear a childish protest and Lily appeared. *The little boy is probably resisting going to bed*, she thought. Lily had a wary look as she approached and motioned that they should step outside.

On first meeting, the two women had gotten off to a poor start, each accusing the other of raising a child in an unsuitable place. However, Betty's longer-than-expected stay in the hospital meant that they now had frequent contact. After the garishly dressed girls from The Last Post had created a stir on the women's ward when they came to see Betty, Clara, normally quite strict about visiting hours, had made an exception for Lily's crew. They could visit after regular hours. This kindness and the ensuing friendly discussions that took place in the patient's room led to an understanding between Clara and Lily of their mutual hardship and difficult choices. Lily had recalled in these chats her happier moments in life: teachers' college in Truro, acting in a play, and a fellow student who planned to be a surgeon, but never asked her out.

Clara recalled, as Lily spoke, a similar conversation with the ship's doctor on her transatlantic crossing. "Was the future doctor quite handsome?" she asked upon hearing about Lily's disappointing romance.

"My future husband was dark and swarthy," Lily said during one of these conversations in Betty's room. "My classmate, however, had boyish looks, auburn hair, and rosy cheeks." Lily paused. "For all I know he was killed in the war. Or he's settled in Halifax, married to a fine girl and working as a doctor. I'd hate for him to see where I ended up."

The certainty that the ship's doctor was the same man had put a smile on Clara's lips.

"We won't be able to stay out here long," Lily said as the two ladies settled themselves on the stoop. She apologized for the lack of chairs. Noticing the matron looking quizzically up and down the empty street, Lily offered an explanation: "The pay packet's blown by Sunday. Were you expecting fisticuffs? On Monday nights we give free dance lessons to our regular customers. Some of them actually bring their sweethearts." Lily laughed.

"I suppose visiting a brothel is one way of preventing the girl you will marry from getting in the child way," Clara said wryly. "Have any of your girls gotten pregnant?" she asked.

"You don't have to be a prostitute to get caught," Lily said. "It happened to my mother, and I'm the result." Her tone sounded bitter.

"All's well that ends well. I'm assuming your parents got married."

"My real father is an Englishman I've never met. My loving father is a Canadian." Lily shrugged as though the word *loving* was something in her past.

"How do you prevent unwanted pregnancies here at The Last Post?" Clara asked.

"My girls are supposed to protect themselves. I don't believe that's the case in the other houses. And of course I can't actually verify that a condom has been used." Lily suppressed a giggle with her hand.

"But how do you get around the Comstock Law? Contraceptives can't even cross the border. Even one as loosely guarded as Montana."

"Pffft! The law is ridiculous. It's the single girls who need condoms; not married couples, as the law states. The pharmacist here in Lethbridge, Mr. Higginbottom, has his source. Because I'm a pharmacist's daughter, he supplies us without a fuss."

"Lily, I think Betty Sanchez may *not* have protected herself."

"Betty is normally a sensible girl," Lily said. "The exception is Dan MacIntyre, who refused to use a condom. Betty told me this, and I warned her of the risk. She didn't follow her father to Mexico because she knew she'd be responsible for the family brood since both parents were sick. I think Betty loves Dan, but not enough to have his baby. On the other hand, I think it's beyond our imagining how much he would want a child. Think about what it would mean to a legless man to become a father. It might make up for his loss." Lily wiped her face with her sleeve. "I feel so responsible for both of them."

Clara shifted to look at Lily. "You are such a young woman to have the world on your shoulders. I hate to see the way you are burdened."

"Why would *you* care, Mrs. Durling?"

"Because I'm fairly sure that I'm your aunt."

Lily turned a shocked face in Clara's direction. "What do you mean?"

"Hear me out. There were too many things adding up in our conversations. I had an older sister who came to Canada to have a baby out of wedlock. I have already connected the dots of my Canadian family through parish records in Halifax. I wrote as soon as I got settled here. Marriage and death records are often the only way to connect families dislocated during the war. I'm aware, however, that lives once established don't like to be disturbed. Your mother may have no desire to see me."

"I can't see how we're related."

"Your mother was the eldest of eight, and I was the second youngest. My parents sent your mother, my sister, Amelia, to a rectory in Halifax to have her baby, you, and that's when she met your 'loving' father."

Lily's demeanour was stiff and unfriendly. "My mother's name is Amelia, but I don't want a relationship with a family that sent my mother away."

"I was only six at the time, but even at that age I was still angry with my parents for what they did. Wouldn't you like your mother to meet her sister?"

"Mrs. Durling, I'm still struggling with this idea that you

are my aunt. I believe you, but … my mother has no idea I run a brothel. She would die if she knew. She had hoped I would marry a doctor."

"Well then, the other news is that Dr. James Barnaby will be in town after Christmas. I wrote him as soon as I figured out who your handsome doctor was. I told him I had met his old sweetheart from teachers' college, and he is most anxious to see you. James is coming to Lethbridge some time in the new year to see Mr. Corker, the cobbler. He is making James a pair of prosthetic boxing gloves."

Lily's face looked stricken. "I know Mr. Corker. He was very helpful to me while I ran the veterans' workshop. He provided leather and allowed the vets to sell through his shop for a small commission. But why does Barnaby need prosthetic gloves? How is he? Married, I imagine. Where does he live? What is he doing?"

"James never got to be a surgeon, but he is a doctor in Edmonton. His extraordinary story didn't include marriage. He will tell you himself if you receive him. You have lots of time to sort out your feelings. His visit is still a few weeks away."

"I'm Lethbridge's most educated madam," Lily said sarcastically "If you are indeed my aunt, I need you to leave well enough alone. I've made the most of a bad situation and I'm happy. Don't spoil it, Mrs. Durling."

CHAPTER 19

Public Health Crisis, 1921

The morning after her visit to The Last Post, Clara sat in her office, waiting to do rounds with Morris. She had decided she would tell him about Betty's use of condoms, with Dan being the exception.

Hearing a commotion outside her office, she opened her door to see what was happening. A nurse was wheeling Betty Sanchez, who was ghostly white, to the operating room. Dan MacIntyre had put on his prostheses and walked alongside her, steadying himself on the gurney. His legs still bothered him.

"Betty took a strong laxative last night that her friend provided and has aborted," the nurse said. Clara followed the stretcher to the operating room where the staff surgeon was waiting to stem the bleeding.

Once her vital signs were re-established, Betty was returned to the ward. Betty looked tearfully at Dan. "I'm so sorry. I just couldn't care for a baby." His fringe was streaked with blood. Clara ached to see the disappointment on his face.

"I would have been a good father," he said. The room was heavy with sadness.

Two days after Betty aborted, she reported that her stomach hurt. On examination, the surgeon determined it was not her lower abdomen where he had operated, but higher up under her ribs. The doctor listened to her irregular heartbeat and ordered total bed rest. Ignoring the doctor's orders, Betty got up in the night to use the washroom rather than calling the nurse for a bedpan. She was discovered lying on the floor beside the porcelain tub with severe swelling at the back of her neck. Betty was put on twenty-four-hour nursing care. Dan watched helplessly as she remained unconscious. She soon died of a stroke due to intracranial bleeding.

Dan was heartbroken. He did not try to hold back his tears, realizing that the girl who had prevented him from killing himself was now dead.

Lily arranged a funeral service in the Catholic church. Delivery boys, prostitutes, madams, and the Chinese herbalist attended the service. The herbalist had known Betty's father, who had often been in the store looking for medicines to cure his emphysema.

Clara understood Dan's heartbreak in the context of what she had seen during the war. Soldiers fell in love with prostitutes despite being told to find more suitable partners. She retained the vivid memory of smacking an undulating bedsheet and a young girl leaping from under the covers and smoothing her dress as she passed. *But war is no longer an excuse for risky behaviour,* she thought, as the last rites were uttered over Betty's modest coffin.

Betty's death exacerbated the old moral divisions. Many citizens, like Mayor Harwood, believed prostitution could not be abolished and thus required regulation. However, clergy and respectable ladies didn't agree and called for city brothels to be ploughed under. Drinkers resisted this mean-spirited approach because brothels assured a man a drink even if he didn't want other services. Many drinking establishments had not renewed their liquor licences, cowed by the local protests. Public meetings and opinion pieces in the *Lethbridge Herald* fired up the debate.

A month had passed since Betty's passing and Easter was fast approaching. Anticipating the pious pleas against sin from the pulpit, Morris and Clara decided it was time to have their own sermon on the medical, rather than moral, consequences of prostitution. Venereal disease was spreading like wildfire throughout the province. Dr. Orr, who was responsible for public health for Alberta, agreed to attend the public discussion. All citizens concerned with public health were urged to attend. Posters were placed in public buildings and private enterprises. Some were torn down, but not before the message got out. Morris expected a big crowd. He asked Dan if he would speak about his war experience. Dan had returned from Edmonton in a good frame of mind after seeing James Barnaby, who had used Dan as a case study in phantom limb and understood his psychology.

On the evening of the meeting, some citizens stood grim-faced outside the Legion Hall, waiting for the doctors to arrive. When Dan turned up looking fit and wearing his artificial legs, many of the unhappy faces turned to smiles. "How're you doing, Dan?" was the chorus. He put a thumb up. Clara, sitting with her nurses in the front row, smiled at the gesture. *That's the resilience of a true soldier,* she thought. Dan sat down next to her, knowing that he held a special place in the matron's heart. Clara, well schooled in grief, had helped him recover from Betty's untimely death.

The crowd had gone inside to see Dan's paintings previously donated to the Legion Hall. These works had not sold because of their macabre nature, but his newer work had become very popular.

Morris and Dr. Orr sat on the stage platform at the front of the room. Floor-to-ceiling black curtains at each side of the stage were a reminder that this hall had been used for entertainment. Morris leaned toward Dr. Orr and quipped, "I'm not sure these walls have heard the word *prostitution* before." Dr. Orr laughed and Morris stood up to bring the meeting to order.

Mormons, women of the Temperance League, Chinese business owners, and clergy — identifiable by their dress — showed the diversity of Lethbridge citizens. Some respectable women, mainly community volunteers, were in attendance along with the nurses and feather-hatted temperance ladies. Lily stood at the back of the hall; she was ready to flee if the discussion got too rough on the prostitutes.

Dr. Orr stood up after Morris's introduction and recited the shameful statistics. "Venereal disease is no way to make Alberta famous," he said. Murmurs erupted and Morris lifted his hand for silence. "Diversity is the mark of your community," he continued. "Lethbridge has widespread differences in wealth, moral standards, and race. But no one in this city or any other should ever be afraid to see a doctor. That includes ladies of the night. They are especially terrified of hospitals. Will the police be called? Will they be arrested? Will they be treated like dirt? These are the questions they ask themselves."

When Morris took his turn, he spoke forcefully. "I was appointed the medical officer of health for Lethbridge, and with this long title comes responsibility. I'm here today to explain how I, and others in authority, rather than acting responsibly, actually did harm. The recent death of the young prostitute,

Betty Sanchez, symbolizes our irresponsibility." Morris looked down at Dan, acknowledging his pain. "Betty's father, sick with lung disease, returned to Mexico, leaving her to fend for herself at the age of sixteen. Some of you knew her as the girl who cleaned at the hospital. But she also supplemented what she made in the hospital by working in a brothel so she could send money to her parents." Morris paused. "Some may think she got what she deserved. She was a prostitute. But that belief ignores the fact that all men and women live under the same heavenly roof."

Vocal eruptions started, and Morris raised his hand again until there was silence.

"Betty Sanchez was recently under my care after she contracted hepatitis. The Randy Bulloch scam is widely known in Lethbridge — I don't have to repeat the details. Betty did not have venereal disease, but either illness is highly contagious and should always be treated by a doctor. So, let her death be the warning that people at high risk must be able to seek immediate medical care."

Dr. Orr got up. "In the context of the war," he said, "we didn't judge soldiers or prostitutes harshly. We've asked Dan MacIntyre, someone who survived the war, to share this reality."

Dan stood facing the audience, leaning against the stage platform. The doctors sat down. A minute passed before Dan broke the silence. He spoke simply and plainly, choosing his words carefully.

"I enlisted because I thought going overseas would be exciting. War isn't exciting. It's awful." Dan gestured toward the wall where his macabre art was displayed. "Soldiers are terrified they might die. So in the short respite from battle, my pals and I would visit a brothel. Those prostitutes kept us human. They were barmaids, laundresses, working girls, widows, and wives.

In a town whose name we'd *always* forget, we *never* forgot the prostitute's. Her name we carried into the next fight."

It looked as though Dan might stop, and Morris leaned forward. "Go on with your story, Dan. It's important for these people to hear."

"I'm a young man without legs. Some of the boys lost their arms. Some can't see. Us banged-up fellas can't court a girl properly. Maybe it's a bouquet of flowers we can't carry, or a walk in a park we can't manage. We begin to feel we have nothing to offer. I have a friend who survived the war and then committed suicide. Another pal contemplated it. I thought of killing myself, but I didn't, because a prostitute, Betty Sanchez, found the person within me that had been crushed or distorted. She made this disfigured man feel attractive." Dan stood staring at the faces. "Betty Sanchez was carrying my baby when she died." Dan sat down suddenly and Clara handed him her handkerchief.

Some of the ladies squirmed in their seats when Dan associated prostitution with motherhood. There was a bit of chitchat and then silence.

"Thank you, Dan," Dr. Orr said. "Our brave soldiers went overseas, and thousands came back with venereal disease," he continued. "But now the war is over, and our frame of reference *must* change." He then handed the conversation over to Morris, who talked about the clinic that would be established at the hospital. Morris stressed that anonymity would be assured to anyone seeking care or consultation.

Snow had begun to fall by the time the meeting ended, and people hurried away.

"A venereal disease clinic won't be effective if prostitutes don't come," Dr. Orr said, as he stepped into a waiting taxi to take him to the train.

*   *   *

Despite the non-judgmental attitude of the clinic, the prostitutes were still afraid to go to the hospital. Lily urged the girls to get examined, with only modest success. Clara thought the girls needed an incentive to come in to be tested for VD. She presented her idea at the next board meeting. "The girls need a reason to come to the clinic," she said. "Perhaps learning to cook in the hospital kitchen. This would be a useful talent if they ever leave prostitution and seek domestic employment. And we could use an extra culinary hand. The girls could do simple tasks such as preparing vegetables. It would give them a sense of helping others. We should keep in mind that the brothel ladies are always generous when there is a town emergency."

A letter from Dr. Orr and a strong word of support from Morris convinced enough board members to allow the girls to use the hospital kitchen after being examined, so long as they tested clean.

Rules of behaviour in the hospital were established. Tuesday, often after a morning of shopping, the prostitutes would arrive in the afternoon for their routine pelvic examinations. If they had a clean bill of health, they went off to the kitchen to try a new recipe or just help preparing food for the patients' trays under Yip's supervision. The girls always arrived in a cheerful mood, anxious to show off their purchases. Lipsticks, rouge, powder compacts, eyebrow pencils, perfume, and witch hazel came flying out of paper bags as the ladies of the night compared bargains. They would sit around the preparation table in the kitchen as they chopped, peeled, or stirred up some concoction while gossiping about their day. Anyone passing the kitchen might hear "that's a bitch" or "bugger my ass," but on the whole they were well behaved and respectful of their surroundings. After a few months, Clara felt almost smug that the kitchen plan had run so smoothly. She knew the board was waiting for an incident to happen and realized after the Bulloch affair that the reputation of the hospital mattered. The arrangement was kept very low-key.

One day the prostitutes arrived at the hospital in their version of conservative dress ready to make cookies for the patients. Lily chose the baking crew from girls who had done well in her literacy class. She made it clear that they were to use language suitable for a hospital.

However, a member of the Ladies' Auxiliary discovered the presence of the ladies of ill repute while pushing the amenities cart past the kitchen. She stopped outside to listen to the unfamiliar voices. A peek around the door confirmed her suspicions. After taking in the girls' dyed hair, garish makeup, and coarse language, she turned on her heel, but not before hearing a shrill voice recount how one of her clients had got his *whatsit* caught in his zipper. "Zippers are quite a novelty," a voice said to raucous laughter. The lady volunteer, abandoning the cart, stormed into Morris's office.

"You're the officer of public health, Dr. Lafayette," she said. "You should object to prostitutes handling food destined for patients." Morris assured her the prostitutes were preparing food for themselves. Although not true, he was unwilling to compromise the goodwill of the bakers.

When Clara arrived in the kitchen, advised by Morris to supervise more closely, the cooks were in a complete muddle. They had misread *teacup* for *teaspoon* and the scent of vanilla extract was overpowering!

"Let's throw out this mess and start again," Clara said.

"I do everything in my head," Yip said, apologetically.

Clara had just donned an apron when Dr. Loring came brusquely into the kitchen, surveying the scene critically.

"A Chinese cook working with prostitutes!" he said mockingly. "I must be in the segregated area, *not* the kitchen of a respectable hospital." The doctor scowled in disapproval. "I think the government should increase the proposed head tax," he added sarcastically. "And perhaps we need a head tax on prostitutes." The girls shot him defiant looks. Yip lowered his eyes, humiliated.

Clara removed her apron. "Those are nasty words and unbecoming of a doctor," she retorted. "Misogyny has no place in a hospital where most of the staff is female. From the maids to the matron, we are all women who deserve respect. And that includes volunteering prostitutes."

Dr. Loring, astonished at her outburst, backed out of the kitchen grumbling loudly.

Clara's equilibrium had more or less recovered from the sparring with Dr. Loring when the mayor, slightly tipsy, arrived at her apartment. This didn't surprise her, given the pressure of city politics. She was just heading to the Sunbeam Ward when he presented himself and she promised to be back shortly to serve him some coffee. Responding to Alistair's mild grumble, she said, "I always do a final check at night before settling in my apartment." The rapidity with which her son Billy had gone from a playful boy to a delirious child had imbedded this evening ritual.

She donned a gown hanging on the isolation room door. The on-duty nurse was sponging a child when Clara entered the ward. Clara first spoke with an eight-year-old boy rocking in a children's wicker chair. He wore blue-and-white-striped pajamas and fuzzy blue slippers with ducks on the toes. His hair was neatly combed and parted.

"Your mommy was here this morning," she said. "I can tell

by your slicked-back hair." The boy began coughing as he tried to speak.

"We'll get that nasty asthma under control," she said. The boy looked up at her with his hand over his mouth.

She compared this much-loved little boy to the child in the next bed who was less cared for. When Clara left, she asked the nurse on duty to give the boy some extra attention.

After leaving the Sunbeam Ward, Clara made a quick stop to chat with a young RCMP officer recently admitted with severe burns. He had been putting out a fire in the woods when a burning branch had fallen on his hands. Content that no infection had set in and that his pain was controlled, she quickly finished her rounds.

It was just nine o'clock when she arrived back at her apartment. Alistair lay stretched out fully dressed on her bed with a half-empty glass of Scotch beside him on the night table. He was snoring contently. When he didn't respond to her voice or the light shaking she gave him, she went out and sat on the sofa and pondered what to do.

She returned to the bedroom to look at him. Tears welled up in her eyes as she thought about the cruel paradox of their relationship. They were like a happily married couple, and there weren't many of those to be found. But she had kept their friendship platonic for fear of losing her job and her respected place in the community. *God has a perverse sense of humour*, she thought. Once he woke, she'd send him out by the fire escape. She dozed on the sofa until she heard him urinate noisily in the bathroom, gargle some mouthwash, and stumble into the living room holding the glass of remaining liquor. Clara gave him a censorious look and he protested that he had not finished his drink. She had already checked the bottle on the sideboard and returned a friendlier grin. "I believe you," she said.

"Clara, you left me to my own devices," he chided, looking sheepishly at the glass. His suit was a rumpled mess.

"It's four in the morning, Alistair Harwood. You can't walk past the receptionist at this hour." Clara shot Alistair a look of exasperation. "That leaves the fire escape ladder as your only exit."

Alistair grinned apologetically.

She smiled affectionately, shaking her head. "Follow me and be quiet. I don't want the probationers to wake up."

She led Alistair into Ivy's room. They tiptoed past Ivy and the probationer, both sleeping soundly. Clara raised the window silently and helped Alistair back out onto the window ledge. She put a finger to her lips to stop his laughing and watched as he carefully backed down the ladder. But seeking the missing last rung, he lost balance and his solid frame crashed to the ground.

"It's my ankle," he whispered. "I've twisted it." And a minute later, he hissed, "I don't think I can walk. Go and find some crutches. I'll never make it to my car."

"Damnation. Your car! Everyone will have seen it," she whispered.

"Get me some bloody crutches," he pleaded. "I think I might have broken my ankle, not just sprained it."

While she rushed off for the crutches, the probationer woke up and stuck her head out the window. "Mayor Harwood, what are you doing lying on the ground?"

"Go back to bed and forget this ever happened."

"Yes, sir."

The probationer crawled back into bed, thinking she was dreaming, and Ivy slept through the whole thing.

Clara ran around the side of the building carrying some crutches. "This is terrible," she murmured as she felt his ankle and determined that it wasn't broken. The ground was hard and slippery from the spring snow. When they finally got him to his car, neither could suppress their laughter.

"I can't drive with this ankle," he declared. "Oh, hell, just call a taxi."

Clara's eyes glistened with tears of frustration. "Why did this have to happen?" she moaned.

"Clara, didn't you want to spend the evening with me?" he asked, looking wounded.

"Of course I did. But while I'm lying to the night nurse as to why I need a taxi at four in the morning, you can think of an excuse for your crutches. And why your car has been here all night! Otherwise, my reputation will be in tatters."

Clara had no idea what she would say as she mounted the steps of the hospital. "How silly," she muttered. "I should have just let Alistair walk out the main door."

CHAPTER 20

Clara Plays Cupid, 1920

Christmas had absorbed all of Clara's free time. Now that it was over, she wrote to Dr. Barnaby to tell him she was looking forward to his visit. They had corresponded regularly, but she had not seen him since they had travelled together on the *Scotian*. Her earlier letter to the doctor indicated that the girl he regretted leaving behind was now living and working in Lethbridge. She also wrote that his former sweetheart had been tragically widowed. Clara related some of her circumstances, but not the whole story.

It amused her to be playing Cupid, but it also gave her joy. Lily was her niece, and James was Dr. Newbury's protégé. She couldn't think of a better pair to be reunited, nor a couple more suited to each other. *So many couples never made it*, she thought as she wrote to Barnaby that she would meet his train. She was pleased that she had overcome Lily's initial resistance to meeting Barnaby at all.

*   *   *

When Clara met Barnaby at the station, she noted that he still had the boyish good looks of someone too young to be a doctor. They walked back to her office, chatting amiably. Over tea, she provided more details of Lily's circumstances: how she was managing a brothel and why that had come about. Clara also explained her family relationship.

As she'd anticipated, Barnaby was not appalled by Lily's current situation, but seemed to take it in stride. This pleased her and fit with the image of Barnaby she had retained from the ship. Barnaby wasn't surprised that Lily had never asked her parents for help. "She was very strong-willed," Barnaby said. "That's what I remember from our days in Truro. Does she know about my hands?" he asked quietly.

"She knows you're here to see Mr. Corker for prosthetic boxing gloves," Clara said. "She told me all about your boxing. She also said you never asked her out." They both laughed.

After tea, they walked together to the pink house in the segregated area, and Barnaby banged the metal helmet. Ginger answered the door. "Oh my God!" she said. "It's Mrs. Durling, and a handsome stranger."

"He's not a stranger," Lily said as she came forward, Teddy shouting behind her to be picked up. Lily smiled as Ginger grabbed him.

"Hello, Barnaby. This is my son. He's a bit spoiled with all these girls doting on him." Barnaby smiled at the girls peeking out from the kitchen. "Nice to see you," Lily said, a blush rising in her cheeks. She turned to the peering ladies. "Dr. Barnaby is an old chum from college. Perhaps we could have a bit of privacy." Lily grinned at their awestruck faces. "Just a friend," she added.

"*Really!*" they chimed and pulled their heads back from the doorframe.

Clara, hands on her hips, looked satisfied that the meeting had gone so smoothly. "I'll be off," she said cheerily. "See you back at the hospital, Dr. Barnaby. I'm leaving you in good hands." Lily was smiling. *She deserves happiness*, Clara thought.

"Thank you, Mrs. Durling," Lily said.

She led Barnaby to the back room that was strewn with books, magazines, and Teddy's toys.

"I'm sorry about Ed's death," Barnaby said. His green eyes were soft and sincere.

"He was a good man, and he lost his life saving mine. I never forget that. Things have worked out, but I admit it's been hard," Lily said softly. She no longer used the defensive tone when she thought people were being critical of Ed.

Barnaby held up his stump. "This is *my* new reality."

Lily made a sweeping gesture. "Well, this is mine."

"I imagine you hear some hard luck stories, but not any worse than your own," Barnaby said.

"I've *never* suffered like these girls," Lily retorted. "If I had wanted to, I could have returned home to the security of my parents. These young women have escaped abuse and poverty. I didn't go back even when things got tough. Would you like to hear how I manage financially?"

Lily watched as Barnaby struggled out of his coat. "I took a small loan to fix up this dilapidated old porch. A bit of insulation and the work of a good carpenter and it became my classroom." Teddy's books were scattered on the floor near the New Silver Moon stove. Barnaby crouched down to examine it. "Did you ever meet my Aunt Marjorie? I inherited this beautiful stove from her when she died; it reminds me so much of my childhood. After her death my father shipped it out west to fulfill my aunt's promise. It was a costly trip for a stove," Lily added, laughing.

A chalkboard was scribbled with homonyms and a cheeky

note: *Screw silent letters.* "This is where my girls learn to speak the King's English. They can charge more if they're good conversationalists. Ask a man about himself and you'll have no end of conversation, I say."

Barnaby leaned back, feigning surprise. "So this is how you use your teachers' diploma?"

"Can you think of a better use?" They both laughed.

"Most of my girls were completely dependent before I taught them to read. Now they can do their own banking, fill out census forms, write letters, and at least read the gossip column in the *Herald*. The girls learn and earn while I pay off my debts. Dan MacIntyre, one of our wounded veterans, is my other source of income. He's an artist, and he pays me a five percent commission on what he sells through me."

"I know Dan," Barnaby said. "Dr. Newbury and I published an article on phantom limb. Dan was the worst-case scenario." He stared wide-eyed at a painting of a blond-haired boy with a pug nose and puzzled blue eyes. "I treated this chap, Lily."

Dan had painted the face of the young soldier with arched eyebrows as though he had no idea what was happening to him.

"He was just eighteen when he arrived at the hospital in Craiglockhart. I remember we had to bring in a dentist to file down his teeth. He was so scared, they constantly chattered. I had no choice but to send him back to the front once his teeth were done. Poor bugger was being treated as a malingerer when he was literally scared to death. I'm so glad he survived and made it home."

Lily began to cry. "I'm sorry, Barnaby. I've had to hold back my emotions. So much has happened since we were students." She wiped her eyes. "If I had lived my life in Nova Scotia as a teacher, I wouldn't have learned all I have coming out west. There's wildness here that I call freedom. People are more settled back home."

Barnaby was to be in the city for a week. The evening after their reunion, Lily recommended they eat at a small Chinese restaurant nearby called Lee Wong's.

"You don't have to eat with chopsticks," Lily assured him. "Ed never learned and Lee always has cutlery on hand, even if it's never as clean as the chopsticks." She laughed.

As they rounded the corner, Barnaby stopped. "Why, that's Sister Durling," he said. He looked sideways at Lily, raising his eyebrows as a question. "Your aunt?"

"I still call her 'Mrs. Durling,' because no one knows about our relationship. It would not be well-received in the segregated area. I have the trust of the girls, and they are afraid of Mrs. Durling."

Barnaby laughed. "I suppose you will *never* think of her as your aunt. She's a great lady, though, and one day you'll be thankful for that."

Clara was tugging an old Chinese gentleman's queue like a bell pull and berating him for spitting in the street. He'd been sitting at a low table on an egg crate, playing mahjong with his friends and enjoying the mid-winter sunshine. Several men bundled in great coats stood watching. The players sucked on cigarettes dangling from their moist lips as they contemplated the moves. Another old man spat a bolus of mucus on the sidewalk, cleared his throat, and spat again. He made no attempt to use the spittoon Clara had dragged over. Lily and Barnaby could hear her clearly as she scolded the elderly man.

"Don't *any* of you remember the days when tents had to be set up outside the hospital?" Clara lamented. The mahjong players shrugged. "When there were too many patients with tuberculosis to be treated *in* the hospital? Spitting helped spread TB. Do you want that to happen again?" She raised her arms heavenward.

"Sister Durling, what are you doing to that poor old man?" shouted Barnaby.

Clara grimaced and waved them over, whereupon Mayor Harwood bounded out of the restaurant, ducking his head to clear the doorframe. "I told Matron I was going to hide while she reprimanded the spitter." He roared with laughter. Several ladies playing mahjong inside the grocery store attached to the restaurant peered out, grinning. Clara gave them a friendly wave and pointed to the spittoon. She nodded her head, urging them to make the men use it. The women bobbed their heads in agreement, and Yip's elderly aunt hurried out.

"Good, you tell 'em, Mrs. Durling," she said. "Spitting is why we keep 'em outside, even in cold, to play mahjong." She straightened her bent spine and said, "We ladies don't do that." She clasped the matron's hand and pulled her inside the store. "You see that government sign," she said, pointing up at the wall over the counter. It read in bold block letters: DON'T SPIT! SWAT THE FLY! "We know both fly and spit carry disease. Our men just laugh at health inspector," Yip's aunt said. "They deserve scolding."

Mr. Wong dragged a table to the large plate-glass window, which was misted with condensation, and the four of them sat down. The cook wiped the table with a filthy cloth, then used it to mop his sweaty brow before returning to his grill at the back of the room. As he worked, he sniffed continuously. Seeing Clara glance disapprovingly at the cook, Harwood said to her, "Now, don't get fussed up if he uses that towel as a handkerchief."

When the different bowls of fish, rice, vegetables, and meat arrived at the table, Lily asked for cutlery.

"Nonsense," Barnaby replied. "I can manage chopsticks." Her eyebrows shot up as he picked up a lump of fish with his chopsticks and popped it in his mouth. Harwood did the same. Seeing Clara muddling with her sticks, Lee came over and demonstrated.

"Maybe Yip serve with chopsticks at hospital," he said, peering over his bifocals. "Cook tell me all about you. He say you very strict, but he like you much the same." Lee laughed and shuffled off in his loose-fitting black canvas slippers.

Later, as they were leaving, Lee handed Lily a greasy package. "I hope Teddy like it." He inclined his head toward Barnaby. "You little-fingers man very good with them chopsticks."

"A Chinese soldier from Nanjing taught me the four-fingered trick."

Lee muttered his approval as he cleared the table. Clara and Mayor Harwood said their goodbyes to Lily and Barnaby and headed off in the direction of the hospital.

The Last Post was lit up and music blared out onto the street. Lily steered Barnaby around to the back. "It wouldn't be good business if the house wasn't full," she said. "And there's only one way to get privacy," she added, laughing. They stepped into the unlit classroom. Except for the orange light emanating from the panes in the door of the New Silver Moon, they were in darkness.

"I feel I'm looking through stained-glass windows on a sunny day," said Barnaby. He tapped one of the panes. "Why, this is mica. We had a woodstove, but not nearly as decorative as this masterpiece." The soft light brought out the rosiness of his cheeks and strawberry-blond hair. He opened one of the small doors and Lily dropped in a lump of coal.

"I have to be careful not to overheat this small room. These stoves are not a precise science."

"How I wish we were still students," Barnaby said softly.

"You haven't lost your Truro boyishness, Barnaby, in spite of everything you've been through."

He circled the room slowly, stopping to read a sheet of paper sticking up from an old Underwood. "Looks like an interesting script." He stood in front of the painting of the chatterer whose teeth had been filed down. "Lily, you're amazing! I can't believe how you've managed." Muffled music and laughter filtered in from the next room.

"Tonight is dance lessons," she explained.

Barnaby put his arms around Lily, burying his face in her thick curls. He was afraid he might explode if he kissed her.

The fog of sadness that had settled on Lily was lifted by the thought of spending a couple of days alone with Barnaby before he left.

"Enjoy yourself! You deserve a little fun," Ginger shouted as Lily rushed down the stairs into the waiting taxi. Seeing Teddy's lack of concern as she sped off, she smiled. *That's what happens when so many girls are looking after him*, she thought. She waved. She couldn't recall feeling such happiness.

"Is there a bridge tournament going on here?" Lily asked, as she and Barnaby entered the smoke-filled lobby of his hotel. About twenty or so nattily dressed men bantered back and forth as they waited to register at the front desk.

"You're looking at the Alberta Boys' Club, or the ABCs, as they call themselves," Barnaby responded quietly. "It's a group of homosexual men who meet at the Lethbridge Hotel once a month and take over the second floor. They come from all over the province. According to the woman who checked us in as Mr. and Mrs. Barnaby, they have a whale of a time. She told me, 'Them queers are good business because they don't just eat the daily specials like our regular clients.' She recommended we take a room on the fourth floor to avoid the noise."

"I've never met a homosexual," Lily said.

"How do you know? They don't wear name tags."

"My sister, Beth, shared an apartment with a man she thought was of this persuasion. But I never met him." She felt cold recalling Beth's failed abortion. She put her arm through Barnaby's as they mounted the stairs to their room.

When they reached their room, Barnaby scooped Lily into his arms awkwardly. "I should have done this years ago." He set her down in the middle of the spacious room. There were floor-to-ceiling windows on either side of a brass bed that had been plumped up with pillows. A blue-and-white patchwork quilt was fashioned into a butterfly shape at the foot of the bed.

"Grandest bathroom I've ever seen," Lily said after inspecting it. She put her handbag on a writing desk to the left of the bathroom door, then walked over to the window where she could look down at the luxury cars parked behind the hotel. A short, slim man with a cropped mahogany beard and brown hair retrieved his suitcase from a dual-toned Buick and headed into the hotel. She felt an overwhelming shyness. Images of Truro floated in her mind. She was acting on a stage, while Barnaby watched from the sidelines. She turned around and walked into his arms.

Minutes later, Barnaby let out an expletive. "I'm having trouble unbuttoning my trousers," he said, tears showing his frustration. "I think I'm nervous. I can usually do this."

Lily reached out to help him and Barnaby rocked back onto the bed. He pulled her down beside him. "This isn't the first time I've been embarrassed by my inept left hand. When I was at Craiglockhart, I was on a high-fluid diet and often had to get to the water closet in a hurry. On one occasion, I dashed in to relieve myself while two senior officers were waiting for me outside. They wanted to discuss a patient I had sent back to the front. I couldn't unbutton my uniform trousers fast enough and my bladder exploded. I had to walk out of the WC with a sopping pair of pants and squeaking boots. When I apologized for taking so long, the officer responded, 'I've experienced worse. No one lives through a war without soiling himself.'"

Lily wriggled out of her dress, slipping demurely under the sheets.

Later, they cuddled on the bed, telling stories of the years they'd been apart.

"Barnaby, I feel I've arrived in heaven."

"Do you? Even with a chap who's handicapped?"

Lily sat bolt upright and stared at him. "Maybe you should spend some time at The Last Post. No one uses that word there."

"And which lady would I see?" he teased.

An hour later, they sat end-to-end in the large claw-foot tub. Lily stretched her long legs on either side of Barnaby. He pushed his foot gently against her abdomen. "Let's call our baby Soap."

In the evening, they joined the bridge players in the dining room for a drink. They circulated around the room. A man with peppery-grey hair and a slight build with whom they fell into conversation introduced himself as Dr. Henry Spalding from Calgary. He had a residual British accent. "I'm one of the ABCs," he said, waiting for a reaction.

Lily shook her head. "Lethbridge is such a paradox."

"How so?" Dr. Spalding asked.

"Well, in spite of the conservative citizenry, prostitutes work safely and homosexuals take over the second floor of a hotel!"

"And what do you know about prostitutes?" Dr. Spalding asked with mock suspicion.

"I run a brothel called The Last Post."

"Good heavens! Well, I never. You fit right in with us queers!" Henry said, grinning boyishly. "My patients regularly scout on my behalf for a potential wife. If they learned I fancied men, they would never come to see me," he said, embracing his younger companion around the shoulders with one arm. "I am what I am. And these card-playing social occasions allow me to enjoy that."

Lily wished Dr. Spalding a good tournament and Barnaby suggested they get to the far end of the dining room before someone else took their reservation. Seated at their table, he held the menu between his left hand and the stump of his right. The elderly waiter looked concerned. "Would you like me to ask the cook to slice your meat?" he asked.

"Only if it's tough."

"The chef's beef is usually so tender it can be cut with a fork," the waiter said.

"Thank you," Barnaby said. "Then my four fingers will do." He smiled, looking up at the waiter. "I've had to learn to say that. I used to resent gestures of help. It was nice of you to offer it."

"I'll bring a knife just in case," the waiter said cheerily.

They were halfway through their meal, and deep in conversation, when they were interrupted by the voice of Dr. Spalding. He stood by their table with his younger companion. "We're having trouble finding a seat. Can we join you?"

"Please, sit down," Barnaby said. The four of them soon fell into conversation. "I'm a doctor, myself," Barnaby said. "Patients are so nosy. How do you keep your personal life private, Dr. Spalding?"

Dr. Spalding stretched back in his chair and let out a loud laugh. "I play the role of a typical bachelor in Calgary. Ladies cluck that I'm wasting my good looks." The doctor gave his partner an affectionate glance. "So the trick is to put people off your scent. I let it be known that I go occasionally to a brothel, but that brothel I visit happens to have one male prostitute who also serves as a bouncer. No one questions now when I travel with another man. They think we're probably both looking for prostitutes."

"Clever," Barnaby said. "Very clever."

The following morning, the Calgary group was sorting out luggage and making plans for one month hence. Barnaby had an early appointment with Mr. Corker, the saddle maker. Before rushing off, he and Lily found Henry Spalding in the dining room.

"We wanted to say goodbye," Lily said. She leaned forward and whispered: "Next time you're in Lethbridge, come and have a drink at The Last Post. Who knows? Maybe we *will* have a man to entertain you."

"I dare say one or two men might like that." Dr. Spalding grinned.

"Not me!" Barnaby laughed. "I'll stay among the handicapped." He grabbed Lily's hand and dragged her off to Mr. Corker's.

Black, brown, and light-tan hides hung from poles sticking out from the walls of the tanning operation. Lily walked around breathing in the pungent smell of new leather while Mr. Corker measured the length and circumference of Barnaby's stump and recorded the figures in a book. He had been a godsend to Lily, providing her with scrap leather to be used for projects in her workshop. The veterans tooled the leather and then sewed the pieces into billfolds that Mr. Corker sold, keeping 20 percent of the profits.

"Shall I send the gloves to Edmonton, Dr. Barnaby?" he asked after taking his final measurement.

Barnaby grinned. "No, sir. I'll pick up the gloves myself." Mr. Corker winked at Lily. They left the shop and found a taxi to take them to the train station.

Barnaby embraced Lily as the train hooted and hissed its imminent departure. "We owe our happiness to the soldiers who didn't make it," Barnaby said, not hiding his emotion. He hoisted himself onto the last car.

"Get ready, Mrs. Parsons, you're about to become Mrs. Barnaby!" he shouted as the train pulled away. He hung over the safety rail, shouting, "I love you, Lily Parsons!"

Lily laughed and blew him a kiss.

The words that were so hard for Ed to say came so easily to Barnaby, Lily thought. She was smiling as she walked back to The Last Post. Neither Ed nor Barnaby had proposed to her on bended knee.

CHAPTER 21

Los Angeles, California, 1922

During the summer, Dr. Morris Lafayette attended a public health symposium in Los Angeles. The Americans did not have more venereal disease than Canadians, but their approach to social hygiene was more advanced. They did not limit sex education to adults and, in fact, some states had actually made sex education in the classroom mandatory. In Canada, the discussion of a venereal disease threat was limited to medical journals. The Americans put the subject out in the open through posters and public forums.

The Los Angeles conference called on doctors, teachers, and legislators to give their perspectives on eradicating venereal disease. However, it was a diminutive retired prostitute by the name of Jasmine Prym who captured the audience. She was no more than five feet tall, delicate-boned, and seemingly of Asian heritage. Standing on the stage in a fitted red brocade dress with her shiny black hair swept up in a topknot, she looked highly exotic. Morris compared her to the wholesome, buxom, farm-bred prostitutes at home and wondered how such a fragile figure had survived as a lady of the night. But she had obviously done well to retire in apparent good health at thirty-five.

Miss Prym began by holding up her self-published manual, *Safety in the Sex Trade*, and Morris expected her to talk about the dangers inherent in her work. He was stunned when she proved to be a self-taught scholar.

"A professor of history gave me an appreciation of books," she told the audience. "Until he taught me to read, I couldn't even sign my name." She clasped her hands in front of her and lowered her head. When she looked up, her eyes were moist with tears. "Once I was capable of understanding written words, I set out to trace the roots of prostitution from antiquity to the present day — using the professor's library," she added, smiling. "I donated the five hundred dollars I earned from my book to the Children's Hospital of Los Angeles. I would love to have a child, but, like so many prostitutes, I am barren. It was Charles Darwin who first suggested that excess exposure to semen could lead to infertility. Furthermore, if prostitutes do get pregnant, they end it in an abortion, which can also lead to barrenness." Delegates stirred uncomfortably, exchanging thoughtful looks.

"Venereal disease is another contributing factor to child-lessness," Miss Prym continued. "But there are things prostitutes can do to avoid such sad circumstances. Recognizing the signs of venereal disease in a client is the first step. A second protection against unsavoury clients is to charge more for sex." She paused and glanced coyly over her audience. "That isn't to say rich men are always healthy." There was a suppressed laugh. "Increasing the price and decreasing the number of clients and refusing to service a dirty customer is a sound strategy." She screwed up her nose. Morris shook his head, smiling at the woman's courage as she put up an admonishing finger and wagged it, saying: "No girl should work on the street. Women who sell their bodies deserve supervised brothels and the care of health professionals who have earned their trust."

Morris's enthusiastic clapping was followed by general applause. As soon as Miss Prym came down from the stage, he rushed to intercept her.

"May I speak with you?" he asked. Miss Prym nodded and smiled. "There will be a symposium in Montreal in the spring on 'Threats to the Family,'" Morris said. "I wondered if I could invite you to speak at the symposium."

The tiny woman drew back, looking confused. "You just heard me speak about prostitution. What would *I* have to say about families? We ladies of the night don't have families."

"Let me explain," Morris said quickly, hoping she wouldn't walk off. "The Catholic Church believes that prostitution is one of many factors eroding the family and destroying the church. I have been asked to put together a panel to discuss what we call the Lethbridge model. I'd like you to be on that panel. Lethbridge has a unique way of keeping prostitution in check, not unlike what you advocated in your talk here, and I believe yours is another useful voice."

"But I don't speak French," she said, laughing. "And a trip to Montreal would be costly."

"We have a budget that will cover your travel costs and there are others on the panel who don't speak French, either."

"You mean there's no fee," she said saucily. She shrugged provocatively, and Morris smiled in agreement. "I suppose a trip to Montreal would be fascinating."

"Then you accept," Morris said, smiling with pleasure. She nodded and the doctor dropped his professional manner, encircling her shoulders with a squeeze.

Morris had no idea if the hospital board would approve

a trip to Montreal. He hoped he hadn't invited Jasmine Prym prematurely.

At the monthly meeting in the mayor's office the following week, members of the board expressed their surprise when Morris described how the Americans were more advanced in their approach to public health and told them the story of Jasmine Prym.

"Not all of America has liberal ideas, but sex education is mandatory in Los Angeles public schools," Morris said. "They don't want their poor young girls becoming prostitutes to survive."

"I'm not sure I agree with that approach," a board member chimed in. "It would be better to improve the economy and guarantee every man a job."

Morris interjected. "May I remind you that Mrs. Parsons is now married to our colleague, Dr. Barnaby? She had no choice but to run a brothel when her first husband died. Single mothers do not always have a choice." Morris had attended the quiet civil ceremony joining Lily and Barnaby in marriage, and Dr. Barnaby had then joined the staff at the Galt. "It's no more surprising that a prostitute, due to good circumstances, became an amateur historian than a schoolteacher, due to bad circumstances, became a madam. Think, had Dr. Barnaby not met his old sweetheart, he might have remained in Edmonton with Dr. Newbury."

"Could we change this salacious conversation to the hospital's approach to public health?" Mr. Sick interjected, leaning forward on his cane. His advanced age and brewery wealth made his quiet voice respected. The normally outspoken board members fell quiet.

Morris spoke out. "The Catholic Church in Montreal is putting on a symposium billed 'Threats to the Family': namely prostitution, women's rights, and the vote. The Quebec clergy has roundly denounced Nellie McClung." The board members chuckled. Nellie was a thorn in all masculine hides as she campaigned province-wide for the enfranchisement of women. "The Lethbridge approach to prostitution as a matter of public health should be represented at the symposium."

In the end, the board agreed to pay travelling expenses for those coming from Alberta, but not for Miss Prym, who would be arriving from California. Morris offered to pay out of his own pocket.

The mayor adjourned the board meeting, stating that he and the lady superintendent would also be at the conference. Members of the board chuckled, and one member asked him not to be an embarrassment to them all.

In the course of a conversation in the hospital corridor, Alistair mentioned the Montreal symposium to Barnaby. A neurologist who had read Barnaby's papers on phantom limb had invited him to visit Montreal for a consultation. Barnaby suggested he arrange his meeting with the neurologist and join the Montreal-bound group. Alistair had indicated they were to travel across Lake Superior on the famous SS *Assiniboia*. Barnaby loved the travelling plan, pleased that Lily could have a well-deserved rest. She was managing the VD clinic full-time and was pregnant with their first child.

Barnaby's case studies on veterans who suffered from postwar nightmares had also aroused interest in the nascent psychiatric community in Montreal. They wanted to study the link between shell shock and phantom limb. His first study reported a patient having a recurring nightmare of blown-off legs being used to shore up the crumbling sides of a trench. His second patient suffered from daytime visions of rats chewing on corpses and refused to go outside. The third veteran tried to commit suicide because of the guilt he felt for not burying his friends, as the frozen ground had made interment impossible. He was a young veteran who sat beneath the Lethbridge town clock every Saturday evening and howled. Most times, the police took him home; occasionally, they would call Barnaby. He would head for the clock with Lily driving. The boy had been a signalman and had fallen asleep on his watch. As a result, fifty soldiers had died in an unexpected German ambush. These reported cases had suffered amputations, and all three of them experienced phantom limb.

Clara didn't think the hospital would pay for an extravagant form of travel such as that provided by the *Assiniboia* and proposed that she cross the country by train. Alistair had travelled with Clara to medical meetings, but the *Assiniboia* seemed a perfect opportunity to avoid prying eyes. Private time thus far had been confined to his evening chats in her apartment. And these were tempered by the fact that his wife Jessie had been admitted to the Galt. Alistair would visit his wife during mealtime because eating was at the root of her health problem. He would encourage her to eat and feed her small mouthfuls. She was now alarmingly thin and wasting away almost daily. Barnaby had diagnosed melancholia. Mrs. Harwood was a sweet, gentle soul: a mismatch for the blustery mayor. Clara made sure she had the best care the hospital was able to provide and Yip served up special dishes to tempt her.

Clara's evenings with Alistair — now that his wife was in the hospital — were mixed with happiness at seeing him and the guilt that he should spend the evening at her bedside. But, frustrated in coaxing Jessie to eat, he would flee to Clara's apartment. "What the devil has she got to be sad about?" he would moan, then apologize, suggesting it was being married to him.

As the plans materialized to travel by ship, Alistair made a pitch to Clara. "There's one way of cutting the cost on the *Assiniboia*," he said, putting his hands on her shoulders. "It's time you stopped walking away from love. You won't lose your job sharing a cabin with me." He sighed heavily as he fixed his gaze on Clara. "I have not been intimate with my wife in years." Clara blushed at his candour.

She didn't meet Alistair's eyes and declined his offer to share accommodation. Jessie Harwood was discharged from the hospital in a weakened state. Clara's emotions ranged from sorrow for Mrs. Harwood to understanding the frustration of the mayor. She packed her silk kimono. "It's high time I wear this," she muttered, but indecision filled her mind.

They boarded the steamship at Port Arthur, both looking back proudly at the towering grain elevators, the mark of the West's success. Alistair's large cabin was on the port side of the ship, near the bow, and it became the room designated for pre-dinner drinks for their group. Clara and the others — Morris, Lily, and Barnaby — had modest cabins the size of dressing cupboards close to the engine.

Relaxed and happy, she and Alistair won handily in an afternoon bridge tournament. A six-piece band accompanying a black jazz singer from Chicago provided after-dinner entertainment. As the travellers strolled the deck on their way back to their cabins, Lily confided that she and Barnaby were expecting a child. Clara could hear the contentment in her voice. She and Lily had both travelled a tough road, she thought, but Lily's journey was ending in love and happiness. She gave her niece a rare hug.

Morris heard the lonely clank of Clara's door well before ten. He guessed her probity was about protecting Ivy. He put down his book and crawled deep below the covers. He fell asleep and dreamt of Jasmine Prym.

The doctor who had invited Barnaby to Montreal met him at the train station while Lily went on to the conference centre with the mayor, Clara, and Morris. The abundance of birettas, white collars, and black capes in the main foyer was the signal that "Threats to The Family" was largely a Catholic symposium. Lily smiled broadly when she recognized Father Michael from Glace Bay amongst the clerics. His overcoat did not disguise the white collar.

"I don't believe my eyes!" she exclaimed, smiling broadly and shaking his hand. She introduced the Lethbridge contingent, indicating they were part of a panel.

Clara looked puzzled and then brightened as she placed him. "Why, you're the priest who informed the Sampsons that the Bishop of Montreal might challenge their adoption of Florence. I'm the nurse who was in charge of Florence after her mother's suicide."

"Yes, you're right. I remember that case. I was working at that point here in Montreal in the bishop's diocese. Believe me, I was just the messenger. How did that all turn out?"

"Fortunately, Florence was already well away from Quebec when the bishop got involved," Clara responded. She bore no grudge against the young priest. "Percy Sampson, as you must know, threatened Madam Dupuis with a charge of involuntary manslaughter; accusing her of writing a misleading letter that led directly to the young mother's death. It was only a bluff, but the bishop let the matter rest. I visit Florence quite often in Calgary, you know. She's thriving."

The conversation was interrupted by the arrival of Jasmine Prym. Father Michael, when introduced, shook her hand awkwardly. The rest of the group moved on, leaving Lily to catch up with the priest.

"I haven't lived in Glace Bay for some time," he said softly as they slid into their seats in the conference hall. "But I did learn about Ed's death and your remarriage to a doctor," he continued. "I keep abreast through the parish newsletter."

"I loved Ed in a completely different way than I do Barnaby," Lily said, feeling awkward. "You know, his last words were, 'my mother ...' I struggled for a long time to find meaning in what he said, but now I realize that's what I *was* to Ed."

Father Michael squeezed her hands. "I left Glace Bay soon after you. I knew too much about Father Mac and could no longer sit comfortably in his former office. I was a military chaplain for a while, and then came here to Montreal after the war. I'm a teacher now at the Jesuit college."

When the delegates broke for lunch, Lily stood with Father Michael, waiting for her friends to appear. They came striding out, talking animatedly.

Father Michael put his hands on his hips, grinning boyishly. "What would you think of a priest touring you through Montreal?" he asked the group. "How about tomorrow?"

Alistair was about to retort that he knew the city well when Clara jabbed him in the side with her elbow. He grinned and shrugged. Arrangements were made over lunch and then all but Lily returned to the conference. She returned to the hotel to rest and to wait for Barnaby.

The following day they stood under the mid-afternoon sun, looking up the mountain at Brother André's newly constructed church. They could see supplicants walking or limping with hands held in an attitude of prayer, hoping for a miracle at the shrine. Lily thought of the healing that occurred at The Last Post and she wished these faithful people would find happiness.

"That's it for religious touring," Father Michael said, after their single stop. "I've ordered a *calèche* to take us up Mount Royal."

His eyes crinkled as he helped Miss Prym into their carriage. She admitted she had never met a priest. "What a waste of good looks," she said saucily. He laughed embarrassedly and sat down beside her.

Mount Royal was teeming with activity. Police officers on horseback trotted by, keeping a semblance of order as children played ball or flew kites. Nannies pushed healthy-looking babies in prams, chatting with each other. Three ladies holding parasols walked briskly in tandem with purposeful faces.

"Out for their constitutional," Barnaby commented, nodding toward the ladies.

A police officer cantered by, exciting the *calèche* horses. They, too, started to canter for a few frightening and rocky moments, threatening to send the *calèche* out of control. The driver, a grizzly-looking man from the Turcotte Stables, hollered, "Whoa, *doucement!*"

Miss Prym looked terrified. "For a moment, I thought I'd never see California again," she said breathlessly, clutching Father Michael's arm. Her dark eyes glistened when she saw the redness creep into his cheeks.

Another police officer dismounted to take charge of the bottle a burly man brandished as he weaved cheerfully through the crowd.

Looking down the south side of the mountain, they could see the grey stone buildings of McGill University. "I imagine Dr. Newbury strolled on these paths during his McGill days," Barnaby said. "I must write to tell him we saw his alma mater."

In the evening, Alistair took charge, squiring the group to a restaurant on Peel Street. Father Michael, meanwhile, had disappeared with Miss Prym. The restaurant was alive with conversation and filled with smoke, eliciting a complaint from Clara. "You'll have to be tolerant," Alistair said. "It's *de rigueur* in Montreal to smoke an after-dinner cigar."

Barnaby commented that everyone, including the waiter, spoke English. "Montreal is a funny place," Alistair said. "The Scots have the power, and the French do the work."

"I hope Father Michael doesn't meet any staff from the college," Lily said. "They're not all clerics. I suppose if they encountered Father Michael in a red-light district, they'd think he was doing missionary work. Strange that Miss Prym wants to poke around that area with a priest."

"She spoke about the lack of safety for streetwalkers at the Los Angeles conference," Morris said. "She's very passionate about the protection of prostitutes."

Alistair gave the doctor a curious look. "Good Lord, Morris, I think you fancy her!" He shot Clara a wink.

A man in his thirties with wavy blond hair lumbered toward their table. He twisted his torso slightly with each step. "Dr. Barnaby, isn't it?" His dinner companion had followed him over. "I'm Dr. Hurley, and this is my colleague, Dr. Smith. We're both interested in your work, but I'm the one with the phantom foot." He stomped his right shoe. "I was in the Quebec medical corps, the Van Doos." Lily looked puzzled. "The 22nd Regiment, the English slang for the French 'vingt-deux.'"

"I can't speak French, but I at least know my numbers," Lily piped up.

"My wife was a teacher," Barnaby said, laughing. "Will you join us?" He nodded to the waiter to pull up two chairs.

"Is your beef from Alberta?" Alistair asked the waiter as they all examined their menus.

"Who's Alberta?" the waiter snapped with a slight French accent.

Alistair ignored the slight and ordered a 1918 Margaux.

The waiter looked surprised. "It's not just the French who know good wines," Alistair said belligerently. The waiter lifted his hand to suggest he wasn't arguing.

Barnaby asked the waiter to have his meat cut into small bits. He held up his stump. The waiter left the table with his notepad, shaking his head.

When a round of cigars was offered after dinner, the ladies excused themselves and headed back to the Mount Royal Hotel.

An hour later, Alistair knocked at Clara's door, smelling of brandy and cigar. "Up for a nightcap?" he asked.

"I'll come over in a few minutes if you order some tea."

Ten minutes later, Clara, dressed in her cream silk kimono, tapped lightly on his door. She could hear his loud snoring. The room-service boy blushed, thinking he had caught her in an indiscretion as she stood there in her nightwear.

"Follow me with the tea," she said and returned to her room. She gave the lad a small tip, then closed the door and wept.

After an hour of sleeplessness, she got up and knocked on Alistair's door again. She listened for a few minutes to the soft, rhythmic nasal sound and returned to her room. *Maybe I should have knocked louder.*

She lay awake the remainder of the night.

The cocky reporter who had hassled Clara when she'd got off the ship was covering the health conference. His presence reminded her that she had been in Canada for three years. She spoke to the reporter, who indicated he worked for the *Montreal Star.* After a few minutes he smiled with sheepish recognition. His face seemed less flushed and he looked healthier. They chatted for a while, having established why they looked familiar to each other. On the last day of the symposium, he stopped Clara as she came out of the lecture hall and handed her the letter written by Madame Dupuis. "The fateful letter," he said, "the one you gave me that day on the dock. I thought that when that little girl grows up she might want to know why her mother jumped overboard. I never did write the story. It was just too much for me, how love ended in such a sad way for both of her parents. One killed by war and the other by suicide. Tell me about the English girl, the mother, Mrs. Durling?"

"She was beautiful, and, as we learned tragically, had every reason to trust Réjean Dupuis. He spotted her in the mess hall when she served him food as a volunteer. As you know, romance during the war was hurried and intense. There's nothing like fear to concentrate your emotions."

Alistair came up behind her and grasped her hand. "Are you being pestered?" he asked. "I remember this young reporter from my last trip here."

"Oh, no. This gentleman has just done something very kind," Clara said, turning toward the man. "I had hoped he would hand the letter back. I fretted all the way to Lethbridge about my impulsive gesture in giving it to him. That letter might have been necessary if the Dupuis ever tried to take Florence."

"You mean the letter telling that poor girl that her lover was already married?" Alistair said. Clara nodded.

"If I were to do a piece on Lethbridge's segregated area for the *Star*, when's a good time to visit?" the reporter asked. "I'd love a trip to Alberta, and what a good excuse."

"Anytime," Alistair offered. "Come anytime. You know how to get in touch with me."

Clara leaned on his arm as they watched the reporter depart. She hoped that Alistair would ask why she was so tired. If he asked, she was going to tell him that she'd knocked on his door the evening before and again in the middle of the night. But he didn't ask, and she had no opportunity to tell him after that.

The morning of their departure, Clara arrived in the hotel dining room to hear Alistair's voice comparing Montreal to Lethbridge for the benefit of several health professionals.

"The Catholic Church in Quebec denies so many of the freedoms we take for granted out West," he said, motioning for Clara to join him. As she walked across the room, she could sense the men's assumption that she and Alistair were having an affair. And there was Morris, standing beside Miss Prym. She wondered if others thought *he*, too, was having a clandestine relationship. She sighed and went to join Alistair. She looked attentive as people talked about the symposium, but her stomach churned with dread at the thought of a three-day journey back to Lethbridge. She imagined Alistair would heal his wounded pride by ignoring her — a far cry from their first journey to the West, when he had lifted the gloom of Annabel's suicide by his unabashed excitement about what they would do together to improve the Galt.

She turned toward Alistair as he talked. He fixed her with a resigned gaze and smiled. She nudged his hand. "Best I go up and finish packing. We leave within the hour."

She walked out of the dining room with her usual brisk step, hoping no one could sense the confusion in her heart. The return to Lethbridge was quieter than when she'd travelled for the first time with Alistair three years earlier. Clara knew she had missed an opportunity and wondered if the chance for love would ever come again.

CHAPTER 22

Lily's Second Marriage, 1920

Soon after returning from the visit to Montreal, Barnaby got wind of a house for sale in the north part of town. He was overjoyed that Lily was having their first child and wanted to move to a bigger house well in advance of the birth. He planned to keep his office in the segregated area where most of his patients lived, and he wanted to assure McKlintock of his plans before he found another occupant. He made an appointment with the real-estate agent to confirm his intentions.

"I plugged my nose and bought a house on a respectable street," Barnaby said, laughing as he spread the real estate section of the *Lethbridge Herald* on Sam's desk.

"Wow! That's quite a house," Sam said, gazing at the advertisement. "How could you afford such a place?" Only Sam would ask such a direct question.

"Horse stable," Barnaby said. "The house is across from a small stable. It put buyers off. The owner decided to sell it privately at a lower price, just to get rid of it. She was elderly and could no longer manage. John Iverson told me about it. But we've made friends with the stable owners, Mr. and Mrs. Black. Their sixteen-year-old daughter, Missy, gives lessons in a paddock attached to the barn. I'll lease a pony for my son when he's old enough. In the meantime, Teddy sits on the fence watching Missy ride the horses."

"Are you happy to be moving out, now that The Last Post will be converted into a home for crippled veterans?"

Barnaby massaged his stump while he reflected on Sam's question. "The segregated area has been good to us, Sam. We appreciate its liveliness. Lily received a great deal of kindness during a difficult time. We won't turn our back on the area."

"So where will you locate your office?"

"Right here, where it's convenient for my patients. Very few have a car, and the office is close to the hospital."

Sam got up from his desk and came over to Barnaby. "Not many people like me in this town, Dr. Barnaby. But I can say sincerely I have enjoyed dealing with the likes of you and your wife. Lending money to people who can't get financing from the bank gives me a bad reputation. Some of my clients are engaged in illegal activities and if they don't come up with the cash I'm owed, I expose them. But I never worried about Mrs. Barnaby paying me back."

"I didn't know my wife had asked *you* for a loan!" Barnaby retorted.

"When she renovated the back porch. After scouring demolition sites for affordable building supplies, she still needed one hundred dollars. She actually stopped the bulldozing of a small warehouse until the windows, roof joists, and flooring were removed and deposited at The Last Post. What's going to happen to the girls once the conversion is complete?"

"Thanks to Lily, the girls can read and they speak much better. They can carry on intelligent conversation. Maybe former clients will hire these girls in their offices or shops. They're hard workers and quite adaptable."

"I'm not sure office work is what they'll be offered," Sam said. "But they will be in high demand." He laughed.

"I'm sure the girls are sad to be leaving The Last Post," Barnaby said. "It's been home to them. But Dorothy Haslam, an occupational nurse from Edmonton, has already begun the adaptations to the house. Dan MacIntyre will use the renovated porch for his art studio and the bedrooms will be filled with cots. Nothing major, but it will be home to a different set of occupants; some of whom have already spent time there." Barnaby laughed.

"Will it still be called The Last Post?"

"Can you think of a better name?"

Jane Barnaby came into the world full of opinions. Her brown eyes popped open as though she had a question for the doctor. Her head was a matted mess of blond curls. Barnaby cuddled his daughter in his arms, grinning with pride. The doctor who delivered Jane and the assisting nurse left the birthing room just as Clara shepherded Teddy and Ivy in.

"Rules are to be broken," she said. Neither child showed much interest in the new arrival. Both were anxious to tell the adults about their latest riding escapade, when Missy had taken them for a ride in the park. This privilege came to a temporary halt when a young man complained that the riders had scared "his girl," who was afraid of horses.

Clara preferred a stricter approach than Barnaby to these childish misdemeanours on horseback, but Barnaby persuaded her that taking privileges away was less effective than adding responsibility. He made the children dismount and walk their horses as they picked up the garbage in the park.

They promised never to scare anyone again.

A few weeks after Jane was born, Lily resumed her work at the venereal disease clinic, which she had begun under Clara's supervision while she was still pregnant. Her job was to compile numbers to see if the incidence of new cases was down. It appeared there was reason for celebration, and she decided to have a dinner in her new home to acknowledge the success. She invited Alistair and Morris, who accepted her invitation, but she was disappointed their wives had declined. Lily still felt judged by a few of the town's respectable ladies.

Health policy, local politics, and the new women's court were lively topics of conversation during the dinner. The recent appointment of Emily Murphy as magistrate was still controversial. The mayor expressed doubt that a woman could administer the law. Lily countered this prejudice by saying: "Emily Murphy would *change* the law. I don't hear many protests coming from the east."

Seeing the ladies getting riled up, Barnaby turned the conversation back to the clinic's success, the reason for the dinner party. Just as the guests were leaving, Lily held Clara back.

"Barnaby and I would like you to be Jane's godmother." Lily grinned. "Clara, I will never think of you as my aunt, but I do think of you and Ivy as family. At least I no longer call you Mrs. Durling."

Clara laughed. "What a lovely gesture. Where will the baptism take place?"

"St. Augustine's Church," Lily said. "It didn't hurt to tell the minister that you would be the godmother."

Clara laughed again. "Did you tell Reverend Parker how we're related?"

"I'll leave that up to you. But I would like Ivy to know that Teddy and Jane are her cousins." Lily smiled. "Ivy already treats

Teddy as a younger brother and they both ignore Jane. Being a cousin may seem like a demotion."

Ivy took her new relationship with Teddy in stride. Literally. Now that they lived across from a horse stable, she preferred to go there rather than the Iversons'. Sergeant Stuart, while convalescing in the hospital after a riding accident, had stirred up her horse enthusiasm. He was the officer in charge of the RCMP stables. The officers had their own three-bed ward next to the matron's office at the Galt. During his six-week stay, Ivy would sneak past her mother and dart in to ask the sergeant to tell her his horse stories. He had no end of horse heroics, and he promised to find a suitable mount for a ten-year-old when he got out of the hospital.

In due course, when the invitation came from Sergeant Stuart to visit the RCMP stables, Ivy didn't disguise her pleasure. But arriving at the barracks with her mother, she groaned upon seeing Katherine Iverson standing with her mother at the door to the barn. Ivy was overshadowed by Katherine's popularity at school.

"Did you invite *Katherine*?" Ivy asked, looking crossly at Clara.

"Ivy, I don't have many ways I can thank Etta for all she does."

"Then, why didn't you just invite Mrs. Iverson?"

Clara returned her daughter's rolling eyes with a stern look.

"I've organized a little show to thank you for getting me back on my feet, Mrs. Durling," Sergeant Stuart said as he strode out of the barn. Clara looked pleased with the attention.

Etta laughed. "Mrs. Durling does have her admirers."

Sergeant Stuart led his visitors to the end of the corral. They watched intently as the officers galloped their horses, stopping suddenly, turning them on the spot, then making them sidestep, back up, and stand still.

"All this is necessary for a horse to work in a crowd without hurting the bystanders," Sergeant Stuart explained. The show lasted an hour, and then he invited everyone to join the officers for lemonade in the barracks.

Etta watched as Clara helped Sergeant Stuart pour glasses of lemonade. *She only has to give him a nod and he will be courting her*, she thought, as she shooed Ivy and Katherine outside after extracting a promise from them not to go in the stable.

"Sergeant Stuart says he's going to find me a horse," Ivy said. "I've been taking lessons with Missy across from Dr. Barnaby's."

"She only has ponies," Katherine said disdainfully.

Katherine's haughtiness left a knot in Ivy's stomach. She wanted to say, "I'll have a horse, but your parents can't afford one." Instead, she blurted, "When I get a horse, I'll let my friends ride it."

Katherine lifted one shoulder in a gesture of *who cares* and said, "I'm going to look in on the horses." There was a dare in her voice, and Ivy followed her into the barn. At the far end, a wheelbarrow, rakes, shovels, and pitchforks were neatly stored in a corner. The farthest stall was piled high with hay. The stalls on either side of a dirt aisle were empty except the one by the door where a horse, head down, munched on hay. Horizontal wood slats nailed up the wall adjacent to the stall served as a ladder to reach the loft. Katherine scrambled up the slats as the horse continued to eat. Suddenly, letting out a whoop, she leapt onto the horse's back. The mare reared and she was thrown off. Ivy screamed and ran to tell the adults.

"Katherine's been tossed," she said breathlessly. "She's in the barn."

Everyone raced toward the stable, where they found the stable hand standing in the aisle shaking.

"She gone jumped on the mare's back while she was just eating quietly in her stall."

Sergeant Stuart threw open the stall door and grabbed the horse just as she kicked out, narrowly missing Katherine's head. "Easy, girl," he said as he slipped a halter over her head and led her into the aisle. Clara knelt down by Katherine, who was crying. "It's her right arm. I'm sure it's broken, but we'll need an X-ray to see where."

"You're lucky it's your arm and not your head that's broken," Etta said, fear and anger in her voice. "Why would you do such a foolish thing?"

Clara marched Ivy out of the barn. "Let Etta and Sergeant Stuart deal with Katherine," she said, her voice shaking. "She could have been killed if that hoof had hit her head. I hope you'll never be so foolish."

In the aftermath of the accident, Katherine's classmates rushed to sign her plaster cast. The story of the rearing horse had given her a daredevil reputation that Ivy both envied and resented. *Katherine only plays with me because her mother makes her,* Ivy thought bitterly, watching the admiring crowd. She concocted a plan to make new friends other than Katherine; a plan to make other children like her.

She decided to make the hospital sound interesting, particularly the morgue in the basement. She whetted her classmates' appetite by bringing to school a metal device used for relieving gas. Ivy had found it in the instrument sterilizer. Her classmates crowded around to see what she had. This elicited giggles and rude noises at recess. Over the next few weeks, she brought a pair of forceps, a tooth extractor, a stethoscope, and an instrument to remove nose and ear hairs. But after a while she ran out of props and her show-and-tell routine no longer drew a crowd at recess. She decided it was time to offer up the morgue.

"Have you ever seen a dead body?" she asked a group of

girls. "I know how to get into the hospital morgue," she added, when questioned where they would see a corpse. "Patients die every day. It's easy."

Katherine challenged her. "That's not possible. All morgues are locked."

"What would your mother do if she caught us?" one girl asked in a hushed voice.

"Nothing. She'd just shoo us away. After all, the person's dead, so what would it matter? Do you want to see a man or a woman?"

It was agreed that they did not want to see a dead man.

Not long after her proposition to view a dead person, Ivy overheard that Mrs. Brody had died. The next afternoon, she brought her friends to the hospital, entering through the kitchen near Yip's shack.

"Miss Ivy? You and friends want eat some cookies and milk?" Yip asked.

"Yes, we'd like that."

The girls toured the kitchen, bug-eyed. "I've never been in a hospital," one girl said.

"Well, not since you were born," another one corrected.

"What you do here today?" Yip asked.

"We're doing a project on dead people," Ivy said.

Yip frowned, then laughed. "You no be serious."

"I was joking," Ivy said, and the girls giggled.

They walked out of the kitchen and Yip called after them. "You come back after you do homework, and I make you something special. You like cake?" The girls nodded excitedly and headed through the breezeway and down into the basement.

They tiptoed down a corridor until Ivy opened an unmarked door. A gurney under a metal lamp sat in the middle of the cement-walled room. A white sheet covered the body. "It smells horrible in here," a girl bleated, putting her hand over her nose.

Ivy put her finger to her lips when she heard voices coming down the hall.

"Follow me," she hissed, swinging open a large door and beckoning for the girls to get in fast. "This is where they keep them from rotting," she whispered. The girls trembled with fear. A hushed conversation near the cadaver was too quiet for the girls to overhear, but soon the voices retreated and the girls came out of the cold room.

"Let's have a quick look and then run," Ivy said. One of the girls backed up and there was a crash as a bottle of embalming fluid broke all over the floor. A nurse came flying in and gasped.

"What are you doing in the morgue, Ivy? What would your mother think of what you're up to?"

"We haven't looked yet," Ivy squeaked, glancing at her friends, hoping not to lose face. She no longer felt like a gang leader. A pungent odour wafted through the room and one of the girls started to retch.

"Follow me to matron's office," the nurse said.

The girls rushed out of the morgue, gagging and plugging their noses. They marched behind the nurse, exchanging terrified looks. They knew Ivy's mother was strict.

"I'm sure Ivy was the ringleader," Clara said after she heard where the girls had been found. "I'll have to talk to all of your parents." She got up and came round from her desk to stand before the girls crowded into her office. "Peering at a dead body for excitement is a grievous violation. I imagine all of you have had someone die in your family. You wouldn't want your relative to be stared at for fun."

"We didn't see the corpse," an older girl said. All of them were in tears.

Ivy stayed in the office as the girls departed. Clara watched, heartbroken, as they shot Ivy dirty looks as they left.

"Mummy, it's so lonely growing up here." Ivy's shoulders shook as she added, "I wish I were that dead body."

Clara could barely understand her words through the sobbing. She decided that Ivy had been punished enough for now and asked the nurse who had marshaled in the prurient girls to take Ivy back to the dormitory.

"It will be okay, Ivy. Wait and see. Your mother will let Dr. Barnaby smooth things over. He's quite respected in the hospital." The nurse put her arm around Ivy's still shaking shoulders. "It's hard, I know, not to have a home."

The next day, several concerned parents asked to meet with Clara, who set up a meeting with them. She indicated that Dr. Barnaby was an expert in nightmares and called him in to offer his advice to the parents.

"Young Ivy is only ten, but she knows all too much about death," he told them. "Death or even a corpse wouldn't mean the same to her. That's why she didn't see how upsetting it would be for the girls to be in the morgue."

"I think my daughter was more upset that I would get angry than she was about seeing a corpse," one mother piped up, trying to be conciliatory.

Another mother raised her hand to speak. "Mrs. Durling, I was at the air show last year when my daughter and her friends went for a plane ride." Her face saddened. "The nurse who accompanied your daughter refused to let her go up because she had not asked your permission. I was heartbroken to see Ivy standing on the ground watching the plane take off. I remember Ivy saying bravely, 'Next time, my mother will bring me to the air show.'" The woman put her hand on Clara's. "You mustn't be too strict, Mrs. Durling. Otherwise Ivy won't fit in."

Dr. Loring was furious when he learned of the incident. He

260 · SHARON JOHNSTON

came roaring into Clara's office, berating her for her laxness in overseeing Ivy's conduct.

"At the bottom of your vindictiveness, Dr. Loring, is the fact that I would not set a nursing entrance examination that your daughter could pass after she failed the exam twice."

"My daughter would be smart enough to know that a morgue is no place for children."

"Ivy *is* a child, Dr. Loring. A ten-year-old. I'm sorry your daughter didn't qualify to be a nurse. But I remember you laughed when a patient put his hand up a probationer's skirt and the poor girl fled to my office in tears. Why on earth would you want your daughter to be a nurse if she might suffer such rudeness?"

"Mrs. Durling, from the time you arrived I have said you are unsuitable to run this hospital. I have asked myself many times what Dr. Newbury was thinking to recommend you as matron."

"And you continue to attack me. I'm tired of this. The board has publicly commended me for innovations and sound financial management of the hospital, yet you went on air to criticize me for mismanagement, forcing Mayor Harwood to counter your statements. You know the headline in the *Herald* last week said: 'Galt ready for certification by American College of Surgeons.' You know perfectly well that I had a guiding hand in that. The accreditation would not have happened without me dealing directly with the college for weeks on end. You have no good reason to continue to attack me."

As reasonable as this conversation seemed, she knew the doctor would eventually launch another public attack. She had no idea why he hated her. When he left her office, she didn't shake his hand.

~~~

Lethbridge, Alberta, 1925

Nineteen-twenty-five is going to be a good year, Clara thought as she flipped her desk calendar to the month of June. The hospital was running smoothly, and she had become more relaxed. She dined with the final-year probationers and cheerily oversaw the arrangements for their graduation dance. Ivy and Katherine were to present flowers to the newly graduated nurses.

Clara had finished her late-evening rounds and was heading back to her apartment when a probationer came running down the breezeway. "Mrs. Durling, Ivy's hurt." She raced behind the girl to the nurse's residence. Cold air was rushing out the door of Ivy's room.

"What's happened?" she demanded. Ivy was nowhere in sight, but the window was open. She looked out to find Miss Popplewell, a second-year probationer, kneeling beside Ivy. A young man stood beside them holding a thick rope and Ivy was crying.

Miss Popplewell started blubbering. "It was an accident."

Through her tears she explained that she had arrived at the

hospital after curfew, and, afraid of the matron's reaction, tried to make her entry by the escape ladder.

Clara was furious. She had been kind to this somewhat scattered girl. She announced angrily that the graduation dance would be cancelled and Miss Popplewell would stand out for six months. Strong objections from the girls' parents forced her to change her mind on the dance, but the probationer was not allowed to return until the new year.

"Why not let Ivy have a year with the Sampsons in Calgary?" Alistair asked the next evening, sipping his Scotch in Clara's apartment. He closed his eyes and leaned back on the sofa. "Let her have a normal home life. And after a year you can see how you feel. Percy has offered to send Ivy to St. Hilda's School, which is more than you can afford. It's a generous and genuine offer." Alistair put his arm around Clara, playing with her nursing veil.

"Ivy's so happy at the Iversons' and even more so at the Barnabys' now that she knows they're related," Clara said. "But she will always struggle with being an only child," she added, resignedly. "I suppose the morgue and the rope were her way of acting out her frustration, trying to be liked. She often says she misses Florence. It's hard to believe that Florence will be starting school next year. Annabel's suicide seems such a long way away." Clara sighed and leaned her head on Alistair's shoulder. They sat on the sofa, holding hands in silence.

Clara had taken Alistair's advice reluctantly and let Ivy move to Calgary to live with the Sampsons and attend St. Hilda's. Meanwhile she had thrown herself into her work, finding reliable suppliers, improving the nursing school, and pushing for certification by the American College of Surgeons. But none of these pressing issues had lessened the pain of Ivy's absence.

Ivy returned for the too-short school holidays and summer vacations, but Clara never got used to having her leave again for Calgary.

Two years passed and she decided it was time for Ivy to come back to the hospital for good. As her train sped toward Calgary, she felt the weight of her task. She would bring Ivy home despite her tearful objections.

Mary Sampson was at the station waiting with a taxi since she didn't drive. "It's so good to have you here," Mary said, throwing her arms around Clara. "The girls are dying to see you." When they arrived at the house, Ivy and Florence came bursting out. Clara dreaded what she would have to say: *Home is with your mother, even if that means living at the Galt.*

"Percy won't be home until late," Mary said. "He spends too much time at the office, but I'm used to that." The Sampsons had moved to a much bigger house the previous year, so money didn't seem to be a problem. But there was a cloud hanging over the household, and Clara didn't know why. Percy was no longer a partner in the R.B. Bennett law firm, she knew, and he travelled frequently and worked late. Was it just Mary's loneliness that she could sense?

When Percy came home that evening, he smelled of alcohol, and Clara could sense the belligerence.

"We want to adopt Ivy," Percy said, plopping himself at the dining-room table. "What kind of a home can you provide for her at the Galt?"

"Percy, I gave you Florence, but I can't give you Ivy. She's my daughter. This is not about a home, but about family."

Mary intervened. "Percy, Ivy's listening." Clara turned to see Ivy standing in the doorway to the dining room. Her long lashes balanced the tears until they were too heavy and spilled down her cheeks.

"You're taking me back, aren't you?" Ivy said. Her words sounded as though she was being returned to jail with a life sentence.

"Ivy, it's hard for everyone. You're old enough to know I didn't plan my life this way. If there hadn't been a war, followed by the terrible flu, you and I would be living in England with your brother and Daddy." Ivy rushed upstairs sobbing, not waiting to hear her mother out.

"Mary's a better mother for Ivy than you can ever be," Percy said.

Clara winced at his caustic words. "And you are less of a father than Ivy needs," she countered, regretting immediately her unkind retort. "Percy, I'm sorry."

She went up to Ivy's room and sat on the bed beside her. "It's a beautiful room," she said sadly, glancing around at the lavender and green decor. Mary had graduated from design school in New York and the room showed her talent. There was fluidity of colour and texture in the curtains, wallpaper, and bedspreads. "I promise you'll have your own room, and Mary can help us decorate. Katherine Iverson is glad you're coming back."

Ivy moved away from her mother. "Not a single friend will stay overnight at the hospital. I can have friends at Mary's anytime. I love you, Mummy, but why do I have to live there with you? Couldn't you work here in Calgary?"

Clara recalled Percy's cruel words. She thought of Alistair saying, *you're the only lady superintendent I've ever liked.*

"Ivy, I'm in Lethbridge because that's where I'm most secure. I have some special surprises for you when you get home."

Sergeant Stuart had found a suitable horse for Ivy's return, and Clara had adopted a cat as an added surprise. Clara didn't fool herself, though, thinking that these enticements would make Ivy happy, but it was the best that she could do. Home for Ivy was with the Sampsons.

Ivy was to receive a book prize at her school's end-of-the-year ceremony. In the school auditorium, Mary pushed through the clumps of parents comparing summer plans, followed by Ivy and Clara, and found three front-row seats. Clara could see how sad Ivy was to be leaving this school and her many friends behind.

When the headmistress came to the podium and announced that Ivy Durling had won the book prize for having a story she had written published in the children's section of the Calgary newspaper, Ivy looked doleful as she traipsed across the stage to receive her award. The headmistress handed Ivy a box containing the two leather-bound volumes of *The Jungle Book*.

"Ivy, would you like to tell the audience why you love the stories in Rudyard Kipling's *Jungle Book*? For that is why we chose it as your prize. It's also a going-away present as we know you will not be back next year at St. Hilda's."

Ivy stood holding the books — a skinny twelve-year-old with long blond hair in a loose braid down her back — looking out at the audience, being careful not to lock eyes with her mother. "I loved the story of Mowgli best. He had wanted to remain with the wolves that raised him as a boy. But one day, running through the jungle, he realized he was a human. His life with the wolves had been false. I've been living with Mr. and Mrs. Sampson like Mowgli living with the wolves. Now I'm going back to Lethbridge to live in the Galt Hospital with my mother. Like Mowgli, I must live with my kind."

The headmistress turned her head slightly to wipe her eyes. She looked at the expectant faces in the audience that were waiting for her to speak. She put her arm around Ivy. "One day you will be a writer, Ivy, and write stories of your own. We are going to miss you at St. Hilda's. You kept us on our toes." The headmistress kissed Ivy on the cheek, and Ivy walked off the stage holding her prize. She sat between Mary and Clara and opened it.

"Ivy, Sergeant Stuart has chosen a beautiful horse that you can ride as soon as we get back to Lethbridge," Clara whispered, having held back her news until this moment. "And I've bought a cat. He doesn't have a name yet." Ivy looked at Clara and gave her a sad smile. At the reception that followed, she chatted happily with her friends. But, despite Ivy's brave words when she'd accepted the prize, Clara could feel the girl's anger and sadness. She shook hands with the headmistress and spoke to some parents.

"Your daughter has such poise," a mother offered.

"Yes," Clara said. "She's had some very adult experiences at such a young age."

"Will you keep my uniform, just in case I come back?" Ivy asked Mary the next morning as they were preparing to leave.

"I would buy you a new one in that case. These are a better size for Florence. She'll be going to St. Hilda's next year." Mary held Ivy in a tearful embrace. "Be good to your mom. She deserves this."

Ivy went upstairs to have a last look at her bedroom. Clara followed and put her arms around her daughter as they sat on the bed. "Spoon and jam?" she asked, holding her.

"There's no more spoon and jam, Mummy. I'm too old for that."

Back in Lethbridge, Ivy wandered about the hospital grounds morosely, or curled up to read, stroking her new cat whom she had named Presto. Summer holidays allowed for very empty and cheerless days. That changed when Sergeant Stuart arrived on horseback leading a feisty fifteen-hand mare that Clara had leased. The sergeant looked splendid in his RCMP uniform. He dismounted at the Newbury hitch in front of the hospital, tied up the horses, and strode to the reception desk.

"I'm here to fetch Miss Ivy," he said, as though he were making an arrest. The nurse at reception scurried to find her.

"Put on your riding habit," the sergeant advised when Ivy rushed into the foyer.

She turned pale. "You mean I'm ... I'm going to ride right now?"

"We are going to ride to the barracks."

Ivy stared at the sergeant wide-eyed, looking a bit scared.

"I'll be right beside you," he said, seeing her indecision. "The mare's a high-spirited horse, but you can handle her at a walk."

Ten minutes later, Clara arrived with Ivy in tow. Ivy was dressed in a crisp white blouse and beige jodhpurs. The riding boots, although used, were polished like new. A black ribbon held back her fine blond hair.

Sergeant Stuart handed her a short leather crop. "Make sure you don't smack her rump accidently," he said, laughing.

Staff members gathered around Clara. "This is just what the doctor ordered," a nurse said.

"What's the horse's name?" Ivy asked.

"I've named her Mystery, because her breeding is unknown."

Ivy put her left knee in the sergeant's cupped hands and to the count of three swung her right leg over the horse, settling in the saddle. The sergeant adjusted the length of her stirrups and leapt up onto his own horse, leaning forward to untie him.

"We're off! Take a firm but gentle hold of the reins, Ivy, and sit up straight. If you lean forward like a jockey, the mare will think you want her to go faster."

Clara watched until they turned right onto 5th Avenue. She felt a swell of pride at her daughter's gracefulness.

On Saturday mornings Clara would stand on the board fencing, watching Sergeant Stuart teach Ivy in the schooling paddock. At first she rode only in wide circles with Mystery attached to a lunge line. Sergeant Stuart snapped the line onto the bridle, cracking a long whip occasionally to urge the horse from a walk to a trot. This allowed Ivy to develop a good seat in the saddle without having to control the horse. She soon learned not to resort to her hands to slow the horse down. Sergeant Stuart used a metronome to teach her how to pace her stride. To practise her rhythm, she cantered on foot down the hospital corridor, clicking her tongue to the cadence of the metronome.

Seeing she was ready to ride at a faster pace, Sergeant Stuart shouted at Ivy from the sidelines, "Sit up, sit deep, and tighten your belly." It seemed like magic when Mystery responded.

Teddy began lessons about a year after Ivy. Barnaby had leased the pony across the street. Once the pony was deemed road safe, Ivy would ride down 5th Avenue to the Barnabys' and call out for cousin Teddy to saddle up. Then they would set off, with Teddy urging his pony to pick up its pace, and Ivy slowing her horse down.

Clara had shown little interest in cricket while living in England, but after Alistair took her to a Sunday baseball game at Sam McKlintock's farm that was being played by some women from the segregated area, she became an enthusiast of the game. It was not just the pent-up energy unleashed by the young women, but the feeling that they were so normal. *Without being told*, Clara thought, *no one would distinguish them as prostitutes.*

She had looked at Sam as a bit of a charlatan, but changed her mind after learning that every Sunday he gave over his farm to the ladies of ill repute.

To avoid the ongoing controversy of prostitutes "hanging around the hospital," the board decided to rent space in a building owned by several Chinese businessmen. Entrance to the clinic, which was located at the back of the building, was via the Natural Medicine Store, popular with many non-Chinese. Bachelors, married men, and wives who were worried they might have VD looked at the various potions while they waited to be examined. Tuesday, the day prostitutes could go into town, was the day for checkups.

The segregated area had changed since Lily's days of running The Last Post. Foreign girls, particularly Koreans, had gravitated out west looking for work. They had no local attachment. There was a code among the various brothels to move the girls around every six months. Madams often received a new crop of prostitutes, having exchanged with a brothel in another part of the province or occasionally as far away as British Columbia. This avoided the kind of romantic obsession that had so disrupted the life of Dan MacIntyre.

The initial reason for segregating an area for brothels was to keep prostitution out of the public eye. Now that it was a tourist attraction, it was painful for Lily to see the gawkers. She gave a man and his wife a piece of her mind when they taunted a veteran limping his way to the The Last Post. *I'm getting to be like Clara*, she thought, laughing as the couple fled.

Dr. Newbury had invited Barnaby to Edmonton to speak about phantom limb. Barnaby wanted Lily to meet the man who had salvaged his career. The doctor greeted them at the train and took them directly to the hospital. He was just as Barnaby had described: small in stature, loud in voice, and addressed as "Colonel" by the people he passed in the corridor. His eyes sparkled as he listened to Barnaby talk about his recent work in neuropsychiatry.

Lily sat at the back of the lecture hall while her husband spoke. She swelled with pride as students crowded around him to discuss his work. *Life is full of second chances*, she thought, as Dr. Newbury stood beside him, proud of his protégé.

They spent the evening dining at the hotel because Mrs. Newbury was "ailing." Dr. Newbury asked Lily and Barnaby for news of Mrs. Durling. He spoke of the war years and how much he had admired her courage. The doctor recounted many of his hospital jokes, and Lily wondered if he knew about The Last Post. Lily wanted to tell him that the two people he had helped and admired were indirectly related, but she decided an explanation would be too complicated.

While Barnaby was busy at the university, Lily met with Dr. Orr, who was still the provincial director of public health. He was pleased with her monthly reports that indicated a decrease in new cases of VD. But like her, he was distressed that street-soliciting and foreign workers were making prostitution more dangerous and harder to regulate.

The visit with Dr. Newbury had been bittersweet. Barnaby was deeply pleased to see his now elderly mentor so full of enthusiasm for the future. But the doctor was frail and he felt sad that he might not have a chance to visit him again. "The combination of treating patients and continuing my research will make it hard to get away again," he said wistfully as the train sped away from Edmonton. "I'm glad you met Dr. Newbury, Lily." Barnaby gripped his stump with his left hand and pushed them toward Lily. "He didn't see these as an obstacle."

Lily frowned. "Barnaby, you make war seem positive!"

Barnaby drew Lily close, ignoring the glances of other passengers. "If I hadn't been injured, I would be living in Halifax, and not married to you. Dr. Newbury set me on a new course and I couldn't be happier."

Lily laughed, shaking her head. "You always have seen the bright side of things."

CHAPTER 24

Kidnapping, 1927

Clara followed with a critical eye the local teams playing in the park near the hospital. Soon she was an avid follower of baseball games and was often at the sidelines, cheering the players on. It was after one of these games, when the players had departed, that she decided to see if there really were thirty strides, or ninety feet, between bases. Satisfied that the distance was correct, she headed to the outfield, imagining what it would be like to catch a fly ball. Two teenage boys wearing peak caps at a cocky angle had just thrown candy wrappers on the ground. She hustled over to them.

"We mustn't leave garbage in the park," she said, taking hold of one of them by his jacket and leading the culprit back to his mess.

"It's just paper," the boy said, trying to tug away from her grip. The janitor from the hospital was on the volunteer cleanup crew, and he approached the boys, handed them a pole with a nail on it and held out his sack. They picked up the papers, crumpled them, and pitched them in.

"You're bossy," one of the boys shot back as she walked toward the southwest corner of the park. Clara was about to give them a further talking-to when she noticed a short, stocky man leaning against a tree, pulling on a cigarette. She grimaced as he flicked its glowing butt into a nearby bush. *I'm not going to end my day in admonishments*, she thought. She walked well away from the man, once she was sure that the janitor would stomp out the cigarette, knowing the woods were dry.

Bob Glimp had just been released from an Alberta prison when Clara noticed him at the park. Angry and broke when he arrived back in Lethbridge, he was still hoping to find work. He discovered bitterly that no mine would hire him and an assault conviction in the United States made returning to West Virginia a bad option. His trial had been complicated. There had been clear testimony from the police officer who emerged from the bushes just as Bob uncoupled the cart that hit Ed. Lily had not been called to testify because she had not seen the cart racing toward them, nor who had uncoupled it.

The prosecution argued that the American miner had willfully committed an act that resulted in death. The defence argued that Ed Parsons, by stepping in front of the cart, had caused his own demise. A plea bargain in the end had put Bob away in a medium-security prison on the charge of aggravated assault causing death.

After many unsuccessful attempts to find work in the mines, he was told by one of the baseball players that Sam McKlintock needed a handyman. The following Sunday, Bob walked the two miles to Sam's farm, where he was offered twenty-five cents an hour to fix up the old barn at the back of the property. The bonus was the use of Sam's old car to fetch carpentry supplies.

There was, however, a condition attached to the job. Sam

was to make himself scarce on Sunday. "I don't need anyone leering at my baseball players," Sam said. "You're to skedaddle before the girls arrive."

Bob had first spotted Lily boating in Henderson Park with her lively family. Bitterness filled him as he thought that it had been Lily who had sent him to jail. *She had no business coming to a striking mine*, he thought. He knew Lily had borne a boy soon after the accident. A boy of about ten sat on the shore waving at the boaters and Bob assumed the young boy was Lily's son. *I'd like to take the smirk off that kid's face*, he thought. He had never forgotten Lily's haughtiness at the hospice.

Lily allowed Teddy to ride his horse in Henderson Park so long as he was with Ivy. Ivy had graduated to a bigger horse named Awesome, and Teddy had inherited Mystery. On a warm summer day, they saddled up their horses, leaving Lily, who was pregnant again, to enjoy the serenade of crickets and warm air. She leaned back in the well-cushioned wicker chair and rested her legs on a stool. Her daughter Jane was shrieking with glee as the babysitter pushed her high on the swing in the back garden.

Lily jumped up, angry that the clip-clop she heard coming down the street was more than a canter. The children had been told that they must walk their horses unless they were in the park. *I'll give those two a piece of my mind*, she thought. She hastened to the curb to scold the young riders. In an instant, her anger turned to fear. Ivy was galloping toward the house with Mystery tethered riderless behind her. Lily rushed out onto the street.

Ivy, breathless and shaking, dismounted and held the two horses. "We were just going into the park when a man stopped his car," she whimpered. "We … we thought he was asking for directions so Teddy jumped down and the man got out and pushed him into the back of the car. I didn't know what to do so

I galloped back here. I thought of riding after the car, but I got scared." She broke into sobs, unable to speak.

"It's not your fault, Ivy," Lily said hiding her fear. "Teddy's so accustomed to patients coming to the house he wouldn't suspect a thing." She hurried into the house to telephone Barnaby and the chief of police and did her best to soothe the distraught Ivy until they arrived.

"Tell me all you can remember, Ivy," Chief Gillespie said softly. "Every detail will help."

"I didn't hear what he asked Teddy. The man wasn't dressed very nicely," Ivy said shakily. "He didn't have a hat. He had scary eyes. The car made a loud bang when he drove off." Ivy began crying again.

"If you try any funny business, I'll tie you up where no one will find you," Bob said, as he drove the car into the south end of Sam's barn. "All I want from your parents is money. I went to prison on account of your ma, but I don't plan to go back to jail for murder."

Bob needed to think how to get a message to the Barnabys. If he wrote a note, it could possibly be traced back to him, and he knew his voice would give him away over the phone. Everyone in town would recognize his West Virginian accent. He realized he had to frighten the boy into co-operating, but not so much as to make him speechless.

Sam only used the farm on Sundays, so Bob had free access to the phone in the house during the week. He dragged Teddy into the farmhouse and warned him that he would have to do everything he was told. He asked the operator for Dr. James Barnaby's residence and thrust the phone at Teddy, who took it with a shaking hand and lifted it to his ear. "Hello, Mom."

Bob was close enough to faintly hear the voice at the other endof the line.

"Hello, Teddy. Are you alone, son?"

"No. The … the man wants five … five hundred dollars," Teddy stammered. "He wants fifty ten-dollar bills."

Bob grabbed the phone and hung up the receiver.

"Can I to go to the toilet?"

"Go use the john, and be quick about it. We'll let your parents stew for a bit."

As Teddy exited the bathroom, Bob held a gun to his shoulder. Tears streaked down the boy's face as Bob marched him back to the barn and forced him to climb a ladder to the hayloft.

Bob sliced two yards of thick braided cord that hung from an overhead beam. "Sit down with your back against that post," he barked. He bound Teddy's arms and torso to the post, and then checked that the binding was secure before scrambling back down the ladder.

He sat in the old car that was parked in the barn, figuring out how he would escape town with money in his pocket. He would have to pay his way across the border. The image of the rigid Galt Hospital matron popped into his mind. He had been hanging around the back of the hospital, hoping to see the probationers undress when she had suddenly appeared and chased him away with a broom.

Soon after this humiliation, he had been heading for a brothel when a pretty brunette rushed past. Not noticing her uniform in the dark, he offered her two dollars. The young nurse had scoffed at him. Now Bob snapped his fingers when the idea came into his head that the broom-toting matron should make the drop-off. He grinned, thinking it was his turn to scare her. *Serve her right*, he thought. He dozed off while contemplating his spiteful plan.

Night was closing in on Teddy as he sat on the dusty, hay-strewn floor, tied to the post. He listened to a chorus of frogs, a dog barking, and the man snoring below in the car. The moon cast shadows as it shone through a windowless opening and then disappeared. He wet himself, afraid to wake the man to untie him. He cried and then dozed off, focusing on his last image of his parents. Suddenly, the man was kicking him in the leg, saying they were going to make another call.

"It's four in the morning," the man said. "Time to alert your good-for-nothing parents where to drop the money."

Meanwhile, at the Barnabys', Chief Gillespie had explained his strategy as they awaited another call. His police officers were out searching, but he didn't hold out much hope that they could cover enough territory to find the boy, who could be any-where by now. Lily was trembling with fear, and Barnaby was grim, but as they waited for the call that didn't come, and the wait stretched into the night, they eventually both fell asleep. Bill Gillespie woke them to tell them he was going home for some sleep as well and they should call him as soon as they heard anything.

"If we make the kidnapping public, you can be sure his abductor will panic, and get rid of the boy who can identify him," the chief said.

Barnaby, normally high-coloured, looked ashen.

The telephone operator was unaware of the unfolding drama. When the call came, she assumed it was a patient of Dr. Barnaby's and, once the connection was made, dutifully tuned out.

Barnaby dived for the phone. "It's Teddy, Dad." The boy's voice came out in a barely audible gasp.

Barnaby swallowed hard.

278 · SHARON JOHNSTON

"Put the man on the phone, son," he said.

There were some muffled voices, and then Teddy came back on the line. "He says he won't talk to you."

Barnaby recalled a patient with a war-damaged vocal box, but didn't think he was capable of such a crime. It must be someone whose voice was recognizable, or who spoke with an accent. Lethbridge was filled with Chinese, Eastern Europeans, British, and Americans.

"Where do I leave the money?" Barnaby asked. The line went dead.

Late Saturday afternoon, the phone rang again. Barnaby cringed at the dry lassitude of his son's voice. There was none of the bravado that was the usual mark of his boy. After several background conversations, Teddy came back on the phone and repeated the kidnapper's directions.

"Mrs. Durling must wait for a taxi in front of the hospital tomorrow." There was a pause before Teddy continued. "One o'clock with fifty ten-dollar bills. She's to get in the front seat." His voice faded and the line went dead.

That evening, the phone rang again. This time, Barnaby interrupted Teddy. "Tell the man I'll do the drop." Barnaby strained to hear the muffled conversation.

"Mrs. Durling," Teddy said when he got back on the phone. "No one else. He has a gun."

"Where are you?" Barnaby shouted into the phone, but there was a sob and a click.

Two minutes later, the phone rang again. "Someone will call." Then silence.

Clara and Chief Gillespie were also at the house, waiting with the Barnabys for further instructions.

"There must be two people involved," Barnaby said.

"Clara, you can't do the drop-off."

"Oh, but I will, James. Tomorrow you will have your son. Nothing frightens me anymore, other than losing Ivy." Then she added, "*Your* son is *family*. I will do whatever I can to bring him back safely."

Chief Gillespie interjected. "The kidnapper was driving a car when he picked up Teddy. Tell him to drive his own car to meet Mrs. Durling at an open spot out of town. He can check that no one has followed, collect the cash, and let the boy out. This man is too mean and too clever to be trapped by a false drop-off. We must co-operate, Dr. Barnaby. It's our best chance of saving your son."

Suggesting this alternate plan when the next call came was met with Teddy's dry voice. "Mrs. Durling in the front seat of the taxi."

Saturday night was spent in morbid silence. Sergeant Stuart patrolled the streets with a posse of six, looking for anything untoward. Since the prostitutes were considered reliable informers, he stopped at the five brothels.

"Anything new?" he asked at the green house.

"No one's reported a crime," a girl said. "Can you tell me why you're asking?"

"Just making the rounds on a Saturday night."

The young woman hesitated but decided not to mention that Bob Glimp had been around a few days before. He had done his time. There was a code of conduct regarding tattling amongst the prostitutes. A client had to be a danger to the public before the girls reported him to the authorities.

Sunday morning, Bob woke with the rising sun. "Wake up, kid," he yelled. Teddy didn't budge. Bob untied the rope and yanked him up. "It's nothin' to me if you die of starvation." He pushed

Teddy into the house and told him to use the john and drink some water, giving him a jab toward the bathroom. Bob opened the icebox and pulled out some sausage.

"I need the energy more than you," he said, chomping on the meat.

The house was close to the barn, but the field where the women played ball was two hundred yards to the southeast of the farm buildings. Bob always left before the girls arrived, knowing Sam would check. But in the evening after the girls had departed, he would climb up into the hayloft to see the signs of Sam's escapades. He envied him, and he laughed thinking of how Sam's hayloft tumble would be foiled when he discovered the boy up there.

As they walked back to the barn, snot filled Teddy's nose. Bob shook his arm. "Ya ain't gonna breathe too well through my handkerchief if ya keep on blubbering."

Teddy climbed the ladder to the loft with the butt end of a gun pushing on his backside. Bob tied his arms and legs, dragging him to the exact spot where Sam had his flings. "Sam McKlintock is sure to find ya here," he said, smirking. "Ya'll put a kibosh on his antics." Teddy lay motionless, staring at the enormous barn beams overhead. His eyes had become a translucent blue-black.

Bob drank two big glasses of water, pissed off the back stoop, and left on foot for Lethbridge. If he could slip into the States unnoticed, he'd be free. He'd be well into Montana by the time Sam discovered the boy.

Bob trekked along the edge of the Oldman River until he found an unlocked fishing shack with tackle. He grabbed a rod and sat on the bank flicking out the occasional cast. Filled with nervous tension, he nodded curtly as fishermen, looking for a shady spot, sauntered past. At 11:30, he made his way up the southeast bank of the coulees to the flats and headed for a taxi stand.

While Bob was negotiating a cheaper price for longer mileage with a cab driver, Sam was watching the women play ball. They were wearing loose cotton pants with elastic at the ankle and sleeveless tops. It would be a toss-up between Hazel's big breasts or Maggie's red hair. Sam felt a slight stirring in his trousers thinking about the loft. Then Mable Cross slid so provocatively in to home plate that Sam changed his mind. At three o'clock, with the game still in play, Mable got the nod and smiled. All the girls were happy to be with Sam.

Just before 2:00 p.m, Clara stood at the front entrance of the hospital, as instructed, with a brown envelope in her large purse. She wore warm clothes and sensible shoes in case she was released far from the hospital. She felt comforted knowing that Alistair was watching from her office. When the taxi pulled up, she inhaled deeply, climbed into the front seat, taking a quick look at the man in the back. Her heart pounded. This was the man she had seen in the park. He leaned forward, gripping the back of the front seat and pointing the gun at the driver. As the taxi pulled away, the man began a rant about Lily Parsons. In that instant she realized this must be Bob Glimp, the man who had unleashed the coal cart. "Is the boy still alive?" she asked softly.

"Yeah. He's in Sam McKlintock's loft."

They were well beyond the city outskirts when Clara, still looking forward, said, "You've just come out of prison, Bob. I'm sure you're angry. But surely you don't want to go back. Why don't you take the car and let the driver and me walk back to town." The driver started to protest about losing his car, but she shot him such a stern look that he closed his mouth. She looked back at Bob. "You will end up having to kill us both," she said. "Then you'll spend the rest of your life in jail if you're caught. The police are looking for me." Her eyes bored into Bob. He cocked the gun with his right hand, pointing it at her and then at the driver.

For an instant Bob seemed to be weighing her proposal. Clara grabbed the steering wheel with both hands and turned it violently to the right, knocking the gun out of Bob's hand as he flew sideways. She took the hand-crank on the seat and brought it down hard on Bob's neck as he bent and tried to grab the gun. She continued to strike him until he slumped to the floor in the back. She leaned over the back seat and grabbed the gun. As she leapt from the car she saw that the driver had hit his head on the doorframe and was unconscious. She tossed the gun into some bushes but immediately realized this was folly. She would need it if Bob came to. She scrambled into the thicket to retrieve it, before peering at Bob, who remained sprawled on the floor.

"Things look bad," Bill Gillespie said as everyone assembled in Clara's office. "No one has called to report where we can find Teddy. The matron is in serious trouble if the kidnapper uses her as a hostage. I'll go down to the radio station and put out a plea to call with any information to Mrs. Durling's office. Someone out there must know something."

"But you told us going public would scare the kidnapper," Lily said.

"Things have changed," said the chief.

A nurse took Lily's arm. "Mrs. Barnaby, let the men do their work. Come with me and lie down. I'll keep you informed. Your son will need you when they find him."

At four o'clock a call came in to Clara's office. "Dr. Barnaby, please," the operator said. "I have a call for him."

Barnaby took the phone but heard only silence. After a few seconds a tentative voice identified herself as Ginger. "I'm the redhead who used to work at The Last Post. Now I'm at the blue house across the street. I think I know the person you're lookin' for. It's someone Sam hired to fix up his barn."

"You mean Sam McKlintock?" Barnaby asked, controlling his impatience for fear the girl would hang up.

"We don't like to finger folks unless they're a real nuisance, but I can't stand to think something might happen to Lily's son. We girls helped to raise him."

"*Please* tell me who you think is behind this kidnapping," Barnaby asked softly. "Every minute we stay on the phone, something terrible might happen."

"I think you should look for Bob Glimp," Ginger blurted out. "I was with him this week. He remembered I worked for Lily and said she was the reason he went to jail. I hope it isn't him, 'cause he just got free." There was a click and the operator came back on.

"Dr. Barnaby, I've put several calls through to you from Sam McKlintock's farm. I didn't listen in on any of your calls until I heard you speak on the radio. I'm sorry if you think I was being nosy."

"You and Ginger might have saved my son." Barnaby hung up and raced to Chief Gillespie's car.

Teddy, hearing someone approaching, felt a rush of scalding fear. He clenched his fists so he wouldn't cry. He was burning with the heat in the barn, and it was getting harder to breathe as the gag became saturated. He could hear a man and a woman's voice below him. It was Mable, who had slipped out of her cotton trousers and climbed the ladder to the loft with Sam coming up behind her. She screamed when she saw the boy and tried to

284 · SHARON JOHNSTON

descend the ladder, but Sam pushed her up all the way.

"Good God! It's Dr. Barnaby's son. What the hell is he doing here?" Sam quickly removed the gag, untied the boy, and helped him to his feet. Sam then started down the ladder first, straight into Chief Gillespie's upturned face. Behind Gillespie was James Barnaby.

"Sam McKlintock, you're under arrest."

Mable poked her head over the ladder. "Sam and me was just gonna have a little fun," she said. "Why's Sam under arrest? He ain't done nothin' wrong."

"Shut up, Mable," Sam said. "Bill, I don't know what's going on, but I found this boy here just now. I think this has something to do with Bob Glimp. He's been working for me. I hired him to repair my barn."

Teddy backed down the ladder straight into his father's arms.

"He's clever, that monster," Chief Gillespie said. "Glimp obviously knew that you would end up in the hayloft after the ball game. He knew you would call the police when you discovered the child. We have to figure out where he might flee. He is likely holding Mrs. Durling hostage."

Chief Gillespie poked his head into Sam's old car that was parked in the barn. "Look!" he said. "There's a map of Montana. That's probably where he's headed unless he left the map here to mislead us."

A constable who had just arrived offered to drive Barnaby and Teddy to the hospital so the boy could be cleaned up before he saw his mother. Lily had begun to bleed and was resting on the women's ward. Barnaby looked at his son's blank face and realized he had shell shock. He decided it would be best to put him on the Sunbeam Ward to be monitored. He would tell Lily that Teddy was in a deep sleep from exhaustion. For a moment Barnaby felt his family was falling apart. As a doctor, he was aware that Lily might lose the baby.

Clara dragged the taxi driver into the passenger seat. She tore a strip from her petticoat and bound Bob's hands and ankles so tightly it would cut off his circulation before too long. She went around to the front of the car and shoved the bloody crank into place, giving it a quick turn. When the engine sputtered to life, she whipped her hands out of the way; she had treated many crank injuries. She drove forward a few yards and braked, repeating this until she was able to steer without over-correcting, and then started back to Lethbridge. Smiling wanly, she recalled the time she'd stepped hard on the gas rather than the brake and had shot into the Oldman River with Alistair. If she got back alive with the culprit, he'd be proud of her. Her hands were almost numb from clutching the wheel.

Clara sped up as she approached the hospital. She came to a jerky stop at the main entrance, where a crowd of agitated people was milling about. She saw Alistair and Chief Gillespie standing to the side. Everyone rushed forward, jostling to see inside the cab. The new chief of staff, Dr. Bryan, ordered them back and called for two stretchers.

Clara handed the gun to Gillespie as she stepped out unsteadily. She explained to him in a few words what had happened before Alistair took her by the arm and led her a little way from the car.

"I thought I'd lost you," he said. "Teddy is safe. You can relax now. Chief Gillespie will look after the rest."

A nurse poked her head in the car and let out an audible gasp. "Is he dead?"

"He'll wish he was," Chief Gillespie said. "Kidnapping a child will put him away for life. You certainly knocked him out," he added with an astonished grin.

Alistair accompanied her to her apartment, explaining, on the way, the dreadful state in which Teddy had been found and that the child was now in the Sunshine Ward.

Clara changed quickly then hurried directly to the ward, where Teddy lay mute, his blue-black eyes staring at his parents.

Barnaby stood looking at his motionless son. "Not unlike shell shock," he said. "I suppose it's my fault for teaching him to trust strangers."

CHAPTER 25

Lethbridge Politics, 1927

The abduction of a child in broad daylight struck fear into the hearts of Lethbridge families. Lily had miscarried with the extreme stress and those that knew her took this to heart. The Barnabys were flooded with casseroles and offers of help, but there was a sense that their family had been dealt too many blows. For a short time the city as a whole turned its attention from nasty politics to public safety. But soon the residents' festering discontent with municipal affairs reared its head again, and Alistair was preparing for a fight. He had barely won the previous mayoral election against his leading opponent, Dr. Loring.

Clara showed her partisanship openly during the election campaign. She was criticized in an editorial in the *Lethbridge Herald* for showing favouritism. Called before the hospital board, she argued until 2:00 a.m. that she had not given the plum job of answering her phone to a nurse because she had promised to vote for Mayor Harwood. Dr. Bryan, the chief physician, supported her, insisting that she campaigned on her own time and not in the hospital, Clara also refused to be daunted by Dr. Loring, who stated on a radio broadcast that he would fire the present lady superintendent of the Galt as soon as he was elected mayor and *ex-officio* chairman of the hospital.

Two weeks after her public scolding, Clara sat eating her usual breakfast of egg and toast. As Yip bowed his way out of the apartment, Alistair came crashing in. He flung the *Herald* on the table. Her cup of tea sloshed onto the newspaper.

"And good morning to you, Alistair. Would you like some tea?" She passed Alistair her cup and he took a sip. He opened the newspaper to the editorial section and plunked it down again in front of her.

"Read this nonsense," he said.

She put on her eyeglasses and motioned for him to sit. He thrust himself into a chair.

The editorial supported council's decision to hold a plebiscite on the form of municipal government. The councillors believed the current system of three commissioners put ultimate authority into too few hands, with the mayor and two other commissioners controlling everything from finance to public works.

"Maybe a city manager might be more democratic," said Clara. "Rightly or wrongly, Alistair, people are worried you have too much power and not enough checks. It may seem unfair to attack you this way, but you need to allow for different points of view. I think you should go back and read Kipling's poem: 'If you can trust yourself when all men doubt you, but make allowance for their doubting too' ... Neither of us suffers fools gladly. But people don't have to agree. I'm sure they'll come to their senses in the polling booth and vote for you."

"My own integrity is all the check and balance necessary," Alistair replied. "Seven aldermen selecting the mayor from amongst them will be less accountable than three full-time commissioners. And the appointment of a city manager will no doubt be rife with cronyism."

"Dr. Loring thinks I'm *your* crony, Alistair. Maybe he hates you for giving me such power in the hospital." Clara refilled her teacup, put marmalade on a piece of toast, and passed it to Alistair. "Eat this while I get dressed."

Clara winced at her tired-looking countenance in the bathroom mirror. She thought of the second Christmas party she had thrown in the ballroom of the Lethbridge Hotel. The hospital was too small for her extensive guest list. The society column "Milady" had called it the social event of the season. No one had found it strange that in spite of their fifteen-year age gap, she and Alistair had danced like long-acquainted partners. When she decided they'd danced enough, she'd suggested to Alistair that he dance with one or two of the wallflowers and abruptly walked off the dance floor. The day after the party, an auxiliary lady laughed and confessed that guests thought she'd had an argument with the mayor. "We couldn't believe it, because no one ever stands up to Mayor Harwood!"

Clara decided she needed a break from the political machinations of the hospital. The following Friday she left with the Barnabys for a weekend at Waterton Park. They had invited Sergeant Stuart to make up a fourth so that they could play bridge. He was to replace Alistair, who, fearing a conspiracy to oust him, had refused to budge. Sergeant Stuart had helped Teddy recover from the shock of his abduction, taking him out for regular riding lessons; this weekend away was Barnaby's grateful acknowledgement.

As Sergeant Stuart settled in the room beside her, Clara recalled the intense longing she had felt knocking on Alistair's door on the steamship *Assiniboia*. She wished he could have

290 · SHARON JOHNSTON

been with her this weekend at the hotel. But he was right; there could be prying eyes at this popular vacation spot.

The weekend of bridge games and hiking in the mountains restored Clara's equilibrium, yet she questioned her own common sense. She had spent the entire three days wishing Alistair were with her, despite the presence of an eligible bachelor. Sergeant Stuart was a shy man, but she knew his eye had been cast on her since his hospitalization. Once he was discharged, there would have been no impropriety in seeing him, but from the moment Alistair Harwood had blustered into the Montreal immigration office Clara had felt an attraction she had not felt even with George.

Returning from her short vacation cheerful and longing to see the mayor, Clara arranged a dinner for them in her apartment. *I'm like a hand in his glove*, she thought as she marched along the corridor to meet Alistair. She decided the next time she vacationed at Waterton Park it would be with him. *I don't have to worry; I'm secure in my job.* She smiled broadly the moment she saw him coming toward her.

"How was your weekend?" Alistair asked when they were back in her apartment. "Did you get in plenty of bridge?"

"I did, and a fair bit of hiking. But I suppose you've noticed I've gained weight."

Alistair leaned toward her and whispered, "How can I tell with your clothes on?"

Her moss-green eyes softened as she scanned his large frame. *He's in such political hot water*, she thought, pushing the idea of dragging him away with her to the back of her mind.

"Just leave the dishes on the sideboard," she said to a nervous-looking first-year probationer as they sat to eat. "We'll serve ourselves."

"Would you like me to put up the Do Not Disturb sign?"

"Please do. And come back in an hour with some coffee. I won't need you until then." The girl smiled and let out an audible sigh of relief.

"You scare the living daylights out of these girls," Alistair said, taking her hand and shaking it playfully.

"Go on with you. They're afraid of Mayor Harwood." They laughed, pointing an accusatory finger at each other. Clara sighed. "Alistair, I need to talk to you about Henry Dobson's proposal to expand the existing hospital."

Alistair laughed. "Since Dobson has become the chairman of the Lethbridge Advancement Committee, he seems intent on showing off his newly acquired wealth on the stock market."

"That is not a very English attitude, is it?" Clara retorted, frowning in disapproval. "In my opinion, the economic boom will bust before construction is completed. Henry has accused me of being obstructionist. When I met with the committee, he suggested my fiscal prudence fit poorly with burgeoning philanthropy in Lethbridge. I had proposed modifying the present building rather than starting a costly building project with so little advance capital."

"I won't have much to say in the matter if Robert Burrows replaces me as mayor," Alistair said. "He certainly will have a better chance than Loring."

"My Lord!" she said, letting out an exasperated huff. "First, Dr. Loring gives me a headache and now it's Robert Burrows. His complaint that I purchase from friends is absurd since I have never favoured *any* business. From food to maintenance, purchases have always been made based on the quality and price offered to the hospital. I wouldn't give his grumbling a second thought except that he's a great friend of Loring. I believe he goes to their spiritual séances on Friday evenings."

"God help Lethbridge if I'm replaced by the owner of a paint shop."

"Alistair, Robert Burrows is a respected businessman."

"And I'm not?"

"Please don't get yourself exercised over Robert Burrows, or your ulcer will become cancerous. No one is suggesting you're not a great mayor." Her voice had a forced cheerfulness.

For five weeks, calm reigned in Lethbridge. But then Alistair, fed up with public criticism, wrote a four-column opinion piece in the *Herald* to defend his record, and by extension, the commissioner form of government. He commented on the failure of the managerial system in other cities. "Neither English Westmount, nor French Outremont in Montreal succeeded as managerial forms of government," he wrote. "I am perfectly conscious of my ability, both from an innate knowledge of my own brainpower when stacked against the other person's. I have been maligned and abused to such a degree that I am tired of sitting still and taking abuse from those who are not my equals."

He's finished, Clara thought when she read the article. *Voters will not forget such bombast and arrogance. The editor of the* Herald *must hate him*, she surmised bitterly. *Alistair has been an excellent mayor, and the newspaper's editor would have known that Alistair's diatribe was out of character.* She realized with a cold clarity that her demise would not be far behind; she had so publicly declared herself in favour of Alistair that she was tarred by the same brush.

Clara begged Alistair to retract his statement and apologize. But his exhaustion altered his normally good judgment in political matters. The next day, she marched into the office of Amos Rostock, the *Herald*'s publisher, and scolded him for letting down a friend. "You should have told your editor not to publish the mayor's statement. Haven't you known him since childhood?"

"All's fair in love and journalism," Rostock retorted matter-of-factly. "Politics is not for the faint of heart. You and the mayor have been both highly praised and roundly criticized in my newspaper. We publish the truth as we see it, not as you want it to be told."

"I understand that, but Alistair Harwood's words were born of exhaustion."

Rostock came around from behind his desk and put his hand on her shoulder. "Mrs. Durling, you are much more of a wife to him than Jessie Harwood. Help the mayor to give up the reins. We *are* heading for a managerial system of government."

At the end of 1927, a plebiscite roundly rejected Alistair Harwood's position. It ended with an eighty percent majority in favour of a managerial system to replace the commissioners. Alistair was humiliated and hurt by the outcome of the vote, but he was not bowed; he immediately used his connections in the provincial parliament, while he was still the mayor, to lobby for a return to the commissioner system.

Clara watched the political machinations as though she had moved to a new community. She could see the hospital board preparing for the end of the Harwood era. She felt deep relief when the *Herald* congratulated the hospital on its excellent performance; the second time the newspaper had publicly acknowledged her sound management. She felt a surge of pride as she read: "The Galt Hospital now has a first-class nursing school and accreditation by the American College of Surgeons, thanks to the lady superintendent's strong leadership."

Impulsively, she hatched a plan.

CHAPTER 26

Waterton Park, Alberta, 1928

Clara sat in her apartment reflecting on her relationship with Alistair. They both needed to get away from the machinations around them, but Alistair was reluctant to escape, fearing the malevolent political forces would take hold. Jessie Harwood was no longer an obstacle to having an affair. Wasting away in the hospital, she had told Clara that she could not make her husband happy and thanked Clara for bringing him joy. Her words: "He deserves what I can't provide," seemingly inviting Clara to have an affair. But Clara wasn't fooled. She was beginning to understand Mrs. Harwood's psychology. She liked to be in control. Even of her husband's sex life. *She controls every morsel of food that goes in her mouth so why not my happiness?* Clara thought as she sat contemplating going away for the weekend with Alistair. *This is my choice, not Jessie Harwood's.* Ivy was now a popular sixteen-year-old and Clara felt secure in her job. The *Lethbridge Herald's* article on the Galt Hospital had buoyed her confidence.

Comfortable that spending the weekend with Alistair would

do no harm to either of them, Clara proposed they take up John Iverson's offer to use his father-in-law's cabin at Waterton Park before it was advertised for rent. Clara pointed out the amusing paradox that it was now she who was suggesting they share a cabin. With suitcases packed with hiking clothes, libation, and books, they set off in Alistair's car for their short holiday.

John Iverson had instructed Waterton Park's elderly caretaker to light the fire and stock the fridge with basics for Mr. and Mrs. Harwood. As Alistair and Clara stepped into the cottage, they were enveloped in the mix of mustiness and burning wood. Green wicker furniture with well-worn chintz cushions and a studio chesterfield that could be made into a bed faced the puddingstone fireplace. A wood box was filled with kindling and split logs. Alistair pulled back the fire screen and threw on some kindling and then a log, poking at the embers until flames appeared. Alistair brushed his hand along the fireplace. "These colourful stones come from a small island close to Sault Ste Marie. We would have passed it when we were on the *Assiniboia*."

"This is heaven," Clara said softly. "Let's check out the rest of the cabin."

A white enamel table, slightly chipped, and painted chairs with caned seats took up most of the space in the kitchen. Alistair lifted the rusty handle of a pump at the side of the sink. "Not bad," he said, as he leaned over to gulp some water. "Only a mild taste of iron." They stepped onto the back porch where a wooden icebox stood. Opening it, they were pleased the old man had indeed put in all the food essentials.

"Would you like to go for a walk?" Alistair asked. He came up behind her and encircled her shoulders with his arms.

"I'd love that. Let me change into my walking shoes first,"

Clara said, retrieving her suitcase. As she pulled back the curtain screening the bedroom from the rest of the interior, she felt a wave of shyness. A small window above the iron bed was open, and worn lace curtains fluttered in the breeze. She picked up a clump of chinking that had fallen on the bed and sniffed a piece of brown wool that clung to the cement.

"Creosote," Alistair said as he stood watching her. "It prevents mice getting in." She looked doubtful as she sat in a chair lacing up her shoes.

She took Alistair's hand, and as they walked through the woods, talking about past vacations — she admitting she'd had very few — they saw a boy and girl filling a pail with spring water as it gushed down the length of a hollowed log. They approached the pair.

"What do you do with that water?" Alistair asked.

"We're fetching it for our grandpa," the girl said. They peered suspiciously at the grit floating in the pail. "The dirt settles after a while and the water is clear as can be. Our grandpa doesn't like the water from the well." Alistair took the ladle offered and dipped it into the pail.

"Oh, that *is* good." He filled the ladle and handed it to Clara.

She picked out a small stick and laughed. "You can stir your drink with this."

"Someone had our cabin all warm and cozy," Alistair said. "Was that your grandpa?"

The children smiled and nodded. "He's the caretaker."

The two scooted off, lugging the pail along a narrow path strewn with exposed tree roots.

Alistair and Clara walked past the line of cabins on the edge of the lake. Cattails and wetland grasses surrounded the shoreline. Alistair stopped abruptly and pointed into the reeds, putting his finger to his lips. "A bull moose," he whispered. "We won't be welcome if there's a female around. It's rutting season. We should back away before he sees us. Happily, we're downwind so he won't pick up our scent." Slowly they made their way back to the cabin, both nervously eyeing the surrounding forest.

"I'm going to go back and fetch some of that spring water," Alistair said when they returned to the cabin.

"The moose will still be in the woods, Alistair. I think going out just as it's getting dark is a silly idea."

"Well water will ruin the Scotch." You're the one who scolds me if I take it neat. I won't go farther than the spring." Alistair grabbed a metal can from the back porch, kissed Clara, and headed back into the forest.

Wildlife had both fascinated and scared Clara since her arrival in Canada. She stood on the back stoop anxiously waiting for Alistair to return. She had no idea how to interpret his pleased look as he backed out of the woods and stepped up on the porch clutching the jug.

"I encountered a bear just as I filled the container, but I just backed away, keeping my eye on her — ready to throw the can if she charged me. I suspect she was seeking a place to hibernate and I didn't look as though I would be much help." Alistair laughed.

"Alistair Harwood, you're crazy." Relieved, Clara opened the bottle of Scotch and poured him a drink with the spring water, careful not to stir up the debris. "I'd love some of that water with a splash of Scotch."

Alistair threw a fresh log on the fire and plopped down beside her on the creaky sofa.

"Mrs. Durling," he said, "I wish you were Mrs. Harwood."

"I'll get cold feet if you say things like that. I don't need any reminder that I'm not Mrs. Harwood. Clara thought of the Hippocratic oath *to do no harm*. And yet she had, over the past six years, personally looked after Jessie Harwood. Once a month she had been admitted by Morris to regulate her diet. And the only person she listened to was Clara. *She inserted herself into our relationship in the hospital but I mustn't let her do that here,* Clara thought. *Who knows if we'll ever have a second chance to be completely alone?*

"A penny?" Alistair said, sensing Clara's mixed emotions. He kissed her softly on the mouth, slipping off his shoes and pulling her closer. The rusty springs squeaked and they both laughed.

In the middle of the night, Clara pulled herself away from Alistair and sat bolt upright. The room was lit by a full moon.

"What's wrong?" he asked.

"I hear something."

She put on her dressing gown and crept into the living room and peered outside. The edge of the woods was completely illuminated. A moose was rubbing and banging his antlers on a tree, grunting and tossing his head. Beside the tree stood a female. The moose rose up on his hind legs and mounted her. Clara watched spellbound at the rawness of nature.

The next morning, Alistair suggested hiking on a marked trail. He knew she was nervous about what could be encountered in the bush. "I was lucky yesterday," he said. "When I surprised that bear, her cub was behind her; I was able to just back away and leave them to scrounge for Saskatoon berries — a last gorge before hibernation. When we're out walking, we should clap or talk loudly to alert any animals. All they want, poor souls, is a warning so they can wander off and ignore us."

I don't feel as confident as you," Clara said as she produced a cowbell from the mantelpiece. She shook it. "Is that loud enough?"

Alistair tossed the bell on the couch and grabbed her. "Da, da, da, da, da," he hummed. She quickly recognized the samba and moved forward and back to the beat.

"I spent six months in Brazil with a mining project when I worked as an engineer," he said, sidestepping deftly to miss the couch. "I wish you had moved here twenty years ago when our third floor was renovated as a dancing room. Back then, people flocked to our house."

She pulled away and set her eyes softly on him. "Let's not talk about home, Alistair." She grabbed the bell and they set out for their walk. "Let's just enjoy this weekend," she said as she put her arm through his. "This happiness cannot last."

CHAPTER 27

Joy and Sorrow, 1929

In July, seven elected aldermen chose Robert Burrows as mayor. He thus replaced Alistair as chairman of the board. Clara was frustrated by Alistair's despondence. "I'm a teller of fortunes and yet couldn't predict mine," he said morosely. "So many of my predictions have turned out to be correct. How strange that I didn't foretell that I was hated."

"Alistair, you're being self-indulgent. No one hates you. Lethbridge chose a different form of government. They weren't voting against you."

Robert Burrows as chairman rescinded virtually all the rights Alistair had established for the lady superintendent. Clara was no longer welcome at board meetings, her responsibility for purchasing was taken away, and finally he refused to pay for her travel expenses. She felt wounded. She knew she was on the wrong side of politics but resented that it was affecting the hospital. What were all these people going to do if the economy collapsed? Certainly not build a new hospital.

In the months that followed, she looked discreetly for other positions, even in other cities, but nothing matched her present situation.

Finally, in August of 1929, she decided to leave for England on an extended holiday with Ivy and the Barnaby family. Lily had invited her mother to join them, meet her younger sister, and thus reunite with her family, but Amelia had declined. Lily didn't press the matter. In many ways, Clara had fulfilled Lily's emotional need of belonging. She often threw her arms around Clara, thanking her for breaking the silence and for being her family. Barnaby planned a short jaunt to Scotland to see old friends while there. Clara had invited Alistair, but he was still too embroiled in politics and his own business affairs.

The crossing took five days. On the third day on the ocean, Barnaby received a wire from his stockbroker. The message contained just three words: "Sell, sell, sell." Clara had the same broker, and although she had only a modest amount invested, she followed suit.

Lily made a last-minute inspection of her two children before disembarking at Southampton. "We must make a good impression," she said, adjusting Teddy's tie and rearranging Jane's mop of blond hair. Then she turned her eye to Ivy.

"You're better at that than I am," Clara said. She felt a swell of pride that she could introduce Lily, until now the unknown niece. She accepted that Amelia had no interest in resurrecting her past; she was settled and happy. But Clara wanted Lily to meet her grandfather, William, who was now a widower with crippling arthritis. Mr. Ives had moved in with Clara's sister Addy and her husband Miff after his wife died.

As the ship manoeuvred into the Southampton Port, Addy and her family could be seen waiting for them on the quay. Clara broke into a broad smile when she saw Di Shaw beside them.

Introductions and handshakes over, Miff hustled the visitors and their luggage to the train station. Once settled in the compartment, Clara answered a barrage of questions. It didn't surprise her that Miff was anxious for news about Francis Newbury.

"He has stepped down as head of the department of surgery, but still seeing patients," Barnaby interjected. Seeing Miff's surprised look, he explained his longtime relationship with the doctor.

When asked about the hospital, Clara admitted that her position was precarious.

"You've always known how to strike a new path," Addy said, admiringly. "You can do it again if need be."

"My wife's cut from the same cloth," Barnaby said. Lily shot him a cross glance, at his allusion to her managing a brothel to make ends meet. Then she settled back in the carriage content that two families, separated by an ocean, were getting on so well.

When the group arrived at Addy and Miff's house, Pickwick Place, the gardener was waiting on the street, ready to carry the visitors' luggage. The man placed the bags in the rooms and everyone congregated in the living room where they were introduced to Lily's grandfather. He was an elderly man, hard of hearing, but he possessed an engaging smile and had a twinkle in his eye. Lily crouched down so he could hear what she was saying. Her children politely shook his arthritic hand and then scooted off.

To Lily, Mr. Ives didn't seem like her grandfather, but just an elderly stranger. Nevertheless, she related to him her mother's happiness in Canada, imagining he cared. He acknowledged his heartless decision to send Amelia away, but thanked God that she had married a kind man with a good livelihood.

To welcome her visitors, Addy had arranged a typical British dinner of roast beef and Yorkshire pudding with treacle tart for dessert. She wanted the children to sit at the table with the adults. Addy had not inherited her mother's fertility and as the years had passed with no news of a child, Clara had thought many times about how happy her sister would have been with Florence. *But timing is never perfect*, she thought.

In the evening, the conversation turned to horses so it could include Teddy and Ivy.

"Aside from horses, what's so special about western Canadians?" Miff asked.

"People from the West don't care if they're seated below the salt, and they don't call red wine claret," Clara said, grinning.

"Touché," Di said.

Clara took the train into London for a few days to visit friends and show off Ivy. She also popped into St. George's Hospital, having learned that a former classmate was the new matron and wishing to congratulate her. Memories of late nights, tough exams, and grateful patients flooded back. She was pleased to be able to wander the hospital and to see the modernization of the old wards.

Another day, while Di took Ivy shopping, Lily and Barnaby visited George and Billy's grave with Clara. On the drive to the cemetery, Clara felt as though her present and past were finally coming together. The vicar at St. Katherine's Church met the Canadian visitors at the south door. As the three scanned the memorial plaque that listed the parishioners who had died in service of their country, including George Durling, the elderly vicar stood at the back of the church, ready to accompany them to the grave.

"A prayer?" he asked at the graveside. Everyone bowed their heads.

"May George, who died for peace and freedom, live forever in our hearts. May Billy, whose young life was taken, remind us that our lives are on loan."

Clara suppressed the thought that God still hadn't given her a sign as to the meaning of her loss. Feeling her spiritual doubt, she made the sign of the cross and prayed silently that she would not face more misery when she returned to the Galt.

A telegram awaited Clara when she returned from a visit to Knockholt. She retreated to her room to read the news that she hoped would be positive. Alistair had been experiencing stomach pains before she'd left for England but had stubbornly refused to be admitted to hospital.

> *Dearest Clara,*
> *Jessie died at home last evening of an overdose of tinc-*
> *ture. Morris reported her death as a heart attack. We*
> *must have no regrets. For almost ten years, with one*
> *exception, I have been faithful, due to your strong will.*
> *I anxiously await your return. I love you.*
>
> *Alistair*

Clara fell down on the bed and wept. Di had come back from shopping and came up to her room.

"Do you want to talk about it?" she asked as she entered. She sat on the bed and put her arm around her longtime friend.

"Di, why has my life been so complicated?"

"What's in the telegram?" Di asked.

"Alistair's wife took her own life." Clara sighed. "My happiness has come at the expense of Jessie Harwood's."

"I'm surrounded by unhappy marriages," Di said, "but most couples prefer an affair to a divorce. It's not unusual." Di began laughing. "Tomorrow we'll take the train to London again and do *your* shopping. A little fancy nightwear is in order."

"Whatever I buy will have to cover this unshapely figure of mine."

"Since I've known you, stress has made you eat. Now happiness will slim you down." They laughed together as they had so often done at St. George's.

Clara spent the next ten days visiting old friends with Ivy while the Barnabys spent time in Scotland. Receiving a wire from the Galt that Alistair had been admitted to hospital, she wired back that as former chairman he should receive the best possible care. *All the stress of the past few months has probably activated that nasty ulcer,* she thought.

Soon after the Barnabys returned from Scotland, the two families said their tearful goodbyes and embarked on the ship for the crossing back to Montreal.

As Clara stood on the foredeck one evening, watching the rolling ocean crash into the bow, she recalled so vividly her chilly evening chats with Annabel and cried a little.

When Barnaby spotted her, he stopped. "What are you looking so pensive about?"

"I was thinking of Annabel and Jessie Harwood."

"Suicide is complicated, Clara. What I've observed over the years, treating patients for emotional problems, is that some threaten and never do it, and others never say a word and then suddenly they're dead! Jessie Harwood stood between these two extremes. Starvation is not the usual way to threaten *or* commit suicide. I imagine the extreme disturbance to her metabolism contributed to her death as much as the laudanum. You didn't contribute to her death. Believe me Clara."

Barnaby's words helped Clara put Jessie Harwood, Dr. Loring, and Robert Burrows out of her mind for the remainder of the voyage. She drew up a low-acid diet for

Alistair and planned a vacation for them to Vancouver. She felt breathless thinking about her plans.

As soon as they'd cleared customs in Montreal and were settled into the Windsor Hotel, she rushed to put through a call to the Galt Hospital. Helen Hope answered the office phone. She had fallen ill as a first-year probationer and couldn't write her exams. Clara had personally tutored her during the summer, and by her third year, she was at the top of her class. It was she who had been given the coveted responsibility of answering the lady superintendent's telephone.

"How is the mayor?" Clara asked. "Did you receive my wire?"

"Mrs. Durling ..."

There was a catch in Helen's voice that made her grip the phone. Helen had often witnessed the mayor arriving morose and leaving happy from the matron's apartment.

"Mayor Harwood died at eight o'clock this morning. I'm so very, very sorry."

Clara could not speak. She hung up, but asked Barnaby, who was waiting there with her, to call the hospital back and find out the details. He came away from the phone and put his arms around her. "They found Alistair in your apartment. Miss Hope said he had a major bleed of a stomach ulcer, probably causing his heart to go into arrhythmia. He died of a stroke. They found him lying on your sofa in his pajamas."

"His oasis," she uttered softly.

"Do you want me to delay the funeral until we're back?" Barnaby asked.

"That wouldn't be appropriate," she said. Sorrow spread from her stomach to every part of her body. "We started and ended in Montreal," she whispered.

CHAPTER 28

Hospital Politics, 1929

Clara eased herself into mourning Alistair's death. The first night back in her apartment, she lay on the sofa looking up at the ceiling with her head on the seat cushion where he had habitually made himself comfortable, nursing his drink. Her heart beat so fast she thought she might have a heart attack; and pain, which she had no words to describe, snaked through her entire body. No matter how much she tightened up and relaxed, she could not rid herself of the ache left by his sudden passing. Around midnight, the dreadful image of him staggering in his pajamas toward her apartment, shouting at the nurses to go away, faded from her mind. She was back at Waterton Park with Alistair, sipping spring water mixed with Scotch, watching a crackling fire. He put down her drink and pulled her up from the studio couch. Cold night air filled the room as they snuggled under the mass of covers. An owl hooted. Clara laughed. "We're both aging," she said at one point. They had made love and slept until she crept out to see the rutting moose.

The next morning, she awoke and slid her hand across the

sofa, looking for Alistair. Yip came into the apartment holding a breakfast tray.

She stood up. "I'm exhausted from travelling," she said as she smoothed her dress.

"Mrs. Durling, I know you sad you see Mayor Harwood no more. He so happy in your apartment that he come die here."

After Yip left, Clara pushed her breakfast aside, took a hot bath, and put on her uniform. She took a few minutes in her office with the door closed to gain her composure before beginning a new day.

As she made her rounds she realized she was now sailing uncharted waters with Robert Burrows in charge. The new mayor was well aligned with Dr. Loring, and she could still feel the challenge to her authority upon her return.

The first incident occurred when she cancelled a requisition to paint the men's ward. The contract had been given to Mayor Burrows's commercial sign company without competing bids. Burrows sent her a note reminding her that she no longer purchased for the hospital. When she ordered storm windows to replace those rotted on the south side of the hospital, she discovered they had already been ordered, and she was reminded again that purchasing was no longer her responsibility. When she wrongly accused the local legion of taking away a hospital refrigerator, she was forced to submit an apology to the newspaper.

"I'm being fed misinformation to make me look incompetent," she said to Morris when he visited her office.

"The politics will blow over in time," he said.

"I'm not so sure. Over the past two weeks a board member has toured the hospital several times. Yesterday, Robert Burrows stood talking with several members of the board in the foyer. When I walked out of my office, they became silent. It was obvious the conversation had been about me."

"The board is made up of well-heeled men," Morris said. "They're nervous their world is about to come crashing down."

A week after her conversation with Morris, Dr. Newbury arrived in Lethbridge. Now seventy-four years old, he came into her office, looking frail. "I've come to deliver my research papers to James Barnaby," he boomed, the strength of his voice surprising her. "He's been like a son to me. I'm so glad you two are related. I'm meeting with the hospital board tomorrow. James said they're harassing you. Tell me what's been happening."

She explained her protracted difficulties with Dr. Loring and more recently her diminishing responsibilities now that Robert Burrows chaired the board.

"Barnaby told me that the atmosphere at the Galt is poisonous." Dr. Newbury shook his head sadly.

Dr. Newbury stayed with the Barnabys and Clara joined them for dinner that evening. As expected, Dr. Newbury filled the house with laughter, telling stories about his days at the Maidenhead Hospital. The next day Lily drove her husband and Dr. Newbury to Mayor Burrows's office where the meeting was to be held. "I'm going to give them hell," he said to Barnaby as they got out of the car. Barnaby, who later recounted the doctor's words, said that he did just that.

Dr. Newbury reminded the board that he had recommended Mrs. Durling for the position of lady superintendent because she had the character that the other superintendents had lacked, and that from all accounts she had done an excellent job. Dr. Newbury countered the argument that the matron lacked tact by suggesting he did too. "But it never stopped me from being an excellent surgeon," he said. His parting words were, "Gentlemen, we're heading for a crash. This is no time to build a new hospital." He suspected Clara's prudent objections had been the reason why Mayor Burrows had stripped her of authority. "I've known Mrs. Durling both professionally and socially for well over a decade. Stop harassing her, and let her get on with her work. If you have a complaint, deal with her directly, not behind her back."

After the meeting, Dr. Newbury and Barnaby came to Clara's office. She ordered tea and they chatted about the economic uncertainty that was making everyone nervous. When it was time to order a taxi to take the doctor to the train station, Dr. Newbury put a hand on Clara's shoulder. He looked tired, as though being in the Galt where he'd started as a young surgeon was reminding him of the passage of time.

"You and I are very much alike," he said to her. "We should both be more diplomatic. I've retired and nobody cares any longer. But *you* can be hurt. Be careful. These are challenging times. I'm not sure the board members, preoccupied with their own worries, won't just ignore an old man's rant."

Dr. Newbury waved in salute as the taxi pulled away. Clara wondered if a single member of the board understood that a great man had just spoken to them.

The board members who had publicly opposed Clara continued to roam the hospital like a mob seeking someone to lynch. Dr. Newbury's visit had heightened her sense of isolation. *He's right*, she thought. *They just ignored him.*

Clara had a feeling that she would not see her loyal advocate again. The people who had believed in her competence and appreciated her efforts were largely gone. Over the years, Dr. Newbury had kept in touch with Barnaby, and Mrs. Newbury had extended annual invitations to Clara to spend Christmas with her boisterous family of four married sons and their wives and a granddaughter Ivy's age. Clara had always refused, saying that at Christmas her place was at the hospital. The prostitutes were no longer allowed in the kitchen, so Lily arrived that Christmas morning at the hospital with what she called bordello cakes, made by the brothel ladies in their own modest ovens. Patients gobbled them up, asking for the name of the bakery.

By the summer of 1930, the effects of the Depression had wormed their way into the hospital. Two nurses left for better-paying jobs in the mine offices. And one probationer, one month into her first year, left to work on the family farm because her parents, two brothers, and her sister were all without employment.

Having lived through rationing during wartime, Clara became a master of invention with this return to austerity. She called the hospital's kitchen staff into her office. "We need to reorganize the way we serve food," she said. "We have to avoid waste, but at the same time we must never forget that a patient's diet is essential to the healing process." Yip, whose greatest joy was pleasing the patients, nodded in agreement. "So much food is left on plates that we cannot reuse," she continued. "We will begin serving meals on smaller dishes and let patients ask for second helpings once they've cleaned their plates." The kitchen staff smiled. They had heard the matron use the same expression with Ivy, who was a picky eater. A trolley with plated meals, followed by a second one with food in serving dishes, soon began rolling onto the wards. The most frequent request was for more mashed potatoes.

Years earlier, hoping to understand Jessie Harwood, Clara had ordered a copy of Dr. Lulu Hunt-Peters's book on calories. As she flipped through the pages now, looking for ways to boost calories, she was suddenly overcome with the memory of Alistair. She took in a deep breath and let it out slowly, trying to ride out the pain. Pain that she had neither fully succumbed to his advances, nor entirely pushed him away.

Economies were introduced throughout the hospital. To save on laundry costs, top sheets became bottom sheets before going to be washed. Previously, the entire bed had been stripped daily. Clara was asked by the board to justify this and every other change in practices. She would write a report for the board members, and they would send it back saying it was inadequate. Their ultimate insult was to send her the lady superintendent's reports from the Medicine Hat Hospital, advising her to follow the woman's example. Clara found comfort in food. She hadn't thought her weight gain was noticeable until she had to order new uniforms.

She escaped as often as possible to the home of the Iversons, or the Barnabys, where she immersed herself in bridge games. Ivy was content to spend time at either place. She and Katherine Iverson fought, made up, and argued again. But Teddy looked up to Ivy and she basked in his admiration. Jane, who was an uppity eight-year-old, didn't show the same respect. She had a contrary opinion on everything.

CHAPTER 29

Lethbridge, Alberta, 1930

When a wire arrived informing Clara of Dr. Newbury's death, she closed the door of her office and wept. He had been out for a walk when he'd collapsed from a massive heart attack. He was slight enough for a passerby to carry him to the nearby hospital. Through shock and tears, his son, also a doctor, acknowledged that his father had died as he wanted: suddenly and without pain. Francis Newbury was to be buried with full military honours, and Clara made the necessary arrangements to go to his funeral.

As her train sped north to Edmonton, she looked at the flat passing landscape and longed for her Kentish hills. The trip to England had made her realize how much she missed her homeland. She could not imagine such indecent harassment occurring at St. George's.

When the funeral service was over, Francis Newbury's grandson raised his bugle to play the "Last Post" and Francis's four sons rolled the casket to the back of the church. Turning in her pew, her eyes following the receding casket, Clara felt very alone.

*   *   *

Home from the funeral, Clara threw her energy into further economies in the hospital. She met with Yip and the dieticians at the beginning of each day to review menus. The most frequent complaint from the patients was that they were given milk instead of cream with their coffee. She negotiated for a few jugs of cream from the local creamery to be delivered daily and had it mixed with the milk.

"Now that we've solved the cream crisis," she said to the dietician, "let's examine our monthly inventory of food supplies." The dietician apologized for the delay in getting numbers on paper, citing overwork. Having previously worked at a hospital the same size as the Galt, she suggested comparing purchasing patterns between the two hospitals; staples such as flour, sugar, salt, plain custard, and chocolate powder, as well as perishables such as vegetables and fruit. In the following months, it became clear that sugar, chocolate powder, butter, and fruit were being used twice as fast as expected.

The dietician came to see Clara. "I think food is being pilfered. "We can't be going through food supplies this quickly!"

Clara went to the window and looked out at the driveway. "I wonder ..." she said softly.

It was common knowledge that Yip played mahjong with his aunt until late on Wednesday nights. On a quiet evening, when calm reigned in the hospital, Clara, with a notebook in hand, slipped into the dietetic kitchen off the main cooking area. It was almost midnight when she heard muffled voices coming in from the hall. She remained motionless, peering through the crack of the doorframe as Ivy's old wagon with its red slats was dragged alongside the large food preparation table. Ivy had used it to deliver bottles to Sick's Brewery, buying her mother a birthday ring with her earnings. Clara choked with indignation that her daughter's wagon was being used for theft.

She heard cupboard doors being quietly opened and closed, and large sacks being dragged across the floor. Then she heard a metallic clatter.

"You stupid ass," someone hissed. "Someone will hear." The pungent smell of chocolate reached her nose, indicating the crash was an upset tin of chocolate powder. Clara boiled inside. "Get a spoon and scoop the powder back into the can. You've got to be more careful."

Clara could clearly distinguish the voice of Thelma Hicks, who had worked as a maid at the hospital for eight years. Clara had just promoted her to head of housekeeping.

The sound of the latch on the cooler room door was followed by another hiss: "Grab the oranges. They keep better than apples."

"D'ya think there's anything in the diet kitchen?" whispered a second voice.

"Not much for people starving, but it's worth a look."

As the door squeaked open, Clara fainted.

"That big bump you got there, Mrs. Durling," Yip said, handing her a tray. "I not know why you be in diet kitchen. You worry bout your weight, maybe? But you look good all the same. No need get smaller. Good you keep up your strength."

"Yip, food was being stolen. I was in the kitchen and heard it all."

"I no see sign of it."

"Didn't you see chocolate powder on the floor? I heard the can drop and then smelled chocolate. It was unmistakable." Clara knew she was babbling.

Yip gave her a curious glance. "You rest now, Mrs. Durling."

She went into the bathroom and stared at herself in the mirror, wincing. She remembered being helped back to her apartment by the night nurse, with only a cursory explanation. The nurse had heard noises coming from the kitchen and gone to investigate. She touched her temple, feeling the emerging bruise.

Her head throbbing, Clara tried to reconstruct the conversation in the kitchen. This was important; she hadn't actually seen the thieves. She remembered the second voice had a lisp. That must be Daisy Bain, who had begun working at the hospital only a month ago. She was a young girl with no housekeeping experience. Clara had hired her on a trial basis.

She ate her breakfast, put on her uniform, and marched off to fire the two women. "Thelma, you've worked at the hospital for eight years," she said. "Stealing food is no way to show your loyalty. I heard your voice in the kitchen last night."

When Daisy began squawking, she said, "You're going, too."

"We was selling the food to them that needs it," Daisy said, giving the matron an exasperated look as though she had failed to see the altruism.

Clara gasped in disbelief. "Even knowing the hospital runs a food bank, you simply decided to help yourselves or sell to desperate people?" Clara stood abruptly. "I never want to see either of you in the hospital again. You're both dismissed!"

Thelma and Daisy walked silently out of her office, and Clara, seething, began penning her report to Mayor Burrows. In the past, she had never had to justify her hiring or firing practices. When she had finished, she held her pen poised for a moment above the paper, and then signed her name to the report.

Two days passed before she heard from the mayor. He sent a cryptic note asking her to meet him in his office. She put on the only outfit that still fit her: a dark blue suit with a fox collar. When Clara arrived, she was escorted into a room that looked more like a courtroom than the mayor's office. Thelma and Daisy sat in chairs with their parents standing behind them. Clara looked at their shabby clothes, wishing she were somewhere else. Like sentinels, a lawyer stood at the side of each girl. Both lawyers were young, and Clara recalled she had played bridge with their parents.

"Mrs. Durling, Thelma and Daisy are being represented," Mayor Burrows said.

"I can see that," she replied, looking at the young men.

"I understand you heard voices in the kitchen," the mayor said. "You didn't actually see anyone. But the next day you fired these ladies." He nodded toward Thelma and Daisy.

"My goodness!" Clara exploded. "You make it sound as though I was having hallucinations. Working with employees, one gets to know their voices. And Daisy is the only one with a lisp."

"But nothing was missing from the kitchen, nor was chocolate spilled on the floor as you described. I've spoken with your cook. Perhaps you should tell us why you were in the diet kitchen at two in the morning. For that was the hour that Nurse Lubrick found you."

"I was trying to catch whoever has been stealing our inventory. I should have put this in the hands of the police. Instead, I took the dietician's word that basic food items were being depleted twice as fast as they were at her previous hospital of the same size. Given that you have asked me to write my board reports following another hospital's model, you shouldn't be surprised that in this case I used another hospital as a comparison."

Mayor Burrows's face reddened with anger. *This man is not outwardly explosive like Alistair,* she thought. *He will be completely underhanded.* She felt the dizziness that had brought her down in the diet kitchen. Clasping her hands in front of her, she asked to sit down. She refused to fall in front of her adversaries. Reflexively, she touched the sensitive bruise on her temple.

"Mrs. Durling, the hospital isn't prepared to defend you against these charges of unfair dismissal," Mayor Burrows said.

The young lawyer who was representing Daisy spoke. "Mrs. Durling, you said you heard the voices of thieves, yet you never confronted them. Miss Lubrick indicated the kitchen was spotless when she found you sprawled on the floor. There was no evidence that food was missing."

"What on earth would Thelma and Daisy be doing in the kitchen in the middle of the night if they were not stealing supplies? The dietician's calculations suggested someone *was* pilfering our inventory."

"You would take inanimate numbers over the word of two young women who have denied stealing?" Burrows asked.

"I have a note of apology from Thelma," she said. "That's proof of her guilt." She looked at Thelma, expecting her to admit her wrongdoing.

Thelma's lawyer interjected. "Who *wouldn't* write such a note if one thought it was the only way to regain a job so necessary to support an impoverished family?"

The mayor asked Thelma and Daisy and their representatives to step out of his office. "Mrs. Durling," he said when they'd left, "the board has not been happy with your performance over the past year. We are willing to accept your resignation to avoid a public fuss."

"Fuss?" Clara bristled. "You'll have to fire me. I will not resign."

She swept past Thelma and Daisy, down the stairs of the municipal offices, and out onto the street. She went straight to her office and called Barnaby.

"James," she said, "I need to talk with you."

"In your office or mine?"

"I'll come to you."

Clara knew the end was coming, but had to decide whether she would be fired or resign. She looked at the photograph of Ivy on her horse and dreaded telling her daughter she might be uprooted again. At sixteen, Ivy had finally settled in with a nice group of friends and a measure of popularity.

Clara needed to weigh the possible consequences of a public battle versus a quiet departure. She was torn between the justice she deserved and public embarrassment.

"What can I do for you?" Barnaby asked when she arrived in his office.

"James, Mayor Burrows has asked me to resign. I refused. I said he would have to fire me. It's a terrible injustice to push me out after all I've done to improve the hospital."

"Let me take your blood pressure before we have a chat." Barnaby pumped up the inflatable cuff and listened through his stethoscope. When he was finished, he relieved the pressure and removed the cuff. He pulled up a chair. "Clara," he said, "it wasn't Alistair's ulcer that killed him. It was his battling nature that led to his stroke."

"What are you trying to tell me, James?"

"You choose the hill you want to die on." Barnaby shook his head. "The war taught us many things, including when to go head-on into battle. Your blood pressure is sky-high, and I would strongly suggest you resign. Forfeit the battle. You can still win the war. You've transformed the Galt Hospital. And even those on the board who want to see you go know that. Accreditation from the American College of Surgeons, a first-class nursing school, and a hospital with standardized practices;

that will be your legacy no matter what. Fight it out, and *you*, not the Depression, will be the reason the hospital expansion is cancelled."

Barnaby leaned forward, placing his stump on her knee. His hazel eyes caught the light from the window. "Lily and I are moving to northern Ontario. Come with us. Leave all this cruel nonsense behind you."

Clara found it hard to speak. The thought of losing such loyal friends was frightening — first Alistair and then Dr. Newbury and now the Barnabys. She had already lost a husband and a son, and now she was threatened with losing her family. Her stomach churned the way it had when she'd left England. "Why, James? Why didn't you tell me? I thought you and Lily loved Lethbridge."

"We do. I should qualify my words. We are *thinking* of moving. Northern Ontario needs a pathologist." Barnaby laughed as he squeezed her hand. "Four-fingered doctors don't have many choices." Through Barnaby's trademark boyish grin she could see his tiredness. "I've helped many people come to terms with the war. But dealing with emotions (or more often the absence of them) has been hard work. Working as a pathologist would be easier. In any event, Lily and I are going next month to check things out."

"But why northern Ontario?"

"The coroner up there reported an unusual number of Indian deaths at a residential school in Sault Ste Marie. At first the Department of Indian Affairs gave the information a bureaucratic shrug. Most deaths were attributed to tuberculosis. But then the department learned that children's remains were found in nearby woods, suggesting the Indian students were running away from the school. I've been asked to investigate. Join us in our little reconnoiter. You might want to move there and have a fresh start. We aren't sure, either, but it's worth checking things out." Barnaby shrugged. "Lily still receives the occasional snub. And this bothers me. A clean slate for all of us."

"Nothing ventured, nothing gained," Clara said. "I'll join you on this exploratory mission." She felt a surge of hope. "James, you are a very wise friend."

"Tell no one of our plans, not even Etta Iverson," Barnaby advised. "Don't give Burrows the satisfaction of knowing you might resign."

Clara experienced a lightness she had not felt in months. *I've dealt with uncertainty before*, she thought, when she passed the surprised looking faces of board members as they wandered through the hospital. They probably expected her to have a fighting demeanor or a look of sad resignation. But she had neither.

She set out to buy a new outfit that accommodated her larger size and then find a hat to match. In the clothing store the saleslady asked, "How are things going at the Galt?" She reminded Clara about the hospital picnic at Henderson Lake. "Oh my," she said, her eyes glowing, "how I remember the cars lined up to park; old buggies, new models, and luxury cars. Three generations piled out of those automobiles. You were the clear hostess and the crowd acknowledged this with such a loud hand clap." The lady raised her hands as though she was going to break into applause. "You raised your punch glass in a toast and said: 'Here's to the Galt Hospital.'"

Clara choked up thinking how much she had loved being matron of the hospital. During the short walk to the hat shop, she realized how her love for the hospital was interwoven with her love for Alistair. She stepped into a side alley and let the tears

322 · SHARON JOHNSTON

flow. How so little seemed so much now: a shortened marriage, a small boy's rose garden, and a weekend at Waterton Park. She searched for her handkerchief and wiped her eyes.

When she strode into the hat shop, Clara said firmly, "I'm wanting a new hat." She smiled, thinking it was her signal that she was going east with the Barnabys. She tried on various models; floppy hats, cloche hats, pillboxes, and berets. She chose a grey felt cloche that accommodated her thick, wound-up hair. The saleslady put two hair combs in the hatbox with a broad grin.

"These are to thank you for all you've done for this community," the saleslady said.

"Now I remember," Clara said. "Your young grandson was in the hospital to stabilize his asthma. He had fuzzy blue slippers with ducks on the toes. How is he doing?"

"Very well, thanks to your soft spot for that little boy. The nurses said you came up twice a day to check on him."

"I do have a special place in my heart for small boys."

Before the trip to northern Ontario was realized, Miss Lubrick, the nurse who reported finding Clara on the floor of the diet kitchen, accused her of being absent from the hospital without leaving adequate directions. The board accepted Miss Lubrick's side of the story without ever looking at the directions. Seeing the nail in her coffin, Clara resigned a few days later and accepted a job as lady superintendent of the much smaller Fort Macleod hospital. Helen Hope, now a full-fledged nurse, but grateful for the special tutoring Clara had provided, packed up her leather-bound books in the matron's office: prizes she had won as a probationer. Helen tried to console Ivy, who hung her head in shame. She had witnessed her mother's lack of compromise on many occasions. Ivy was old enough to understand that her mother had been fired, and had not resigned, although face-saving had mercifully been allowed.

Not surprisingly, Miss Lubrick took Clara's place. Barnaby postponed the trip to northern Ontario so Clara could get established in her new position. If she didn't like the area, she would still have the position in Fort Macleod.

Humbled but still proud, Clara rented a hall to celebrate Ivy's seventeenth birthday. Everyone invited accepted the invitation despite the Great Depression, which had curbed so much of the social life in Lethbridge.

CHAPTER 30

Sault Ste Marie, Ontario, 1931

In two months, Clara, true to her demanding reputation, fired a nurse for incompetence and riled up the small Fort Macleod board. "It's time for you to check out the North," Barnaby had said, smiling, handing Clara a train ticket on her first trip back to Lethbridge. One week later she and the Barnabys were in Sault Ste Marie, Ontario.

While Barnaby went to be interviewed by the medical establishment, Lily accompanied Clara to her interview with the director of the residential school.

A shabbily dressed couple sat beside them in the dreary foyer. They were distinguishable as Indians by their weathered brown skin and hair tied back in ponytails. They spoke so softly it was hard to hear their story; they had come a thousand miles from the Fort Hope reservation to see their six-year-old daughter.

Clara stood when a woman indicated the director was ready to see her. As she marched down the corridor, she heard screams. She opened the door to see what was happening, just as a grey-haired woman, her head bent in determination, raised a thick leather strap. She brought it down with great force on a little girl's outstretched hand. Clara stiffened at the child's pained sobbing. She stepped forward, grabbed the strap and the woman's hand, and gave her one fierce lash. She dropped the strap as the woman howled.

"Now you know how this child feels," she said.

ACKNOWLEDGEMENTS

Matrons and Madams is fiction based on facts. I gratefully acknowledge Greg Ellis, the former archivist at the Galt Museum in Lethbridge, who provided the Galt Hospital board notes from the end of the Great War to the onset of the Great Depression. It was during this time that my grandmother was the matron of the hospital. The archived *Lethbridge Herald* newspaper articles provided the social and political background to the novel. I am indebted to Amy Viel, a graduate student at the University of Lethbridge, for her meticulous historical research. In-depth conversations with people who knew my grandmother in England and Lethbridge captured the events impacting on her life. *Red Lights on the Prairies*, written by social historian James H. Grey, gives an authentic description of prostitution in western Canada.

A grand thank-you to Joe Kertes, dean of the Humber School of Creative and Performing Arts, who mentored me to a published product. And I am indebted to Margaret Hart for her wise council on book publishing. My appreciation also goes out to publisher Kirk Howard, editors Sylvia McConnell and Shannon Whibbs, and the rest of the team at Dundurn Press.

Finally, upon discovering a dozen letters written in 1929 by Lethbridge doctors and public figures extolling my grandmother's virtues, I asked the question, "Why would she need so many commendations?" I booked a plane ticket to Lethbridge to find out why, and that is how the story began.

CPSIA information can be obtained at www.ICGtesting.com
Printed in the USA
LVOW10s1228271115

464347LV00002BA/59/P

9 781459 728967